Inside An Lộc

Inside An Lộc
*The Battle to Save Saigon,
April–May 1972*

VAN NGUYEN DUONG
with NGHIA M. VO

McFarland & Company, Inc., Publishers
Jefferson, North Carolina

RECENT WORKS ALSO OF INTEREST AND FROM MCFARLAND
Legends of Vietnam: An Analysis and Retelling of 88 Tales, by Nghia M. Vo (2012); *Saigon: A History*, by Nghia M. Vo (2011); *The Viet Kieu in America: Personal Accounts of Postwar Immigrants from Vietnam*, by Nghia M. Vo (2009); *The Tragedy of the Vietnam War: A South Vietnamese Officer's Analysis*, by Van Nguyen Duong (2008); *The Vietnamese Boat People, 1954 and 1975–1992*, by Nghia M. Vo (2006); *The Bamboo Gulag: Political Imprisonment in Communist Vietnam*, by Nghia M. Vo (2004)

LIBRARY OF CONGRESS CATALOGUING-IN-PUBLICATION DATA

Names: Duong, Van Nguyen, 1934– author. | Vo, Nghia M., 1947– Co-author.
 Title: Inside An Lộc : the battle to save Saigon, April–May 1972 / Van Nguyen Duong with Nghia M. Vo.
 Description: Jefferson, North Carolina : McFarland & Company, Inc., Publishers, 2016. | Includes bibliographical references and index.
 Identifiers: LCCN 2015040400| ISBN 9780786499342 (softcover : acid free paper) | ISBN 9781476621210 (ebook)
 Subjects: LCSH: An Lộc, Battle of, An Lộc, Vietnam, 1972. | Vietnam War, 1961–1975—Personal narratives, Vietnamese. | Duong, Van Nguyen, 1934–
 Classification: LCC DS557.8.A5 D86 2016 | DDC 959.704/342—dc23
 LC record available at http://lccn.loc.gov/2015040400

BRITISH LIBRARY CATALOGUING DATA ARE AVAILABLE

© 2016 Van Nguyen Duong and Nghia M. Vo. All rights reserved

No part of this book may be reproduced or transmitted in any form or by any means, electronic or mechanical, including photocopying or recording, or by any information storage and retrieval system, without permission in writing from the publisher.

Front cover: An ARVN soldier peers out from a bunker in a position north of Chơn Thanh in South Vietnam on May 7, 1972

Printed in the United States of America

McFarland & Company, Inc., Publishers
 Box 611, Jefferson, North Carolina 28640
 www.mcfarlandpub.com

To the valiant ARVN soldiers who fought at the An Lộc Battle.

To the brave U.S. advisers and pilots who supported the ARVN during that battle.

To the people of An Lộc who suffered so much during the battle.

Table of Contents

Abbreviations	viii
Introduction	1
I. The Border War	9
II. General Lê Văn Hưng and I	35
III. Prelude to the Bình Long Battle	48
IV. The Fall of Lộc Ninh	62
V. Crucial Decisions Made to Save An Lộc	77
VI. The First Attack on An Lộc	94
VII. A Clash of Personalities	117
VIII. The Siege	134
IX. The War Game in Chơn Thành	146
X. Breaking the Siege	154
XI. Releasing the Pressure on An Lộc	172
XII. Besieged Towns	196
XIII. Return to the Mekong Delta	208
XIV. Hell in a Very Insignificant Place	215
Epilogue	221
Appendix: War Self-Immolation in Vietnam (Nghia M. Vo)	225
Chapter Notes	238
Bibliography	249
Index	253

Abbreviations

APC	armed personnel carrier
Arc Light	B-52 bombing strike
ARVN	Armed Forces of the Republic of Vietnam
CARP	computerized aerial drop system
CBU	cluster bomb unit
COSVN	Central Office for South Vietnam (communist)
CP	command post
CPV	Communist Party of [North] Vietnam
DMZ	Demilitarized Zone
DRAC	Delta Regional Assistance Command
DRV	Democratic Republic of [North] Vietnam
FAC	forward air controller
FRAC	First Regional Assistance Command
FSB	fire support base
GVN	Government of [South] Vietnam
HALO	high altitude, low opening
HEAT	high explosive anti-tank rocket
IRC	Indochinese Resource Center
JCS	Joint Chiefs of Staff
JGS	Joint General Staff (RVNAF)
KIA	killed in action
LAW	light anti-tank weapon
MACV	Military Assistance Command, Vietnam

medevac	medical evacuation
MIA	missing in action
MR	Military Region
NLF	National Liberation Front
NVA	North Vietnamese Army (we will use PAVN and NVA interchangeably)
PAVN	People's Army of [North] Vietnam
PF	Popular Forces
POW	prisoner of war
PRG	Provisional Revolutionary Government
RF	Regional Forces
RPG	rocket-propelled grenade
RVN	Republic of [South] Vietnam
RVNAF	Republic of Vietnam Armed Forces
SAC	Strategic Air Command
SAM	surface-to-air missile
SDS	Students for a Democratic Society
SRAC	Second Regional Assistance Command
TF	task force
TOC	tactical operations center
TOW	tube-launched optically tracked wire-guided missile
TRAC	Third Regional Assistance Command
VC	Việt Cọng (communists in South Vietnam)
VM	Việt Minh (communists in North Vietnam before 1954; interchangeable with PAVN or NVA)
VNAF	[South] Vietnamese Air Force
WIA	wounded in action

Introduction

An Lộc represented one of the defining moments in the history of the Vietnam War in general and of the Republic of South Vietnam in particular. It was in 1972, a place where one South Vietnamese division stood its ground against three North Vietnamese infantry divisions (NVA) and won. Throughout the two-decade war (1954–1975), all the battles had been fought in the countryside, swamps and villages of South Vietnam or the hills of central Vietnam, with the possible exceptions of Huế, Saigon probably Quảng Trị. But An Lộc was almost an urban war, with house-to-house and street-to-street fighting, where opponents shot at each other at close range.

An Lộc was only 11 city blocks long by six blocks wide, so small that its aerial photograph could fit onto one book page. Tucked in the middle of vast rubber tree plantations, it was in 1972 a provincial town with 15–20,000 inhabitants at its peak. The tallest buildings were the scattered two- or three-story houses that lined the main city streets. One could have easily missed the town while driving on the ground. No heavy fortifications dotted the landscape because it was home to no major army unit, installation, or ordnance depot. For this reason, no one thought the communists would launch an attack on a rural town with such low strategic value—so low that U.S. then South Vietnamese troops did not build any heavy fortification to strengthen it.

However, it turned out to be a town where brand-new 36-ton T-54 enemy tanks[1] roamed through until they were destroyed by valiant ARVN[2] soldiers carrying anti-tank rocket launchers. The town was physically so small that one could see ARVN soldiers chasing after tanks in order to have a better shot at them at close range.

For more than 60 days,[3] that unprotected small rural town was pounded daily by 1,000 rounds of shells, mortars and more. It was so thoroughly shelled that almost nothing was left standing after the battle, except for five or six crumbling buildings riddled with holes and bullets; a few weeks into the battle had rendered visibility across town almost perfect from north to south and east to west.

The An Lộc battle ranked high in the history of strategic battles, probably at the same level as Điện Biên Phủ and Khe Sanh: all these battles had been savagely fought on Vietnamese soil. The significant strategic and military differences of these battles will be discussed in Chapter XI.

An Lộc was one of the three battle sites where the NVA waged war against the South Vietnamese in their 1972 summer offensive that was fittingly called *Mùa Hè Đỏ Lửa*, the Fiery Red Summer. The others were Quảng Trị and Kontum in the northern and central parts of South Vietnam. This was the three-pronged attack engineered by Hanoi to destabilize the South Vietnamese government. An Lộc was also one of the bloodiest battles in Vietnam in which more than 20,000 soldiers and civilians died in a few-square-mile area. This was how heavily contested that area was in 1972.

The An Lộc battle came at a time when U.S. troops were leaving Vietnam, turning everything over to the Vietnamese as a consequence of the Vietnamization of the war.[4] Only a small contingent of U.S. troops remained on the ground in 1972. At the An Lộc battlefield, a dozen U.S. *cố vấn* or advisers at most worked on site. No foreign reporters, except maybe one or two, showed up in town later; which means that one of the bloodiest battles of the war was ignored, under- or mis-reported by world press.

An Lộc was a lengthy, bloody, and ugly battle that looked more like World War I trench warfare than a modern-day battle. Whichever side lasted the longest would win it. It was a battle of attrition rather than a fast-paced and decisive battle where one side just overwhelmed the other either by force or power. Although force and power were employed in An Lộc, they neutralized each other effectively to a stalemate in the beginning until the communists had no more force to throw into the siege. When it ended, the town lay wasted like a huge pile of rubble. It looked like the devastation left behind by a Category 4 or 5 hurricane that had just touched down smack in the middle of town. A hurricane would have been better for the townspeople; it would have come unannounced and left as fast as it arrived. The pain and sorrows would have been short-lived. After a short but tragic nightmare, people would be ready to rebuild their lives. The war in An Lộc, which lasted for more than two months, on the other hand, left daily evidence of killings, ravages, and destruction. People and soldiers suffered from the shelling, noise, destruction, killing, horror, fatigue, hunger, thirst, pain, and grieving almost daily for almost three long months. They bore down and lived in hell during that time, trying to survive day by day. Their physical and psychological wounds broke open, bled, and re-bled daily without getting time to heal. Even the dead were not allowed to solemnly die in one piece; their bodies were shelled and shelled repeatedly until they were shredded into thousands of small pieces that scattered over a large area. If bodies were shredded into pieces, how could their souls remain intact in one piece?

No town had been so thoroughly and so much shelled and bombed as An Lộc had been. Andrade, a westerner, rightly called it "Hell in a Very Insignificant Place,"[5] for An Lộc was an insignificant small provincial town smack in the middle of nowhere, among its well-known and age-old rubber plantations close to the Cambodian border. Its importance lay in the mind of the North Vietnamese communists who were determined to conquer it at all costs to make it their "capital" in South Vietnam, a place to boost their legitimacy and a base to conquer Saigon. From there, they could roll their tanks down Highway 13 and be in Saigon in a couple of hours. They could make it the terminus of the Hồ Chí Minh Trail and cut down by more than half the travel time for their troops from North to South. In the process, they would leave their troops exposed to U.S. and South Vietnamese air strikes. But they were willing to take this gamble: sacrifice tens of thousands of their soldiers for the conquest of a town. Otherwise, in a sparsely populated province, which was no larger than an average eastern U.S. county, An Lộc held minimal strategic value. The goal of "liberating" a town ended up tearing it apart, destroying it, and laying it into ruins. Conquest had become murder, killing and destruction. This was how murderous the communist mind could be.[6] Strangely, world news reporters and anti-war activists had never mentioned the cruelty and savagery of the communist leaders during all these fights. Where did all these T-54 tanks and all these artillery guns come from? Did the communists build these fancy, top-of-the-line killing machines in the jungles of South Vietnam, or had they been shipped from Hanoi to South Vietnam? If they had been shipped from faraway lands, Hanoi had simply invaded South Vietnam.

An Lộc's population may have doubled in size with the arrival of the soldiers of the ARVN 5th Infantry Division. The latter just showed up for this battle: although it was not their home, it was their sacred land to defend. They came, dug their own foxholes, and put up bunkers made of sandbags around the periphery of An Lộc to protect themselves and the town. A few concertina wires were spread here and there and that was all. The few rare heavy fortifications left behind by the Japanese during World War II and the Americans later explained the reason why enemy tanks rolled so easily into the middle of the town, which was basically a lowly residential, commercial, and rural town, not a fortified military camp.

An Lộc was the story of its defenders who bravely withstood more than two months of endless shelling, fatigue, hunger, suffering, and misery to survive and fight another day. Major General James H. Hollingsworth said, "The real credit goes to the little ARVN soldier. He is just tremendous, just magnificent. He stood in there, took all that fire and gave it back."[7] It was the story of a brave commander General Lê Văn Hưng who vowed to "die with An Lộc" until it fell. It was the story of a U.S. TRAC commander who promised to rain down enough bombs to dislodge the attackers and prevent them from capturing the town.

If one looks at the map of South Vietnam, one is surprised to see that the Cambodian border is only 100 kilometers away from Saigon, the heart of the Republic of South Vietnam. Hanoi had opened since 1955 the so-called Hồ Chí Minh Trail that began in North Vietnam, went through the mountainous jungles of Laos and Cambodia, and finally ended in Cambodia across the border from the Bình Long Province of South Vietnam. By skirting the South Vietnamese border, the communists avoided major military air strikes on the movement of their troops and trucks. Once in Cambodia, they settled down in the Parrot's Beak and Fish Hook areas—fancy names for the Cambodian territorial indentations into South Vietnam—and could then aim straight into the heart of Saigon. It was no wonder that their aim in 1972, when the U.S. had withdrawn most of its troops out of Vietnam, was to target An Lộc and use it as a "liberated town" to promote the National Liberation Front, a front cover for the Hanoi communist government. Once this Vietnamese border town was taken, they could just roll down Highway 13 and within two hours be in the heart of Saigon. This was how strategic and important An Lộc had become to the communists.

An Lộc was not only one of the biggest battles of the war; it was also bigger than Điện Biên Phủ or Khe Sanh (Chapter XI). It was a full battle with infantry, tanks, aircraft, artillery and anti-aircraft missiles. Yes, the enemy brought down the huge Russian-made M-54 tanks that frightened any foot soldier, to mount attacks on the town. But An Lộc was not the only battle; it was also a complex three-part battle with the prelude in Lộc Ninh north of An Lộc, the main battle at An Lộc itself and the third one south of An Lộc—for the latter city to be freed, the southern corridor from Saigon to An Lộc should be freed. Attempts to downgrade these three phases would be ignoring the multi-dimensional strategy of this bloody battle.

An Lộc would only be saved if two conditions were to occur:

1. It had to hold its own despite being shelled 1,000 plus rounds each day and attacked three or four different times with infantry and tanks.

Introduction 5

2. Reinforcement troops could only come from the South through Highway 13.[8]

Since Highway 13, which ran in a south-north direction through the province before crossing An Lộc, was blocked by enemy troops at Tàu-Ô Stream, to liberate An Lộc the ARVN had to take down the dense blockade at Tàu-Ô Stream north of Chơn Thành. Otherwise, An Lộc could not be resupplied and peace could not be reestablished in the province. Although the battle had ceased by the end of the second month in An Lộc, it lingered on for another month south of town—the time it took ARVN soldiers to uproot the blockade north of Chơn Thành.

The book is divided into 15 chapters and one appendix.

Chapter I, "The Border War," details the different parties involved in the Vietnam War, namely the U.S., the Army of the Republic of Vietnam Armed Forces (RVNAF), and the North Vietnamese Army forces (NVA) and the Việt Cộng (VC). The border war involves cross-border fighting against communist forces stationing in neutral Cambodia. These latter forces, if not neutralized, would later cross the border to wage war in An Lộc.

Chapter II, "General Lê Văn Hưng and I," discusses the educational and training relationships between the author and Lê Văn Hưng, who would later become the commander of the ARVN's forces in An Lộc.

Chapter III, "Prelude to the Bình Long Battle," details the strategy and forces involved in this bloody and little-discussed battle of the Vietnam War.

Chapter IV, "The Fall of Lộc Ninh," describes the sudden communist attack on Lộc Ninh, a 3,000-people village used as an ARVN firebase across the border from Cambodia and 30 kilometers north of An Lộc.

Chapter V, "Crucial Decisions Made to Save An Lộc," details how General Lê Văn Hưng's crucial decisions made while flying over the Cần Lê Bridge, 15 kilometers north of An Lộc, eventually saved the town from imminent disaster. General Hưng's vow to take a stand and defend the town until death galvanized local defenders.

"The First Attack on An Lộc" is described in Chapter VI along with details about communist shelling of civilians who tried to escape from the war zone; the two hospitals that treated thousands of injured people, civilians as well as military personnel, during this battle; and the ranger group, the Airborne brigade, and the Commando group that were involved in the battle.

Chapter VII deals with the intimate details of "A Clash of Personalities" between General Hưng and his U.S. adviser, Colonel Miller.

"The Siege" of the town is detailed in Chapter VIII, along with a discussion about the tactical assessments of the battle between General Hưng and his adviser.

Chapter IX, "The War Game in Chơn Thành," details the second front south of An Lộc where enemy forces used "choke points" to try to prevent reinforcing forces from relieving the pressure around the besieged town. This was a miniature war of the trenches.

Chapter X, "Breaking the Siege," describes the brutal attack on the town, which received close to 10,000 rounds of mortars and shells on the first day of the third attack but survived to repel the attackers; the battle between TOW rocket launchers and tanks; and the feats of the Airborne battalion.

The unique strategic moves made by General Nguyễn Văn Minh to bring reinforcement troops to An Lộc underline the war games played by General Minh and his opponent, General Trần Văn Trà, in Chapter XI, "Releasing the Pressure on An Lộc." Also discussed are the counterattack mounted by Lieutenant Colonel Nguyễn Văn Đinh and his paratroopers; the village of Phú Đức that took care of wounded patients displaced from the destroyed An Lộc hospital; and President Thiệu's visit to the liberated town of An Lộc.

The three major sieges and battles waged in An Lộc (1972), Khe Sanh (1968) and Điện Biên Phủ (1954) during the Vietnam War had major implications on the course of events in Vietnam. They are discussed in Chapter XII, "Besieged Towns."

General Lê Văn Hưng's reassignment to the Mekong Delta is detailed in Chapter XIII, "Return to the Mekong Delta," where he became the deputy commander of the IV Corps and IV Military Region until his death in 1975.

Chapter XIV, "Hell in a Very Insignificant Place," describes the significance and insignificance of this An Lộc battle in a remote southwest corner of South Vietnam close to the Cambodian border. The Vietnam War finally ended three years later with the self-sacrifice of five South Vietnamese generals and scores of other officers—the largest number of self-immolated generals in a war—who could not stand to live without their defeated country.

The epilogue discusses the significance of the loss of South Vietnam.

As the former chief of the staff's intelligence unit of the ARVN 5th Infantry Division, or J-2/5th Div/ARVN, Van Nguyen Duong was privileged to be present for the duration of the siege of An Lộc. Duong lived in the same bunker as the divisional staff of the ARVN 5th Division and attended meetings with General Lê Văn Hưng, the 5th Division commander. As all the staff officers of the S-3 Operations staff of the division were killed in the early stage of the battle, except its chief, he was the officer—with the help of his two captains—who recorded the history of the An Lộc battle and later submitted it to the Division of History Branch of the J5/JGS/RVNAF. This is an accurate depiction of battle as it was submitted in 1973. It contains unique features only known to Duong and the ARVN. However, since memories are not always accurate with years passing by, we have added various other sources, mostly South Vietnamese, that are not known to or have been ignored so far by western reporters.

It is therefore our privilege to present the battle of An Lộc as well as the strategy and perspectives of General Lê Văn Hưng, the man who stood in the "trenches" to lead our forces during the more than two-month bloody siege, endured the tens of thousands of artillery shells and bombs that rained down on the tiny town like any foot soldier, and fought the attackers until the end. It is our hope that this presentation will convey a better and more comprehensive view of one of the most important battles of the Vietnam War and in extension the Vietnam War in general.

Finally, this book is dedicated to the brave ARVN soldiers who courageously stood in their foxholes and trenches day and night for three months in An Lộc ready to fight against an army of invaders led by huge T-54 tanks and supported by long-range artillery and anti-aircraft guns, to the few valiant U.S. advisers still on the ground, and U.S. and VNAF pilots who day and night supported An Lộc defenders.

I

The Border War

"When the NVA[1] crossed the DMZ and invaded Quảng Trị Province on 30 April 1972, the Joint General Staff was still having serious doubts about the enemy's real objective." So wrote General Ngô Quang Trưởng.[2]

Huế was the main threat because it was a historic capital and easily accessible from the north. The Central Highlands were also a possibility because of enemy buildup there. But little attention was paid to the Military Region III (MR3) and An Lộc because they were at the end of the Hồ Chí Minh Trail where supplies and reinforcements would be difficult for the communists to deliver. But the three-pronged attack against Quảng Trị (MR1), Kontum (MR2), and An Lộc (MR3) would give the enemy some "flexibility" because an "initial success of any thrust could be reinforced and turned into the main effort." Andrade, however, argued that the capture of An Lộc would be symbolic but insignificant because "American B-52 [would] soon unseat the North Vietnamese."[3] This may be true, but for the communists, who did not control any city or town in South Vietnam in 1972, symbolism could mean a lot of things.

The real prize was always Saigon, the capital of the Republic of South Vietnam and the nerve center of its army, the Army of the Republic of Vietnam or ARVN. Saigon was also the political nemesis of Hanoi, the opposition center of communist expansion throughout Indochina. No matter what the communists did and said, they never took their eyes off that city. This was where the power was; this was what they aimed for. All the rest was secondary. Besides, Saigon was only 100 kilometers from the border with Cambodia where large NVA units had been stationing in plain view of the world along with huge armament caches in very safe sanctuaries inside Cambodia. And the Vietnam War could not be won without these safe sanctuaries.

The main question that needed to be answered was how did Hanoi manage to bring its troops from the North all the way down to Cambodia to take aim at Saigon, the heart of South Vietnam? How did Hanoi manage to create sanctuaries inside neutral Cambodia where it could rest its troops, replenish their reserves, and send them back to fight in Vietnam? This was a long story that began back in Geneva in 1954 where the U.S. attempted to block Hanoi from expanding its hegemony all over Indochina but could not.[4] The Geneva failure would later come back and haunt the U.S.

Washington's War

The War in Laos (1954–1962)

Indochina was from the 9th to the 14th centuries home to a huge and powerful Indianized culture.[5] One just has to look at the pharaonic temples of Angkor Wat and Angkor Thom to realize its past greatness and might.[6] The Khmer (Cambodian) empire then encompassed present-day Cambodia, Laos, Thailand, Vietnam and Malaysia.[7] That vital and important culture slowly ebbed in the 15th century from internecine rivalry and outside attacks by rival states—Vietnam, Thailand, and Malaysia—that slowly nipped at its fringes. By the end of the 17th century, Cambodia had become a vassal to Vietnam,[8] which had transformed the Khmer fishing village of Prey Nokor in the Mekong Delta into the Vietnamese Saigon in 1698. By the 1800s, the king of Cambodia each year had to come to Saigon to wish well to the king of Vietnam on the New Year Tết celebration.[9]

When the French arrived in Vietnam in the late 19th century, they lumped three neighboring but different states (Vietnam, Laos, and Cambodia) together to form Indochina. That tour of force held on its own for many decades until French Indochina broke apart after World War II. Although they were Asian neighbors, these three states were racially, culturally, and socially different: Laos and Cambodia formed the "Indo" side while Vietnam was the "China" side of the Indo-China equation. Laos and Cambodia were heavily Indianized or Hinduized, while Vietnam was Chinese influenced. The former used the Sanskrit alphabet and the latter the Chinese alphabet. The Indianized (Hindu, Buddhist) and Chinese (Confucian) civilizations clashed inside the peninsula for centuries before the latter finally prevailed in the 17th century with Cambodia becoming Vietnam's vassal. The northernmost extension of the Hinduized civilization which once reached all the way to present-day Huế and Quảng Trị Province in the third century AD, was slowly pushed back by Vietnamese southward advance (*nam tiến*).

By the 1950s, the North Vietnamese communists attempted to reconstitute a new Indochina under their control and at the same time to expand the realm of communism in Southeast Asia. In that sense, they were *not* truly nationalists but internationalists: they were fighting not for Vietnam, but for international communism and its worldwide spread. For them, Vietnam was secondary to their primary goal of supporting communist expansion.

In Geneva in 1954, the U.S. among other nations negotiated the partition of Vietnam through the 17th parallel, creating two new countries: North and South Vietnam. In fact, the U.S. wanted more: they wanted to lock the belligerent North Vietnamese forever inside North Vietnam but could not. The plan did not work because the Vietnamese communists who already had troops in Laos refused to withdraw from that country. This may be one of the reasons why the U.S. opted not to sign the Geneva Accords.

In 1961 the Republican Averell Harriman became Kennedy's roving ambassador for the complex Laotian problem with its continuous infighting between the various factions: Laotian nationalists, neutralists, and communists (Pathet Lao). The central Laotian government was too weak to fight against the Pathet Lao who were supported by Hanoi's communist troops. Despite being a veteran politician and diplomat, Harriman had minimal experience in Southeast Asia. When he visited Diệm in May 1961, the latter advised him to "stop the communists from taking over Laos," and South Vietnam could defeat the Việt Cộng.[10] Harriman, however, suggested a diplomatic solution by promoting Laos as a neutral country. He believed he could rely on the Soviet Union to control the North Vietnamese communists who were stationing in Laos. After witnessing the various battles occurring in his kingdom, Laotian King Savang quickly realized that the Americans did not want to open a new front in Laos by fighting the Pathet Lao and the North Vietnamese communists. Left to defend his kingdom on his own, the king knew he would soon lose his power to the communists. The realistic Cambodian King Sihanouk, seeing the communists advancing militarily in Laos while the Americans remained passive and knowing he could not unilaterally fight against the communists, also decided from that time on to accommodate communist Hanoi.[11] Laos and Cambodia, which eventually became neutral countries, basically gave the green light to the communists to forge ahead militarily to conquer South Vietnam. This was where Harriman had failed: by ignoring or turning a blind eye to the North Vietnamese aggression, he de facto acknowledged their expansion into Laos and stimulated their continuing aggression into Cambodia and South Vietnam. Laos was the first step in the conquest of South Vietnam.

The 1962 Geneva Accords on Laos thus sanctioned the neutralization of Laos and the withdrawal of all forces from that country.[12] If correctly implemented, neutral Laos ideally would have become a shield protecting the western flank of South Vietnam. However, the North Vietnamese not only refused to withdraw from Laos, but also continued to expand their control on the eastern part of Laos. The Transport Group 559 and NVA infantry began building a trail leading to South Vietnam.[13] Worse, they helped the Pathet Lao, the communist faction of the Laos government, control the southeastern side of Laos,[14] through which the North Vietnamese built the Hồ Chí Minh Trail to subvert South Vietnam.[15]

The failure of Hanoi and the Soviet Union to live up to the neutralization of Laos, agreed upon in Geneva in July 1962, angered President Kennedy and prevented the possibility of another retreat in Southeast Asia.[16] The decision was made to pursue some paramilitary operations to block the North Vietnamese expansion: it only confirmed by 1963 that it was physically and logistically impossible for the U.S. to prosecute a major war in Laos even from Thailand.[17] This did not prevent the U.S. from attempting later to cut off the building of the Hồ Chí Minh Trail through bombing, South Vietnamese cross-border invasion into Laos (Lâm Sơn 719), or setting up nearby observation bases (Khe Sanh, Khâm Đức) by Studies and Observation Groups (SOG) to perform strategic reconnaissance missions on the Laotian side, although by that time it was too late because the communists controlled eastern Laos.

Ambassador Ellsworth Bunker once confided, "In retrospect, I am more certain than I was in 1967 that our failure to cut the Hồ Chí Minh Trail was a strategic mistake of the first order."[18] Nixon even compared the similarities of North Korea's and North Vietnam's invasion. He wrote that, knowing that North Korea's blatant invasion across the border in the Korean Peninsula gave the U.S. a justification to intervene, "North Vietnam shrewdly camouflaged its invasion to look like a civil war. But in fact, the Vietnam War was the Korean War with jungles."[19]

Westmoreland's War (1964–1968)

The U.S. strategy in Vietnam in 1963 was also confusing as the position of U.S. Secretary of Defense McNamara remained a key mystery. It was ironic that "Dean Rusk, the top diplomat, favored a military solution while McNamara, the senior military manager, advocated diplomacy." McNamara then recommended against "military actions against North Vietnam."[20] He flew to Vietnam in December 1963 to see firsthand reports about the trail. What he saw alarmed him: "Current trends, unless reversed in the next two or three months, will lead to neutralization at best and more likely to a

I. The Border War

communist controlled state." He ordered U2 aerial photography of the Laotian-Cambodian border of Vietnam, which showed evidence of road building along the trail, including heavy construction equipment. This dispelled doubts about the need for robust cross-border interdiction.[21]

With the war inside Vietnam deteriorating, President Lyndon B. Johnson poured U.S. ground troops into South Vietnam in 1965 to help stabilize the country. He accepted the recommendation of building up to 175,000 men but disapproved the call-up of reserves.[22] He was also unwilling to commit all his efforts to win the war while at the same time trying to build the "Great Society" and wage the "War on Poverty" in the U.S. However, concentrating on one project meant not investing enough on the other because of budget constraints. As the hope of defeating the enemy through a war of attrition could not be sustained[23] and as the 1968 election year approached, President Johnson looked for a political solution out of Vietnam: he switched to Vietnamization and made the decision not to seek reelection.[24]

General William C. Westmoreland, commander of the U.S. Military Assistance Command, Vietnam (MACV), was also a controversial warrior. He believed his role "was not to *defeat* the North Vietnamese army," although on other occasions he claimed his main role was to defeat the enemy and to pacify the country.[25] He had the correct idea of wanting to cut off the Hồ Chí Minh Trail by sending in U.S. infantry troops, but he was hamstrung by Johnson and McNamara who believed that widening the war could worsen the stalemate in Indochina. Besides, U.S. Ambassador Sullivan to Laos also opposed an invasion into Laos to control the trail because it would violate Laos's neutrality and could lead to Chinese intervention.[26] Although Sullivan was correct in principle, he simply "forgot" that Hanoi already had 30,000 troops in Laos. Unable to wage the war outside Vietnam or control the inflow of North Vietnamese soldiers and supplies into South Vietnam, Westmoreland was left with fighting a war of attrition based on search-and-destroy missions.[27] The strategy was "costly in terms of time, effort, and materiel, but often disappointing in terms in terms of results,"[28] besides the fact that "chasing [the enemy] around the countryside was futile." Alexander Haig called the tactic "a demented and bloody form of hide and seek."[29] The mission, which in the luxuriant jungles of Asia and in a country where the Việt Cộng (VC or communists in South Vietnam)[30] looked like civilian bystanders, proved to be a difficult and frustrating task. Besides, the enemy also hid deep underground (first phase of "revolutionary" or insurgency war), a factor that U.S. troops were not used to dealing with.

Westmoreland also used the body count—which, initiated by McNamara, often "did not add up" and was called "inflated"—to evaluate the progress of the war effort.³¹ The difficulty in differentiating a VC from an innocent villager caused many mishaps to both troops and villagers. The wily VC often fired at U.S. or ARVN troops while hiding behind villagers. By firing back, the troops could endanger the villagers' lives; by not firing back, they could get injured themselves. If an innocent villager killed inadvertently during an encounter was counted as a dead enemy by mistake, the body count had been artificially increased. However, the main problem lay in the fact that no westerner could believe the VC had suffered heavy losses during the war—a number so large that no army from any civilized country could afford to lose it. But the wily VC again hid the huge losses to its own people and the world and pretended they had never occurred. It was only after the war that Hanoi revealed it had lost 1.2 million soldiers—that is, more than 6 percent of its population: a staggering number indeed. The number seems to vindicate Westmoreland, no matter how inflated his numbers were. Only the communists could sustain such losses and get away with it. By 1966–1967, the war of attrition proved to be laborious and costly: on one occasion in 1966, 25,000 U.S. troops looked for the enemy in War Zone C, a notorious communist refuge north of Tây Ninh, only to find 20 VC after a daylong search.³²

Westmoreland also ignored two other crucial aspects of the war, improvement of South Vietnam's armed forces and pacification,³³ that were essential to the success of the war effort. He was not imaginative enough to use ARVN forces to bolster his own. That would have achieved two additional goals: first, to build up Vietnamese forces and shore up their confidence and ability to wage war; second, to turn the fight over to the ARVN (later called Vietnamization) and to withdraw, thereby cutting down U.S. losses. In the end, it was not an American war, and the U.S. should have realized that it was a Vietnamese war. Had Westmoreland thought about these goals, both Westmoreland and the ARVN would have won the war, or at least fought to a stalemate.

In a war of attrition, whichever side lasted longer would win. In fact, Westmoreland thought that with America's technological might and deep pockets, he would outlast the NVA. But he did not count on the deep pockets of the Soviet Union and China and the stubborn resolve of Hanoi. Hồ Chí Minh once mentioned he was willing to lose 10 of his own troops for one U.S. troop killed and he still would prevail.³⁴ By the end of the war, the U.S had lost 58,000 troops and withdrew while the communists accepted the loss of 1.2 million troops and won the war. Hồ Chí Minh's bravado had escalated the 10/1 troop-loss ratio to a staggering and insane 20/1 ratio. This was not the end of the story, however, because as early as a decade after the war, the two countries had diverged from the economic, social, and military points of view. Burdened by the huge human losses and the war-devastated economy, communist Vietnam became an economic third world country that could not even feed its own people, an oppressive, corrupt, and illegitimate regime that was shunned by its people and neighbors and from which escaped more than three million boat people. On the other hand, the U.S., after having lost the war, soon reestablished itself as a world economic and military power that easily defeated its nemesis, the Soviet Union, in the Cold War conflict.

Westmoreland also failed to count on the American people's antipathy to friendly losses. When he told Senator "Fritz" Hollings from his home state of South Carolina, "We're killing these people at a ratio of ten to one," Hollings responded, "Westy, the American people don't care about the ten. They care about the one."[35]

In the aftermath of the 1968 Tết attack on 15 June 1968, General Abrams assumed command of MACV replacing Westmoreland, who became U.S. Army chief of staff. The VC guerrillas, having lost the bulk of their forces during the Tết attack, were no longer a threatening force. Abrams decided to go after the North Vietnamese troops inside South Vietnam, especially those hiding in Cambodia.

However, the war was primarily lost in Washington by those who decided the war over the head of its MACV commander and his generals in South Vietnam. They were the "bureaucrats" whom American historians named the "Lunch Bunch Powers." For years, Johnson had ignored the role of the "Old Guards" at the Pentagon and had chosen to use the "politicians" in their places: planning and leading strategic and tactical operations both in Laos and Vietnam—including air war and land war in North and South Vietnam.

Saigon's War

Although the Government of Vietnam (GVN), or the Republic of Vietnam (RVN), only wanted to preserve its status and existence—survival and independence, eliminating the VC, driving out the North Vietnamese, and building a strong nation that could survive the communist threat[36]—their actions were at times uncertain, if not erratic.

First, they should have put more effort into it and fought more aggressively than the VC despite the fact that rebuilding the post-colonial country, searching for a democratic and economic path, and conducting the war at the same time in a country with limited resources was challenging to say the least. They should have had their own goals and plans, besides those required by the U.S., and should not have totally relied on the Americans to save them. Personal effort was not only needed; it was essential in this war of attrition. Bùi Diễm commented,[37]

> There was no sense of purpose or direction among the high officials of the government and strangely enough, in a country so pressed by the requirements of war, not a single member of the government, including the President himself, had any sense of urgency about the situation.

It was not because leaders did not have a sense of urgency; many did. But rebuilding the country and its infrastructure, shoring up the economy, establishing a new democracy, and waging a new war all at the same time were such overwhelming tasks no one was able to handle it. A democratic country cannot be built in 5 or 10 years; that effort alone may take two or more generations. Although some leaders had the vision and dream of winning the war and reunifying the country under their colors, their actions in an emerging country were not focused and strong enough to drown out the enemy's destructive zeal. The RVN once had thought about reunifying the country under its flag but was dissuaded by the Americans, who only accepted to fight a "limited war" inside Vietnam for fear of irritating China and the Soviet Union or causing them to get involved in the war.[38] The U.S. had failed to realize the Soviet Union was already involved in Vietnam by supporting Hanoi and sending them armaments and ammunition. Besides, it was not wise for the U.S. to telegraph beforehand to Hanoi that it would "limit" its war to certain regions. Knowing U.S. limitations, Hanoi simply used Laos and Cambodia as transit territories with minimal fear of retribution or attacks by the U.S.

Vietnamese leaders should have asked their people to sacrifice more in order to achieve the final goal. People would have been more than willing to do it had they been asked repeatedly. Just like after the 1968 Tết Offensive, civilians, although having already contributed their own blood and lives to the war effort, spontaneously felt they should give more to their country and volunteered in great numbers to enroll in the army to defend their country. The RVN should have invested in more propaganda work or even mind control because this was a total war: if the war were lost—it was—they would lose everything.

Seeing the Americans elbowing them away to take over the war effort, many ARVN leaders and troops became frustrated. They seemed to tell the Americans, "If you want to wage *your* war, go ahead. Do it yourself." For the South Vietnamese, it was a question of legitimacy, credibility, pride and self-consciousness. Because if they could not defend their own country, they would have a hard time rallying their people under their flag, for only a "self-reliant GVN could defeat insurgency."[39] This was Colonel Lansdale's "x factor," which dealt with the human, political side of the war. Đặng Văn Sung, a South Vietnamese nationalist and editor/owner of the Chính Luận newspaper, said,

> The anti-communist fight in Vietnam is seventy-five percent political and twenty-five percent military. Yet, everything the Americans did is directed to the twenty-five percent and nothing to the seventy-five percent.

The U.S. indifference toward the South Vietnamese nationalistic aspirations as well as inattention to the destructive impact of massive U.S. troop intervention on the structure and culture of Vietnamese society had damaged Saigon's position in the eyes of their own people.[40]

Despite these drawbacks, the South Vietnamese should not have become passive and withdrawn into their shells. They should instead have redoubled their efforts: fight with the U.S. to share the war effort and do the counter-insurgency part. Had they done an excellent counter-insurgency job and cleaned out the VC from the villages, they would have won the war—and the U.S. too. This was a common effort toward the same goal. Unfortunately, South Vietnam was not blessed with enough smart leaders who could figure that out.

Second, the South Vietnamese had been battling against the communists all along: first alongside the French during the First Vietnam War (1945–1954), then with the Americans during the Second Vietnam War (1955–1973) and then by themselves (1973–1975). Those who said that the ARVN stood by while the U.S. waged the war simply did not know what they were talking about.

The First Vietnam War had cost the French 59,745 dead and missing in action. The Vietnamese National Army (South Vietnamese) lost 58,877 dead and missing in action. About 400,000 civilians had died, of which 100,000 to 150,000 had been assassinated by the communists.[41]

By the end of the Second Vietnam War, the ARVN had lost an additional 300,000 soldiers, or five times as many casualties as the Americans. For a South Vietnamese population of 17 million people in 1975,[42] the 1.76 percent loss was indeed a huge one. Extrapolated to the U.S. population of 250 million people, that loss would equal 4.4 million people.

Table I. War Casualties by April 1975

	Military Casualties	Civilian Casualties	Wounded
United States	58,000	—	300,000
South Vietnam	294,000	450,000	1,600,000
VC/NVA	1,200,000	70,000	

However, a defensive approach alone would never win the war because South Vietnam had to defend a large territory and vital areas like cities, towns, storage areas, bridges and open borders with Cambodia and Laos as well as its own people. The communists by taking the offensive only needed to gather their forces and strike at Saigon's weak points, then run away. By the time rescuers arrived at the scene, the enemy had literally disappeared in the "bushes." For the majority of the war years, this was a low-grade insurgency war except for 1968, 1972, and 1975 when the enemy launched simultaneous multi-divisional attacks at different targets. Stretched thin, the ARVN could not defend all targets and simply was overrun. Besides, although troop mobility was essential, the ARVN was not allowed to build lots of mobile units and strategic reserves to defend against communist attacks.[43]

Third, the ARVN had always been outgunned by the communists, who were supplied with top-of-the-line armaments from their Russian or Chinese comrades. By 1964, while the communists used the famous Soviet AK-47 assault rifle, South Vietnamese forces were still equipped with World War II vintage arms like the U.S. M-1 rifle. Lieutenant General Đồng Văn Khuyến stated,

> the crisp, rattling sounds of AK-47s echoing in Saigon and some other cities seemed to make a mockery of the weaker single shots of Garand and carbines fired by stupefied troops.[44]

It was only after the 1968 Tết Offensive that some ARVN units were given the first shipment of U.S. M-16 rifles.[45] A four-year period was a long time in that war and could account for major battle losses. The U.S. 105 mm and 155 mm howitzers could hit a target at 11.27 and 14.6 kilometers respectively while the Soviet 122 mm and 130 mm had a range of 23.9 and 27.5 kilometers respectively. The NVA outgunned the ARVN in long-range artillery duels.[46]

With 11 infantry divisions, one marine and one airborne division, and some ranger forces, for a total of 1.1 million men under arms, the ARVN was spread too thin to defend all villages, hamlets, bridges, and cities. On the other hand, the communists had 300,000 troops alone in South Vietnam, besides local troops belonging to the National Liberation Front. By April 1975, Saigon was surrounded by 17 NVA divisions.[47]

After the 1973 Paris Accords were signed, the U.S. began to reduce its aid to South Vietnam while the Soviet Union doubled its assistance to North Vietnam to 1.5 billion dollars. This allowed the Hanoi communists to infiltrate 100,000 cadres and soldiers and to send 600 tanks, 500 heavy cannons, 200 anti-aircraft weapons, and many SA-7 rockets to South Vietnam. Their pipeline system was able to supply gas to their troops all the way up to 80 kilometers from Saigon.⁴⁸ In the meantime, the ARVN suffered from severe cutbacks, with U.S. aid decreasing from 1.5 billion to 750 million in 1974. Ammunition was running short as well as fuel for choppers, fighters, ships, and trucks. This led to operational flight time that was cut in half. VNAF reliability and efficiency gradually decreased with time. Spare parts for planes were difficult to get. Of the VNAF fleet of 30 C-130s, only five planes were able to fly. This cutback created tactical problems for field commanders on top of the lack of ammunition, which caused a morale problem for troops that obviously did not like to fight with insufficient ammunition. Soldiers going to battles used to get 400 rounds for their M-16 guns. Because of ammo shortage, they only received half that amount, which severely affected their fighting capability and morale. For anti-tank weaponry, instead of using the LAWs, they reverted to the 3.5 rocket launchers, which were World War II vintage weapons. The TOW rocket was not only expensive—$3,000 a piece—it did not do much good in killing enemy tanks. Damaged APCs or M-48 tanks had to be sent to the U.S. for repair and rebuilding, which not only increased repair costs, but also cut down on their availability. The M-16 rifle required three different types of oil to grease them while the communist AK-47 was simpler to fire and maintain.⁴⁹

Fourth, there are marked geographical, cultural, economic, political differences between northerners and southerners. The bounty of southern nature and its tropical climate offer a plentiful and laid-back lifestyle to southerners: rice from the expansive and rich Mekong Delta fields, fruit from their backyard gardens, and fish in ponds. By Vietnamese standards of the time—one cannot and should not compare it to the U.S., which had more than 180 years of democracy based on the Constitution—everyone had more than enough to eat in the South. Northerners, on the other hand, had to struggle against nature (cold weather, chilly winds), small agricultural plots, and crowdedness. In 1967–1968, North Vietnam's population exceeded 18 million people while South Vietnam only controlled 12 out of 17 million people.⁵⁰ "They [northerners] work harder, endure more, and know less of creature comfort"⁵¹ and therefore are more resilient than southerners. Southerners are "unrestrained to the point of indiscipline ... ready to laugh or to cry, quick to flare in anger and almost as quick to forgive and forget." They are cosmopolitans, at ease with foreigners, and know how to enjoy themselves.⁵² Politically, southerners lived under a somewhat free society: they were free to follow any religion they liked: Buddhism, Catholicism, Cao Daism, etc. They could protest, take to the streets, shut down the government, or make their voices heard. Foreign reporters were free to roam anywhere and ask any question they wanted. Under communism, northerners at the time could not speak to strangers or take to the streets; they had to follow strict communist rules and could not worship any religion they liked. One has to remember the cruel Land Reform (1954–1956) and Literary Reform (*Phong Trào Nhân Văn & Giai Phẩm*, 1956–1957) where tens of thousands of civilians were killed in the North. Western reporters could not roam anywhere they wanted or ask any question to civilians. There was essentially no freedom of choice and speech in the North.[53]

People have compared the South Vietnamese to the sunny, easygoing Italians and northerners to Germans. A closer analogy would be to compare northern (communist) and southern Vietnamese to the 2012 U.S. Republicans and Democrats, respectively. This is a comparison about attitude and societal control, not about freedom, which the North Vietnamese did not have. The South Vietnamese were in many ways similar to the 2012 Democrats, who, despite their discipline, tend "more toward anarchy than hierarchy."[54] The Republicans on the other hand are more regimented and "exercise more authority over policy and candidate selection than does the Democratic counterpart.... They prefer hierarchical, well-ordered organizations, and are much more willing to cede authority to those in power.... [They] crush insurgent candidates and select the next in line." As the 2012 Republicans are ahead of the Democrats as an "institutional force capable of command and control," in the 1960–1970s the communists were years ahead of the South Vietnamese nationalists in terms of organization, hierarchy, and propaganda.

Fifth, Saigon's leaders being "neither as unified nor as zealous as their counterparts to the north"[55] seemed to be the corollary of the above. The French, by staying around in South Vietnam until 1956 (they had vacated the North in 1954 but hung around in the South for a few more years), prevented the South Vietnamese from exercising and maturing their political and administrative acumen. By 1955, the communists had more than a decade of military and political advantage over them. When southerners finally got their freedom, it was like a dam breaking loose: all the various sects and political parties vied for power and fought against each other. No one listened to anyone: this was also the expression of the newly found freedom in the South. In 1954, Ngô Đình Diệm had to battle against the Hoà Hảo, Cao Đài sects, the Bình Xuyên, the state army, General Hinh, and the French who were still lingering in Saigon, more or less at the same time, in order to reestablish control of the state over these disparate entities.[56]

In the North, the communists had no qualms about suppressing and silencing their nationalist opponents. The Đại Việt (Greater Vietnam) and the Việt Nam Quốc Dân Đảng or VNQDD, both right-wing nationalist parties, fought against the communists, but to no avail.[57]

The communists just killed people right and left, forcing the opposition to hide as no one dared to raise his voice or head for it would be chopped off. This was how uniformity and strict control were accomplished under Hanoi's leadership. When Hanoi spearheaded its Land Reform, which killed more than 50,000 peasants,[58] the West stayed mum. But when Diệm tried to control the Buddhists, western papers raised its opposition and Lodge plotted to get him killed.[59] Either westerners did not want to acknowledge this difference in treatment or were plainly biased against the southerners. By staying mum and trying to downplay communists' bad behavior, they only encouraged the communists' cruelty and expansionist vision.

To state that South Vietnam lacked a sense of national identity[60] is not entirely correct, for Diệm had expressed his non-communist strain of modern Vietnamese nationalism that was present and had stood in opposition to that of the communists since the 1920s.[61] The Republic of Vietnam was proclaimed on 23 October 1955, "according to constitutional and legal procedures in contrast to the illegal and illegitimate takeover in Hanoi" by the communists.[62]

> In the present task of national revolution and reconstruction it is the anti-communist spirit that counts. It is the strongest and most comprehensive spirit because it includes all others. Those who have the anti-communist spirit are well qualified to be entrusted with the noble mission of liberating the people from oppression and slavery. So the main factor in our national revolution is the spirit, the will to fight communism.[63]

Historically, Lord Nguyễn Hoàng, one of the high officials of the northern monarchy (Hanoi), moved to Thuận Hoá (present-day Quảng Trị) in 1558 to serve as governor of a region that would become part of South Vietnam. In 1602, he turned away from Hanoi to dedicate himself to the building of the South or Đàng Trong. His successors broke away completely from the North or Đàng Ngoài then waged against it a 50-year war that ended in a stalemate (First Vietnam War). Thus, for two centuries (1602–1802), Đàng Trong and Đàng Ngoài co-existed as two separate and independent countries until Nguyễn Ánh (Gia Long) reunited the two regions into Vietnam in 1802.[64]

Vietnam then existed as a free and united country under the Nguyễn dynasty until 1861 when the French took over the South in 1859 and then the whole country in 1868. After World War II, the communists seized the power in the North while the South remained a French colony. The first modern Vietnam War broke out and concluded with the division between North and South through the 1954 Geneva Accords, with North Vietnam becoming a communist country while South Vietnam followed an open, although modified western-style republic under Ngô Đình Diệm's leadership. Diệm argued for an authoritarian government that would lie midway between communism and western-type democracy. For him, communism was an inhumane and foreign ideology while western liberalism would not pay enough attention to the poor and the community. Vietnam, a fractious country dominated for a long time by an authoritarian culture, would be more receptive to his brand of political ideology, which he dubbed *personalism*.[65]

The South Vietnamese formed a disparate group of freedom fighters who had not been unified under a strong leadership while Hanoi reigned supreme in the North because the communist party suppressed all nationalist non-communist parties.[66] When President Diệm tried to impose his authority on southerners, westerners labeled him an authoritarian leader who needed to be gotten rid of.[67] On various occasions between 1954 and 1963, Diệm and the U.S. had different and competing agendas for building a new South Vietnam. Although their visions were not so dissimilar as to make collaboration impossible, differences were real and substantial to the point of leading to the murder of the president and his brother. Americans among themselves also had different views about nation building in Vietnam. So did the Vietnamese politicians in South Vietnam. All these competing views collided, broke into the open and caused the unraveling and failure of the U.S.–Diệm relationship. "Nationalism in twentieth century Vietnam was nothing if not a contested and fragmented phenomenon." The latter phenomenon, although prevalent in the old Vietnamese Republican days, persisted under the communist post-war Vietnam.[68] This is to say that the Vietnamese, be they communist or non-communist, would be contesting about nationalism and nation building for years or decades to come, simply because "infighting was the[ir] primary chord."[69]

Sixth, to mention that "the exactions and cruelties of communist practice were acceptable [to peasants], however unpleasant," was far from the truth. This statement was not only derogatory, but also demeaning to Vietnamese peasants. Were they just less "human" than Americans and other westerners? People and peasants dreaded the violence of the VC but could not do anything about it because they were either confined in VC territory, had land and properties in these areas, or were not allowed to get out of these territories. Civilians were maimed by mines, caught in ambushes, had their houses burned down and were recruited against their will in the VC army.[70] Had they had a choice, they would have moved out a long time ago. Such was the case of the post-war period when millions of boat people just got out of the country knowing they might die from lack of food and water, engine breakdowns, sea storms, or in the hands of pirates.

The primary author (VND) personally had witnessed the arrest, torture, and execution of "suspected collaborators" in the 1940s in Cà Mau, South Vietnam. People were thrown in groups of three or four to be drowned alive in rivers (*mò tôm*).[71] My family was forced to escape to another province before returning two years later to our hometown. But soon, we had to move to Bạc Liêu to avoid persecution by the VC.[72]

Seventh, Saigon as a benevolent benefactor failed to rally peasants by not linking benefits to obligations. The VC awarded land to peasants only on condition that they become active participants in the revolution, send their sons to the VC army, and provide intelligence and material support for the insurgents. Saigon, on the other hand, by distributing land unconditionally in 1970, failed to generate any improvement in peasant allegiance to the government.[73] The peasants' outlook had not changed significantly for centuries. They were local, apolitical people who were more interested in their plots of land than national matters, Marxist theories, or collectivization of agriculture. All they wanted were tranquility and some material well-being; and they were less nationalistic and cared less about policies than city dwellers. They welcomed benevolent authoritarianism as long as it allowed them to work in peace. In the same vein, they approved good leadership or people with skills and determination, because hopefully the latter would leave them alone. Therefore, they were easily swayed in one direction or another by strong-arm tactics.[74] However, their attachment to any political institution was superficial and temporary in nature. They were above all opportunistic and never strongly trusted any government.

South Vietnam in the 1950s and 1960s was a complex society that was just emerging out of colonialism with groups having diverging aspirations and agendas. Because of its openness, its strengths and weaknesses lay bare like an open book for friends and enemies to see and target. Its nationalism—based on its anti-communism and free market economy—could not be contested. However, its leaders could not achieve their goals because of the wide diversity of opinions and views, which still persist to this day in postwar Vietnam. At least South Vietnam was freer and more democratic than North Vietnam during the war.

Hanoi's War

Communism is a foreign ideology that was introduced into Vietnam and imposed on the Vietnamese by Hồ Chí Minh and his party in the 1940s. By essence, it was alien to the Vietnamese and their culture. To force them to accept that ideology required a lot of coercion, brutal force, and mind bending. But northern communists proved better in "propaganda, depth of commitment, and, one must add, deception than the non-communist South Vietnamese leaders or governments."[75]

Hanoi's goal was always to conquer and unite the country under the leadership of the Vietnamese Communist Party (VCP).[76] "They [Americans, French, and South Vietnamese] would not allow us to unify our nation in a manner favorable to our side."[77] Having conquered the North by force in 1954, they proceeded with the conquest of the South again by using communism as their tool in order to get military support from China and the Soviet Union. South Vietnamese president Diệm, knowing the communists' intentions, tried to distance himself from the Americans—although he needed their help to fight off the communists—lest he be called a U.S. puppet. He also did not want to invite too many foreign troops into South Vietnam because Hanoi would frame the foreigners as colonialists and the war as a war against American colonialism. Therefore, when the Americans landed in Vietnam in 1963, from pursuing itself a war of conquest, Hanoi happily framed it as a war against "foreign aggressors," sold it as a patriotic war against foreign invaders, and thus seized the high moral ground.

Thanks to aggressive propaganda ploys like the one above, millions of Vietnamese unwittingly fell into Hanoi's trap and died thinking they fought for the right cause; many Americans who sided with the communist regime formed the Hanoi Lobby of the Indochinese Resource Center (IRC) in an attempt to influence Congress to cut aid to South Vietnam. As U.S. college students faced the prospect of being inducted into the army and sent to Vietnam if they scored low on their course grades, the group "Students for a Democratic Society" (SDS), besides sponsoring anti-war demonstrations on campuses, distributed a counter-exam on 14 May 1966 at 900 Selective Service System sites. The counter-exam destroyed the standard government propaganda on the war. A typical question reads,

> The war in South Vietnam is supposed to be part of our policy to contain communist Chinese aggression. How many communist Chinese troops are actively engaged in combat in Vietnam? (A) None (B) 1,000 (C) 50,000 (D) 100,000 (E) 500,000. The answer: (A).[78]

Sadly these student groups played into the hands of the communists—who of course approved and supported them—by challenging their own government and supporting the communist cause. They, however, did not even know the true answer to their own question. From declassified data, the Chinese had been helping the North Vietnamese since 1946, and by 1967 there were 15 Chinese AAA divisions with a peak strength of 170,000 men in North Vietnam.[79]

I. The Border War

The anti-war movement, the Hanoi Lobby of the IRC, the communist party of the USA (CPUSA) and other groups were successful in adversely influencing the U.S. Congress.

> The aid cut, approved by the Senate in September [1974], greatly hampered South Vietnam's fighting ability. Air operations were restricted, ammunition was rationed, and morale plummeted. The reduction also worsened Thieu's economic and political problems.[80]

Tom Wells concluded his book by mentioning that the American movement against the Vietnam War "played a major role in restricting, deescalating, and ending the war."[81] Although he may be correct about the adverse actions of the anti-war movement, the latter did *not* end the war, which continued until 1975 when the North Vietnamese, in full violation of the 1973 Paris Accords, invaded South Vietnam with their 17 divisions. Sadly, Wells and his anti-war movement, which could be defined as the U.S. fifth column, did not mention anything about the northern invasion.

The U.S. press (William Prochnau, David Halberstam, Neil Sheehan, Malcolm Browne, and others) wrote articles detrimental to the GVN cause.[82] Besides, newspaper editors would refuse to print any article beneficial to the South Vietnamese government. Bob Sharplen told Tom Polgar that for an "entire year not a single one of his articles got published," forcing him to part ways with the *New Yorker*. One correspondent for *Time* magazine was told about writing an article on the defection problem in the South Vietnamese Army. When he completed his article, which dealt with a worse defection problem in the communist army compared to the ARVN, only the section on the ARVN was published. There were good and bad newspeople. "Frances Fitzgerald was about as dishonest as they come, though…. She was interesting as a woman. But as a journalist she was another one that if the news didn't fit, she wouldn't print it."[83]

Hanoi did not care about the will of the people or the South Vietnamese. There was not a single inch of democracy in the North Vietnamese regime. Central to the communist effort was the use of "terror and violence in the broad sense of assassinations, kidnappings, sabotage."[84] Besides, the survival of the Hanoi government was never at stake, as U.S. leaders had made clear through both official statements and U.S. actions—a major mistake on the part of the U.S.[85]

Despite signing the Paris Accords which prohibited any interference in the South, Hồ Chí Minh in December 1957 at the 13th Plenary Session of the Party Central Committee stated, the preservation and growth of *our* revolutionary forces [italics ours] in the South is the factor that will directly determine the success of the revolutionary struggle in South Vietnam.[86]

In other words, Hồ acknowledged back in 1957 that he had military units in South Vietnam ready to fight and to take down that part of the country. In 1959, Hanoi was ready to send the 338th Division, composed of Southern regroupees (southerners who had moved north during the 1954 division of the country) and a number of northern infantry regiments to the battlefields of South Vietnam. The Group 559 (May 1959) was established for the purpose of opening a road from Đồng Hới City in Quảng Bình Province to Khe Hồ in western Vĩnh Linh, which then crossed the Bến Hải River dividing the two sides of the country down Route 9 in Thừa Thiên Province (part of South Vietnam) along the eastern slopes of the Trường Sơn Chain (Annamite cordillera, which forms the backbone of Vietnam), and advancing toward the South.[87] Once the South Vietnamese discovered the infiltration route and tightened control along the Bến Hải River,[88] the trail from Khe Hồ was shifted eastward, crossing into Laos before heading south along the western edge of the Annamite Mountain range and ending in western Cambodia.

That route, known by Hanoi as the "Trường Sơn Strategic Supply Road" because it hugged the western side of the Trường Sơn cordillera, was labeled by westerners as the Hồ Chí Minh Trail. Almost 100,000 Vietnamese and Laotians worked on the trail at its height.[89] The number of "confirmed" cadres and *bộ đội*[90] sent down the trail rose to 4,000 in 1961, 5,300 in 1962, and 4,700 in 1963. There were an additional 12,850 probable infiltrators.[91] NVA General Võ Bẩm confirmed that 20,000 cadres moved along that route in the early years.[92] The infiltration rate increased to 12,400 in 1964, 36,300 in 1965, 92,287 in 1966, and 101,263 in 1966.[93] It remained a vibrant and active highway of invasion of the South. Hanoi sent 100,000 troops down the trail in 1973 and 80,000 more during the first half of 1974. By that time, the roads were macadam or paved all the way to the South Vietnamese border.[94] It was no wonder that as soon as Westmoreland destroyed one NVA battalion a new one had already emerged to take its place.

Throughout the war, Hanoi repeatedly denied having invaded South Vietnam or having troops in that part of the country although evidence was widely available. Lê Duẩn in May 1959 through Resolution 15 had sanctioned armed force to support the political struggle in South Vietnam, the first stage of Lê Duẩn-Lê Đức Thọ's campaign for total war.[95] In December 1963, one month after the murder of President Diệm, Lê Duẩn at the Ninth Plenum of the Central Executive Committee of the Communist Party elevated the Vietnamese civil war to an international Cold War conflict by formulating the

Tổng Công Kích Tổng Khởi Nghĩa plan (General Offensive General Uprising) to take over South Vietnam by force.[96] Hanoi, by infiltrating troops and armaments into South Vietnam, had not only violated the 1954 Paris Accords but also started the Second Vietnam War. Since it had planned the war back in 1959, Hanoi and the Communist Party should bear all the responsibility and consequences of their actions.

Hanoi also established a sea infiltration route in South Vietnam under Group 959, a parallel naval unit[97] with a base set up on the Gianh River in the province of Quảng Bình and a communication base high on the Hải Vân Pass in Quảng Nam, central Vietnam, to broadcast navigation directions. Group 959 would send out soldiers and cadres disguised as local fishermen in wooden boats for local infiltration. Later, they sent larger Chinese ships[98] loaded with soldiers and armaments that eventually disembarked at Sihanoukville, formerly named Kompong Som, a Cambodian port on the Gulf of Siam. From November 1966 to January 1969, 34 ships suspected of unloading ordnance had docked at Sihanoukville. Twelve that were well documented had delivered more than 14,000 tons of ordnance from November 1966 to October 1968.[99]

All these shipments through Laos and Cambodia would not have been possible with the complicity and/or weakness of these governments. These two countries claimed to be neutral because they were too weak to even defend their territorial integrity. They hoped that a neutral status would save them from an invasion. But Hanoi did not care about anything, even world opinion. It used Laos and Cambodia as transit routes to move armaments and troops from North Vietnam to western Cambodia, without any of these two countries raising a problem. Hanoi even used Cambodia as a huge army camp to station its forces as well as storage areas for guns, tanks, ammunition, and food to be later dispensed for use inside South Vietnam. The U.S., by respecting their neutrality, simply played into the hands of Hanoi. The Vietnamese have an expression for Hanoi's attitude: *"vừa ăn cướp, vừa la làng"* (loud mouthing while stealing). It was fine for them to abuse the neutrality of these two countries, but once the South Vietnamese moved into Laos, they cried foul forcing the U.S. to pressure the South Vietnamese back home.

The communists controlled the minds of its people. They used radical methods to destroy the links between the recruit and his family, forcing him to devote completely to the revolutionary cause. By killing individualism and inserting him into a cell of three people to control one another, they built a socialist and communist man dedicated not to his family or society, but to the party. The recruit was then subjected to daily indoctrination and self-criticism. Corralled by the other people in his cell, the new recruit had no chance of escaping from the system.[100] They set up a well-regulated propaganda system with loudspeakers blaring off all kinds of propaganda all day long, forcing civilians/soldiers to think one way. By 1975, indoctrinated northerners, although very poor, still believed they were waging the war to "liberate" the South from imperialist oppression. They believed southerners were so poor they did not have rice to eat and bought cheap-quality rice from the North. Only when they arrived in Saigon did they realize southerners were much better off than northerners. A female writer—a youth brigade volunteer and party member—Dương Thu Hương, was amazed to see all kinds of books displayed for sale in the open markets of Saigon: "I could see all the great authors, Russian, American, and so many others.... I could buy Marx in Saigon, but I couldn't buy the authors of different opinion in Hanoi."[101]

They made the world believe that they were fighting the war alone while they not only received aid from both Moscow and Beijing, but also played one off against the other in order to get the best deal possible. Although aware of Hanoi's game, to maintain unity within the communist group they gave the "fraternal assistance" Hanoi requested. The Soviet Union provided advanced military weaponry and personnel to defend the skies of North Vietnam against American bombing.[102]

China not only sent billions of dollars in aid, but also dispatched "half a million technicians, advisers, and combat troops to assist Hanoi in its struggle."[103] The Chinese provided missiles, artillery and logistics, railroads, engineers and minesweeping forces. They built and repaired Vietnamese infrastructure damaged or destroyed by U.S. air strikes. Chinese anti-aircraft artillery troops peaking at 150,000 men in 1968 would claim credit for downing more than 1,700 U.S. aircraft over North Vietnam. The massive Chinese force was also used as a shield to prevent any potential invasion of North Vietnam.[104]

In 1971, the NVA lowered the draft age from 17 to 16 and raised the upper age from 30 to 35 to fill their 15 divisions, 14 of them located outside North Vietnam. The average training time had been reduced from six to five months. Between October 1971 and March 1972, the USSR delivered 271,000 tons of POL (130 percent of requests) to North Vietnam. By the end of 1971, the NVA personnel strength increase from 390,000 to 430,000. They were equipped with technically advanced air defense systems: the Strela or "SA-7 Grail," a handheld, heat-seeking surface-to-air missile (SAM) that could destroy aircraft flying up to 10,000 feet. Larger Soviet-made SAMs could destroy B-52 bombers. They also had .51 caliber machine guns; 23 mm, 37 mm, 57 mm, 85 mm, and 100 mm anti-aircraft guns; and ZSU-24s that fired anti-aircraft rockets.[105]

The Vietnam War was not only a war of aggression, but also an international one. Without foreign troops and huge amounts of sophisticated and modern foreign equipment, Hanoi could not have achieved its conquest of the South. As a war of aggression, of conquest, there was no such a thing as greatness or nationalism in Hanoi's goals.

The Border War Under Generals Đỗ Cao Trí and Nguyễn Văn Minh

Bound by Washington's "limited war" and reservation about expanding the war to Laos and Cambodia, Westmoreland had minimal intelligence on the specifics inside each of the communist Cambodian sanctuaries. His intelligence chief MACV J-2, Lieutenant General Philip Davidson, stated that he never had half a firm grasp on these sanctuaries although he knew of the NVA order-of-battle information.[106] But as soon as the NVA emerged from the sanctuaries, fought a battle, lost prisoners or dead soldiers, the order of battle was immediately known to the U.S.

At least two North Vietnamese regiments marched through Laos into Northern Cambodia in 1953–1954.[107] The 1954 Geneva Accords assured Cambodia's independence under Prince Sihanouk as well as the withdrawal of northern troops from Cambodia, although the latter never left Cambodia. Sihanouk then faced the determined Vietnamese communists on one side and the softer South Vietnamese and the Americans on the other side. Between the communists or American imperialism, he made the fatidic choice of helping the former.[108] He allowed them to receive Chinese arms shipments through the port of Sihanoukville and derived some income from the transportation of these shipments to the safe sanctuaries in western Cambodia. That deal sealed his demise and his country's.

Cambodia was therefore essential to Hanoi because from there it could send troops into the South Vietnamese highlands or III and IV Corps (a dozen eastern provinces and the Mekong Delta, respectively) and then withdraw back to the safe Cambodian sanctuaries without fear of being pursued. It could rest its troops and rearm them for the next battle. But the borders between Vietnam and Laos and Cambodia stretch over 600 miles beginning from the western end of the DMZ line to the Gulf of Siam. Watching this border was difficult and manpower/resource demanding since the area is mountainous and sparsely populated.

Besides using the Hồ Chí Minh Trail to feed these sanctuaries, Hanoi also used the maritime approach. It shipped weapons in October 1966 to the port of Shihanoukville with the "tacit approval of the Cambodian government."[109] Although the Cambodian leader, Sihanouk, sought to preserve his country's autonomy, he was faced with aggressive requests from Hanoi whose troops were already in Cambodia; he relented and made a deal with Hanoi, which eventually led him and his country downhill. What was worse was that his family profited by letting Hanoi move its supplies from the port to western Cambodia.

An NVA ship would dock at Sihanoukville every three months and supplies were trucked to depots west of Phnom Penh. From there, arms and ammunitions moved through regional facilities at Svay Rieng, Kratie, Kampong Cham, and Stung Treng before reaching one of eight communist bases in western Cambodia[110] where the communists controlled a swath of land 10 to 15 kilometers along the border. U.S. bombers easily targeted these communist bases in Cambodia. Although it was a military success, it lost public and congressional support, which drastically cut down U.S. military advisory effort and military aid to South Vietnam.[111]

In January 1969, newly elected President Richard Nixon decided to bomb NVA bases in Cambodia. The strike began in March 1969 and lasted until August. Operation MENU, the secret bombing of Cambodian sanctuaries, targeted six of the 16 sanctuaries along the Vietnamese border that posed significant threat to Saigon and surrounding areas.[112] The secret bombing of Cambodia cemented the adversarial relationship between Secretary of Defense Laird and the Nixon White House, forcing Laird to push for faster withdrawals from Vietnam.[113]

Nixon, recognizing the Americans' disenchantment with the war and the decline of U.S. power,[114] began the pullout process. Some 25,000 men left in August 1969, 40,000 more in December and 50,000 by April 1970. A total of 115,000 soldiers, or one-fourth of the U.S. forces, were withdrawn in the span of nine months. Another 90,000 more were scheduled to depart by December of 1970.[115] This withdrawal was associated with cuts in U.S. tactical air and B-52 operations.

Then on 1 May 1970, U.S.–ARVN launched a cross-border attack into Cambodia. The advance rarely moved farther than 15 kilometers inside the Cambodian border and cleared both banks of the Mekong Delta all the way to Phnom Penh. All the forces returned back to South Vietnam by 1 July.[116]

Lieutenant General Nguyễn Văn Minh was promoted commander of the ARVN III Corps and 3rd Military Region (III Corps and MR3) after the most brilliant ARVN officer, General Đỗ Cao Trí's, helicopter was blown up while flying above the province of Tây Ninh on 23 February 1971.

During his tenure, the ARVN had made many military operations from all four corps against communist strongholds along the Cambodian and Laotian borders and pushed them deep into the Laotian and Cambodian territories. At the high-water mark, the ARVN had more than 29,000 troops in Cambodia and the U.S. about 19,300. One NVA cache yielded 1,300 individual- and more than 200 crew-served weapons, along with a million and a half rounds of AK-47 ammunition. Huge treasure troves of intelligence were found, more than a million pages of documents and 32 cases of cryptographic material in just the first three weeks of the cross-border operation.[117]

Operational units from the III Corps and MR3 under Lieutenant General Đỗ Cao Trí had achieved the highest results. From April 1970, they had pushed the North Vietnamese Army 7th Division (7th Div/NVA) and the VC 9th Division (9th Div/VC) of the COSVN out of their strongholds in the Fish Hook area on the northwest border of Bình Long and the Parrot's Beak on the southwest border of Tây Ninh respectively. They had also destroyed the strongholds, big and small, of the COSVN (Central Office of South Vietnam—the political and military nerve centers of northern communists in South Vietnam), killed more than 11,000 PAVN soldiers, taken 2,200 troops prisoners, and confiscated hundreds of tons of ammunition and armaments. The VC 5th Division (5th Div/VC) had pulled back into Cambodia and been followed closely by the ARVN IV Corps and MR4.

Up north, along National Route 7, tank units from the III Corps and MR3 crossed the rubber plantations of Mimot, Krek, and Chup, all the way to Tonle-Bet on the eastern side of the Mekong River across from the city of Kampong Cham—the headquarters of the FANK, 1st Military Region (FANK/MR1) of Brigadier General Fan Muong from the National Cambodian Armed Forces (Forces Armées Nationales Khmères, or FANK). In the south, along National Route 1, other tank units from Lieutenant General Trí moved to the outskirts of Sway Rieng to support the forces of Colonel Dap Duon, the governor of this eastern Cambodian province that lies across the border from Tây Ninh of South Vietnam.

While staying on Cambodian soil for close to one year, the ARVN worked with the Cambodian military government to repatriate approximately 20,000 Vietnamese living in Cambodia. The main goal of Lieutenant General Đỗ Cao Trí's "*Toàn Thắng*" (Total Victory) operations was not only to destroy communist forces and their strongholds in Cambodia and to support the weak and young forces of General Lon Nol (who was the chief of staff of Cambodian forces that overthrew Norodom Sihanouk in March 1970 when the latter was out of the country), but also to free the tens of thousands of jailed Vietnamese who were suspected by the local government of siding with the communists. In mid–April 1970, I was assigned by General Trí to be the liaison officer in the province of Sway Rieng in place of Colonel Lê Đạt Công, then the chief of 2nd Bureau (in charge of military intelligence), III Corps and MR3 (ex–III Corps and 3rd TZ). I received instructions and understood the worries of General Trí with regard to the Vietnamese living in Cambodia. Therefore, after knowing the needs of Colonel Dap Duon, province chief of Sway Rieng, and satisfying a few important matters, my first job was to request Colonel Duon to allow me to meet with the 2,000 Vietnamese being held prisoner at the local primary school. In front of the school gate, I promised to the representatives of the Vietnamese to transmit their wishes to be repatriated to Vietnam to General Trí. That I have done.

In May 1970, I was assigned to Kongpong-Cham as a liaison officer at the headquarters of Brigadier General Fan Muong, along with a group of 10 officers and NCOs of the 2nd and 3rd Bureaus and communications of III Corps and MR3. In Kongpong Cham, I had also requested Lieutenant Colonel Ly Tai Sung, deputy of General Fan Muong, to let me see the Vietnamese being held prisoner by the Cambodians. More than 2,000 Vietnamese, including women and children, huddled in the deep and wide trenches within the perimeters of the FANK/MR1 headquarters. This happened only in the morning after I requested General Trí to send South Vietnamese Air Force (VNAF) jets to relieve the blockade around the headquarters caused by the VC J-16 Sapper Battalion and the NVA forces the night before. Pointing to the Vietnamese in the trenches, Ly Tai Sung told me in Vietnamese in straight terms, "If you did not call the Air Force to free us up, these people would be shot dead."

From the time we arrived to Kongpong Cham, we communicated with Major John Fernandez, the chief of staff; Ly Tai Sung, deputy commander; and Brigadier General Fan Muong, commander in French since we did not speak Cambodian and had never heard them speak Vietnamese at any time before. When I heard Ly Tai Sun utter these words, I told him, "You are thus a Vietnamese. Do you mean that you would kill the Vietnamese prisoners and our group too?"

He smiled.

"You have underestimated the huge consequences of your action," I told him.

Ly Tai Sun or Lý Đại Sơn did not say any other word. I went inside right away and told Brigadier General Fan Muong about Ly Tai Sun; I then reported to General Trí who sent helicopters and some airborne troops to take us back to Biên Hòa in the afternoon. Maybe Brigadier General Fan Muong later apologized to General Trí. The important problem was to solve the problem of thousands of Vietnamese being held prisoners by the Cambodian

I. The Border War

government many months earlier before the North Vietnamese communists and the Khmer Rouges began their attacks on Cambodian cities and the capital of Phnom Penh. A few days later, Major Nguyễn Văn Lý from the 2nd Bureau, III Corps, and another liaison team were sent to Kong Pong Cham. Later Colonel Trần Văn Tư replaced Major Lý.

Although I was not privy to the high-level relationships between the government of South Vietnam and Cambodia on that May of 1970, VNN (Vietnam Navy) and ARVN missions continued and brought back tens of thousands of Vietnamese in the months of May, June and July of 1970. During that period I was assigned to the 2nd Bureau, III Corps, under the leadership of Colonel Lê Đạt Công, sometimes at Biên Hoà, other times at Hiếu Thiện, Tây Ninh and rotating around to advise him about army intelligence until General Trí passed away.

After Lieutenant General Minh replaced General Trí and following the latter's solemn funeral, the military situation in the III Corps and MR3 had significantly changed for two reasons.

First, the communists significantly increased their forces in all the battlefields in Laos and Cambodia with offensives in Tchepone and along Route 9 all the way to the border with Khe Sanh; along Route 7 from the rubber plantations of Minot, Chup, to the Vietnamese-Cambodian border, the Parrot's Beak and the Fish Hook area. The 8th Regiment and an armor unit of the ARVN 5th Infantry Division (5th Div/ARVN) suffered heavily and withdrew from Snoul, Cambodia, at the end of May 1971. The only remaining place that the RVNAF III Corps and 3rd MR still maintained on Cambodian soil was the combined U.S.–Vietnamese firebase located at Krek, at the intersection between Highways 7 and 22 going to Tây Ninh, about 12 kilometers from the Viet-Cambodian border.

Second, Lieutenant General Nguyễn Văn Minh, a thoughtful man, preferred defense rather than offense. He was not a tiger like General Đỗ Cao Trí, but more like an intellectual general. Besides, strategy had changed after the Lâm Sơn 719 Operations in lower Laos. He fell into a difficult command situation for having graduated from Class IV of the Dalat Military Academy while his two subordinates were from a senior class. Major Generals Nguyễn Văn Hiếu and Lâm Quang Thơ, commanders of the 5th and 18th Divisions respectively, graduated from Class III of the Dalat Military Academy. After the withdrawal from Snoul, Major General Hiếu was transferred to another post. Colonel Lê Văn Hưng, province chief of Cần Thơ, had been promoted to succeed Major General Hiếu. Shortly after, Major General Lâm Quang Thơ was replaced by Colonel Lê Minh Đảo.

In the first week of June 1971, I was ordered to report on the positions of enemy forces inside and outside Vietnam that III Corps had to deal with to Colonel Hưng, the new commander of the ARVN 5th Infantry Division. The bulk of the report was no different from what I have written here. Of course, no mention was made about Generals Trí, Minh, Hiếu, and Thơ. I discussed about the NVA and COSVN local communist forces operating close to the Vietnamese-Cambodian border after the ARVN withdrew from Cambodia; the strengths, equipments, and territory of operation of each of these units according to our latest news; and speculations about their future plans. I thought that we needed to decrease the pressure exerted by NVA troops that gathered to attack Krek following the presence of COSVN in the Snoul area and the reactivations of the NVA secret bases close to the border of Bình Long and Tây Ninh. I thus gave the usual report on enemy strengths at the military divisional level. Colonel Hưng apparently heard me well and did not raise any question. After I completed the report, he turned to General Minh and said, "General, Dưỡng was not only my classmate, but also in my platoon." He stood up, walked to the podium, shook my hand and embraced me. This was the first sign of friendship he had shown 15 years following our graduation from the Thủ Đức Military Academy in January 1955 as 2nd lieutenants. At the time of the report in 1971, I was a major, a member of the 2nd Bureau III Corps while he was a colonel, commander of a division. Positions in the military were indeed a world apart.

The border war was just delaying the final outcome of the war by containing the NVA inside Cambodia. When allied forces left Cambodia, the NVA just stepped up and rebuilt their forces in the safe Cambodian sanctuaries to get ready for the next strike across the border. For as long as the NVA could safely maintain troops and armaments in Cambodia, they had the upper hand in the war. From there, they could rest their troops and infiltrate new units to whichever regions of South Vietnam they liked.

One could see that Washington had restrained itself in a "limited" war while Hanoi used a multi-pronged attack against Saigon and brought the war to the heart of Saigon.

II

General Lê Văn Hưng and I

The first time I met Lê Văn Hưng was at the Thủ Đức Military School Center, about 15 miles northeast of Saigon, where we went through a yearlong military training to become reserve officers in the new South Vietnamese Army in 1954.

Formative Years of the South Vietnamese Army

On 1 May 1950, President Harry S. Truman by approving a $10 million grant for needed military assistance items for Indochina made the formal commitment to militarily support the Government of Vietnam (GVN). From 1950 to 1954, the U.S. contributed $1.1 billion to France to prosecute the war in Vietnam including $746 million worth of army materiel to the French Expeditionary Force in Indochina. Following the signing of the 20 July 1954 Geneva Accords, the U.S. began to directly assist the GVN under President Diêm. The U.S. Military Assistance Advisory Group in Vietnam (MAAGV) was limited by the Accords to 342 individuals. It was only in February 1955 that a joint Franco-American Training Relations and Instruction Mission (TRIM) was established to develop a program to train the Vietnamese Army. Since the French still retained a portion of their army in South Vietnam until 1956, its chief, General Paul Ely, was head of the TRIM and U.S. General O'Daniel's operational superior.

The work of the TRIM was severely limited because of the internal and political situation in South Vietnam. This affected the South Vietnamese Army, which lacked trained leaders, equipment and adequate logistical capabilities at all levels. Logistical matters were still controlled by the French who withdrew their advisers only on 28 April 1956. Following their departure, they took with them the best equipment in the quantities desired for their future needs, leaving the Vietnamese with obsolete or inadequate materiel, which could not be upgraded because of lack of Vietnamese logistical system.

By September 1959, the South Vietnamese Army was reorganized into seven divisions of 10,450 men each and three Army Corps headquarters. Each division consisted of three infantry regiments, an artillery, a mortar, an engineer battalion, and company-size support elements. The airborne troops were organized into a five-battalion group.[1]

The Civil Guard Corps (Regional Force or RF) created in April 1955 assisted regular forces with internal security duties and local intelligence collection. Initially placed under the control of the president, it was turned over to the Ministry of Interior in September 1958. The People's Self-Defense Corps or Force (PSDF), officially established in April 1956, policed villages and protected the population from subversion and intimidation. Their numbers were 46,000 and 40,000 respectively.[2]

Military Training at Thủ Đức

The Thủ Đức Reserve Officers School was established by the French in October 1951 to train cadres and specialists of all branches of the South Vietnamese Army including the infantry. After the 1954 Geneva Accords, the management changed from the French to the Vietnamese armed forces. The school changed its name to the Thủ Đức Military Academy in 1955 and to the Infantry School in July 1964. From 1952 to November 1969, it graduated over 40,900 students and continued to be the largest source of officers in the Vietnamese armed forces.[3] Thủ Đức offered nine months of military instruction to high school level officer candidates, and graduates received a reserve commission, the rank of aspirant (CW5 or chief warrant officer 5), and a four-year active-duty obligation.[4] The latter could mean ten to 15 years of active duty as the war progressed without end. Many well-known generals had graduated from this academy, including Nguyễn Khoa Nam, Ngô Quang Trưởng and Lê Văn Hưng.

The Vietnamese National Military Academy (VNMA), which was founded in Huế in December 1948, was moved to Dalat in the Central Highlands because of better local weather. When the Vietnamese assumed control of the academy in 1954, they changed its name to Dalat Military Academy. After 1955, under the American advisory effort, the curriculum was extended from one to two years (1956) and then to a four-year degree-granting university under President Diêm in 1959. However, because of short-term demand for junior officers, it only graduated three-year classes. It was only in December 1969 that it graduated its first 92 cadets from its four-year program. During 1970, a second-year VNMA cadet was the first Vietnamese to be accepted for entrance to the U.S. Military Academy, West Point.[5]

The number of cadets of Class V, *Vì Dân* (For the People), at the Thủ Đức Military Academy totaled more than 1,300. This included two infantry companies that were sent to the Dalat Military Academy for training while the remaining cadets were dispatched to the Thủ Đức Military Academy in May 1954. Lê Văn Hưng and I were assigned to the 8th Platoon of the 2nd Infantry Company under the command of 2nd Lieutenant Nguyễn Hưng Chiêu. We slept in the same mixed room as cadets of the 7th Platoon of 1st Lieutenant Lê Văn Sỹ. In this mixed central room, each platoon had 12 men; two main rooms located on either side of the mixed room housed 24 cadets of these two platoons each.

In this Class V were two infantry companies and six specialized companies: armor, artillery, engineering, signal, ordinance, and administration. The 1st Infantry Company included the 1st, 2nd, 3rd and 4th Platoons; the 2nd Company was composed of the 5th, 6th, 7th, and 8th Platoons. My 8th Platoon had 36 students, of whom I remember more than 30 names. Platoon 8 of Company 2 of 2nd Lieutenant Nguyễn Hưng Chiêu was the only platoon to have produced two major achievements: graduate a valedictorian and the only general for the whole class who would later become famous nationwide. The latter was Brigadier General Lê Văn Hưng, from Hóc Môn, province of Gia Định. He, along with four other generals, committed suicide on 30 April 1975 following the fall of Saigon.[6]

At that time, cadet Lê Văn Hưng compulsively blinked his eyes: the tic persisted when he became a general. Whether it was congenital or acquired in his youth was not known; but by the time I knew him as a cadet, he had already acquired it. In the dorm room, he was always bare chested, wore a red Cambodian sarong with dark green stripes and a gold necklace threaded through a small boar tooth. Like many South Vietnamese, he rarely spoke, but he was very likable because he frequently smiled—a gentle smile that captured the heart of many ladies. His skin was somewhat dark, but he was tall like a hero rather than a student. He was also married at that time. Close to the completion of the first phase of the training and after being allowed to wear the alpha sign of a cadet, we were released every other week to allow us to visit families and relatives. For each platoon of 36 cadets, one-half would remain in the camp while the other half took leave each weekend. I was in the same group as Hưng, whether on leave or in the camp.

As Vietnamese, we all faced moving experiences, and I was not the exception. When I entered the Thủ Đức Military Academy, I was a single student from a poor family who had no nearby relatives. Two months after my enrollment into the school in May 1954, my country became divided into two states following the signing of the Geneva Accords. My small birthplace of Cà Mau, in the southernmost region of the country, became the rallying center for all the communist and insurgent armed forces in the southern part of Vietnam before they were relocated to North Vietnam according to the agreements of the Geneva Accords. During the same period, almost one million northerners migrated to the South by various means, most likely ships from allied forces.[7]

My father and elder brother moved to Bạc Liêu to work for the government. In spite of my small cadet salary, I did send some money to help my parents, my younger school-aged sister, my widowed sister and her two children.[8] During weekdays, when practicing in the fields, I carried the leftover breakfast that other cadets did not consume—mostly bread, chocolate, and cheese—to use it during class breaks while other well-to-do classmates scurried around local vendors who provided fresh food. At dinner time, I used to take back to the dorm a can-size bit of white rice to use as an evening snack while more fortunate cadets frequented the mess or the many vendors (usually wives of camp staff soldiers) who brought dessert for sale on the doorsteps of the dorm. I quietly took my rice along with a bottle of soy sauce, sat on the steps at the beginning of the sewer system being built on a stream close to a row of dormitories, and ate it under moonlight or in total obscurity. I swallowed these cold rice grains on many nights with feelings of self pity. And one day, I don't remember which one, Lieutenant Nguyễn Hưng Chiêu caught me eating rice in the dark. He shone his flashlight in the can of rice and the bottle of soy sauce while I was standing in a salute position as a cadet would do in front of his superior. He did not say a word; he let me stand there and went back to the dorm. I quietly returned to the dorm with a lot of apprehension in my heart and fear of having committed some kind of infraction against one of the school rules; I was waiting for punishment. On the contrary, I received a 100-piaster bill—which was a huge amount at that time—that was slipped into my notebook when the company commander returned it to the cadet. He quietly gave me the cash to let me know he understood my economic situation. For more than six decades, I felt I still owed him for having made me into an ARVN officer and a compassionate and righteous person like him. I did not dream of returning the

II. General Lê Văn Hưng and I   39

favor to him in this life because I knew of nothing comparable to his magnanimous heart. On the other hand, the person who did him a huge favor was General Hưng through his brilliant military career and his self-sacrifice; he was another cadet that Lieutenant Chiêu had trained and educated.

At that time, I rarely took weekend leaves. When I did, I got out on Sunday morning, strolled around the big downtown district of Saigon, watched a movie, and waited for late afternoon to go to Hai Bà Trưng Street behind the National Congressional Building where the academy's GMC trucks were waiting to take us back to the camp. When not taking leave, I dressed up in full military gear and mingled with northern cadets who were made "orphans" like me by the 1954 Geneva Agreements. Many northerners either had families stranded in the North or were relocated far from Saigon. We then strolled around the camp's flagpole where rows of trees, although rare, projected their shade on the grass and where cadets used to meet their visiting families when they were stuck in the camp.

The peacefulness, happiness, and vibrant vitality generated from this family environment were also seen in the mess and kiosks, dining stands around the mess. Naturally, among the crowd of visitors, there was no lack of beautiful, smiling ladies who were the sisters, relatives, girlfriends, or wives of the cadets. One of them was Hưng's wife. From afar, one could tell she was beautiful. The fact that she was tall, thin but strong and well proportioned made her look like a European lady. Her face was bright and her skin fair. Her composure and clothing placed her in the middle class. Each time she came, she brought with her a one-year-old daughter. And the family huddled together and looked very happy. But one could not predict what the future would bring to people.

At the end of the training, we said good-bye to one another, and each of us went his own way. Absorbed in our military as well as personal life, we did not keep in touch with each other. Nine years later, toward January 1964, I suddenly received news about Hưng. During the 1 November 1963 overthrow of the government, President Ngô Đình Diêm and his brother were assassinated. Colonel Nguyễn Văn Phước, the second bureau chief of the Joint General Staff of the Republic of Vietnam Armed Forces (II Bureau/JGS/RVNAF) was jailed and replaced by Lieutenant Colonel Hồ Văn Lời, commander of the Cây Mai Intelligence School. I followed him and became the Administrative Branch chief of II Bureau/JGS or J-2/JGS.

While reading the mail one day, I noticed a transfer order from the Ministry of Defense releasing then Lieutenant Lê Văn Hưng back to the Military Intelligence Branch under the control of J-2/JGS. Before the overthrow, Hưng was the district chief of Trà Ôn District in southwest Vietnam. He could thus have gone through an intelligence course or held a job in the field of military intelligence, which I was not aware of. Later, I received his personnel file indicating that by graduating high in the class at Thủ Đức, he chose to serve the 15th Regiment in Gia Định in the III Military Region, which at that time comprised the present III and IV Corps with Major Lê Thọ Trung as the regiment commander. Later when Hưng became a general and commander of the 5th Div/ARVN, then Lieutenant Colonel Trung became Hưng's chief of staff.

Less than one week after he was transferred to the J-2/JGS/RVNAF, a lady requested to see the colonel, chief of J-2. I met her as an administrative representative of the bureau in place of my supervisor. She stated she was Hưng's former wife but had divorced him. I then realized that she was the lady I saw a decade earlier at the Thủ Đức Academy. She was thin and still beautiful for a middle-aged lady. She carried a document requesting that his salary, according to a court's verdict, be sent directly to her in Gia Định. I wrote down her request, although could not make any decision because Lieutenant Hưng had not shown up for duty at the bureau yet.

Not long after, I received another memo from the Personnel Directorate of the Ministry of Defense transferring Lieutenant Hưng to the 21st Infantry Division (21st Div/ARVN). Therefore, up to 1971 I still had not met Hưng because he showed up for duty at the 21st Div/ARVN instead of the J-2/JGS/RVNAF. By the end of 1967, I unintentionally met his ex-wife again one evening at the Victoria Dancing Club in Tân Định close to the JGS Headquarters where she was a dancer. Although I recognized her, she did not remember seeing me four years earlier. At that time, I was a major and Hưng a lieutenant colonel, commander of the 31st Regiment of the 21st Division. A short while later, I heard he was made colonel and province chief of Cần Thơ. From 1967 after the meeting at the dancing club, I had no further encounter with Hưng's ex-wife. That was more than half a century ago.

Intelligence Work

After the June 1971 briefing, Lieutenant General Minh invited Colonel Hưng, commander of the 5th ARVN Infantry Division, and I to have lunch in his trailer that lay in the front yard of his residence in Biên Hoà. I might not have had the privilege to be invited to have lunch with the two commanding officers had it not been for the fact that Colonel Hưng had mentioned me as his classmate. The other reason why I was included in this high-level meeting was that in early 1955 when I was transferred to the 61st

Vietnam Battalion to serve as chief of the personnel office until August 1955, then Major Minh, recently promoted commander of the 61st Vietnam Battalion and district chief of Đức Hòa District of Chợ Lớn Province, had assigned me to serve as the Secretary Office chief of the battalion and the Đức Hòa District. After the election of the South Vietnamese Congress and the president of the First Republic of Vietnam, Major Minh was promoted lieutenant colonel and province chief of Sadec. I was transferred to the 1/43 Battalion of the 15th Light Infantry Division and stationed at Dục Mỹ, Nha Trang.

During the Second Republic, Minh was rapidly elevated, from colonel and commander of the 21st Division to brigadier general, major general, then lieutenant general and commander of the Saigon Military Zone, and of the III Corps and MR3. He had not forgotten that I had worked for him some 15 years earlier. As to the third reason, I only heard it at mealtime: Colonel Hưng had asked General Minh to let me serve as chief of the 5th Infantry Division's Intelligence Staff or S-2. As that request caught me by surprise, I asked to have time to think about it. General Minh also did not make his decision then. After dinner, Colonel Hưng flew back to Lai Khê while I was given a week of leave in Saigon so that he could reshuffle his personnel.

At that time, since General Minh did not trust Colonel Lê Đạt Công, chief of J-2 at III Corps and MR3, he transferred him to the 21st Div/ARVN. Although the S-2 staff had many other lieutenant colonels, I managed most of the work at the bureau despite not holding any official title. I expected that Lieutenant Colonel Mạch Văn Trường, a protégé and former J-2 chief of General Minh who had recently been transferred to III Corps and MR3, would be nominated as its intelligence chief. The speculation turned out not to be correct. I had been notified that Colonel Hưng had sent two official memos requesting my transfer to the 5th Infantry Division. General Minh told me to go to Lai Khê to help Colonel Hưng, and Lieutenant Colonel Mạch Văn Trường became commander of the 8th Regiment. Lieutenant Colonel Trần Văn Bình, S-2 chief of the 18th Infantry Division, was elevated to S-2 chief, III Corps and MR3. The move was logical, for Lieutenant Colonel Bình had a lot of experience and was the former chief of the Intelligence Branch at the J-2/JGS/RVNAF.

I was saddened by General Minh's decision, not because I wanted to escape the responsibility of becoming the S-2 chief of a division, which I felt was important. But I felt ashamed of having to serve under a classmate. What I was afraid of most was that any mistake, any casualty, military or civilian, and any lost outpost related to my work could affect and sap our friendship as well as cause trouble for him and me to handle. I then valued our friendship a lot and was afraid to lose it. Working for another commander who would be impartial in his judgment would make me feel much safer. Reward and punishment would be accepted and tolerated in a thoughtful manner had I been successful or failed on the job. But as a soldier, I had to accept the leader's decision. I thus called Colonel Hưng and told him I would present myself at the division headquarters on 16 June. That day, around 14:00, Colonel Hưng sent his own helicopter to pick me up at Biên Hòa for the trip to Lai Khê, the division headquarters. In the commander's office, he shook my hand and held my shoulder expressing his happiness at seeing me. Later, I assumed the position without official transfer because my predecessor, Lieutenant Colonel Nguyễn Công Ninh, had left his post a week earlier. While I was meeting with officers of the division intelligence staff, the commander's secretary chief, Captain Nguyễn Đức Phương, called and informed me that Colonel Hưng had invited me to have dinner with him in his trailer after the daily 17:00-hour meeting at the TOC (Tactical Operations Center of the division).

The military trailer, protected all around by sandbags, stood behind the commander's residence, parallel to the row of offices of the division's S-2, where I worked that afternoon, and separated by a mesh for protection from B-40 rockets. There, for the first time, I was officially introduced to his wife by Colonel Hưng himself. Her maiden name was Phạm Kim Hoàng. I thought she was a right fit for him: she was thin and strong with a bright face, soft voice and fair complexion. She appeared friendly with her husband's colleagues. As for him, he did not ask me about my family or whereabouts since graduating from school. He and I talked about events larger than the world of III Corps and MR3 as equals, without any affected style like I did in front of any superior in the past. After that dinner, I felt I could work with Colonel Hưng without carrying any guilt complex. On the other hand, I thought I should work harder, get more involved in my job so that he could understand me better and at the same time prove that I had enough knowledge and skills so as not to betray his trust.

That was not the only time Colonel and Mrs. Hưng invited me to dinner in the trailer at his compound at the Lai Khê headquarters; in fact, this was a frequent happening during my tenure at the 5th Division under his command. Each time they threw an intimate family reunion, the only friend to be invited was me. Also, if in the morning he scratched my name off the list of people to be promoted or be given the Medal of Valor at the divisional order, which Colonel Hưng—as commander of a division—had the power to bestow at the suggestion of the chief of staff, Lieutenant Colonel Lê Thọ Trung, Mrs. Hưng always invited me to dinner with them. During dinner,

Mrs. Hưng always said in order to comfort me, "My husband is like that. Don't take it personally," while Colonel Hưng sat there and smiled. The smile expressed not only an intent to comfort, but also to convey the idea that he did not want other people to object to the promotion and that the Medal of Valor was not reserved for staff officers. The person who understood these rules would be Lieutenant Colonel Lê Thọ Trung, Hưng's former superior. I suspected that Lieutenant Colonel Trung had also been invited to such private dinners with the Hưng, because Colonel Hưng did not forget that Trung was his former superior when he just graduated from school. Of course, the person who understood the relationship between commander Hưng and myself was Mrs. Hưng. These dinners not only occurred at the 5th Division/ARVN, but also later at his residence in Cần Thơ when he became the deputy commander of IV Corps and MR4.

The Commander of the ARVN 5th Infantry Division

After working with Colonel Hưng for a short while, I became impressed by his competence and fairness. As for his competence, his thinking was fast and accurate and I will elaborate on this later on. As for his behavior and dealing with others, he was straight like an arrow, energetic, although deeply emotional—the two examples were his dealings with Lieutenant Colonel Lê Thọ Trung and me.

He could appear difficult and rigid on the outside because of his tall stature, strict demeanor, and the few words he uttered here and there. In reality, he loved his soldiers, NCOs, and lieutenants, which he chose with care to fill the leadership positions of squads, platoons, and companies. At the battalion level, he always chose young, courageous, battle-hardened captains and majors who cared for and loved their soldiers. He told me that if these leaders knew and cared about their soldiers, he did not have much to worry about. Therefore, he was always close to leaders of squads, platoons, companies and battalions. At times, he remembered the names of certain squad and platoon leaders of certain companies, which few division commanders paid attention to. But the division commander could not make any decision about the regiment commander because the latter's selection and/or dismissal came under the purview of the Corps commander or higher.

The ARVN 5th Infantry Division with its 11,000 troops was composed of

- three regiments, 7th, 8th, and 9th;
- an armored squadron, the 1st Armored Squadron;

- four artillery battalions: the 50th Battalion with 155 mm guns and the 51st, 52nd, 53rd battalions with 105 mm guns;
- one combat engineering battalion;
- one signal battalion;
- one logistical battalion;
- one medical battalion;
- one reconnaissance company;
- one military intelligence detachment;
- one technical company; and
- one transportation company.

The 7th Regiment was under the command of Lieutenant Colonel Lý Đức Quân (later promoted to colonel then late brigadier general when he passed away). He was a highland minority Nùng like most officers, warrant officers, and soldiers when this regiment was formed under the designation of 4th Field Division, which was later called the 5th Infantry Division. As the ARVN expanded, most of the Nùng minorities were regrouped into the 7th Regiment. Lieutenant Colonel Quân was an ideal, religious, competent, and experienced leader whom Colonel Hưng was very fond of.

The 8th Regiment had been assigned by General Minh to Lieutenant Colonel Mạch Văn Trường. Upon graduating from Class 12 of the Dalat Military Academy, Trường was sent to the U.S. for training as company leader. On his return, he was assigned to Military Intelligence Branch and had never commanded a company. As a regiment leader, he would be promoted to colonel. Knowing his lack of battle experience, Colonel Hưng had assigned Major Huỳnh Văn Tâm, a young officer who was a former battalion commander, to be his deputy.

The commander of the 9th Regiment was Colonel Nguyễn Công Vĩnh, who was one of my relatives. When I met him the first time after many years of absence, I thought he should have requested a transfer to a central office position instead of fighting in the battlefield. However, under him were two excellent officers: Major Trần Đăng Khoa, his deputy, and Major Võ Trung Thứ, the battalion commander of the 1/9 Battalion who graduated as valedictorian of Class 15 of the Dalat Military Academy. The commander of the cavalry unit was Lieutenant Colonel Nguyễn Đức Dương.

In early March 1972 in Lai Khê on the anniversary of the formation of the division, Colonel Hưng was promoted to interim brigadier general, and Lieutenant Colonel Mạch Văn Trường to interim colonel. The person General Nguyễn Văn Minh left out was Lieutenant Colonel Lê Thọ Trung, the division's chief of staff, who was not promoted despite his seniority in rank.

II. General Lê Văn Hưng and I

General Hưng was very strict toward officers, especially those on the division staff. That was the reason why Colonel Lê Nguyên Vỹ, the division deputy commander, and other officers from major and above were frequently "rectified" by General Hưng right during meetings at the Tactical Operations Center (TOC). One evening, after Vỹ had been rectified I did not remember how many times, I followed General Hưng after the meeting to his office. As he was still steaming, he was surprised to see me walking in but did not say anything. I immediately began: "Excuse me. May I say something?" Before he had the chance to utter any word, I continued: "I believe you have been too harsh with Colonel Vỹ. He cannot work if he is constantly 'rectified.' Colonel Vỹ and we, high-ranking staff officers, have the duty to express our opinions, right or wrong.... If we are rectified all the time in front of our junior staff, we would not be able to talk freely."

"That's none of *your* business," General Hưng exploded.

"Excuse me, General. If it is not my business, I'll go." I saluted him and left.

That was the first and last time he called me by *mầy*—like "*toi*" in French—a word used only to address subordinates or very close friends,[9] and I felt that he used that word because we were close "buddies"—classmates who graduated from the same school—and not because he saw me as his subordinate. Sensitive about causing any hurt feelings, from that time onward he dropped the word *mầy* from his vocabulary. And he certainly understood that the word "General" I used conveyed my dissatisfaction with him. I usually called him general in front of everyone; however, when we were alone or in front of his wife, I just called him *anh* (brother) because he was slightly older than I. He was born in March 1933, and I in January 1934, although we were both from the same lunar calendar year: Quý Dậu—precious rooster. He usually called me "Hey Dưỡng" or "Hi Dưỡng" without any "toi," any "cậu," or "*mầy*."

The next morning, I swung by the office of the chief of staff and submitted my request for transfer before heading to the airport to accompany General Hưng in his visit to the units. After he stepped down from his jeep and before getting on his helicopter, he shook Lieutenant Colonel Trịnh Đình Đăng's hands and mine. When he shook mine, he smiled but did not say a word.

After we returned to Lai Khê in the afternoon, at around 14:00 hours, Lieutenant Colonel Trung called me to his office and told me that he had met General Hưng about my request. He repeated General Hưng's word, "Dưỡng was making a fuss; just throw the request away." I was not making any fuss but really intended to request for a transfer. I was not embarrassed when I met General Hưng before the late-day staff meeting. However, a few days later, he met with me in private and told me that he and Colonel Lê Nguyên Vỹ did not get along well. A week later, General Minh transferred Colonel Vỹ to the III Corps and made him deputy for Operations, III Corps and MR3.

The position of deputy commander of the 5th Infantry Division was left unfilled. Colonel Bùi Đức Điềm, province chief of Long Khánh, was transferred to the 5th Division because he was not trusted by General Minh who dismissed him. When he arrived at the division, he became the chief of staff for Field Operations, but not deputy commander or deputy of Operations to General Hưng. Colonel Điềm was a veteran officer, a man who accomplished a lot in the battle of An Lộc a month later. He was left out like an old oak in a forest of trees somewhere in Bình Long. It was only by the end of 1972 that the division had a new deputy commander in the person of Colonel Nguyễn Bá Long aka Thin, formerly province chief of Kontum who had accomplished a lot in preserving the city of Kontum; maybe there was also some unfairness related to this officer.

I will write in particular about the injustice that had occurred during the battle of An Lộc as it happened in reality, which is different from what some other authors have written, although I realize that what I touch upon may not only make certain people unhappy, but also may bring some adverse reactions to myself. I accept them when I write about the truth and only the truth. Many people knew about the truth, although they were not able to talk about it. I would have liked to forget it for the past few decades but could not. I just wonder whether the aura of many ARVN heroes had been overshadowed by a small cast of inept leaders whose shadows loomed so large as to completely obstruct the former. I have pondered for a long time and held my tongue too long when I did not mention about the injustice suffered by General Hưng or Colonel Điềm and others who were victimized by their superiors. As of today, some of them have also been "victimized" by outsiders who did not know about the truth. If I know about it and do not speak out, then who will? I am the witness, the insider, although my knowledge only allows me to mention the least and the most civil event of all.

I write for those who are still alive, especially for Hải and Hà, General Hưng's children who were still young when their father passed away. Now that they have reached maturity, they need to know the turbulent and difficult life of their father. I will mail a copy to Mrs. Hưng, who lives somewhere in the States, to tell her I am proud of having shared the miseries and dangers with a hero I did not know then.

A hero is different from a mortal by his stature. Those who long for power, position, and glory but avoid the danger, who run away when the tide turns, leaving behind soldiers and flags, though they be generals, are simply mere mortals. Generals who consider their lives and their families as too important cannot be heroes or gods. But generals who die for their country may become heroes or gods. The adage says, *"Born as a general, die as a god."* Vietnamese history is still there; our behavior will be reflected by the mirror of posterity. The five generals who sacrificed themselves on the last day of "Black April" will have their names forever inscribed for posterity.[10]

III

Prelude to the Bình Long Battle

When General Nguyễn Văn Minh replaced General Đỗ Cao Trí whose command helicopter blew up in the air above Tây Ninh for unknown reasons in February 1971, it was not known why he did not use the valuable talents left behind by General Trí. He first transferred Colonel Lê Đạt Công from the III Corps' intelligence staff to the 21st Infantry Division and did not use Brigadier General Trần Quang Khôi, commander of the 3rd Armored Cavalry Brigade who had just returned from high-level training in the U.S. General Minh then dispersed the cavalry brigade and the III Corps Assault Force previously built by General Trí and under the command of Brigadier General Khôi, basically demoting the latter without taking away his star. General Minh's operational tactics changed with the evolution of the battlefield. He gradually withdrew all his units from Cambodia to buff up the defenses in his assigned area of responsibility. The III Corps thus became a tactical defensive force instead of an offensive force like under its former commander.

This may have to do with the rapid withdrawal of U.S. forces, which suddenly created huge defensive gaps in the III Corps and MR3. In 1968, the MR3 was home to a formidable U.S. fighting force: the 1st Infantry Division, the 25th Infantry Division, the Tropic Lightning, the 199th Infantry Brigade, the 11th Armored Cavalry Regiment, two brigades of the 1st Cavalry Division, and one battalion of the 17th Air Cavalry Regiment. By December 1971, U.S. troop strength was down to one squadron of the 17th Air Cavalry, a portion of the 1st Aviation Brigade, one squadron of the 11th Armored Cavalry Regiment, a provisional brigade of the 1st Cavalry Division, and a battalion of combat engineers.[1] At a time when the NVA was building up, the U.S. was drawing down. The tactical shift allowed the NVA forces to rebuild their units in Cambodia and get ready for an all-out across-the-border attack on Bình Long Province.

However, in the last quarter of 1971 with the reinforcement of a Marine brigade and an Airborne brigade, General Minh who organized an offensive inside the Cambodian territory along Highway 7 in order to relieve enemy pressure on the last U.S.–Vietnamese firebase at Krek in Cambodia before abandoning it had inflicted severe damage to NVA units. That was the last South Vietnamese victory on Cambodian soil. After the attack, he withdrew from Krek to reinforce his troops along Route 22, on the northern side of Tây Ninh, and to reshuffle his units in the III Corps.

The III Corps oversaw the 5th, 18th and 25th Divisions. It also had

- a brigade of armored cavalry
- a battle group of rangers,
- a reserve force used for out-of-the-country offensive battles under the Đỗ Cao Trí years, and
- units of artillery, engineering, air force and navy.

The 18th Infantry Division's military range encompassed the MR3's eastern provinces: Biên Hòa, Long Khánh, Phước Tuy, Bình Tuy and the town of Vũng Tàu with its headquarters at Xuân Lộc. That division would become famous in the late phase of the war in 1975.

The 25th Infantry Division took care of the southwestern provinces of MR3: Tây Ninh, Hậu Nghĩa, and Long An with its headquarters at Củ Chi. The Capital Special Zone—later Capital Military Region—included Saigon, Chợ Lớn and Gia Định, which were under the purview of the III Corps and 3rd MR.

After taking over the command of the 5th Infantry Division from Major General Nguyễn Văn Hiếu in early June 1971, General Hưng consolidated his forces and opened some offensives at the regimental levels (usually with the combined forces of an infantry regiment plus an artillery battalion and an element of cavalry) into communist strongholds in the north-central provinces of MR3: Bình Long; Phước Long; Bình Dương and the Iron Triangle; Long Nguyên, Bến Than; and VC secret zones along the Saigon River—mainly secret zone D on the right side of Bé River—south of Đồng Xoài, known as bloody theaters between the U.S. and ARVN forces and communist forces in the 1960s. The command center of the 5th Division was located at the rubber plantation in Lai Khê, Bến Cát District, province of Bình Dương.

The ARVN 5th Infantry Division

Tây Ninh, Bình Long, Phước Long, and Bình Dương, four of the northern provinces of the III Corps, form the southern foothills of the Trường Sơn

Range and constitute a buffer zone between the Central Highlands in the north and the Mekong Delta in the south. The area contained some of the richest rubber plantations in the world and was traversed by two important highways, 13 and 14. Highway 13 linked Saigon to Cambodia while Highway 14 led to Ban Mê Thuột and the Central Highlands.

Highway 13 ran the whole length of Bình Long Province from north to south and bisected it into two almost equal sections. It traversed the southern district town of Chơn Thành, the Bình Long capital of An Lộc, and the northern district town of Lộc Ninh before crossing the border into Cambodia. A 2,240-square-kilometer area, Bình Long was one of the smallest provinces in South Vietnam. Phan Nhật Nam, a soldier-writer, lyrically wrote about the soon-to-be-famous Highway 13:

> This road [Highway 13], a dark black line between the rows of green-leafed rubber tree plants, stands out against the reddish brown earth. Its unlucky number and the color of the earth suggest that fate had planned everything: a road with the number of death and dirt the color of dried blood.[2]

The areas of responsibility of the 5th Infantry Division comprised three provinces from north to south: Phước Long under Colonel Lưu Yểm, Bình Long under Colonel Trần Văn Nhựt, and Bình Dương with Colonel Nguyễn Văn Của as province chief.

The divisional forces were distributed as follows: the Task-Force 9 (TF-9), under the command of Colonel Nguyễn Công Vĩnh, included the 9th Regiment with three battalions 1/9, 2/9, and 3/9; the 53rd Artillery Battalion with 14 105 mm howitzers and four 155 mm howitzers (from the 50th Artillery Battalion); and the 1st Armored Cavalry Battalion. It served the northwest region of Bình Long from Fire Support Base (FSB) Alpha (10 kilometers north of Lộc Ninh) to the Vietnamese-Cambodian border on Highway 13 and toward the east through the intersection of Lộc Tấn between Highways 13 and 14 to the district of Bố Đức of Phước Long Province.

The headquarters of the TF-9 was located at the main base of the 74th Ranger Battalion situated at the end of the Lộc Ninh airfield runway on the western side of Highway 13 and from the market that ran parallel to the runway to the rubber plantation west of the Lộc Ninh village.

The 74th Ranger Battalion controlled FSB Alpha close to the Vietnamese-Cambodian border with four 105 mm howitzers placed under the operational leadership of Lieutenant Colonel Nguyễn Đức Dương, commander of the 1st Armored Cavalry Squadron. The headquarters of the 1st Armor Cavalry, located at the Lộc Tấn intersection, was upgraded with four 105 mm howitzers and two armored companies, the 3/1 Cavalry and the 1/1 Tank; overall it had 40 tanks, including 14 M-41, 26 armored cars of different types, as well as trucks, jeeps and GMC trucks. These units operated on Highways 13 and 14 north of Lộc Ninh.

The whole 1/9 Battalion camped at the Bố Đức District on Highway 13, on the left side of the Bé River, province of Phước Long on the border of the Bình Long Province.

The 2/9 Battalion that operated on the northwest side of Lộc Tấn collaborated with and supported the 74th Ranger Battalion.

The 3/9 Battalion, a mobile unit, operated in an area from three to five kilometers southwest of Lộc Ninh. Each battalion left behind a company to protect the headquarters of the TF-9, while the 9th Reconnaissance Company operated on the border of Bình Long-Tây Ninh, north of Tống Lê Chân Base where the 92th Ranger Battalion stationed, close to the Saigon River north of Bến Than and northwest of the Chơn Thành District, province of Bình Long.

The 53th Artillery Battalion headquarters of Lieutenant Colonel Hoàng Thông and other artillery units from the same base were located on a line parallel to the air strip at about 400 meters from the headquarters of the TF-9 and 200 meters from the headquarters of the district and Lộc Ninh Subsector. Major Nguyễn Văn Thịnh, district chief and commander of the Lộc Ninh Sub-sector had two companies of provincial Regional Forces (RF) and two platoons of People's Self-Defense Forces (PSDF) to care for the security of the headquarters. In addition, there were four companies of RF and other platoons of PSDF within the province and a platoon of police located at the Lộc Ninh market. The RF and PSDF were drawn from the local populace and were responsible for the defense of their towns and hamlets. RF battalions and RF companies were assigned to provinces and districts respectively, while PSDF platoons were controlled by hamlets and village chiefs.[3]

All NVA artillery guns, designed by the Soviet Union and manufactured either by the Soviet Union or China, had very long reach. The Soviet D-74 122 mm gun had a range of 23.9 kilometers, and the Soviet M-46 130 mm gun could strike at 27.5 kilometers. All ARVN guns came from the U.S. The 105 mm howitzers—the M-101-A1 and the M-102 used in South Vietnam— could fire 10 rounds per minute, and the sustained rate of fire was three rounds per minute. A standard six-gun battery could strike 60 rounds per minute but only at 11.27 kilometers. The 155 mm howitzer could hit only at 14.6 kilometers. The NVA thus outgunned the ARVN in long-range artillery duels.[4]

About 15 kilometers south of Lộc Ninh lay the Cần Lê River, which connected the Saigon and Bé Rivers. A sturdy concrete bridge spanned across the Cần Lê River on Highway 13. There stationed a company of 2/9 Battalion, a combined 155 mm and 105 mm artillery company, a fighting engineering company, and two companies of RF, all under the leadership of Lieutenant Colonel Nguyễn Văn Hòa. About four kilometers north of the Cần Lê Bridge, on the left of Highway 13, was the 20-kilometer-long provincial route 17, which headed westward toward Tây Ninh. About two kilometers from Highway 13 heading west was the Hùng Tâm base camp, which housed the two battalion-sized bases located respectively north and south of route 17. At the request of Brigadier General Hưng, General Minh sent him the Task Force 52 of the 18th Infantry Division on 28 March 1972 which would be stationed at these two Hùng Tâm bases. This unit comprised the 2nd Battalion of the 52th Regiment (2/52) and the 1st Battalion of the 48th Regiment (1/48), a reconnaissance company and four 105 mm and two 155 mm howitzers, and an engineering company.

At nine kilometers south of the Cần Lê Bridge sat the provincial town of An Lộc, which also served as the headquarters of the military zone of Bình Long. Colonel Trần Văn Nhựt, chief of the province and the military sector, was an experienced Marine officer, a former commander of the 43rd and 48th Regiments of the 18th Infantry Division. A brave officer, although modest, subtle, and skillful with dealing with people, he was respected by superiors and subordinates. U.S. advisers often praised him, probably because of his cleverness. From An Lộc, he commanded two battalions of RF and many platoons of PSDF for a total of 2,000 soldiers who were scattered throughout the province. In An Lộc and nearby sites like Windy Hill and Hill 169 were stationed 800 soldiers with some old V-100 armored cars and artillery platoons of 105 mm and 155 mm howitzers.

General Hưng placed his forward command post of the 5th Division in the town of An Lộc itself. On the outskirts of the town heading north was Base Charlie where the headquarters of the 7th Regiment were located. Two battalions, the 2/7 and 3/7, and the 7th Reconnaissance Company operated around the province and its northwest area. The two companies of the 1/7 Battalion operated on the northeast of the village while two other companies stationed at Quản Lợi airfield and base about seven kilometers northeast of An Lộc. One could also find there a company of RF and a company of Lôi Hổ. The main base of the 7th Regiment was still in the Phú Giáo District, Bình Dương Province. The district of Chơn Thành, province of Bình Long, 30 kilometers south of An Lộc, was guarded by two companies of RF. Thirty kilometers south of Chơn Thành was the Lai Khê rubber plantation where the headquarters of the 5th Infantry Division were located, in the province of Bình Dương about 20 kilometers west of the village of the same name.

The 8th Regiment of the 5th Division was located at the divisional headquarters at the Lai Khê base, which was protected by one battalion of the

8th Regiment and a recon company. Another battalion was being trained at the divisional training center in Bình Dương while a third battalion operated at Dầu Tiếng District in the province of Bình Dương on the left side of the Saigon River.

In the beginning of February 1972, in the area of responsibility of the TF-9, its units had fought on many occasions with squads or platoons of NVA troops in the northwest border with Cambodia, close to the Fish Hook area or along the Saigon River at the border of Bình Long and Tây Ninh and outside Bến Than on the west side of Chơn Thành. They had taken down a small number of enemy soldiers mostly from the reconnaissance units of the 5th, 7th, and 9th Divisions of COSVN (Central Office of South Vietnam). Documents retrieved from the bodies of soldiers included those related to "combined attacks of cities with infantry, artillery, and tanks." We had also detected newly formed divisional units that were prepped for the battles of Tây Ninh and Bình Long. There was the Bình Long Division or the C30B Division with the 271th Regiment that recycled cadres from the 271th of the 9th Div/VC; the other regiments were the 24th, 205th and 207th which were composed of soldiers recruited from the Central Highlands. Based on these documents, I had suggested to General Hưng to open an operation against Bến Than, north of Route 13, about 15 kilometers west of Chơn Thành. The 1st Airborne Brigade, which was attached to the 5th Infantry Division, thus began an attack on Bến Than VC secret zone on the second week of February 1972. We destroyed 100 tons of rice and food, confiscated 1,000 personal guns and destroyed tons of ammunitions that were newly brought from bases in Cambodia to be stashed there.

Intelligence Estimates

Around mid–February 1972 during a reconnaissance operation five kilometers north of Lộc Ninh and three kilometers west of Highway 13, a reconnaissance company exchanged fire with a squad of communist soldiers: it shot four of them dead and caught one with a short gun and two other soldiers. The prisoners were brought back to the intelligence unit of the division for questioning. As the divisional chief of the intelligence staff at that time, I participated in the interrogation. The one with a short gun was a northern officer who had infiltrated into the South two years earlier. He was first assigned to the 7th Div/NVA then transferred to the Reconnaissance Battalion of the 69th Artillery Division (69th A.Div/VC)—or the 70th Artillery Division of COSVN.

This officer, a 1st lieutenant, stated that he came along with the reconnaissance battalion commander of the 69th A.Div/VC and two other officers and a squad of soldiers to look for placement sites for artillery guns. The main goal was to destroy the headquarters of the TF-9 of the 5th Div/ARVN at the end of the Lộc Ninh airfield runway, the 1st Armored/5th Div/ARVN and the 74th Ranger Battalion at Lộc Tấn intersection, and Alpha Base on Route 13 that connected with Route 14A north of Lộc Ninh in the next total offensive. The latter would be a major assault as it involved infantry and long-range artillery against the city.

The prisoner seemed to be truthful during the various encounters with me. He gave me extensive information during the interrogation process due to a combination of soft interrogation technique, good food which was provided to him, and my personal enquiries about his family in the North. He said that the 69th Artillery of COSVN had changed its name to 70th Artillery and had received huge artillery guns and ammunition from North Vietnam. He, however, could not tell when the attack would happen and whether tanks would be involved or not. He mentioned that once the reconnaissance unit established the *sa bàn* of the region—a tactical sand table of enemy targets—figured out the placement of guns, and received approval, the attack would begin a week later. But since the reconnaissance unit had been caught and gunned down, he could not be sure about the date. As for the tanks, he did not see any in his area but was told during discussions that they would be involved.

Having nothing else to learn from him, I transferred him to the III Corps Interrogation Center, following which he opted to switch to our side as a *hồi chánh*—a rallier.[5] A week after the battle of An Lộc began, this reconnaissance officer, who was wearing an ARVN outfit and a gun, followed a U.S. adviser and came to see me at the divisional headquarters in An Lộc. The reason I describe this event in detail is to convey the fact that we were not caught by surprise by the NVA summer offensive. The reality was that, being a lowly NVA officer, he was not privy to all the details and full extent of the planned attack during the 1972 Fiery Summer. Although it was possible that he did not reveal all the information he knew, I was pretty convinced he was truthful. So was the III Corp Interrogation Center since they allowed him to be a *hồi chánh*.

Assigned to the duty of gathering intelligence for a unit the size of a division, not only I but all the military intelligence chiefs at ARVN divisions carried a heavy responsibility toward our units and commanders. My responsibility toward General Hưng seemed heavier than normal and our relationship closer because he was not only a strict superior, but also a close friend.

III. Prelude to the Bình Long Battle

After the attack by the Airborne Brigade at Bến Than that destroyed important COSVN storage centers in the province of Bình Long, based on the declarations of the above-mentioned officer and two other prisoners from the 69th Artillery Division along with documents confiscated earlier, I presented to General Hưng on the third week of March 1972 an estimate of the aims and possibilities of the COSVN in their attempts to attack the area of responsibility of the 5th Division and III Corps and MR3. As far as aims were concerned, three points needed to be mentioned:

- A communist attack against the III Corps would be imminent during the spring or early summer months, although the exact timing was unknown. This was an important element that required further assessment and evaluation. Eventually, the enemy launched its "offensive on the night of 30 March in MR-1, on 31 March in the B-3 front [MR-2], and on 1 April in western MR-3.... We [U.S. intelligence] had expected the offensive to begin around 20–25 February.... The earlier timetable was delayed due to B-52 and tactical air strikes, Island Tree interdiction, allied preemptive ground operations, and the high state of alert of allied forces."[6]
- From the prisoners of the Reconnaissance Battalion of the 69th A Div/VC and documents of large communist units retrieved from the bodies of communists, the attack would be a combined infantry, artillery and tank attack on the cities of Bình Long. We knew all about the communist infantry units, except for the newly formed Bình Long Division. The 69th Artillery Division had been renamed the 70th Artillery Division and augmented with artillery and anti-aircraft guns. It had received ammunitions from North Vietnam through waterways, from the south of the Khone Falls on the Mekong River then into the Chllong River in the province of Kratie in Cambodia.

The presence or absence of enemy tanks in the area of conflict had raised an important but puzzling question for us. Yet, despite a very thorough search in Vietnam as well as in Cambodia, we were unable to physically document the presence of any tank. Although this failure had been one of our most important intelligence failures under my watch, General Hưng was prepared to deal with them should they show up on the day of attack. Troops had been armed and trained with anti-tanks guns as we shall see later on. General Thi had reported that Colonel Vinh had told him in 2006 that "roaring noises of tank engines" had been heard and "underwater bridges built with logs were discovered in certain stream locations on the Song Be River."⁷ Back in 1972, we did investigate all these leads, which turned out to be non-conclusive. Prisoners did not give out any important information, except for the fact that COSVN was very strict about keeping a tight schedule for receiving guns and ammunition that were transported on barges on the Mekong River on Cambodian soil. All the artillery guns and ammunition had been received on commercial ports on the Chllong River at a predetermined time for each night. There were no daytime transactions on any of these commercial ports, and all the vestiges of any night transactions had been eliminated. I believed that the NVA transported tanks from North Vietnam via the Hồ Chí Minh Trail to Khone Falls where they were camouflaged then loaded onto barges that brought them on the Mekong River to ports on the Chllong River every night for at least three months before "D" Day. Tanks were then hidden in tunnels carved on the side of mountains that abutted the river. Therefore, despite using all available technologies and manpower, like air surveillance, air photography, informers, and recon agents who were dropped in Cambodia disguised as NVA soldiers in an attempt to detect the presence of any tanks, we were unable to find pipelines, tank tracks on the Cambodian soil. We had not left any stone unturned and had even explored another area. The Vietnamese-Cambodian border in the forested area at the end of the Trường Sơn mountain range on the northern end of the provinces of Bình Long and Phước Long to Kratié was full of mountain roads and bridges that were used by trucks carrying logged wood. If these trucks could pass through mountain roads, then tanks could too. This fact had worried me a lot. I still believe that tanks were being transported by barges on the Mekong River although I could not prove it. We no longer had air support and could not bomb targets in the Cambodian territory. However, I had marked all the bridges that crossed falls or rivers so that we could bomb and destroy them in case of an attack on An Lộc.

- Although I could not identify the exact timing of the attack or find tank tracks, I believed the attack would occur in late spring or early summer 1972. The 2nd Bureau of the III Corps thought so too. The J-2/JGS/RVNAF had also found warnings of an imminent attack, although the timing and date were unknown at that time. In the MR3, I informed General Hưng that the communists intended to take over one of the two provinces, either Bình Long or Tây Ninh,

III. Prelude to the Bình Long Battle

to show off the Provisional Revolutionary Government of South Vietnam (PRGSV), which was led by Nguyễn Hữu Thọ, Trịnh Đình Thảo, Huỳnh Tấn Phát and propped up by Lê Duẩn and the Communist Party. The appearance of the PRG was necessary for the North Vietnamese to prove to the world that they were holding some territory in South Vietnam while the dialogue between Kissinger and Lê Đức Thọ took place in Paris. Which of the two provinces was the main target and which one was the decoy remained to be determined. Both these provinces were under the control of General Hưng.

In my estimate, Bình Long was the main target for the communists in order to show off their PRG; therefore, the battle would take place in Bình Long. The main reason was cultural and religious in nature. The province of Bình Long was a newly formed province under the First Republic. It comprised three cities: Lộc Ninh in the north, An Lộc in the middle and Chơn Thành in the south with a total provincial population of 60,000 people. The latter was heterogeneous and came from all over the country except 4 percent, or 5,000 people, who were from the Stieng minority. More than 75 percent of the people worked for the huge rubber plantations at Lộc Ninh, Quản Lợi, Xa Cam, Xa Cát, and Xa Trạch, and 10 percent were merchants. The remaining people were government officials, military personnel, and their families.

Geographically, Bình Long sat along the main axis of Highway 13. In Cambodia, Highway 13 joined Route 7 at Snoul; from there, it went southward, crossed the border, entered the towns of Lộc Ninh, An Lộc, and Chơn Thành in succession, then Bến Cát of Bình Dương, and finally ended up in Thủ Dầu Một of the same named province. In South Vietnam, the north-south Highway 13 sat in the middle of the province, about 15 to 18 kilometers from two rivers: the Saigon River on its western side and the Bé River on its eastern side. The rubber plantations thrived between the two rivers. The northeast and northwest of Lộc Ninh contained huge forests of precious wood with large tree trunks spaced out about 4 to 5 meters from each other through which tanks could easily roam without being detected. Kratié, a Cambodian province north of Phước Long, and Bình Long formed the COSVN den from where the communists could direct the battle. From Bình Long, they could control the battlefield in South Vietnam more easily.

On the other hand, the Tây Ninh Province with a population of 300,000 people shared the same border with Sway Rieng of Cambodia at the Parrot's Beak. The latter housed an important complex of communist bases that served as depots for guns and ammunition shipped from North Vietnam many years earlier. After General Đỗ Cao Trí became commander of the III Corps and MR3 until February 1971, these bases had been totally destroyed and not yet repaired except for bases along Route 7 on Cambodian soil on the north end of Tây Ninh. In case of a major attack, the communists could only move on Route 22 all the way to Tây Ninh. On the east and northeast, the grass was dry or marshy, with open spaces that were susceptible to ground shelling or bombing by VNAF. The most important element was the population, which was very homogeneous and four times larger than that of Bình Long, with 70 percent of them being from the Cao Đài sect.[8] The latter were fiercely anti-communist and had battled against the communists in the 1940s and 1950s. Years of warfare had hardened these Cao Đài making them fierce fighters. Also, the locals had settled in the area for many generations that dated back to the time when the lords Nguyễn from central Vietnam began their expansion and conquest of the south in the 17th century. Therefore, a battle in this province would lead to the destruction of Tây Ninh and cause a lot of anger and resentment from the populace. Besides, North Vietnam was fighting for real estate, for a place to show off its provisionary government. Since land grabbing was the main objective, the fewer people who stood in the way the better it was.[9] From these geographical and demographic conditions, Tây Ninh might just be a decoy area and Bình Long the real target.

General Minh, commander of the III Corps and MR3, believing in these estimates, reshuffled his forces and gave additional ones to General Hưng's 5th Division. An airborne brigade was sent to Chơn Thành and opened an offensive at Bến Than. The TF-52 of the 18th Division/ARVN was reassigned to the Hùng Tâm bases as noted above.

Some authors, Vietnamese and American, have erred when they wrote that Colonel Lê Nguyên Vỹ was General Hưng's deputy. This was not correct. As mentioned earlier, when the battle of An Lộc broke out, Colonel Vỹ was General Minh's operational assistant, a title he held when he was reassigned to the III Corps following his tactical disagreement with General Hưng. Once General Minh agreed with the assumption from Lieutenant Colonel Trần Văn Bình, chief of intelligence staff of III Corps and MR3, and mine, that the communists would attack Bình Long, he decided to move his Forward Operational Command Headquarters from Tây Ninh to An Lộc. He therefore sent Colonel Vỹ and an engineering platoon to An Lộc to organize the place in order to eventually house the III Corps' Tactical Operations Center (TOC).

The place where Colonel Vỹ had reorganized in the city of An Lộc was a row of houses with concrete walls facing Nguyễn Huệ Street and a small villa located behind the row of houses. A large underground bunker, which

III. Prelude to the Bình Long Battle 59

lay beneath the garden behind the villa, was left behind by the Japanese after World War II.[10] This garden was surrounded by barbed wire and lay next to the administrative building of the Bình Long Province, which was the former headquarters of a Special Forces unit.

When the battle of An Lộc broke out, General Minh's Operational Command had not moved to the bunker yet, although Colonel Vỹ was already there. When the Forward Command Post of the 5th Division/ARVN, located by the train station area in a bunker built with sandbags by the division engineers,[11] was heavily damaged by enemy rockets and mortars on the first day of the attack, Colonel Vỹ and the staff of the division had suggested to General Hưng to move his headquarters to the labyrinth of underground tunnels described above. The communists, therefore, did not know the exact location of General Hưng's new command center in the city after the move. At one time, one of the enemy battalions was just one street away and attacked the area furiously, although they did not know which unit was resisting them. This was how close the victory could have gone to the other side. Two T-54 tanks drove by the command headquarters, and when they tried to turn around, Colonel Vỹ shot at one of them point blank, blowing it up. For three months, rockets and mortars had been falling on the old command center that faced the province chief's compound, ripping it apart and eventually flattening the whole area. Had the divisional headquarters stayed there, the victory again could have gone to the other side; but luckily no rocket fell directly on General Hưng's new command center. Although westerners do not believe in these signs, Asians do. General Hưng and his staff were twice close to being wiped out, although the war gods had favored them and helped them survive the ordeal.

My report to General Hưng suggested that the NVA would use known units stationed in Cambodia, like the communist COSVN's 5th, 7th, and 9th Divisions as well as the 429th Sapper Regiment, the revamped 69th Artillery Division and the Bình Long Division. According to my estimate, the enemy would have two strategic options when planning their attack of Bình Long with the use of a total force of 40,000 to 45,000 troops, infantry and artillery units.

The first strategic option was the "concentration attack" strategy—*Tập Tấn*—during which enemy forces would concentrate most of their forces on one target at a time, jump to the next one on Highway 13, then mass their units for the final assault on An Lộc. If the enemy adopted this strategy, they would use one division to attack the 5th Division/ARVN units on the northern end of Highway 13 such as the 74th Ranger Battalion and the 1st Armored Cavalry unit at Alpha base and Lộc Tấn intersection at the same time as the

1/9 Battalion at Bố Đức on Route 14A. At the same, they would use another division along with tanks to attack the 9th Regiment headquarters, the 53rd Artillery Battalion, and the headquarters of the Lộc Ninh Sub-sector that stood along the road parallel to the Lộc Ninh airfield runway. They would be protected by the 70th Artillery Division with their well-known motto: "Artillery first, then infantry." The third division would block the northern end of Highway 13, between the Cần Lê Bridge and Lộc Ninh District. Another regiment would block Route 14A between Lộc Tấn intersection and Bố Đức District and at the same time attack Quản Lợi Airfield to prevent reinforcements from coming in from Saigon. The 70th Artillery Division would also support the local guns and directly target An Lộc to neutralize the ARVN 5th Infantry Division. After taking care of the small targets in the district of Lộc Ninh, COSVN would mass two divisions, a sapper unit and an artillery unit to attack An Lộc while a third division would ambush on Highway 13 south of the rubber plantation Xa Trạch and north of Chơn Thành.

The second option was to use the "dispersion attack" strategy—*Tấn Tấn*—during which enemy forces would simultaneously attack three sites: Lộc Ninh, An Lộc and Lai Khê. The first attack on Lộc Ninh would comprise an infantry division supported by strong artillery, anti-aircraft artillery, and a sapper battalion attacking two sites: first, the headquarters of the 9th Regiment, the 53rd Artillery Battalion, and the town of Lộc Ninh; the second site would include the 1st Armored unit and the 74th Ranger Battalion at base Alpha and the Lộc Tấn intersection. These small bases would be flattened by artillery first before the infantry launched its attack. The second attack would take aim at An Lộc, which at that time had only two battalions of the 7th Regiment patrolling the outskirts of this capital city of Bình Long Province. The defense also had two companies of Regional Forces (RF) stationed at the nearby Windy Hill and Hill 169 and two other companies inside the city—also called military sector. The communists would use an infantry division, two artillery regiments, an anti-aircraft regiment and two sapper battalions. They would also attack the units at the airfield and at the Quản Lợi plantation. The third attack would focus on the headquarters of the 5th Infantry Division at Lai Khê and use a sapper battalion to destroy the reserves and ammunition while artillery would level the area. An infantry regiment supported by an anti-aircraft battalion would block reinforcement on Route 13, south of Lai Khê.

Luckily, when the communists launched the so called "Nguyễn Huệ" campaign, they adopted the concentration strategy and focused on the peripheral bases in the district of Lộc Ninh before attacking An Lộc.

III. Prelude to the Bình Long Battle 61

Had they chosen the second option and applied their strategy *dương đông kích tây*, or "show up in the east and kick in the west,"[12] for three consecutive days, especially with the assistance of tanks, the South Vietnamese units in III Corps and MR3 would have crumbled in disarray; unable to reshuffle units around fast enough, An Lộc would have fallen on the third day. The nail having been placed on the coffin, the ARVN, even if they were willing, would not be able to retake An Lộc. If they pulled major units like the Airborne Division, the Marines, and the rangers to protect the distraught Saigon, they would lose Kontum and Quảng Trị. Had they moved two divisions from the Mekong Delta, the IV Corps would have been in disarray too.

Using their motto "fast forward, fast victory" at that time, communist leaders simply did not think clearly enough, whether it was Võ Nguyên Giáp, Văn Tiến Dũng, or the party in Hanoi. The main reason was that they were so confident in their anti-aircraft SA-7 missiles and the most modern artillery guns, and their Russian T-54 and PT-76 tanks, that they abandoned their dispersion attack technique and simply used the concentration attack strategy or the Chinese communists' "human wave" tactic. They did not believe that the powerful U.S. Air Force and the ARVN that had matured with time would blow them away. Using the mass invasion strategy simply meant losing the battle in this case.

IV

The Fall of Lộc Ninh

The first attack fell on Lộc Ninh, a tiny district town on the northernmost end of Bình Long Province, although diversionary attacks were launched somewhere else.

Diversionary Attacks on Southern Bình Long

What I had predicted about the communist attack on the III Corps and MR3 that summer had been presented to General Hưng; and my counterpart, Lieutenant Colonel Trần Văn Bình, had also presented his report to General Minh. Of course, we both had given private communications to these two commanders earlier. They later had discussed among themselves and their staff and in the end had suggested the above-mentioned troop reinforcements. ARVN units were thus ready and prepared for the attack that summer.

What was missing was that the Forward Operational Command of III Corps had not moved yet to An Lộc when the attack broke out. General Minh was at that time still at his general headquarters in Biên Hòa and would later move his forward command post from Tây Ninh to Lai Khê, the main base of the 5th infantry Division, to coordinate the battle during the subsequent months.

It should be remembered that if any province in the III Corps and MR3 had been lost, Saigon would have become jittery and Washington might have been in disarray because the Vietnamization of the war had not been completed yet. The U.S. internal politics would have become feverish when the elections would take place later that year. In that aspect, had General Nguyễn Văn Minh won the An Lộc battle, he would be the hero who had saved not only An Lộc, but also Saigon and Washington by extension. And Nixon and Kissinger would have thanked General Minh.

IV. The Fall of Lộc Ninh

However, when the attack occurred, there were rumors in Saigon and Washington that the ARVN was caught by surprise. The reason behind the rumors was the following: At 02:00 hours on 31 March, the communists fired rockets at all the bases belonging to the TF-49 unit of the 18th Infantry Division along Route 22 from the forward base of Xa Mat at the Vietnamese-Cambodian border to Thiện Ngôn on the northern end of Tây Ninh. Defenders of the base of Lạc Long, in particular, who were unable to withstand the barrage of attacks, decided to withdraw all their forces, about a battalion of infantry, artillery and tanks. On their retreat route to Tây Ninh, they fell into an enemy's ambush and suffered heavy casualties.

That morning, General Minh ordered General Hưng and me to meet him at the forward command post in Tây Ninh. When we arrived, Lieutenant Colonel Bình, the chief of the 2nd Bureau of III Corps and MR3, was already waiting for General Minh in the waiting room of the commander's office at the Forward Operational Command headquarters. General Minh, who flew in from Biên Hòa, walked straight into the room without shaking anyone's hands, including General Hưng. We followed General Minh who, sternly looking straight at Bình and me, exploded: "What kind of intelligence is that? They have already destroyed the 49th Regiment. What do you think? What will happen next?"

Lieutenant Colonel Trần Văn Bình (presently in California), who before 1971 was the chief of the Intelligence Operational Branch of the Joint Intelligence Staff of the Joint General Staff of the RVNAF (J-2/JGS/RVNAF), was an expert intelligence officer who knew exactly the level of communist forces in both North and South Vietnam. He calmly explained to General Minh that COSVN would still attack Bình Long and An Lộc. The attack the night before on Route 22 was just a decoy.

Luckily, at that time an officer of the S-2 III Corps and MR3 walked in and presented to Lieutenant Colonel Bình documents that a unit of the 49th Regiment had retrieved from the dead bodies of the communists during their attack on the base. The documents revealed that the attacking communist unit belonged to the COSVN's C30B Division, newly formed in Tây Nguyên—Central Highland—and later renamed the Bình Long infantry unit. Absent from the battlefield were the communist 5th, 7th, and 9th Divisions that were most likely getting ready for the next attack. After reading these documents, General Minh calmed down and appeared to trust Bình's report. However, he requested that General Hưng return the airborne brigade that had been assigned to the 5th Division/ARVN and was operating at Bến Than, west of Chơn Thành. Helicopters picked up the airborne brigade in the afternoon and dropped it close to Route 22, which was its next target. Another unit of the 18th Div/ARVN and a ranger unit were also sent to the area. General Hưng was also told to return the TF-52 unit stationed at Hùng Tâm and to get the 7th Regiment of the 5th Division/ARVN, which was operating outside An Lộc, ready if needed to be transferred to Tây Ninh the following day depending on the progress of events on Route 22.

But things turned out quite strangely that morning. After attacking the TF-49 base, all communist units withdrew out of the area without collecting their trophies or removing the bodies of their dead comrades. General Minh's reserve units which were brought into the battle did not fire any shots or find traces of enemy forces. On the second day of April, Route 22 in Tây Ninh was considered safe for travel. From that day until 3 April, the whole III Corps and MR3 was quiet without any gunshot. This frightening silence foretold a violent storm that was about to ride in.

It turned out that these were only diversionary attacks that helped to hide the movement of the 5th, 7th, and 9th NVA divisions into Bình Long. The 5th Div/VC positioned itself north of Lộc Ninh, the 9th Div/VC around An Lộc, and the 7th Div/NVA close to Highway 13 south of An Lộc. The main aim was on An Lộc itself, although the ARVN leadership did not know about it at that time.

Attack on Lộc Ninh

Things that should happen eventually happened. The communist Nguyễn Huệ campaign in the III Corps and MR3 soon began.

In 1972, Lộc Ninh was a small district of 3,000 inhabitants, most of them ethnic Montagnards who worked for the rubber plantations. A local airfield sat half a kilometer west of Highway 13 with the 9th ARVN Regiment headquarters located close by, although its forces were scattered throughout the area. There were three small compounds parallel to the airfield: the subsector headquarters compound, the artillery battalion firebase, and the regiment's headquarters at the southern end of the airfield. The FSB Alpha was 10 kilometers northwest of Lộc Ninh. A smaller force of five armored personnel carriers and a single M-41 tank were left at the junction of Highways 13 and 14 about four kilometers north of Lộc Ninh.[1]

In the early morning of 5 April, at 03:00 hours, my phone rang. At the other end of the line was General Hưng. He told me that Colonel Nguyễn Công Vĩnh, commander of the TF-9, reported that the 9th Regiment headquarters, the 53rd Battalion firebase and the headquarters of Lộc Ninh Sub-sector were massively shelled and most likely being attacked. The 3/9

IV. The Fall of Lộc Ninh

Battalion, which was operating south of Lộc Ninh, was ordered to return to its base and was followed closely by enemy forces. The 1st Armored Cavalry Battalion of Lieutenant Colonel Nguyễn Đức Dương and the 74th Ranger Battalion at Lộc Tấn and FSB Alpha were also shelled heavily. General Hưng ordered me to come immediately to the division's Tactical Operations Center (TOC). He added, "They have already attacked. The campaign has begun."

When I arrived at the TOC, the 3rd Bureau chief (operations) Lieutenant Colonel Trịnh Đình Đặng was already there. General Hưng came in a few minutes later. I then heard that earlier, when ordered to go on operation, the 3/9 Battalion heard tanks roaring on the west side of Route 137, which linked Highways 13 and 7 across the forest, from the Cambodian border toward Lộc Ninh.

Lieutenant Colonel Nguyễn Đức Dương, commander of the 1st Cavalry Battalion, stated that none of his tanks' engines were turned on at that time. Therefore, communist tanks had been active in Lộc Ninh's battle zone. This fact embarrassed me and caused me to feel ashamed of my limitations while General Hưng continued to receive report that Lieutenant Colonel Dương's units were heavily shelled. If they remained in place, they would either suffer major damage or be annihilated. Lieutenant Colonel Dương was ordered to move his armored unit out of base Alpha and Lộc Tấn intersection; at the same time, the 2/9 Battalion, which was operating in the northwest of Lộc Tấn, was ordered to accompany the 1st Cavalry Battalion and to return to the headquarters of TF-9 at the Lộc Ninh District. However, Lieutenant Colonel Dương could not execute the order at that time, because it was still dark and the armored battalion, the rangers and the 2/9 Battalion were still being heavily shelled. The 1/9 Battalion was also shelled at Bố Đức District. All these details had been reported to the division's TOC. General Hưng himself would like to report these events straight to General Minh but could not contact him on any audio or telephone system from that time until 09:00 hours of 5 April. Of course, all other generals and officers at III Corps and MR3 had similar difficulty communicating with General Minh.

When General Hưng was able to connect with General Minh, he was flying in the airspace over Lộc Ninh. In his helicopter, besides General Hưng, were Colonel William Miller, U.S. adviser to the division; Lieutenant Colonel Phạm Trọng Phùng, the division artillery commander; Lieutenant Colonel Trinh Đình Đăng, the chief of staff of operations S-3 (Thủ Đức Academy Class 5, like General Hưng and myself; he was promoted colonel after the battle and presently resides in California); and me, chief of staff, intelligence S-2. We all wore combat helmets equipped with headphones in order to listen to communications between General Hưng and unit commanders on the ground, and General Minh and other officials.

Earlier, when his helicopter flew over Lộc Ninh, General Hưng had received a report from Lieutenant Colonel Nguyễn Đức Dương that his armored unit was moving on Highway 13 when it was ambushed south of Lộc Thạnh Hamlet. He asked for permission to destroy four 105 mm and two 155 mm artillery pieces in order to move faster and lighter. General Hưng agreed only after they direct-fired on the enemy before destroying them. The procedure consisted of lowering the elevation of the artillery tubes and firing directly into the enemy. Of course, the orders had been encoded before being transmitted. A while later, Lieutenant Colonel Dương reported back that although the orders had been executed, he could not still move to Lộc Ninh because of enemy ambush. General Hưng ordered him to go back to the Lộc Tấn intersection, wait for the 74th Ranger Battalion, and regroup the two forces together before moving forward to liberate Lộc Ninh. The reconnaissance company of the 9th Regiment, which was also placed under the command of Lieutenant Colonel Dương, was ordered back to Lộc Tấn. All units executed the order. However, around noon, the 3/1 Armored Company with accompanying infantry unit broke through the ambush and moved to Chùm Bao close to Hill 177, roughly one kilometer from Lộc Ninh, but could not move further because it was surrounded and attacked by enemy troops. Lieutenant Colonel Dương could only communicate by wireless telecommunication.

When he finally got in touch with General Minh, General Hưng made his report. He was immediately dissed by General Minh—the first time during the An Lộc battle. General Minh's words sounded clear and loud. "What kind of fight was that? Nothing major has happened yet, and you have already decided to pull back?"

He then hung up leaving General Hưng surprised. Obviously General Minh had not understood the overall picture and the gravity of the situation at Lộc Ninh, which would unfold within the next few hours. Everyone in the helicopter sat quietly and looked saddened following the exchange. Only the loud motor engine kept roaring. The divisional helicopter soon had to leave the Lộc Ninh airspace to let South Vietnamese airplanes move in to bomb NVA soldiers who were attacking the TF-9 base. After the planes did their job, General Hưng's helicopter turned back toward Lai Khê for refueling.

A while later, Colonel Miller, the division's U.S. adviser, asked, "What did General Minh say, 45?"

Although General Hưng's code name was 45, he did not answer. No other officer in the helicopter had the courage to answer for him because there were certain things that an ARVN officer could not disclose to a U.S.

IV. The Fall of Lộc Ninh

adviser. These "things" were personal in nature and had nothing to do with war or strategy. The relationship between General Minh and his subordinate General Hưng being a personal topic, the officers would simply refuse to discuss it with an adviser, although a stranger who is not blood related, like Colonel Miller. There was no offense intended because they simply believed that dirty laundry should not be aired in public.

This attitude has to do with "face," which is a Chinese concept that has been around for millennia. Other Asians, the Vietnamese included, have adopted that concept and made it their own. Face in Asia often symbolizes the "soul," the personality of a person. Saving face is therefore crucially important to Asians and is akin to the English "preserving honor, prestige, good name, or reputation." Since being yelled at by one's boss could lead to a loss of prestige or reputation in Asia, not talking about it would seem to be a natural way to preserve someone's "face" in public.

Westerners, on the other hand, are not too sensitive about the issue of "losing face." Being more open than Asians, they see "yelling" as a way to express their anger, their disapproval about something or somebody. Therefore, yelling has become a fairly common process in certain milieus to the point of being considered normal. As such, a westerner does not take it as personally as an Asian does. Being more pragmatic, he just accepts it and moves on. This is part of the cultural environment.

While a westerner may interpret silence as an attempt to hide or cover something, an Asian would see it as a time to draw down, an attempt to help someone save his face. For the Asian, not talking about something does not mean hiding; it is a civil way to avoid embarrassing someone. Again, personal things need to be dealt with on a personal level, not in public. And there were many such personal "things" during the battle of An Lộc that General Hưng could not disclose to Colonel Miller. This cultural difference eventually may have led to bigger misunderstandings between the two officers during this important battle.

After refueling, the helicopter took off again and flew over Lộc Ninh, but at 3,500 feet to avoid intense enemy anti-aircraft missiles. In the afternoon, General Hưng communicated directly with his commanders on the ground, listened to their report and called for immediate air assistance whenever needed. He had the talent of directing air attack right on enemy positions that were one street away from ARVN positions or ordering an air strike on fixed positions without looking at maps, especially while flying in a helicopter. He could do that because on the map he used daily, he had already marked the coordinates of important locations, like intersections, bifurcations of streets or rivers, villages, high-rise buildings, and important strategic positions. He remembered all these coordinates in the territory under his control. In our daily report with him, we had to be careful about naming positions and coordinates; otherwise he would correct us. He would tell us that the coordinates we had given him were incorrect, and this turned out to be true on many occasions. This method of remembering important positions seemed very neat and useful for commanders. It allowed them to retaliate rapidly to the enemy's attacks either through artillery or bombing or to direct and move troops rapidly and precisely, especially when they were airborne. General Hưng had done this since he was a regiment commander at the ARVN 21st Division. While working with him, I had tried to acquire this technical feat, although I was not always successful.

However, in all the battles that occurred that evening as the VC hung onto unit wings of ARVN forces—from the TF-9 bases to those of the 53rd Artillery Battalion—or to units moving to join a new gathering site, like the 74th Ranger Battalion, 2/9 and 3/9 Battalions, and the 9th Reconnaissance Company, General Hưng was unable to save them all. First, air force planes reported that anti-aircraft artillery was so intense that they could not support moving units except fixed bases along the runway of Lộc Ninh airfield. Second, enemy forces were rather large. Defense forces had effectively pushed back repeated enemy attacks, and airplanes had supported them rather efficiently. Units at the level of companies or platoons had either been overwhelmed or withdrawn and dispersed. The Lộc Ninh market and church had been taken by the enemy. Enemy shelling continued into the night and resulted in heavy casualties. Defending forces were frightened by the intensity and the barrage of the shelling. The fixed and visible positions of ARVN 105 mm and 155 mm howitzers made them sitting ducks for enemy guns.

Enemy units executed orders in a strict but rigid manner. In one example, the COSVN's 70th Artillery Division shelled the 1st Armored Cavalry at Lộc Tấn the night before until the latter unit moved out of its base. Then it suddenly stopped shelling as if its mission had been accomplished. In midafternoon, Lieutenant Colonel Dương who had contacted all the units under his command, ordered them to move toward Lộc Ninh in a two-wing formation across the plantation and parallel to Highway 13 but avoiding its use. After two unsuccessful attempts, Lieutenant Colonel Dương ordered withdrawal back to Lộc Tấn to rest for the night. That night was peaceful as they were not shelled like the night before.

On 6 April, Lieutenant Colonel Dương proceeded again to advance to Lộc Ninh using a two-wing approach. The first wing was composed of the 1st Armored Cavalry with 60 tanks and trucks of all kinds including 14 M-41s and M-113s along with two 155 mm and four 105 mm howitzers. The

IV. The Fall of Lộc Ninh

second wing consisted of the 2/9 Battalion and 9th Reconnaissance Company.

The first wing, under the direct command of Lieutenant Colonel Dương, did not use the west side of Highway 13 like the day before, but crossed the forest deep on the eastern side and then swung back to Highway 13 at the level of Hill 150 north, which lay on the east side of the road but south of Highway 13 and south of Hill 177. These two hills were about one or two kilometers southwest of Lộc Ninh. Hill 150 south sat to the southeast of Lộc Ninh and about two kilometers from Hill 150 north. The day before, when the VC came down from Hill 150 north to take over the market, the church and the local police station, other enemy units also came down from Hill 150 south to attack the headquarters of TF-9, the 53rd Artillery Battalion, along the airport runway. The second wing supported the first one on its eastern side and swung back to Highway 13 to attack Hill 178.

Had the two ARVN wings been able to control Hills 150 north and 178 on both sides of Lộc Ninh, airplanes would have had an easier task of bombing Hill 150 south where a large enemy contingent used to attack the ARVN units along the airport runway, thereby decreasing the pressure while waiting for reinforcement. That was General Hưng's strategy when he ordered all units under Lieutenant Colonel Dương to pull out of Lộc Tấn to move to Lộc Ninh.

Things, however, did not turn out well. When Lieutenant Colonel Dương moved out to Highway 13, it was 08:00 hours. The leading 1/1 Armored Company, whether by error or because of another reason, moved out of the forest at Chùm Bao close to Hill 177—at the same place where the 1st Armored Cavalry was ambushed the day before—instead of close to Hill 150. While tanks moved up the hill, enemy troops as numerous as ants ran downhill, waves after waves, and almost eliminated the 1st Armored Cavalry and the 74th Ranger Battalion. In the helicopter above the Lộc Ninh Region, General Hưng could not communicate with Lieutenant Colonel Dương for many hours afterward. When he relayed the news to General Minh, the latter sneered at him for the second time during this battle.

It was later known that at the battle at Chùm Bao on 6 April, ARVN units were attacked by the VC full 5th Division and the 95B Regiment that came down from the highlands to reinforce the Bình Long units. They had taken Lieutenant Colonel Dương and other officers prisoners.

The second wing was composed of the 2/9 Battalion and the 9th Reconnaissance Company under the leadership of Captain Nguyễn Quang Nghi. From Lộc Tấn, they moved deeper into the forest and took over Hill 178 on the east side of the Lộc Ninh village. Captain Nghi was a well-known battalion leader who had led his battalion and 1st Lieutenant Thái Minh Châu's reconnaissance unit all morning but was unable to move up Hill 178 because of the enemy's superior number. In the afternoon, General Hưng communicated with Captain Nghi and after receiving his report told him to abandon the objective on Hill 178 and to turn around and look for Lieutenant Colonel Dương's units. He followed Highway 13 but could not get into the area where Lieutenant Colonel Dương was located. In the evening of 6 April, Captain Nghi reported that his units had reached the market of Lộc Ninh although they had suffered heavy casualties. Apparently, only a small portion of the unit had arrived at the market; the remaining forces had been harassed by enemy forces all night.

The base of the Lộc Ninh Sub-sector, the 53rd Artillery Battalion, and the headquarters of TF-9 unit of Colonel Nguyễn Công Vĩnh were heavily shelled on the night of 5 to 6 April. The TF-9 base at the end of the runway was heavily damaged and the underground emergency unit had collapsed killing almost all its staff. At daytime, the NVA launched repeated attacks that were repulsed. The reason why this unit was still active was because the close bombing by aircraft on enemy troops near the high earthen wall had protected the unit. The NVA units had also suffered high casualties. The 53rd Artillery Battalion base of Lieutenant Colonel Thông was heavily damaged. All the artillery tubes were hit at close range. Although the number of wounded at these two units was high, no medical helicopter, U.S. or Vietnamese, could land on the runway to pick them up because of heavy enemy shelling.

The 3/9 Battalion operating on the south side of the district, although harassed by the Việt Cộng, reported that evening that they had arrived at the southeast side of the runway, on the border of the rubber plantation. General Hưng told them to remain there to protect the outskirts of TF-9 base camp and to let only one company enter the base to bolster Colonel Vĩnh's forces and another platoon to assist the 53rd Artillery Battalion. The rest of the battalion remained outside, including the 2/9 Battalion and the 9th Reconnaissance unit. Enemy shelling continued overnight, and by 04:00 hours, communication with Captain Nguyễn Quang Nghi, commander of the 2/9 Battalion, and 1st Lieutenant Thái Minh Châu of the 9th Reconnaissance Company was lost. The second wing of the units on the northeast of the district that were withdrawn to Lộc Ninh had ceased to exist. General Hưng lost almost 2,000 troops, more than 80 tanks and armored cars, and 20 105 mm and 155 mm artillery guns. A dark veil fell over the career of General Hưng.

On the evening of 6 April while having dinner with General Hưng in the forward command post of the 5th Division at An Lộc (fortified but aboveground and overlooking the residence of the province chief; we had not yet moved to the underground unit being set up by Colonel Lê Nguyên Vỹ), he recounted to me his life as a soldier from the time he was a 1st lieutenant serving under General Minh at the 21st Infantry Division/ARVN from 1964 to 1968 and how he won battles and praises from General Minh who then took him under his wing, nurtured him until General Minh became commander of the III Corps, and elevated him to commander of the 5th Division and then general. During all this time, General Minh never had any harsh word for him. General Hưng told me,

> Dưỡng, this battle is a dangerous one; life and death could occur at any time. From the same class and unit under Teacher Chiêu, I am a general now while none of you has become Lieutenant Colonel yet. Having achieved a great deal, death seems a natural happening for me. As for you, there is no need to stay here. Go back to Lai Khê tomorrow and send Captain Bé here to me.

Captain Trần Văn Bé was my deputy and chief of the Military Intelligence Detachment (MID) unit of the division. After 1973, he was elevated to major and transferred to Định Tường Province where he became Section 2 chief of the sector. In 1976, he escaped from the VC reeducation camp at Suối Máu, Biên Hòa, where he was kept and was caught along with a captain of the Military Security Directorate. That afternoon, right after these two officers were shot to death, the sky suddenly darkened followed by thunder and storms. Prisoners at the Suối Máu camp remembered the day when sky and earth wept when innocent people were unjustly killed.

I did not answer right away and thought lengthily about General Hưng's suggestion. A moment later, I told him about my firm decision not to return to Lai Khê, but to remain there in An Lộc. The dinner was sad because we had lost a lot of troops during the last few days. I had my share of responsibility because I had underestimated the huge enemy forces stationed on the Cambodian territory, at the Fish Hook, the gathering place of all NVA and COSVN's units and at bases along the Chllong River of the Kratie Province of Cambodia.

Final Hours of Lộc Ninh

The next day, 7 April, was a crucial one for Lộc Ninh.

Early in the morning around 06:00 hours when soldiers in front of the base camp of the ARVN 9th Regiment saw four T-54 enemy tanks rolling toward them, they got scared, although there was no infantry attack like many days earlier. Coming just a few days after the initial attack, the tanks immediately raised concern for the defenders. They rolled on the hilly route while shooting at the hill base. For the average Vietnamese soldier, each T-54 tank looked like a monster, for it dwarfed all other tanks he had seen before; it was almost twice as tall as he was and moved around with a great deal of loud clanking, grinding and roaring. The impressive tank was 6.45 meters long, 3.37 meters wide, and 2.40 meters high and weighted 36 tons. It was powered by a 580-horsepower V-12 engine and could move as fast as 48 kilometers per hour (30 mph). The main gun shot a 100 mm shell that could penetrate up to 0.30 meters of armor a kilometer away. It also had a 12.7 mm coaxial machine gun besides the main gun.

Colonel Nguyễn Công Vĩnh relayed the news to his staff in his underground bunker. He then notified the headquarters of General Hưng: this was his last report before his staff and U.S. advisers to the unit escaped from the base in an attempt to join the 3/9 Battalion that was stationed outside the base at the beginning of the airfield runway. Of course, they were caught by the enemy before they reached their target. Lieutenant Colonel Thông, commander of the 53rd Artillery Battalion running toward the 3/9, was also held prisoner.

Inside the 9th Regiment base camp, Major Trần Đăng Khoa, deputy commander, took over the command in the absence of Colonel Vĩnh and reorganized the defense. Defenders aimed and shot at the incoming tanks with an M-72 light anti-tank weapon (LAW), apparently with no effect as the T-54 continued to roll forward. Why did ARVN soldiers at Lộc Ninh not have any success with the M-72 rocket launchers while their counterparts at An Lộc were able to kill many T-54 tanks with the same launchers, as we shall see later? This may have to do with the fact that the M-72 was incapable of consistently piercing the sloped frontal armor on the Soviet- and Chinese-built tanks used by the NVA. This has happened before at Lang Vei in 1968, Bến Hét in 1969, and during the Lam Sơn 719 campaign in Laos in 1971.

As enemy infantry swarmed into the base, Major Khoa called General Hưng and reported that he had lost contact with Colonel Vĩnh and that enemy tanks were outside the compound, while ARVN soldiers were battling with NVA soldiers above the bunker. General Hưng; Lieutenant Colonel Đăng, 3rd Bureau; Lieutenant Colonel Phùng, artillery commander; 2nd Lieutenant Tùng, General Hưng's aide-de-camp; and I, who were sitting in the command helicopter, heard the message, except for Colonel Miller, who did not understand what was happening. Although he asked, no one answered because they were busy following the tragic events that were unraveling on the ground beneath them.

IV. The Fall of Lộc Ninh

Major Khoa said, "Please drop bombs on my head. They are overrunning the base and shooting at the underground TOC. Please 45, do not hesitate."

"Roger, Khoa; this is 45. I hear you well and will do as you wish. I'll take care of your family." General Hưng answered. These were Khoa's last words,

"Thanks and good-bye, 45," followed by a loud noise.

General Hưng's face reddened and tears ran down his face. We all shed tears. General Hưng switched to another frequency and requested the VNAF to bomb TF-9 base as well as enemy forces that had overtaken the base. When he asked for the bombing, he knew more than anyone else his own drama. When airplanes bombed the overrun base, General Hưng made his report to General Minh and was sneered for the third time—this one badly.

Before getting into his helicopter that morning, General Hưng ordered the TF-52 commander of the two bases at Hùng Tâm north of the Cần Lê Bridge to move his two battalions to the intersection with National Route 13. Contrary to the presumption or supposition of writers who thought that General Hưng ordered the TF-52 unit to head to Highway 13 then to liberate Lộc Ninh, he only told him to move his troops to Highway 13 to set up a defense line north of the Cần Lê Bridge. Close by were stationed two companies of the 5th Division, one from the 2/9 Battalion and the other from the 1/7 Battalion, and two companies of RF of the Bình Long military sector with six artillery guns under the command of Lieutenant Colonel Nguyễn Văn Hòa.

It was only that morning that General Hưng received the report that the 9th Regiment base camp had been attacked by tanks. It was the first time that the presence of PAVN tanks had been officially confirmed. Therefore, he wanted to set up another line of defense north of the Cần Lê Bridge and about eight miles north of An Lộc. General Hưng after losing contact with the 1st Armored Cavalry the day earlier had no hope of freeing the pressure on An Lộc.

However, events on the battlefield were different than what was expected. The TF-52 unit had not reached Highway 13 when it encountered heavy enemy fire from the NVA 5th Division and the 95th Regiment that had ambushed and destroyed the ARVN 1st Armored Cavalry the day before. Before the afternoon of 7 April when General Hưng's command helicopter from Lộc Ninh flew over Cần Lê, the TF-52 unit reported that it encountered heavy fighting on Route 17 but could not receive artillery support because of the risk of firing on friendly forces. General Hưng told them to try to withdraw to An Lộc without trying to get to Highway 13.

What Really Happened in Lộc Ninh?

Contrary to what was mentioned earlier, the American side had a different story about the loss of Lộc Ninh which was related by U.S. Captain Smith as follows: On 6 April, Lieutenant Colonel Nguyễn Bá Thịnh, commander of TF-52 at Hùng Tâm, sent a battalion to link up with the besieged garrison at Lộc Ninh. It was ambushed and had to withdraw back to its base.

On 7 April, the TF-52 unit was ordered to withdraw to An Lộc as well as the two companies at the Cần Lê Bridge. They encountered heavy enemy attack. Thịnh and three U.S. advisers were wounded. On 8 April, U.S. helicopters supported by closed tactical strike succeeded in extracting all three advisers. TF-52 continued its withdrawal and arrived at An Lộc later with only half of its effective force of 1,000 troops.[2]

The situation in Lộc Ninh was desperate by noon after enemy tanks launched an attack on TF-9 compound in the early hours of 6 April. The 9th Regiment held out with close air support. Attacks continued in the night when enemy artillery and rockets hit the hospital bunker killing wounded troops. The ammunition depot was destroyed. Another ground attack was repulsed.

At 07:00 hours on 7 April, the NVA launched another attack. One enemy tank was destroyed at the base perimeter. Based on Captain Smith's account, the only U.S. survivor from Lộc Ninh to tell the story, Colonel Vĩnh, the 9th Regiment commander, rushed out of the compound gate at 08:00 hours to surrender to the enemy. The executive officer hoisted a white shirt as a sign of surrender. But according to Captain Smith, he subdued him, ran the national flag up the pole, and told everyone to go back to fighting.[3]

The attack continued and caused major damage to the remaining troops of the 9th Regiment, although a few bunkers still held on. Smith and his group held on until 18:30 hours when they abandoned their compound and ran south. Smith was caught and held by the enemy in a camp in Cambodia. He was released on 12 February 1973 as part of the provisions of the Paris Accords. He later received the Distinguished Service Cross for Valor for his actions in Lộc Ninh.[4] His account, however, was not free of controversy as "Smith and the army are at odds about what happened that day [7 April] in the bunker."[5] A few other advisers held on in the district bunker until 8 April, when they too tried to escape, but without success.

From the South Vietnamese side, Colonel Vĩnh was the other survivor to tell his story. In a telephone interview with General Lâm Quang Thi in 2006, he denied having surrendered to or colluded with the enemy; his executive officer did not hoist a white flag on the compound flagpole on 7 April.

IV. The Fall of Lộc Ninh

He was instead captured when his compound was overrun by the enemy and then taken to the NVA campaign headquarters in the district of Mimot in Cambodia where he met Lieutenant Colonel Dương, the TF 1-5 commander. They were then blindfolded and transported to a prisoner camp deeper inside Cambodia.

Released in 1973 following the Paris Agreements, he continued to serve at the ARVN headquarters in Saigon until 1975 when the communists sent him to various communist reeducation camps in North Vietnam for a total of 13 years. This was the second time he landed in communists' hands. We have a picture of an elderly Colonel Vĩnh clothed in a pair of black pajamas, exhausted and worn out by the years in the toughest reeducation camps of the country,[6] when he emerged from the Saigon train station in 1988 flanked by his wife and middle-aged son who had come to pick him up. Would a man who had colluded with the enemy serve a 13-year imprisonment and be in such a sorry physical state? While he was first jailed by the communists in Lộc Ninh, western writers had written bad reports about him. Years after his release, he immigrated to the U.S. through the ODP program and settled in Southern California. He was hard of hearing and subsequently wrote to General Thi,[7]

> I commanded a unit responsible for the defense of the border. I was defeated and feel very ashamed. If people say I am weak, I accept that; but don't blame me for what I have not done.

Until today, it appears that the chapter on Lộc Ninh on the afternoon of 7 April 1972 had not been completely clarified except that many troops, U.S. as well as Vietnamese including Major Trần Đăng Khoa as mentioned above, had valiantly defended their positions until the end.

General Thi, who had analyzed the Lộc Ninh battle, wrote,

> The rapid collapse of Lộc Ninh was due in great part to his failure of leadership. [Facing an imminent attack on MR3] Vĩnh had failed to take necessary actions to reinforce the district town. He should have, for instance, secured the section of Route 13 north of Lộc Ninh and recalled the mechanized Task Force back to the district earlier to shore up the defense of the district. On the other hand, Lieutenant Colonel Dương, the TF 1-5 commander, in my opinion, had failed to take appropriate precautions when he received the order to return to Lộc Ninh on 5 April.[8]

General Hưng and his operational staff were in the air above Lộc Ninh on 7 April 1972 and were monitoring the events that happened to ARVN units on the ground that day. The loss of Lộc Ninh deeply affected General Hưng. He thereafter vowed to sacrifice his life to defend An Lộc against the communists.

According to Lieutenant Colonel Nguyễn Ngọc Ánh, former assistant for Operations to General Minh, gave the following tally for the battle of Lộc Ninh[9]:

Enemy: 2,150 KIA (killed in action).
2 T-54s and 1 PT-56 destroyed.
ARVN: 600 KIA, 2,400 captured.
38 M-41s and M-113s destroyed or captured.
8 artillery howitzers destroyed or captured.

In Lộc Ninh, the communists clamped down immediately. On 8 April, all government officials and teachers were rounded up. The head of the local Self-Defense militia along with a sergeant and another militia man were publicly executed: they were shot outright without even the benefit of a "people's court." The rest arrested as "enemies of the people" were trucked to a secure base in Snoul, Cambodia. The communists then ransacked homes and plundered offices of both government officials and plantation employees. Among the most prized booty were half a dozen black-and-white television sets confiscated by the victorious NVA. They were sent to COSVN in Cambodia where high-ranking officials and cadres closed out each work day by watching a program broadcast by Saigon.[10]

In the II Corps on 30 April 1972, after the town of Dak To fell to the communists, Colonel Stephen Bachinski, the Kontum Province adviser, wrote,

> Stories of VC atrocities continue to pour in from those Highland tribesmen who survived the long trek through the jungle from Dak To and points south: clergy murdered; village officials with throats slit; families of U.S. employees killed and slogans posted over their homes; young boys and girls separated from their families and taken into the jungle; and refugees being held forcefully by the NVA in obvious ambush positions in order to avoid B-52 strikes.[11]

General Creighton Abrams wrote to U.S. Secretary of Defense Melvin Laird,

> Enemy staying power is his complete disregard for the expenditure of resources, both men and materiel, and second on discipline through fear, intimidation, and brutality. An enemy decision to attack carries an inherent acceptance that the forces involved may be expended totally.[12]

The atrocities committed by the NVA forces were innumerable, excessive and known to the whole world. That was how they were able to conquer South Vietnam.

V

Crucial Decisions Made to Save An Lộc

Major Decisions on Highway 13

In the afternoon of 7 April, as General Hưng's helicopter flew over the northern end of the Cần Lê Bridge before leaving the area, a long convoy of what appeared to be trucks was seen moving along the Bé River parallel to Highway 13. What was unusual was the presence of what looked like communication antennas that only the headquarters of the NVA or large VC units had while handling emergency operations. Suspecting enemy forces, General Hưng immediately called the air force to strike the convoy. It was a total hit.

While returning back to the sky above Cần Lê, the TF-52 unit reported that it was able to cross the southern end of the bridge, although with heavy casualties. Above Highway 13, although flying as high as 4,000 feet, we then saw a group of people heading toward the Cần Lê Bridge followed by a column of 20 tanks. Both General Hưng and Colonel Miller thought they were tanks, although they could not be completely sure that these were NVA tanks or those of the 1st Armored Cavalry of Lieutenant Colonel Nguyễn Đức Dương that had lost contact the day before. Desiring a confirmation, General Hưng called the 1st Armored Cavalry on its frequency but got no response. Once more, General Hưng made another important decision. In his mind, he was afraid that these NVA tanks were rushing south to attack An Lộc using their famous strategy, "Once victorious, keep moving forward."

On one hand, he called VNAF to strike a column of soldiers and tanks on Highway 13 about eight kilometers north of the Cần Lê Bridge. He then told me to draw two B-52 boxes on the western side of the Bé River and to give them to Colonel Miller to request bombing that evening or night. He commanded Lieutenant Colonel Nguyễn Văn Hòa, commander of the bridge area, to immediately destroy the steel support of the bridge. Under ideal circumstances, it would be better to totally destroy the bridge. He also ordered Lieutenant Colonel Hòa to shell the northern section of Highway 13 each time aircraft left the area to prevent any enemy troops from moving south on that highway, and if the enemy attack was too strong, to destroy the canons. The destruction of the bridge was carried out, and although it was not totally destroyed, the spans of the bridge were damaged to the point that tanks could not roll through.

When he returned to his command post in An Lộc and the helicopter flew back to Lai Khê for refueling, General Hưng went to his TOC to report to General Minh. At that time, Colonel Lê Nguyên Vỹ was not there, while Colonel Bùi Đức Điềm, operational chief of staff of the division, was directing the move of the division's forward command post from its former location to the new one because the night before and that morning, many shells had been falling on the periphery of the former command center. It was suspected that the enemy knew of its location.

Prior to getting into his old command center, General Hưng told me, "I'll be sneered at again."

Correct. It was not a simple sneer but a full frontal attack. The staff furtively left the room as no one wanted to witness the coming storm. I stayed around because of my friendship with General Hưng. General Minh declared that destroying the bridge was like leaving children behind in Lộc Ninh, with no means to return, especially the 1st Armored of Lieutenant Colonel Dương. It is possible that the column on the northern side of Cần Lê Bridge was the 1st Armored Cavalry, which had 60 tanks, armored cars, trucks and a thousand soldiers; and losing contact did not mean total destruction of the unit. Acting like that was like killing your own sons. General Minh thought General Hưng had made hasty decisions without consulting with his superior.

General Hưng just listened without saying a word because what General Minh said might sound logical. He did not have any reason to argue back to his superior, who also was his teacher, except for the fear that the NVA would be attacking An Lộc that evening. If his assessment were correct, he had saved An Lộc from falling into enemy hands that morning. But he dared not argue back. He accepted his perceived "failure" and made up his mind about his future.

Out of the operation room, he grimly walked to the dining mess without uttering a word. When the cook set up the table, General Hưng just asked for water. So did I. How could one eat in such a condition? The losses were high. In a slow but firm voice, he repeated his decision to hold An Lộc at all cost and sadly commented that his career as general was over. On his first battle as a general, he had lost a lot—almost more than one-third of his division. The biggest loss of all was that of his mentor's confidence. General Minh had always trusted his battle leadership until now. Once more, he ordered me to go back to Lai Khê and send my deputy to him.

I told him right then that we had the 5th Reconnaissance Company with several long-range reconnaissance groups that had just withdrawn for other sites. As these troops were battle savvy, they would be glad to protect him. They knew the terrain, were experts in moving through forested areas day or night, traveled easily on all kinds of terrains, hills, valleys, and rivers, and were led by savvy and battle-hardened officers. If General Hưng wanted to kill himself after the loss of An Lộc, we would take his body to the forest, douse it with fuel, burn it, and carry his ashes to Lai Khê in two weeks. I was determined to remain in An Lộc and stay alive to carry his body away. I later notified Captain Dương Tấn Triệu; 1st Lieutenant Lê Văn Chánh, commander of the reconnaissance company; and 1st Lieutenant Nguyễn Đức Trạch, aka poet Trạch Gầm—the son of writer Tùng Long—who were trusted officers in charge of secret missions in zones controlled by the Việt Cộng in the divisional area. These three excellent officers were close and reliable friends.

After dinner, General Hưng gathered his staff for a meeting: Colonel Trần Văn Nhựt, Bình Long province chief; Colonel Lê Nguyên Vỹ, General Minh's operational deputy; Lieutenant Colonel Lý Đức Quân, 7th Regiment commander; U.S. advisers at the divisional and military zone levels; the leadership staff of the forward command post; and Lieutenant Colonel Nguyễn Văn Biết, commander of the 3rd Ranger Battle Group that had been sent to An Lộc as a reinforcement unit. The latter had lost a few officers when their plane was hit by a missile on landing.

This meeting took place at the unique above-ground villa in the new headquarters area at 14:30 hours on 7 April after the two Arc Light boxes had been executed by the U.S. Strategic Air Force on the northern side of the Cần Lê Bridge as requested. At that time, the 1/7 Battalion had withdrawn from the Quản Long Airfield and the 2/7 and 3/7 Battalions, 7th Reconnaissance Company, had also pulled back to the north and northeast of An Lộc City while the headquarters of the 7th Regiment had settled down in the administrative buildings of the province. Only the TF-52 unit and the mixed unit of Lieutenant Colonel Hòa had not withdrawn completely, besides a few units that had crossed rivers and arrived at An Lộc. The 7th Reconnaissance Company and an intelligence team of the division were welcoming these people and waiting for the rest of the unit.

Arc Light was the code name for the massive attacks carried out by B-52 Stratofortress bombers throughout the course of the Vietnam War. The bombers that flew in groups of three B-52s each positioned themselves to ensure their bombs would saturate the target area. Each aircraft was loaded with 84 500-pound bombs carried internally and 24 750-pound bombs under the wings. Two cells (six bombers) would deliver 360,000 pounds of high explosives in a period of a few minutes. Each box would target a specific area of half a mile long and a quarter mile wide.[1] However, when President Nixon insisted that the B-52 fleet supporting the Vietnam War be increased, SAC deployed some of the B-52G fleet that had a significantly smaller conventional bomb load. There was no way for the person on the ground to be able to identify the different models or which model was flying a particular mission. The effect of the Arc Light would be almost the same for the soldier on the ground: it was deadly and frightening. Every living thing was shocked senseless or killed, giant trees were shredded and torn apart, and pulverized rock covered the whole area with a gray powder.

Defensive Setup at An Lộc

After I presented the battle results of the last few days, division losses at Lộc Ninh, and estimates on the battle of that night and the night after, Lieutenant Colonel Đăng listed the positions of the various units protecting An Lộc according to the directions and specifications of General Hưng. Positions were temporary until reinforcements arrived at the scene.

- The 1/7 Battalion and 7th Reconnaissance Company were positioned on the north end of town with 2/7 Battalion at its left. They would leave this position once the TF-52 unit had returned and move left to occupy the northeast section of town. If the TF-52 unit were severely damaged, it would stay behind the 1/7 Battalion.
- The 3/7 Battalion would occupy the western position.
- The 3rd Ranger Battle Group took over the eastern zone.
- The south would be under the control of the PSDF, which also controlled the Windy Hill and Hill 169 on the southwest of town.

Two important issues were raised at this meeting.

First, General Hưng asked that Colonel Trần Văn Nhựt (who later became brigadier general and commander of the 2nd Infantry Division), as province chief, requisition all available trucks and other commercial buses in the province. The 7th Battle Group of Lieutenant Colonel Lý Đức Quân would then use these vehicles as defensive shields to block Highway 13, the road coming from Phú Lố on the west side of town, and the route coming from Quản Lợi airfield. This decision was made because there was no time and no building materials to erect heavy defensive fortifications in these areas. Without these blockades, the enemy would reach the center of town and the forward command post without difficulty.

Second, he asked that Colonel Nhựt advise civilians to evacuate the town because of a potential communist attack. Only essential officials would be kept such as those dealing with water, electricity, and health care, to avoid a wasteful loss of civilian lives.

Colonel Nhựt, with his usual subtleness, did not comment on or argue about these two decisions but later did talk in private to General Hưng. He argued that the decisions made would ultimately affect the morale of the people, and therefore he would present them to General Minh and the civilian delegate of the government.[2]

General Hưng then left for Lai Khê, the permanent headquarters of the 5th ARVN Division to discuss the defense there with his deputy, Lieutenant Colonel Lê Thọ Trung, and to resolve personal family matters regarding his staying in An Lộc. When General Hưng returned to An Lộc in the late afternoon, the town had been shelled a few times and a few hundred civilians had been transported to the local hospital for care. On the north end of town, which served as a commercial zone and town market, soldiers from the 9th Regiment of the 5th Div/ARVN along with civilians from Lộc Ninh began to trickle in. The TF-52 unit after fighting against the enemy west of the Cần Lê Bridge had also arrived at An Lộc; it was positioned north of town. Units of the 7th Regiment of the 5th Div/ARVN had been moving trucks and huge commercial buses to set up a defensive shield on Highway 13 according to General Hưng's orders but without the consent of the province chief.

Around 20:00 hours in the new underground command post, General Hưng was rebuked by General Minh, the fifth and last time before the official battle began, about the requisition of private trucks and buses to shore up the defense of An Lộc. The matter had been brought up to General Minh by Colonel Nhựt. But General Minh made no decision whatsoever—whether to approve or cancel the order—except rebuking General Hưng. One had to acknowledge the wise decision and military acumen of General Hưng who had correctly estimated the importance and severity of the battle that would unfurl in the following days and had made proactive and good decisions that a wise commander should have made on the battlefield. He would bravely accept any untoward consequence resulting from his decisions in front of his superior. As events unfolded rapidly with each succeeding minute or second on the battlefield, it would be difficult for a general to fight a war and report to his superior at the same time. Although deeply saddened following his discussion with General Minh, he changed frequency and called Lieutenant Colonel Lý Đức Quân, commander of the 7th Regiment to inquire about the progress of setting up a defensive barricade on Highway 13.

At 21:00 hours that night, General Hưng and Colonel Miller rode in a jeep to see Lieutenant Colonel Quân, commander of the 7th Regiment on the northern periphery of town. I followed them in a second jeep with Captain Triệu, a 2nd Bureau member, and a few aides. While General Hưng and Colonel Miller made the tour of the defense perimeter with Lieutenant Colonel Quân, I went to the security and reception unit where soldiers and civilians who ran away from the town of Lộc Ninh were processed. After one hour of discussion with soldiers of the 9th Regiment, the 53rd Artillery Battalion, and the TF-52, I began to realize that General Hưng had been correct in his assessment of events at the Cần Lê Bridge.

First, civilians running away from Lộc Ninh stated that they heard NVA tanks rumbling down Highway 13 followed or preceded by soldiers holding their AK-47s and B-40s and marching toward the Cần Lê Bridge. The VNAF airstrike on this column had been effective and deadly as NVA soldiers had to stop to care for the dead and wounded while leaving alone civilians who were hiding in ditches. Had the airstrike not taken place, the enemy column would have easily reached and attacked an unprepared An Lộc. They would have killed or held hostage the civilians to prevent them from warning An Lộc defenders.

Second, the 52nd Task Force unit had battled with enemy soldiers on provincial Route 17 after pulling out of the Đồng Tâm bases. It had gunned down many NVA soldiers, although many more soldiers showed up. But after B-52 bombers dropped bombs down on the requested areas close to the Bé River, north of Cần Lê Bridge, enemy troops withdrew from the area leaving the rest of the task force free to return to An Lộc.

Third, many local Stiengs (minority highlander) living on the banks of the Bé River had seen columns of NVA soldiers walking through their lands toward an elevated and large area close to the river. In the morning when the soldiers pulled up their antennas, the Stiengs, fearing for their lives, ran away toward the highway in the direction of An Lộc. Later they saw small planes dropping bombs, then larger planes dropping larger bombs on the enemy column. They also believed that the bombing had saved them.

From the information gathered, I believe that the assessment of the progress of the battle—NVA mounting a forced march to attack An Lộc on 7 April, when the defenders had not had the chance to set up their defense—

was accurate based on the experience of General Hưng. Therefore, his rapid decisions on Highway 13, Bé River and Cần Lê Bridge had saved An Lộc in its most critical moments and changed the course of the An Lộc battle right then and of the war in Vietnam in the following two years. Had An Lộc fallen on 7 April 1972, what would have remained of Saigon? What would Washington have thought and how would it react? In which direction would the "Vietnamization" strategy of Kissinger-Nixon that was in its latest stage be heading to? Losing An Lộc on 7 April would have dealt a deadly blow to the Government of South Vietnam, and the ARVN had to fight to protect Saigon. Where would Saigon find troops to reinforce Quảng Trị and Kontum? Would the U.S. be forced to reenter the war? Since Washington had made its decision not to reenter the war, that would have been the end of South Vietnam then. That early loss would have dealt a huge moral defeat for the U.S. Therefore, General Hưng's wise and rapid decisions marked not only one of the deciding moments in the Vietnam War, but also saved Saigon and Washington. Had he earned his reputation as one of the most brilliant generals of South Vietnam? If even many insiders had not grasped the complexities of what had occurred before the official battle of An Lộc began, outsiders, no matter how famous they were, who based on this or that person's comments wrote about the An Lộc battle without seeing it, would easily have committed errors.

In summary, these were General Hưng's decisions:

1. Order the bombing and destruction of an NVA divisional command headquarters on the western side of Bé River.

2. Order the 52nd Task Force to move out of the Hùng Tâm bases to Highway 13 and to set up a defensive perimeter north of the Cần Lê Bridge. Although the move had not been completed in time, it held up and prevented another enemy divisional unit from mounting a surprise attack on the bridge. This battle gave enough time for the ARVN unit at Cần Lê to fire at the attacking unit and blow up the bridge.

3. Order the bombing and destruction of an infantry and tank unit that planned to mount a surprise attack after a forced march on the Cần Lê Bridge and subsequently on An Lộc.

4. Order Lieutenant Colonel Nguyễn Văn Hòa to destroy the Cần Lê Bridge to prevent NVA tanks and infantry from moving south and attacking An Lộc at a time when its defense was not yet organized.

That night, the 5th Div/VC was no longer heard on the communication system of COSVN or the operation headquarters of the Nguyễn Huệ campaign until a week later following a report from the 5th Technical Company of the

5th Div/ARVN (this is a telecommunication unit belonging to the 7th Joint Staff of the Joint General Staff of the RVNAF (J7/JGS/RVNAF) that intercepted and dissected orders and news from COSVN and translated all the coded messages for the division's 2nd Bureau to evaluate and assess. Each division had such a telecommunication unit. With news coming from the 5th Technical Company and from soldiers and civilians returning from Lộc Ninh, we knew exactly that the advanced operational headquarters of the 5th Div/VC had been destroyed and the tank and infantry unit that rushed to attack An Lộc had suffered major casualties on 7 April following VNAF airstrikes and U.S. Air Force B-52 bombings.

Since the official attack on An Lộc occurred only on 13 April, during the next six days and five nights, the enemy indiscriminately shelled the town of An Lộc. The 5th Div/VC moved out of the battle zone on Highway 13 into the secret zone Bến Than, then followed the Saigon River to Dầu Tiếng where it reinforced its unit's strength from troops of the C30B Div/VC (or the C30B Div. of the COSVN) in order to return to the An Lộc battlefield. The newly formed C30B division which had once used troops from the 9th Div/VC had fought against the 49th TF/ARVN on Route 22 on 31 March 1972. After that battle, the C30B Div/VC left the area of Tây Ninh to move to the Saigon River area where it operated from Bến Than on the eastern side of the province of Bình Long to the east of Lai Khê all the way to Bời Lời. It attacked all the bases along the Saigon River from the Tống Lê Chân base to Bến Than.

Once reinforced, the 5th Div/VC returned to An Lộc after the town was first attacked by the 9th Div/VC, the NVA's 202 and 203 Armored Regiments, on 13 April. As for the much-weakened C30B Division, it received order to attack posts on the periphery of the Bình Dương Province at the battalion/company level, not at the divisional/regimental levels as before. Failing there, it picked up new recruits along the Vàm Cỏ Đông in mid–May and moved to Trảng Bàng and Gò Dầu Hạ. In this area, it attacked Hiếu Thiện and planned to cut off Route 22 to isolate Tây Ninh but was beaten by the ARVN 25th Infantry Division, following which it moved to the Parrot's Beak area to reinforce itself another time.

The COSVN attack on An Lộc on 7 April had to be delayed because its 5th Division/VC had suffered casualties and the 202 and 203 Armored Regiments were stuck at the bridge. Therefore, General Minh not only did not lose An Lộc that day, but was also able to reinforce General Hưng with new troops. From that time on, General Hưng was viewed as a brilliant general who had defeated the NVA during the summer of 1972 in his area of responsibility.

General Minh had an excellent perception of men that allowed him to select the right person to protect the country in times of upheaval. Although he could get irritated or criticize an officer for the way he moved troops in a difficult and challenging situation in the beginning, all of this was not important. General Minh was overall a good leader whom I have always respected, although I believe his good nature and blind trust of his inferiors had been taken advantage of and abused by a few other persons.

Political Implications of the Summer Attacks

To understand the important roles of the generals on the battlefield of the III Corps and MR3, one has to note the overall spring–summer 1972 campaign of the communists in South Vietnam. One also has to evaluate the position and role of Washington in this important battle in the context of the whole Vietnam War.

After the huge battles between the ARVN and the NVA in Laos and Cambodia in 1971, renowned observers knowledgeable about the world situation and the war in Vietnam had come to the conclusion that the war was about to end at any price, but not as a "peace with honor" as Nixon and Kissinger had always stated. At that time, these two men only considered Vietnam as a sideshow in a larger political context that the Nixon Republican government needed to solve if they did not want the Democrats to win the elections in November 1972. Observers mentioned that Kissinger had almost defeated the ARVN with the scheme of wasting troops in the Laos and Cambodian battlefields after executing his Vietnamization project. From there on, the war would end because South Vietnam would be like a crab without its claws. Kissinger also believed that North Vietnam would land in this same situation.

From July to December 1971, northern and southern troops had suffered massively to the point of no longer being able to fight each other for six to seven months until 1972. During that period, the Paris talks dragged on. Discussions between Lê Đức Thọ and Kissinger went nowhere. The magician Kissinger, although having considered South Vietnam as a sideshow, had pulled out such a masterful trick that even South and North Vietnam were left surprised and fearful; the deeply worried Soviet Union welcomed Nixon but delayed the signing of the Strategic Arms Limitation Talk (SALT) on 22 May 1972. A few months earlier, Kissinger had set up the show with Nixon flying to Peking to meet Chou En Lai, the prime minister of Communist

China on February 1972. Everyone knew that an ultra-secret settlement of world order was about to happen. What happened there was anyone's guess. The Soviet Union obviously saw a threat to itself in this high-level meeting. Lê Duẩn, Lê Đức Thọ, and Phạm Hùng had criticized the "Renovation" of Nikita Krushchev before the IX Central Committee Meeting of Communists and secretly followed China, although they did not let anything showing on the outside. Lê Đức Thọ, who controlled everything on the inside—security and all the material support of the international communists—began purging members in the Politburo and army.

At that time, the government of Nguyễn Văn Thiệu, although afraid of Kissinger's maneuvers, could not do anything, except trust its U.S. benefactor.

The following two factors had forced Hanoi to act within a time frame because otherwise they would cause Hanoi some serious damage.

On 26 March 1972, the Soviet Union defense minister Marshal Pedorovich arrived in Hanoi with a large military contingent to review the whole process of attacking South Vietnam. He had also seen the goals of the White House about Vietnam and given Deputy Prime Minister Podgorny in December 1971 clearance to discuss the process of attacking the South while promising to supply Hanoi with advanced tanks, T-54, T-55 and PT-76, as well as 130 mm and 150 mm artillery guns, fighter planes MIG-19 and MIG-21, anti-aircraft 23 mm and 57 mm guns, anti-tank rockets AT-3 Sagger, surface-air missiles SA-7 Strela against planes like transport, and attack helicopters. All these armaments were transferred to Hải Phòng in huge quantities over many months only after Hanoi had completed its summer attack.

November 1972 turned out to be the election month of the U.S. president, congressmen as well as leaders of the executive and legislative branches of the states. This important election strongly affected world events while the U.S. was still waging war in Vietnam. If the Democratic Party won, the U.S. would have pulled out earlier. Therefore, Hanoi needed to defeat South Vietnam before the elections in order to have a chance to defeat Nixon. Although South Vietnamese intelligence, civilian as well as military, was aware of this fact, it could not assess the intensity of the upcoming battle and its timing because only the U.S. knew about the magnitude of communist armament shipments to the port of Hải Phòng and the degree of troop infiltration through the Hồ Chí Minh Trail. However, on the political side, Washington made strong announcements when Nixon declared on 4 April, "The bastards have never been bombed like they're going to be this time."[3] He then ordered U.S. Air Force to support ARVN forces to the maximum, including the use of B-52 bombers throughout the 1972 Fiery Red Summer conflict.

The NVA had gone through full mobilization during which 16-year-old youths were sent to the three main fronts in Quảng Trị in the I Corps and MR1, Kontum in the II Corps and MR2, and Bình Long in the III Corps and MR3. During this major offensive, Hanoi had shipped approximately 200,000 troops to the South, not including transportation and support forces that accounted for twice or thrice the number of offensive troops. This was equivalent to 14 infantry divisions, 4 artillery and air defense divisions, 4 to 6 cavalry regiments, and 26 specialized units at the regimental level. Overall close to 22 divisions equipped with the latest Soviet and Chinese armaments were thrown into the three fronts in Quảng Trị, Kontum, and Bình Long. Each battle front was potentially dangerous. However, if one province in MR1 or MR2 were lost, the impact on the remaining country was not really critical. It had been estimated that even if the NVA won in both I and II Corps fronts, South Vietnam could still survive from Nha Trang southward. However, had Bình Long or Tây Ninh been lost, the situation would be critical because of the close proximity of Saigon. Therefore, the Bình Long front was utterly critical to the survival of South Vietnam.

The Hanoi-led "Total Offensive of the Fiery Red Summer of 1972" was placed under different NVA leaderships:

- the battlefield of Trị Thiên (south of the DMZ) under the direct command of Hanoi;
- the Central Vietnam battlefield was divided into the highland battlefield under the command of the communist B3-Front or the NVA III Military Region (a communist corps-sized command level) in the Central Highland and the shoreline battlefield under the command of the communist B-5 Front or the Fifth Military Region (also a corps-sized command level); and
- the South Vietnamese III Corps and MR3 and IV Corps and MR4 under COSVN command. The latter after having taken control of Lộc Ninh but failing to attack An Lộc on 7 April had to postpone the attack until 13 April.

General Hưng to Defend An Lộc to Death

Back to the An Lộc battle zone, after General Hưng had ordered the destruction of the Cần Lê Bridge (not Colonel Trần Văn Nhựt as mentioned in some papers), its spans were severely damaged. Under the support of the 31st Ranger Battalion—recently sent to An Lộc for reinforcement—the 52nd

Task Force unit at the Cần Lê area was able to return to An Lộc with 400 able troops. The situation was not as grim as earlier in the morning. Lieutenant Colonel Nguyễn Văn Hòa's units at the Cần Lê base which comprised a company of the 2/9 Battalion, two RF companies, 256 and 257, were able to withdraw to An Lộc in the afternoon after destroying two 155 mm and four 105 mm howitzers because of lack of available trucks to pull them out.

On 7 April, the 3rd Ranger Battle Group of Lieutenant Colonel Nguyễn Văn Biết had been flown in to reinforce An Lộc. It included the 31st, 36th, and 52nd Battalions comprising more than 1,500 troops. Lieutenant Colonel Biết, the battalion and its company commanders were battle-hardened officers.

The next day, General Minh reinforced An Lộc with the 8th Regiment, which was part of the ARVN 5th Division and included the 1/8, 2/8 and the 8th Reconnaissance Company with a total of 850 troops under the direction of Colonel Mạch Văn Trường. The 3/8 Battalion had been kept in Lai Khê to protect the division headquarters and the forward command post of the III Corps. However, during the whole battle, the 8th Regiment (-) was under the command of Major Huỳnh Văn Tâm. When the regiment arrived at the north end of town close to the Đồng Long Airfield, Colonel Trường standing in front of his forward command post watched his troops settle in their positions. A Dodge 4 × 4 running over an M-72 rocket in the far distance caused an explosion, and a fragment of shell got lodged into the soft tissue of Colonel Trường's shoulder. I did not remember which shoulder was injured, because the injury was insignificant. Dr. Hùng, commander of the 5th Medical Battalion of the division after evaluating and examining the wound reported to General Hưng that there was no bony or tendon injury. But the colonel requested to remain at the divisional headquarters for treatment. General Hưng with bonhomie smiled and gave him his small room—reserved for the division commander—at the end of the underground tunnel. He also ordered Dr. Hùng to come and care for the wound every day. For more than two weeks, he did not use that space, which was the safest in the compound, but turned it over to the colonel as a place to stay. General Hưng and Colonel Miller had to use two cots placed at the entrance of the tunnel with a small table between the cots serving as the operational table for the two men. This area became the center of operations. Close by was a long table used for the telephone and other communication gear. Colonel Lê Nguyên Vỹ, Colonel Bùi Đức Điềm, Lieutenant Colonel Trịnh Đình Đăng, Dr. Hùng, I and three or four other essential officers set up our cots on the side of the large table.

General Minh had also received from the RVNAF General Staff the 1st Airborne Brigade and then the 21st Infantry Division to free the VC blockade at Tàu-Ô Stream on Highway 13 north of Chơn Thành. This blockade was not the usual type seen at the company or battalion level at other battlefields; it was a defensive rampart deep and wide on both sides of and on Highway 13 itself with deep and sturdy foxholes, especially on top of the two hills that dominated all this area. The place was a former sturdy U.S. battalion base. The blockade was manned by the NVA's 7th Division (7th Div/NVA), a battle-hardened unit equipped with all kinds of armaments, including anti-aircraft artillery guns and SA-7 surface-air missiles. This 7th Div/NVA had bypassed An Lộc to reach this assigned area while the 5th Div/VC was running down highway 13 to attack Cần Lê and An Lộc. It was successful in cutting off Highway 13 at Tàu-Ô causing An Lộc to be encircled as of 10 April.

On 9 April, a group of journalists from the Saigon daily newspaper *Sóng Thần*, including Dương Phục, Thu Thủy, and Nguyễn Tiến, flew to An Lộc to interview General Hưng. I was, however, assigned to meet them. General Hưng told me to relay to them that he was busy conducting an operation and therefore unable to meet with them. He stated that he would "defend An Lộc to death. He would take his own life if the town were lost." He allowed me to let them know about enemy forces. Among the reporters, Dương Phục and Thu Thủy were my friends during the 1970–1971 campaign in Cambodia under General Đỗ Cao Trí. And I stressed to them the words, "Defend An Lộc to death," as the general had told me. What General Hưng meant was that he had vowed he would not be captured alive. The next day, 10 April, everyone in Saigon and the provinces knew that General Hưng would defend An Lộc to death when the newspaper hit the streets.

He again reiterated his pledge of "not letting the enemy capture him alive" when the enemy tanks were closing in on his command post on 13 April.[4] With this challenge, the NVA responded with another challenge of their own which the 81st Commando Group found on 5 May following a shootout with NVA attackers:

> In the pocket of each dead body, the commandos found a small piece of paper inscribed with the following words: "At all costs, capture the 5th Division commander alive, raise the flag of victory.[5]

On 12 April, President Thiệu visited Lai Khê, the forward command post of the III Corps, to survey the battlefield situation and to stress his role as commander-in-chief. From there, he told senior officials in An Lộc by radio that "district capitals might be abandoned, but provincial capitals were to be defended at all costs."[6] Colonel Miller commented that for President Thiệu, An Lộc was "a Bastogne, a place where a stand and die defense would decide the fate of the enemy offensive closest to the national capital."⁷ It would be more accurate to compare An Lộc to Verdun in World War I and Leningrad, where the fate of the entire nation hinged on the outcome of one single battle.⁸ But by directing that the city be held "at all costs," President Thiệu all but challenged the NVA to take it. And they kept on coming, even long after the battle had been decided in favor of the defenders.

Strategic Moves

In the III Corps and MR3, facing General Nguyễn Văn Minh was VC General Trần Văn Trà who was born in Quảng Ngãi in 1920, joined the Communist Party of Indochina in 1938 (Đảng Cộng Sản Đông Dương), and fought against the French in the People's Army from 1946 to 1954. He was promoted to major general in 1961 and commander of the VC B-2, which comprised the territories of the ARVN 2nd, 3rd, and 4th Military Regions. That year, Hanoi sent to South Vietnam Generals Trần Lương, aka Trần Nam Trung, and Trần Độ to create the COSVN, which was the leading political and military office of the CPV. Nguyễn Văn Linh was the highest political official and General Trần Văn Trà the commander of all communist armed forces in the South. General Nguyễn Chí Thanh, member of the central party, was sent south in 1964 as the commander of COSVN, forcing the other two to move back to Hanoi.

In 1967, Nguyễn Chí Thanh died suddenly in Cambodia while he was on his way to Hanoi, which recalled him for consultation. He probably died secondary to a liquidation process by poisoning. Phạm Hùng, the number four of the Political Bureau of the Communist Party, was then sent south to direct all aspects of the "resistance" of the party in the South. General Trần Văn Trà became the military commander of the National Liberation Front (NLF). At that time, Hồ Chí Minh allowed the NLF of Nguyễn Hữu Thọ and Huỳnh Tấn Phát to be formed. When General Nguyễn Cao Kỳ, prime minister of the Republic of Vietnam, called the NLF "a reality but not an entity," the communists elevated the NLF from an organization to a government. General Trần Nam Trung became the minister of defense of the communist temporary government of South Vietnam, and General Trần văn Trà was made deputy commander of COSVN and NLF forces.

From the U.S. side, MACV had stated that the NVA was the invading force of North Vietnam while the VC units were just the armed forces of the NLF. This was just a smoke screen because, in reality, all the communist forces in South Vietnam were set up and directed by the CPV from Hanoi.

V. Crucial Decisions Made to Save An Lộc

All major communist offensives in South Vietnam were planned and directed by General Trần Văn Trà, including the 1968 Tết Offensive, the Fiery Red Summer 1972 offensive, the attack on Phước Long in 1974, the attack on Saigon in 1975, etc. Therefore, Trần Văn Trà had directed hundreds of battles against the French, then the U.S., before the 1968 Tết Offensive and the Nguyễn Huệ Offensive during that 1972 summer. If one understands General Trần Văn Trà's military talent, one would appreciate General Nguyễn Văn Minh's smartness.

From a military point of view, the communist plan of attack by General Trần Văn Trà, by being too conservative, prevented the NVA from overrunning An Lộc. COSVN had wasted too many troops when it used the concentration strategy. Communist generals often lacked decisiveness and self-belief because all decisions and final plans were drafted in Hanoi. Had they been decisive, the war would have ended before the 1972 U.S. election.

If we looked back at the skirmishes from 3 to 7 April, COSVN had four infantry divisions, one heavy artillery division with two anti-aircraft regiments, two tank regiments, one sapper regiment, and the 95B Regiment that was brought in from the highlands notwithstanding a few other battalions or regiments. In reality, the battle that occurred in the first week of the Nguyễn Huệ campaign could be reported as follows:

- General Trà used the Bình Long Division in Tây Ninh as a ploy, albeit a successful one, on 31 March 1972.
- Four days later, on 4 to 5 April, General Trà threw in almost all his forces to destroy the ARVN 9th Regiment and the 1st Armored Battalion of the 5th Infantry Division and to conquer Lộc Ninh District first.
- He then used a small sapper unit and an artillery unit to attack the fire base and Quản Lợi airfield, six kilometers northeast of An Lộc. He did not fire on or attack the headquarters of the 5th Division at Lai Khê or An Lộc on 4 to 5 April as some reporters have imagined.
- Once Lộc Ninh fell, he sent the 5th Div/VC and the NVA's 202nd and 203rd Armored Regiments running down Highway 13 to attack An Lộc on 7 April.
- Sometime before that date, General Trà mobilized the 7th Div/NVA around An Lộc to establish a bottleneck at the Tàu-Ô Stream about 15 kilometers south of An Lộc and 15 kilometers north of Chơn Thành. The plan was to block any reinforcement coming from the south as well as to prevent any retreat from An Lộc.

General Hưng called such a plan a "concentration attack," the goal of which was to attack one enemy's target at a time. The COSVN used the Chinese Red Army's "flood" strategy. The latter had many drawbacks, including loss of the surprise element and huge losses from artillery and bombing counterattacks by the enemy. As a result of the first week's attack, General Hưng, under attack from two enemy infantry divisions and a division of artillery and tanks, naturally could not hold Lộc Ninh; but despite the loss of roughly 2,000 troops, he had caused severe damage to the enemy at Lộc Ninh and along Highway 13, and at the same time was able to reinforce An Lộc for future fighting. That was the first reaction by General Hưng; the second strike would be delivered by General Minh with his knowledge and military experience.

As mentioned above, General Minh, unlike the aggressive General Đỗ Cao Trí, was a cautious and careful general or simply an "intellectual" fighter. He thought everything through very thoroughly before making decisions grounded on military strategy and troop mobilization. Here is an example. Having heard the report that the 5th Div/VC and the C30B Div/VC had gathered at the Trị Tâm area and Bời Lời secret zone close to Bình Dương—in reality to pick up new recruits after suffering severe damage on 7 April—General Minh told reporters, although not exactly word for word,

> After attacking Lộc Ninh, the VC 5th Division moved to Trị Tâm to work with the C30B Division. These two enemy divisions being present close to Saigon would be dangerous if they moved further south. We need to follow the VC 5th Division closely through potential new battlefields.

By putting it that way, General Minh implied that in conjunction with the C30B, the VC 5th Division, besides attacking Bình Dương and Biên Hòa, including Gia Định, could possibly open new battlefields with local forces in Long Khánh and Phước Tuy. What he mentioned was within the possibilities of COSVN.

In reality, the goal of COSVN in moving the VC 5th and the C30B Divisions to Trị Tâm was not to open new battlefields in Bình Dương and Biên Hòa, but to reinforce the VC Division. However, with General Trần Văn Trà's two divisions close to Saigon, General Minh had reason to ask the Joint General Staff and the president to keep the ARVN 18th Infantry Division (minus the TF-52 which was sent to An Lộc) on the west side of Saigon along National Highway 1 and to move the ARVN 25th Infantry Division stationed in Củ Chi to Tây Ninh, on the west side of Saigon, and the 3rd Tank and Ranger Brigade belonging to Brigadier General Trần Quang Khôi to station in Biên Hòa. These were the basic units of the III Corps that General Minh could use to deal with any new battlefield caused by the VC 5th Division,

V. Crucial Decisions Made to Save An Lộc

while the JGS/RVNAF did request President Nguyễn Văn Thiệu to send additional troops to the III Corps.

The JGS, after moving the 21st Infantry Division, sent the 15th Regiment of the 9th Infantry Division to An Lộc. And to prevent any mishap to Saigon, President Thiệu moved the 3rd Airborne Brigade from the II Corps and MR2 to assist General Minh and sent the 1st Airborne Brigade and the 81st Airborne Commando Group to An Lộc. General Minh thus understood the widespread impact of the An Lộc battle over more than the territory under his care. He had grasped the operational concept of General Trần Văn Trà in the Summer Offensive of 1972 which entailed battling at An Lộc and opening several other battlefields around the capital. From the U.S. side, Creighton Abrams, the MACV commander, and General James Hollingsworth, commander of the TRAC (Third Regional Assistance Command) who obviously understood the situation in the III Corps and MR3, had supported General Nguyễn Văn Minh to the maximum. If one understands the above war strategy, one has to realize the operational ability and military intelligence of General Nguyễn Văn Minh, contrary to past speculations about this cautious ARVN leader.

General Minh had mobilized the necessary units to bolster the defenses at An Lộc, relieve the blockade at Tàu-Ô Stream and keep the basic units in their places to meet the challenges of the COSVN offensive.

VI

The First Attack on An Lộc

The First Attack on An Lộc

Following two days of attack against the small Quản Lợi airstrip about six kilometers northeast of An Lộc, units of the NVA 9th Division overran the ARVN 7th Regiment/1st in the evening of 7 April. Defenders were ordered to destroy their equipment and withdraw to An Lộc. On the same day, at the national security meeting in Saigon, in view of increasing enemy attacks, the three Corps commanders were requesting additional reinforcement troops. General Nguyễn Văn Minh, commander of the III Corps and MR3, argued that the thrust of the NVA attack was aimed at the III Corps instead of the 1st or 2nd Corps. President Thiệu agreed with him and gave him the ARVN 21st Division and the elite 1st Airborne Brigade.

On 8 April during a reconnaissance toward the Đồng Long airstrip on the northeast side of town, the 3rd Ranger Group saw civilians running toward them from Quản Lợi. They were followed by enemy troops who shot at them. Many civilians were killed before reaching the Ranger Group. The rangers shot back at enemy troops who took cover before withdrawing.

ARVN troops rapidly prepared for the defense of An Lộc. The defending forces, which were made up of diverse ARVN units brought together and gradually inserted within the whole defensive system, included the following:

- the 7th and 8th ARVN Regiments, an artillery battalion, the 5th Reconnaissance Company that protected the headquarters of the division (under 2,500 troops);
- two battalions from Bình Long (under 800 troops);
- the 3rd Ranger Battle Group (more than 1,500 troops);
- the TF-52nd/18th Div/ARVN (400 troops including wounded);
- the 1st Airborne Brigade (2,200 troops); and

VI. The First Attack on An Lộc

- the 81st Airborne Commando Group (450 troops) (that arrived only on 17 April).

The grand total was more than 7,500 troops.

The enemy forces included the following units according to J-2/JGS/ARVN:

- 9th Division (7,200 men) with the 271st, 272nd, and 95C regiments.
- 5th Division (5,200 men) with the 274th, 275th, and E6 regiments.
- 7th Division (7,000 men) with the 165th, 209th, and 141st regiments. It was reinforced with the NVA 11th Anti-aircraft Artillery. Its mission was to block Highway 13 at the level of Chơn Thành, about 10 kilometers south of An Lộc. The 141st and 165th Regiments participated in the second and third attacks on An Lộc.
- 70th Artillery Division (4,000 men) with the 42nd Artillery Regiment, the 208th rocket regiment, and the 271st Anti-aircraft Regiment.
- 202nd and 203rd tank regiments (500 men) with T-54, PT-76 tanks, and BTR-50 armored carriers.
- 429th Sapper Group (1,100 men).

The grand total was 21,000 troops—excluding the units that blocked south of Highway 13—or three times the ARVN defensive forces in An Lộc.

Government forces met increased enemy activity with increased air power concentrating on hostile forces, moving supplies and equipment. To reduce the time required to make these strikes, the Bình Long provincial Chief relinquished the authority to approve air strikes to the Commanding General of the 5th ARVN Division.... On 12 April, 200 enemy troops killed by airstrikes were discovered four kilometers west of An Lộc.[1]

On 12 April, enemy artillery began shelling An Lộc all day long, picking up the pace in the evening. The provincial communication center was hit, resulting in seven casualties and seven wounded.

On the night of 12 to 13 April 1972, about 4,000–5,000 NVA rounds of all calibers—82 mm mortars, shells from 122 mm and 130 mm howitzers—were lobbed toward An Lộc, a provincial town that occupied a two-square-kilometer area. Rockets from 105 mm and 155 mm howitzers captured by the enemy in Lộc Ninh were also fired at the town. Although expected, no one had ever dreamed of such a violent salvo. The ground shook and shook as one salvo was followed by another one almost nonstop for hours. Soldiers and civilians were all stunned and frightened by the intensity and violence of the shelling.

After a weeklong lull, the long-awaited attack had finally begun. The ugly beginning did not presage anything good. As the shelling suddenly stopped at daybreak, the NVA launched their first attack with infantry and tanks at the Đồng Long airstrip on the northeast side of town, which was held by an RF battalion. The fuel and ammunition depots at the airstrip were hit and exploded. The RF forces at the airstrip being overrun had to pull back toward town. The forces on the nearby Đồng Long Hill after beating back three successive human wave assaults were also overrun. The capture of Đồng Long Hill allowed the enemy to position its mortars, artillery batteries, and anti-aircraft weapons to aim with good accuracy at ARVN positions located on the northern end of the town as well as on incoming aircraft.

A column of T-54 tanks and infantry attacked the western sector held by the ARVN 7th Regiment. Overwhelmed by superior enemy forces led by armored vehicles, some ARVN units had to pull back from their defensive positions.

Another convoy of tanks accompanied by infantry troops moved slowly toward town from the north. Defenders watched it approach, and when the convoy came within range, they fired their 81 mm mortars on the troops that ran in all directions.[2] Unable to back up, tanks in the front continued their forward progress without infantry protection. Once in town, the T-54 tanks became prey for the 8th Regiment troops who positioned themselves from the windows of buildings on Ngô Quyền Street. When the first tank approached the center of town, an ARVN soldier braving his fear used his M-72 rocket launcher to shoot at the third tank in the column; it struck the tank below the turret. With a flash and a loud noise, the tank came to a stop and burst into flames. While all the tanks behind it stopped, defenders stepped out of their foxholes and managed to destroy three more tanks. The two lead tanks continued their run southward and were destroyed by ARVN soldiers in another section of the town.[3]

The first tank destroyed by An Lộc defenders was scored by an RF soldier. The news spread rapidly among defenders that tanks were not invincible and effectively calmed the long-established fear of these steel monsters. One U.S. adviser who was quite surprised to see that young RF soldier running after a tank commented,

> This little guy goes out to hunt a 40-ton piece of metal with a light anti-tank weapon on his back weighing two to three pounds. That's beyond belief and it inspired me. How do you describe a little ARVN soldier fighting tanks?[4]

Although the M-72 rocket launcher light anti-tank weapon (LAW) may have been new to the 5th ARVN Division soldiers, it was not a new weapon to either the U.S. or South Vietnamese Army. It was first developed in approximately 1963 and landed in the hands of U.S. Army troops as early as 1964.

VI. The First Attack on An Lộc

When it first arrived in Vietnam, it was used almost exclusively as a "bunker buster" in the absence of an enemy armor threat until enemy tanks appeared in 1968.

The tank threat became more apparent after NVA tanks first appeared in South Vietnam during the 1968 defense of the Lang Vei Special Forces camp near Khe Sanh and the 1969 tank-supported attack on the Bến Hét Special Forces camp. ARVN soldiers were armed with the M-72 during the Lam Son 719 Campaign in 1971 but did not understand how to use it. They were not aware of the relatively short range of the weapon, and they probably made the same mistake as the soldiers at Lang Vei and Lộc Ninh. The M-72 was incapable of piercing the sloped frontal armor on the Soviet- and Chinese-built tanks used by the NVA.

During the Lâm Sơn 719 campaign in Laos, the ARVN declared that the M-72 was ineffective. This led to an urgent effort to locate as many 3.5-inch rocket launchers as could be found in U.S. depots and rush them to ARVN troops. While all of this was going on, MACV tested the M-72 and found it to be effective just as the 5th ARVN Division later did in An Lộc. It turned out to be simply a matter of engaging targets within the effective range of the weapon and aiming at the sides or rears of tanks where the armor was thinner and not sloped.[5]

Around 10:00 hours, a T-54 tank rolled aimlessly into the southern sector without infantry protection. It got entangled in concertina and barbed wire and remained stuck in the middle of a street. It then used its 100 mm cannon to fire at the southern watchtower. Colonel Nhựt told Captain Khải, his artillery commander, to destroy the tank with a disabled 105 mm howitzer. As its sight instrument was disabled, Khải pointed the gun directly at the tank and destroyed it with a single round. The captured tank driver reported that he had infiltrated from North Vietnam to Cambodia in February 1972. On 13 April, as his unit attacked An Lộc, his commander told them that when tanks attacked Lộc Ninh, defenders fled in terror. His commander, therefore, decided to send in tanks first to frighten An Lộc defenders before bringing in infantry. He also told them that people would greet them with open arms. Each comrade thus brought with him a new set of uniform to wear in a parade whenever An Lộc would be captured.[6]

An Lộc defenders were lucky during this attack because the NVA had not yet mastered the need to coordinate infantry and armor despite having received tank training in the Soviet Union. Also, the two army branches came under separate command structures and lacked coordination, leaving tanks rolling across town oftentimes without the guidance and protection of infantry troops. Since tank crews had also been told by their political cadres that the town had been liberated, many drove with their hatches open as they did during a ceremonial mission. Believing that their job was to drive to the provincial chief's residence and run the VC flag up the pole, they had become careless and unaware that ARVN soldiers were right there waiting to take a shot at them.

Colonel Walter Ulmer, senior adviser to the 5th ARVN division, later wrote,

> During the battle of An Lộc, the North Vietnamese were skillful in the use of artillery, aggressive in anti-aircraft techniques, but notably amateurish in the employment of armor. Their hesitant, uncoordinated fumbling with some well-maintained Soviet vehicles showed once again that successful armor employment is totally dependent on aggressive spirit and technical skills on the part of the tank crews.
> The close-in destruction of T54 and PT76 tanks in An Lộc is a tribute to the skill and courage of many ARVN soldiers.[7]

The NVA used about 100 armored vehicles against the 5th ARVN Division and the several units attached to it, of which 75 to 85 were destroyed in and around An Lộc. Tanks were used on three main occasions during the many multi-directional thrusts against the town on 12–14 April and 11–13 May. The final use of tanks came on the night of 23 May when a group of six tanks attacked from the south. The largest single axis formation was composed of 12 tanks. In addition to these main attacks, groups of two or three tanks would rumble around town before sneaking in from positions held by the NVA forces.

While ARVN troops were battling against NVA troops and tanks, aircraft circled above town like vultures preying on their targets. There were the high-flying B-52 bombers that targeted enemy logistical installations and staging areas, and slow-flying Cobra attack helicopters, A-37 Dragonfly jet fighters, and AC-130 Spectres that operated above the city in close proximity of friendly troops. The Bell Cobra was a two-person attack helicopter gunship armed with 7.62 mm mini-guns, a 40 mm grenade launcher, and rocket launchers. Some Cobra had HEAT (high-explosive, anti-tank) rockets that were just perfect for the roaming enemy tanks. The A-37 Dragonfly was a converted USAF trainer that was modified for close air support; it could carry six 500-pound bombs or a mixed load of other ordnance. The AC-119 Stinger gunships, which were jet-assisted, propeller-driven, two-engine cargo aircraft converted to serve as fixed-wing gun platforms, were armed with 7.62 mm mini-guns and 20 mm Vulcan cannons.[8]

The B-52 could carry up to a 70,000-pound bomb load per mission, and there were 52 bombers based at U Tapao Royal Thai Air Base, Thailand, and

VI. The First Attack on An Lộc

31 at Andersen AFB, Guam. Flying at 30,000 feet would prevent them being seen or heard by enemy on the ground. They had a combat range of 8,800 miles (14,080 kilometers). They could destroy everything within a rectangular box of a half mile wide by two miles long even through cloud cover. These boxes could be decreased to a half mile by one mile or half by half mile to concentrate the bombs. The degree of accuracy was so high that bombs were dropped sometimes half a kilometer away from friendly lines in An Lộc, although at that range the incidence of broken ear drums; bleeding eyes, ears, and noses; and disorientation increased among friendly troops.

To prevent air collisions, it was decided U.S. Air Force would cover the area three kilometers north of Chơn Thành at the Cambodian border while VNAF would cover the area south of USAF's sector.

The U.S. Air Force had used large, fixed-wing, multi-engine gunships to provide support for troops on the ground. With each new generation of gunships came improved communication systems, targeting systems, weapons systems, and computer technology. In An Lộc, the U.S. also used the Spectre gunship—a C-130 transport plane converted into a gunship equipped with infrared sensors that could detect the heat generated by motor engines, a 105 mm howitzer, a pair of 20 mm Vulcan cannons, and a Boford 40 mm cannon. The computerized fire-control system maximized effectiveness on target. This was a very striking gunship that could destroy tanks and cannon-carrying trucks or NVA mobile cannons at the An Lộc battlefield especially outside the town. Due to their size, they carried a great deal of fuel and could fly over the battlefield for hours; they brought a lot of ammunition and flares and could illuminate the night for hours. They were equipped with FM radios so troops on the ground could talk to them directly.[9]

In An Lộc and the surrounding area, from the beginning of the battle, all the ARVN tanks and trucks had been destroyed, except for a few jeeps that were never used except for travel at night; therefore, the sound of any motor engine at night could only come from NVA tanks or resupply trucks. Since there were two engines running in An Lộc, one from the division headquarters and the other from the Bình Long Sector headquarters, with both having fixed positions, the Spectre gunships, originating from U Tapao Royal Thai Air Base, could not misfire at defenders' units. Dozens of NVA tanks and trucks had been destroyed by Spectre gunships outside An Lộc on the following nights.

Following the violent attacks by the 9th Div/VC and the 202nd and 203rd tank units that had been sent down from North Vietnam, three artillery regiments of the 69th Artillery Div/VC or 70th Div/VC augmented by an NVA anti-air artillery regiment and the 429th Sapper Regiment, the defensive forces of the ARVN 8th Regiment, the 52nd Regiment, and the 3rd Ranger TF on the north and northeast had to retreat to their second line of defense. One section of the city's commercial center north of Nguyễn Trung Trực Street and the Đồng Long Airfield had temporarily fallen into enemy control although enemy tanks had been destroyed in each ARVN area of responsibility.

In General Hưng's forward command post facing Nguyễn Huệ Street, the S-3 (operations) office of Lieutenant Colonel Trịnh Đình Đăng was hit by a 122 mm rocket, which killed six of his staff officers. My S-2 intelligence office, which was in the same row of buildings, encountered only one casualty. Having no staff to assist him, Lieutenant Colonel Đăng, I and two of my captains, Dương Tấn Triệu and Nguyễn Chí Cường, decided to gather details of and to document the operations fought by all units in order to create an operations log of the division at An Lộc. I kept the operations log book until General Hưng passed away.

When the COSVN forces attacked An Lộc on 13 April 1972, the 1st Airborne Brigade and the 81st Airborne Commando Group had not arrived in town yet. The city had 5,500 defenders with the RFs included. On that day, the 1st Airborne Brigade was fighting to unblock the NVA blockade at Tàu-Ô. But because of the attack on An Lộc, General Minh withdrew the brigade to send it to reinforce An Lộc. The ARVN 21st Division took over the battle at Tàu-Ô Creek.

After that first attack, evacuation of the wounded, replacement of troops, and resupply of food, medicine, and ammunitions were no longer possible because of the loss of the Đồng Long Airfield and part of the northern commercial section of the city, along with the loss of Windy Hill and Hill 169. Resupply by C-47 Chinook helicopters was totally interrupted.

Civilians still lived in their houses along the new defensive front, although most had temporarily moved close to the creek along the railway track on the southeast side of the village. In the administrative center south of Hoàng Hôn Boulevard close to the above-mentioned creek and close to the defensive front, soldiers shared their rations with civilians.

On 14 April, cumulative losses in An Lộc were as follows:

Enemy: 169 killed, two taken prisoner;
 3 crew-served and 50 individual guns, 2 communication devices lost; and 14 to 16 T-54s and PT-76 tanks destroyed.
ARVN: 28 dead, 53 wounded, and
 3 crew-served and 42 individual guns lost.

At 04:30 hours on 15 April, the VC/NVA proceeded to shell the town. This was immediately followed by armor and ground troop attacks, which were broken by determined defensive forces and judicious airstrikes. At 10:00, the VC/NVA launched another ground attack, which turned out to be a little bit more effective than the previous one. But their advance was stopped. At 14:00, 10 enemy tanks advanced toward the town defensive lines. Nine of them were destroyed by ground units and air strikes. By nighttime, the attack seemed to have subsided.[10]

Although the defenders did not realize it, the first attack had ended after three days of fierce close combat (13–15 April). By 16 April, the North Vietnamese had lost 23 tanks. With the help from the U.S. Air Force, the South Vietnamese had held the town in the face of violent and dizzying attacks. But they were tired and worn out, supplies were minimal, wounded became a problem, and morale was at a low ebb. The town was heavily ringed on three sides with anti-aircraft guns. The 81st Airborne commando reinforcement group had not arrived yet.[11]

The North Vietnamese were in no better shape. Despite having overwhelming superiority in troops, tanks, and artillery guns, they had not been able to conquer the town. On 18 April, a company from the Border Ranger Battalion ambushed and killed a highly placed COSVN political officer close to Tây Ninh. On his body were the plans of an attack on 19 August, the next day, the details of which were helpful to the ARVN. Another letter contained a critique of North Vietnamese strategy and performance up to that point. The 9th VC Division and its commander were castigated for failing to take An Lộc within the first few days of the attack. The use of armor was considered to be particularly poor.[12]

An Lộc and the Military District Hospitals

As no area in An Lộc had been spared by the shelling, houses, buildings, and even the ground bore the scars of bombs and mortars in the form of huge or small, ragged and irregular craters. At times the ground appeared like a lunar landscape. One of these craters was large enough to sink a T-54 tank that was being chased by ARVN troops. Even the Catholic Church and the railroad station were hit, resulting in heavy damage.

Because of its location on a hill and close to the ARVN 5th Division command post, the An Lộc hospital was regularly targeted. Later, after the division artillery units, originally located in the soccer field on the south side of town, were moved to the east side close to the hospital, the latter was subjected to more shelling. As a result, there was no way to be completely safe, except leaving town, which was not an option because the town was completely encircled by enemy troops. One just had to hunker down in one of those bunkers or crudely dug-out tunnels and hope for the best. Defenders and civilians alike were injured, some mildly others seriously, although that second eventuality was more and more common in view of the frequency and intensity of the shelling.

The number of casualties, most of them arriving almost at the same time after a shelling episode was lifted, stressed the medical capability of the provincial An Lộc hospital. A civilian hospital, it had an attached military section designated as the Bình Long district hospital strictly reserved for military personnel. The provincial hospital was staffed by only three military physicians, of which Captain Doctor Nguyễn Văn Quý was the surgeon; the staff did its best to provide care for the injured civilians in the face of staff and medication shortages. Most of the nurses and technicians at the hospital were civilians. Then, for some unknown reason—whether fear, overwork, stress, need to care for local family members, or a combination of all those, no one knows—they all disappeared after the second attack. They were replaced by a small technical team from the 5th Medical Battalion of the 5th ARVN Division. Captain Quý performed his procedures about 300 meters from the battle zone wearing a flak jacket and a steel helmet. Although it might be safer for him, the outfit was not very sterile. Because electricity was often lacking, the operations were often performed under flashlight held by the nurse anesthetist. The mortality rate was of course high because of the frequency of infections caused by lack of sterile conditions and antibiotic shortage.

Due to the indiscriminate NVA shelling, the hospital had to increase the number of beds from 60 to 120 to accommodate the overflow of patients, which meant, for a small hospital, putting two, sometimes three patients in each hospital bed. Supplies and medications rapidly ran low because of logistical problems. At one time, the presence of 300 bodies in the hospital morgue close to the operating room made people sick because the smell was just overwhelming. The hospital was always crowded during the siege, for families often hung around to comfort, feed, and care for the patients as the nursing staff was overburdened by their work.

Of course, the severely injured patients were evacuated whenever possible. However, because of the dense anti-aircraft and ground artillery, the few brave pilots who dared to fly into An Lộc hovered long enough for wounded patients to hop in; the latter were called the "Olympic" wounded because they still had the strength to board evacuation helicopters by themselves. On occasions, stretchers bearing severely wounded were brought out to the helicopters for evacuation only to be left behind because the stretcher bearers had rushed aboard to escape the hell below.[13]

The communists, who were not known for their humanitarian concerns, did not spare the hospital as long as they could achieve their victory sooner. On 25 April,[14] enemy artillery targeted and destroyed the hospital.[15] Injured patients who were brought there for treatment and their families died from the shelling. Dead bodies were shredded apart by secondary bombing. Blood and body parts were scattered everywhere. This was an unimaginable carnage for the local people of An Lộc who were not used to this type of violence. Once the hospital was destroyed, there were no medical facilities left except for some aid stations scattered here and there. Worse, there was no place to store bodies, except for speeding up mass burials. When the two operating rooms were severely damaged, Colonel Nhựt came to the rescue and provided two underground rooms to be used as operating rooms. Toward the end of May as the situation had somewhat improved, thousands of lightly wounded patients had taken refuge at a pagoda in Phú Đức, southwest of An Lộc.[16]

The medical condition for South Vietnamese troops was equally bad. Once the hospital was destroyed courtesy of the enemy who in their wrath decided to level off the town, church, hospital, and school included, the surgical facility had been moved to a small bunker. Medical care consisted of laying down critically wounded men and assigning their less-wounded comrades to cook, clean and care for them until they could be transferred. Sterilization of surgical instruments was out of the question, although some rare instruments were required to be sterilized. Due to lack of supplies, the surgeon, who had to improvise again, used threads taken from old sandbags to be used as suture materials.[17] Of course, this was not sterile either, but what was the choice?

About the mass burial, Dr. Quý wrote this in his "An Lộc diary":

> When the vehicle was full, the driver left immediately for the common grave. They threw the corpse into the common hole. By eight o'clock in the evening two loads were done. They worked like this continuously through two days before emptying all the corpses out of the hospital. Bulldozers had to dig new holes as long as the schoolyard had enough room left. Past the Xa Cam intersection along the rubber tree orchard, a funeral company dug more common graves that were very large. I heard that a grave held about a thousand bodies…. Here you could die not only once, but two or three times? When artillery rounds hit the graves, pieces of bodies were ploughed up, buried again and then hit again, parts of decomposing bones and flesh strewn all over with a horrible rotten stench.[18]

One day, as he was resting in his room, Dr. Quý was asked to see an American pilot who was doing some reconnaissance work over An Lộc when his plane was shot down. The pilot was able to open the cockpit, eject himself and parachute down. He luckily landed in friendly lines but hit his head on landing. Besides a few forehead bruises, he was in good condition. ARVN soldiers took him to their superior who referred him to the hospital for evaluation. After examination, he was given a tetanus shot and taken to the headquarters to be evacuated later to his unit.[19]

Another gallant surgeon was Captain Dr. Cao Phú Quốc, of the 183rd Medical Company from the 18th ARVN Division. At the beginning of the battle, he was evacuating wounded patients back to An Lộc for care. He had escaped death many times while his regiment was withdrawing from Lộc Ninh, especially at the Cần Lê Bridge where it was racked by enemy machine guns without having a place to take cover. He did his best to alleviate the pain and suffering of soldiers and civilians and was well loved by his unit troops. He was killed in An Lộc by an artillery shell early in the battle while trying to help a wounded paratrooper near the city soccer field.[20]

The Bình Long District Hospital was a military field hospital that was set up in a former underground facility of the Ranger Border Defense Forces. It was about 20 meters long, 6 meters wide and 1.8 meters high. Its corrugated galvanized steel roof was protected from shelling by six layers of sandbags. The ground-level outpatient examination room that sat on top of the hospital was large enough for a small wooden table and two chairs. The belowground hospital was divided into five sections with the nine-meter-long operating room (OR) in the center, which contained three surgery tables and two resuscitation beds. On the right of the OR were the physicians' quarters, and on the left the pharmacy and the non-commissioned officers' quarters.

Lance Corporal Bình was in charge of cooking for the injured soldiers and patients. The kitchen with its outdoor cooking area was protected from the elements by a roof of corrugated steel sheets. Conveniently located near the entrance of the underground complex, it allowed staff to run down for protection once the characteristic departing pop of an incoming projectile was heard. The typical officer fare, after several days of no supply due to the downing of helicopters by enemy fire, consisted of moldy rice, some salted soy paste and salted dry fish.

Each battalion usually treated its lightly wounded patients and only referred the severely injured ones to the hospital for surgery or further treatment. When a fierce battle raged on, Drs. Lê Quang Tín and An T. Thân operated side by side on the two OR tables while medic Xa would suture simple gashes, clean wounds, or apply casts or splints under the physicians' supervision. On many occasions, the surgeons were devastated for not being able to save the lives or limbs of our comrades. All they could do was emergency damage-control surgery and then request rapid chopper evacuation to Cộng Hòa Military General Hospital, a tertiary-care center in Saigon.

As they frequently got shelled, Dr. Thân still vividly recounts instances of death or cheating death. In a heavy bombardment that took place one early morning, the driver of the military ambulance was immediately killed. An older medic warrant officer was seriously injured in the lower jaw and neck. He was suffocating from the bleeding and required immediate tracheostomy. He recovered nicely from the operation. On one another occasion, Dr. Thân came out to the surface to take a cigarette break and enjoy fresh air. For no particular reason, he decided to go back down to the bunker to look for a book to read. As he was shuffling things around in the bunker, a shell hit exactly the spot where he was sitting a minute earlier. It was like fate or luck that forced him to go back down and saved him from a certain death. He had also saved the lives of three communist soldiers and operatives who were ambushed and captured by the district rangers. On one occasion, he had the courage to deny the army intelligence officer immediate access to one prisoner of war to interrogate him before his injuries could be stabilized.[21]

Facing the high casualty rate and the problem of splattered body parts and to prevent the spread of epidemic diseases in a very confined environment, which could lead to disastrous medical consequences, Colonel Bùi Đức Điềm, the operational chief of staff of the division, following an enemy tank assault, found who knew where, a bulldozer, which he himself used to dig a huge hole in the front yard of the town high school. Soldiers of the 5th Reconnaissance Company then gathered corpses and fragments of bodies for a mass burial. Later, another burial site was dug out in a vacant lot between the high school and the hospital. With mounting casualties, mass burials soon became common whenever war conditions allowed. On one occasion, Colonel Điềm's men had buried 956 corpses in one day. This was a sad and gruesome ordeal in the midst of a violent carnage. Everything pointed to a deadly and unpredictable environment.

Colonel Điềm was one of those rare officers who always showed up at the battle sites, in personal defensive holes with soldiers when missiles rained down or while visiting soldiers along the divisional defensive line. He was a brave, courageous and energetic officer. I had never seen an officer like him during my whole military life. It was only at night that he went down into the bunker to sleep close to me after he had everything on the ground under control and did everything he could do that day.

The 3rd Ranger Group

The 3rd Ranger Battalion Group, led by Lieutenant Colonel Nguyễn Văn Biết, consisted of three battalions: the 31st Ranger Battalion was led by

Major Trương Khánh; the 36th Ranger Battalion by Major Tống Viết Lạc; and the 52nd Ranger Battalion by Major Lê Quý Dậu. Prior to the battle, they were conducting a search operation in Cambodia trying to locate the NVA 5th, 7th, and 9th Divisions when they were ordered to report back to An Lộc. The first battalion arrived on 6 April 1972 and the rest the following day. After briefing, they were told that they had encountered enemy rear services and transportation units that were running away from them instead of fighting against them in Cambodia. The main NVA forces were instead gathering and ready to move across the border into Vietnam.

A few days after their arrival, An Lộc was shelled repeatedly with long-range heavy artillery guns such as the 122 mm and 155 mm howitzers the enemy had captured in Lộc Ninh as well as organic artillery, 130 mm artillery units and 105 mm howitzers. It was at that time that civilians abandoned their homes and sought refuge in soldiers' bunkers. They cooked and ate with the soldiers who in return tended their wounds and gave them medicine.

The artillery sounds and the tremendous blasts of shells filled the rangers "with fear and dread" since they never knew when one might hit their location. They were particularly afraid of the "delayed fuse" rounds, a type of 155 mm round that penetrated into the bunker and buried itself in the dirt before exploding, causing tremendous destruction and widespread casualties.[22]

One morning, the Ranger Group headquarters received a call advising them that the enemy had moved in the direction of and occupied the province "Open Arms" Office while firing at the 52nd Battalion. The enemy was in a threatening position because the office was close to the 5th Division command post and the rangers' headquarters. First Lieutenant Nguyễn Văn Hiếu was ordered to retake the office. While commanding the attack, Lieutenant Hiếu was suddenly killed by a sniper when his company was fired on by machine guns and M-79 grenade launchers. With the loss of their leader, the rangers were pinned down and could not move an inch. In the afternoon, another company under 2nd Lieutenant Phước was ordered to take over the job. It got stuck at the same place as the first company despite valiant efforts. Since this government office in An Lộc was located on high ground and had concrete bunkers covered with a tin metal sheet with layer over layer of sandbags, the decision was made to request helicopter gunship support. As VNAF pilots could not fire because of the close proximity of friendly positions, a U.S. Spectre gunship was requested. It fired round after round causing the top of the bunkers to cave in.

The attack occurred during a heavy downpour, and water flooded enemy positions. The gunship was asked to stop firing so that Lieutenant Phước could finish the enemy off. After policing the area, he counted more than 10 enemies killed and captured a medium machine gun, two M-79 launchers and six AK-47s and large quantities of M-79 ammunition. One pallet of parachuted supplies had landed into the Open Arms Office giving enemy troops food rations and M-79 rounds for their use.[23]

One day, one ranger company shot and disabled an enemy tank. The latter drove away but fell into a crater bomb. The rangers sneaked into the tank where they recovered important military and communication documents and a radio. While trying to get out of the crater, they were fired at by enemy troops. Once they returned to the ranger headquarters with their booty, they were shocked to discover among the radio documents the secure radio plan and codes of the 5th Division. The latter was contacted, and Colonel Vỹ and two S-2 officers were sent to recover the documents. Investigation was initiated, and the division's secure radio plans and codes were immediately changed.[24]

The 1st Airborne Brigade

Commanded by a two-star general, the Airborne Division was under the direct control of the country's national leadership. Serving as a reserve force, its units were sent to critical areas where its combativeness, ardor and resourcefulness were needed. Its three brigades were led by colonels and the battalions by lieutenant colonels.

When General Minh rolled out his strategy of reinforcing An Lộc with the 1st Airborne Brigade, Colonel Miller gladly approved it. However, after Colonel Lưỡng was brought to the divisional headquarters at An Lộc for discussion with General Hưng, things turned out differently.

When the Airborne Division was formed in 1966 to serve as the backbone of the ARVN general reserve, the 1st Airborne Group became the 1st Airborne Brigade. It was the oldest and most experienced brigade of the Airborne Division for having participated in all major battles in 1968 and 1971. Colonel Lưỡng, a graduate of the Thủ Đức Reserve Officers School in 1954, rose rapidly through the ranks and assumed command of the 1st Brigade in early 1968. He was born and raised in Bình Dương Province and knew the region well. He proposed a better and more reasonable strategy that proved his talent as a tactician and an experienced warrior.

He suggested that if his 2,200 troops were dropped on the open field between Cần Lê Bridge and Đồng Long Airfield, the first lift, whether by a

Vietnamese or U.S. C-47 aircraft, because of its sudden and unexpected timing would be successful. But from the second lift onward, his troops would become easy prey for enemy troops and artillery, which had been stationed there for a few weeks. Casualties would be high in the order of 50 percent or more. They would be unable to mount an attack against the Đồng Long Airfield after suffering such a high casualty rate, despite leaving the wounded behind or bringing them along. Besides, if troops were dropped at that landing zone, only airborne troops could be released, not the artillery regiment: the big guns would not be available to mount an immediate attack. Even if the airbornes were successful in getting to the airfield, they would not be strong a force enough to dislodge enemy troops stationed at the airport and the north end of the city, the number of which was still unknown. Victory would not be certain, but defeat was looming. Even if the airborne were successful in dislodging enemy troops, with only about one regiment left due to casualties, they could not withstand further attacks from enemy troops. If a strong and elite group became a battered unit, the reinforcement of An Lộc would be futile. With this reasoning, Colonel Lưỡng suggested another strategy.

Colonel Lê Quang Lưỡng viewed his offensive concept of reinforcing An Lộc not only as augmenting troops to a strategic area, but also helping local leaders to boost the morale of defenders. The latter should not only be able to defend from enemy attacks, but also to counterattack when the situation allowed. The reinforcing unit should not be the main force striking at the occupying force, the strength of which could not be assessed at this time. Was it a divisional or inter-regimental level? In reality, we only knew that the enemy's artillery, especially anti-aircraft artillery, was very strong. If troops were dropped in the barren fields south of Cần Lê but north of An Lộc, they would be subjected to constant shelling from the enemy's artillery and then wiped out.

The other option was to drop forces to clear a secret landing zone (LZ) south of town. Troops would land safely because enemy troops would not have time to react and reposition their guns to a surprise landing at the unknown LZ. The 6th Airborne Battalion would immediately attack Windy Hill and Hill 169, the two high elevations occupied by enemy forces about three kilometers south of and overlooking the town. The 3rd Artillery Airborne Battalion would land after the two hills were secured. These two battalions would be led by Lieutenant Colonel Lê Văn Ngọc, deputy commander of the airborne brigade. The brigade headquarters, the 5th and 8th Battalions, would then land in the following days.

The 5th Battalion would support the 8th Battalion's advance toward

VI. The First Attack on An Lộc

Highway 13, which led to the Xa Cam rubber plantation, three kilometers south of town. This highway was 20 meters wide, on each side of which U.S. units had deforested a swath of land about 800 to 1,000 meters, which could accommodate a temporary large landing zone for Vietnamese and U.S. aircraft. Later, the 8th Battalion of Lieutenant Colonel Văn Bá Ninh would take over and control this LZ, allowing defenders to evacuate wounded combatants and receive fresh troops.

The 5th Battalion under the command of Lieutenant Colonel Nguyễn Chí Hiếu would move to the southern defense line of the village and serve as a reserve force for the 1st Airborne Brigade and General Hưng. The brigade headquarters, protected by the Reconnaissance Company, would stay with the Bình Long Military Sector headquarters close to the other two battalions. Colonel Lê Quang Lưỡng said,

> If the airborne troops could open a LZ and protect the area around it south of the town, defenders would be able to evacuate wounded troops and receive fresh ones. Defending troops would be stronger. Then, the RVNAF could interrupt the supply route of NVA troops and isolate this wing from their COSVN base weakening them in the long range. Defending forces in An Lộc would wait until they shook hands with the 21st ARVN Infantry Division that would move northward from Chơn Thành after blasting through the NVA/VC forces located at Tàu Ô. At that time they could open their offensive and take back the northern end of the provincial town as well as the Đồng Long Airfield. That was a safe strategy for An Lộc defenders to resist for a long duration and for enemy forces to wither under continuous bombing attacks by the Air Force, Vietnamese and U.S. That was the recipe for success for we could at the same time hold the fort and fight the enemy.

Based on the battlefield events at the time, Colonel Lê Quang Lưỡng's operational strategy was the best among the options suggested. After an hour of discussion with General Lê Văn Hưng who wholeheartedly supported the strategy, Colonel Lưỡng flew back to Lai Khê to discuss with General Nguyễn Văn Minh, who approved the mission. From the evening of 14 to 15 April, the airlift of the airborne troops was successfully executed causing a big surprise to COSVN General Trần Văn Trà. All the airborne units reached their objective in An Lộc on 17 April with minimal casualties (4 percent) thanks to the surprise element and the carefully chosen LZ. The latter was the local Route 245 that crossed Srok Ton Cui in a southeast direction and close to Windy Hill and Hill 169. All Colonel Lê Quang Lưỡng's operational details had been meticulously executed.

- Lieutenant Colonel Nguyễn Văn Đinh's 6th Airborne Battalion from the LZ moved to the targets and attacked enemy units on the two

hills. On the evening of 14 April, one hour after they landed, the airborne troops had retaken Windy Hill and Hill 169.
- The whole 1st Airborne Brigade composed of the brigade headquarters, the Reconnaissance Company, and the 5th and 8th Battalions completed their arrival by 15:00 on 15 April at the LZ near Windy Hill.

On the same day, COSVN forward headquarters launched a tank and infantry offensive against General Hưng's defensive lines after raining 5,000 missiles on the town. The attack on the west and northwest side of the town appeared to have been hastily executed because tanks arrived without infantry support. In the northeast, the pressure of the attack was heavy. In the southeast, enemy could not attack because the airbornes had already taken over the two hills and the surrounding area. Enemy tanks, which arrived in town in a haphazard manner, without knowledge of targets or topography, were therefore easily destroyed by ARVN troops. The most likely reasons for this showing were the following.

On 14 April, to decrease enemy pressure and cut off enemy resupply lines after they launched a northwest attack on the town on 13 April, and to distract them away from the landing of the airborne brigade, General Hưng had ordered me to draw 10 B-52 Arc Light boxes for referral to Colonel Miller to request for strategic bombing on that same day. Two of these boxes were aimed at ấp Phú Lố about three miles from the town of An Lộc and Ấp Phú Bình, roughly half a mile from the defense perimeter.

That afternoon, U.S. Air Force executed these two boxes on Phu Lố and Phú Bình hamlets on the northwest side of the town. The other eight boxes were aimed along the axis of movement of enemy troops. Villagers had abandoned these hamlets to move into town on 7 and 8 April. Although dwellings were empty, they still served as resting places for enemy troops who would find fresh water from wells and gardens full of vegetables and fruit. We later found out the B-52 bombing on 14 April had completely destroyed the headquarters of the NVA 271th Regiment, its two battalions along with its anti-air artillery. These units were the main forces attacking the northwest side of the town.

On 15 April, without its infantry support, an enemy tank unit roamed aimlessly again in An Lộc without knowing its targets and the layout of the streets. On that day, 10 NVA T-54 and PT-76 were destroyed inside the town limits. On the same day because the LZ had been safely secured, the headquarters of the 1st Airborne Brigade, the 5th and 8th ARVN Airborne Battalions landed safely in Srok Ton Cui. Since An Lộc was under attack, General

VI. The First Attack on An Lộc

Hưng told Colonel Lê Quang Lưỡng to hold his forces around the three hills south of the town.

The following day, Colonel Lê Quang Lưỡng ordered the airborne brigade to move into An Lộc from two different directions.

The first wing, which comprised the brigade headquarters, the Reconnaissance and Engineering Companies, and the 5th Airborne Battalion under the command of Lieutenant Colonel Nguyễn Chí Hiếu, moved into the military zone perimeter via the Sóc Gòn hamlet. A U.S. adviser wrote,

> The paratroopers of the 5th Airborne Battalion were tough, experienced, and totally professional.... The march through the trees was conducted at a cautious but steady pace.... Along a slope of rising ground, they had found the remains of a South Vietnamese company.... There were fifty or sixty Rangers, each one swollen up and turning black and leaking into the bottom of his foxhole.... They had been overrun and killed by a North Vietnamese attack.... Personal weapons were still with the bodies, but the enemy had taken the hand grenades, claymore antipersonnel mines, and tactical radios.... It was hard to look at the dead soldiers' bloody faces and broken heads, torn and shot full of holes, fly covered and rotting in the heat. The bodies were without a shred of dignity, or even humanity.[25]

The second wing was under the direction of Lieutenant Colonel Văn Bá Ninh, commander of the 8th Airborne Battalion whose target was the highway south of An Lộc, close to the headquarters of the military zone through the Phú Hòa Hamlet, which was about one kilometer outside the defense perimeter on the east. Sóc Gòn Hamlet was located about one kilometer northwest of Phú Hòa Hamlet.

Both wings encountered enemy troops. The 8th Battalion entered the Phú Hòa Hamlet first after encountering minimal resistance. It stationed in Phú Hòa on the night of 16 April to support the 5th Airborne Battalion that encountered vigorous attack from a regiment of the NVA 5th Division at Sóc Gòn Hamlet. Enemy troops launched consecutive attacks with tanks and infantry but were repulsed. Colonel Lưỡng's units destroyed four T-54 tanks and took seven crew-served weapons and 20 AK-47s; the enemy left 86 troops killed. The airborne brigade suffered 3 losses and 13 wounded.

In the morning of 17 April, all airborne units had arrived at their planned positions according to Colonel Lê Quang Lưỡng's strategy. The 6th Airborne Battalion and its 3rd Artillery Battalion under the direction of Lieutenant Colonel Lê Văn Ngọc were securely stationed at Windy Hill, Hill 169 and Srok Ton Cui; the biggest part of the airborne brigade under Colonel Lê Quang Lưỡng's command settled at the planned sites. The brigade headquarters and the reconnaissance company stayed at the military zone headquarters, the 5th Airborne Battalion close by. The most important thing was that the 8th Airborne Battalion under Lieutenant Colonel Văn Bá Ninh had secured a large area of the highway south of the town all the way down to the Xa Cam rubber plantation on 18 April. There it exchanged fire with a unit of the NVA 7th Division, causing enemy troops to leave behind 40 dead and many crew-served and individual weapons. Thereafter, the 8th Battalion and the Engineering Company proceeded to clean up an area on the highway to provide a safe landing path for Vietnamese and U.S. Air Force helicopters and Chinooks. This battalion kept the LZ open throughout the rest of the battle. Helicopters flew in and out safely, although they could not avoid enemy missiles, to evacuate hundreds of wounded defenders and bring in new reinforcements, food and light ammunitions, although heavy equipment still had to be dropped by USAF planes.

On 18 April, the 5th Battalion was ordered to disengage and move to a new defensive position on the south side of town with the 51st Company to cover its retreat. As the U.S. adviser was slow to move out, Lieutenant Colonel Hiếu approached him.

> After quickly pointing out the direction the battalion was going to move, he grabbed me by the shirt and pulled me close. Looking me directly in the eye and shouting over the roar of the gunfire, he gave me a message I will never forget—do not stay here long: 51 Company will die today. I'd previously studied the theory of the Detachment-Left-in-Contact in service schools.... It [the company] was going to make the stand so the rest of the battalion could fight the next battle. But the harsh realities had not sunk in.... They [paratroopers] had thrown away their helmets and pull on their maroon paratrooper berets.... Committed to a fight they could not possibly win, those men had decided to face their enemies wearing the symbol that best described who they were. I realized with a jolt they were actually getting ready to die right then and there in that patch of torn-up rubber plantation.... Seeing their willingness to accept their fate, their own impending deaths, really shocked me.[26]

It was also in An Lộc that the oldest lieutenant paratrooper died. He started his career as a boy soldier fighting against the Japanese during World War II. In 1954, as part of the Fifth Parachute Battalion, he jumped into Điện Biên Phủ not once but twice. Captured by the communists, he managed to survive their prison camps. After his release, he joined the Vietnamese Army and his old unit, now designated the 5th Airborne Battalion. Over the years he had been promoted to sergeant major and commissioned a lieutenant because of his experience and leadership quality. Without formal education, he knew he would not be promoted beyond the rank of lieutenant but decided to soldier on until he was killed.[27]

The 81st Airborne Commando Group

On 16 April, the 81st Airborne Commando Group with less than 500 troops under Lieutenant Colonel Phan Văn Huấn's command had been dispatched by the JGS to General Nguyễn Văn Minh and ferried to An Lộc by Chinook helicopters. The Commando Group once belonged to the ARVN Special Forces. When the latter were deactivated in 1970, its personnel were transferred to the ranger battalions or to the Commando Battalion which was then upgraded to the 81st Airborne Commando Group. This unit was expert at night operations, in close combat operations, and in conducting small-unit long-range reconnaissance patrol deep into enemy territory, capturing prisoners, and destroying rear base installations and infrastructures; they were not normally engaged in conventional warfare. The unit was allowed to retain its uniform and its green beret. It had proven its effectiveness in the destruction of enemy *"chốt"* (reinforced blocking positions) like the ones in Chơn Thành.[28]

They landed safely at 17:00 hours at the Ro Falls, close to the Srok Ton Cui LZ of the airborne brigade. Lieutenant Colonel Phan Văn Huấn shook hands with Lieutenant Colonel Lê Văn Ngọc, deputy commander of the airborne brigade, on arrival. On their way to An Lộc, the Commando Group made contact with two companies of the 3rd Ranger Group that had been separated from the 52nd Ranger Battalion, which was defending Hill 169 during the 13 April attack. The rangers had not been supplied for many days. Hungry and exhausted, they were happy to join the commandos in an attempt to return to their unit. The wounded rangers were treated and evacuated by the helicopters that had brought in the commando group. Later, they received a phone order by General Hưng to position themselves on the north end of An Lộc by following the railway tract. However, due to darkness, the Commando Group decided to camp outdoors at whatever was left of the Sóc Gòn village, a Montagnard hamlet that had been abandoned by the enemy after their encounter with the 5th Airborne Battalion.

> They were armed with everything under the sun to include weapons taken from the enemy. Their uniforms were equally diverse with some soldiers in camouflage and others in mixed uniforms. Some of them were wearing steel helmets and others had on soft caps.... They were the toughest looking crew I had seen in many a month. That was saying a lot because up until that point the paratroopers I was serving with were as ferocious as any soldiers I had ever laid eyes on.... They possessed extraordinary bravery and were supremely confident.[29]

On 17 April, the 81st Airborne Commando Group moved to the northern side of An Lộc. They saw corpses of NVA soldiers and civilians scattered all around the streets. Close to the An Lộc hospital, hundreds of unburied bodies were piled up inside two big holes, the stench of which was sickening. The hospital itself was in ruins; most of the roof had disappeared and the collapsed front wall revealed a row of empty beds with sheets and blankets lying on the floor.[30]

The 81st Commandos were assigned the north-central section of the town, flanked on the right by the 5th Division's TOC and the left by the 8th Regiment. A few days later from midnight until 03:00 hours, they moved northward in small groups at the squad level. Buildings had collapsed, and bunkers that civilians had dug out for their own safety were used by the enemy. The commandos moved slowly from house to house using knives and grenades to kill the enemy in their foxholes. They were able to regain a small enclave 400 meters from their starting point. This was a small step for the commandos, but a giant leap for the defenders in An Lộc.

But by moving unilaterally northward, their flanks became exposed. Lieutenant Colonel Huấn, the commander, asked units of the 5th ARVN Division to also move forward. The 5th ARVN Division asked Lieutenant Colonel Biết of the Ranger Group if they could expand northward to cover the right flank of the commandos. The 36th Ranger rapidly occupied the northeastern sector toward the high ground near the airfield, scattering enemy soldiers who fled toward the Quảng Lợi Plantation. The 8th ARVN Regiment under Major Huỳnh Văn Tâm, deputy commander, however, did not move to fill the gap on the left flank of the commandos. The enemy then launched a two-pronged attack against the commandos, one from the north, the second from the west. Fearing encirclement, the commandos withdrew to the market area. By the end of 18 April, they controlled the whole assigned area stretching about 100 meters in the northern direction.[31]

In the night, they started digging graves to bury their fallen comrades following their tradition of working during the day and burying at night. Soon a well-kept cemetery emerged amid the ruins of the besieged city. Old ladies came to burn incense and offer prayers at the graves of these heroes.[32]

Hanoi was so confident about its victory in An Lộc that they proclaimed on the National Liberation Radio that effective 20 April 1972, An Lộc would become the seat of the Provisional Revolutionary Government of South Vietnam. On 19 April, Hanoi unleashed an intense and brutal attack on the northern sector of the town preceded by a heavy artillery barrage followed by tank and infantry assault. The latter was stopped by effective close air support.

The airborne commandos were ordered to counterattack while the enemy regrouped. They crossed Trần Hưng Đạo Street and retook the New Market, the bus station, and the hamlet of Thánh Mẫu (Blessed Mother) abandoned

VI. The First Attack on An Lộc

earlier by the 8th ARVN Regiment. They moved stealthily from one house to another, one building to the next, by blowing holes about one meter high by half a meter wide in the city walls to avoid being observed and shot by snipers. They used hand grenades and M-72 rocket launchers to destroy enemy bunkers, forcing them to retreat to the north. When they reached the pagoda and the Field Police headquarters, the enemy counterattacked by assaulting their left flank. The 5th ARVN Division had to call for B-52 support, which after being diverted from another mission unloaded bombs 200 to 300 hundred meters from the commando line to prevent them from being overrun. The commandos regrouped and engaged in hand-to-hand combat to dislodge the last pockets of resistance. By the end of the day, they had regained most of the lost territory.[33]

From that day onward, the 81st Airborne Commandos racked up many valiant deeds, although they suffered moderate losses from incoming enemy missiles. Captured NVA prisoners admitted they were most afraid of three things: B-52 strikes, the 81st Commandos, and then paratroopers.[34] Their deeds had been published in the Vietnamese military history. Their small cemetery in An Lộc bore two sentences that were used to memorialize them. Although the cemetery no longer exists because the communists after their victory in 1975 erased all traces of South Vietnamese glory and valor including cemeteries, remembering plaques, steles, etc., any ARVN soldier could remember these words:

> On the famous battlefield of An Lộc,
> Airborne commandos have sacrificed their lives for the country.

Also, on the brick wall of the cemetery, one could read Vương Hàn's two sentences that were inscribed in large letters:

> TUÝ NGOẠ SA TRƯỜNG QUÂN MẠC TIÊU.
> CỔ LAI CHINH CHIẾN KỶ NHÂN HỒI
> It's better to go to the battlefield drinking and laughing,
> for from antiquity, not many had come back from there.

This poetic note depicts the gallant attitude not only of the 81st Airborne Commando Group, but also of the common broad-minded, magnanimous spirit of ARVN soldiers. They fought courageously with the ultimate goal of protecting people; they were generous, altruistic, and acted without any hate like the bloodthirsty North Vietnamese Army, known as "Bộ đội Hồ Chí Minh." The latter, "born in the north and dead in the south," killed people en masse during the Tết Offensive in Huế, the withdrawals from the highlands and the I Corps in 1975, and on every battlefield where their goal was to attack and kill everyone, whether soldiers or civilians, without discrimination.

An Lộc that summer was also an example of this genocide of innocent people by "Hồ's *bộ đội*," where old men, women and children were mowed down when they tried to escape the war zone on 7 April under the leadership of Catholic and Buddhist priests. The communists would not spare anyone standing in front of the barrels of their guns. That was their policy.

An Lộc was a provincial town without any system of fortifications or trenches like Điện Biên Phủ. It never was a camp or a military fort. In that town, the proportion of civilians to soldiers was five or six to one. If there were 4,000 to 5,000 defenders, there were about 20,000 civilians or more. Before the battle erupted, thousands of civilians left the village in groups in direction of Chơn Thành or Bình Dương. They were mowed down by AK-47s or killed by incoming VC mortars on Highway 13 over many kilometers from the Xa Cam rubber plantation heading south.

Besides, on the first attack day coming from the east, the communists pushed in front of them hundreds of Quản Lợi civilians using them as shields. This was a cowardly and heartless act. Although ARVN troops had faced such difficult situations, they had tried not to use their firepower against civilians. On the contrary, on the same day, the NVA soldiers fired directly at the An Lộc local hospital and civilian homes on many other occasions causing hundreds of injured people who later died at the hospital. They kept on shelling, causing dead bodies to disintegrate in multiple pieces or into globs of flesh and bones flying all over the place inside and outside the hospital. The following day, the shelling continued as many thousands of shells rained down on the town daily. It was natural for troops to die, but in this case hundreds or thousands of civilians also died while the town totally collapsed under the onslaught of shells and bombs. There was no house left standing, no wall, no street, no tree trunks that did not carry scars from mortars, missiles, or shells, big or small, courtesy of Ho's *bộ đội*. The small local church also was turned into rubble, except for the still-standing pedestal holding the statue of Jesus the Redeemer. It should be remembered that An Lộc was a town, not a system of trenches or fortifications. It was a live dwelling place for villagers, not an armory or a military camp to be turned into a no man's land.

The presence of these two airborne units in An Lộc raised the hope of defenders whether they were the 5th ARVN Infantry Division, 3rd Ranger TF, or soldiers and civilians of the Military Sector of Bình Long. The latter reorganized their fighting positions—they mostly enlarged or deepened their foxholes to be better protected from shelling or attacks. Defense techniques, reliance on M-72 launchers, and a formidable anti-tank armament introduced to 5th ARVN Division soldiers in 1972 raised the fighting spirit of the troops as well as their belief in the will of their leaders, especially their commander, General Lê Văn Hưng.

VII

A Clash of Personalities

One could not remain inside this small bunker in the middle of the besieged An Lộc town without feeling the tension between the two main officers who directed the battlefield from the South Vietnamese side. If everything was hot outside the bunker, it was also "electrically charged" within on various occasions. If bombs and shells exploded outside the compound, verbal explosions shattered the calm inside. If the outside skirmishes affected the tension on the inside, the inside dispute could adversely affect the war on the outside.

Easterner and Westerner

One does not know when the animosity between the two officers began, but even before the first explosion was heard in An Lộc, Colonel Miller had tried to have General Hưng dismissed.[1] This was the first official salvo that the former had "fired" against the latter.

General Hưng, however, did not respond to the offense but continued to work as usual as if nothing had happened maybe because he had the full support of his superior, General Minh. General Hưng did not share anything with me about that topic either. He was a calm and quiet, some say taciturn, officer who rarely discussed his personal problems with anyone. As a true southern introvert—although it is hard to generalize—he kept everything to himself and tried to correct and improve himself through his own effort. Like many Vietnamese, he was an individualist who had been successful so far by that time; that success in turn had given him some inner confidence that allowed him to meet the challenges of the An Lộc battle. Some people may call this attitude "aloof," although many southerners would simply characterize it as an acceptance of adverse events. They thought that if they could not change or refute an event, they simply accepted it. Since General Hưng could not change the mind of Colonel Miller, who bore preconceived opinions about him, he just accepted the fact, went on with his life, and proved himself later on the battlefield.

From the Vietnamese side, accepting an adverse event did not mean ignoring it or ignoring Miller: that would only create more problems down the road. A shunned or discredited Miller could have, for example, held off air support, which could have led to a battlefield disaster. Therefore, General Hưng had to diplomatically maneuver through a minefield whenever he had to deal with his adviser. If at times he would support Miller's ideas and go along with them, on other occasions he would stick to his own ideas and pursue them until he reached his goals. On a battlefield, there was no way to prove beforehand that decisions one had planned to take would always be foolproof, successful or logical. These decisions General Hưng made, derived from the combined years of experience on the battlefield, from "gut feeling," and from the confidence he had in his troops and military reserve. Having fought the Viet Cong for many years, he had the "gut feeling" of how the enemy would react if such or such decision were taken. How could he relay that feeling to an American who had not had that same experience? How could he convey that feeling to a person of a different culture, especially when Vietnamese officers, in general, did not have a good grasp of English to explain everything in detail? How could he convey all the subtleties of the art of warfare, the nuts and bolts of a maneuver, when they both had graduated through different military schools and lived in different cultures? Other factors also played a role in the relationship between the two officers. Although at times he had shared his ideas with Colonel Miller, it was always difficult in the heat of a battle to explain in detail the maneuvers or decisions he had planned to take. Taking time to explain everything could cause him to lose concentration on the rapidly changing events of the battlefield. Although he would like to explain everything to Miller and put him at ease, it was not always possible in all occasions.

Accepting an adverse event, on the other hand, did not mean that he was wrong: it simply meant that two people have two different opinions about an event. In this case, he believed that there was no need to argue or discuss because neither side would budge or change his mind. It was like being a communist and a non-communist in Vietnam. Each side would stick to his argument and believe he was right until time had come for the differences to break into the open and to fight again.

An American, however, would not accept an event/status a priori. Colonel Miller, especially, had opinions or ideas about everything, which he tried to sell to General Hưng on every occasion. He would offer his own ideas—many of them were odd, to say the least—even though they were not requested, to the point of forcing them on his counterpart.

This is where the mind of the Vietnamese (easterner) and the American (westerner) differs. One side is passive, subtle, or introvert and tries not to impress his counterpart; however, when he was convinced he was right, he would proceed ahead anyway, leaving his counterpart confused. The western side is aggressive or extrovert and tries at all cost to smother or dominate his counterpart. Thus, if the Vietnamese may appear difficult for the American to judge or decipher, the American may appear arrogant or abusive to the Vietnamese. Although this is a generalization, it is true in the majority of cases if majority can be defined as happening in more than 51 percent of the cases. Unrefined, an American or a Vietnamese may harbor preconceived ideas about the other, especially if either is tainted by a complex of inferiority.

Although General Hưng did not say anything, I was pretty convinced that Colonel Miller's attempt to replace him by another officer did hurt him. This was a direct and personal attack on his character, ability, and self-worth, and no officer in his right mind would take that affront lightly. A Vietnamese would rarely make such a direct frontal attack, such as asking for the resignation of someone. As a soft or passive person, he would indicate his displeasure in a more indirect way. Born in an open society, an American has been told from a young age to speak his mind; he usually does it without realizing that this attitude could be felt as offensive by Asians. Although it is the purview of an adviser to suggest certain things, such a direct frontal attack may not be "politically correct."

James Bruton, a former military adviser in Vietnam, contrasts the Vietnamese and American psychological differences a little bit further.[2]

American Tendency	*Vietnamese Tendency*
Individualistic outlook	**Collective outlook**
Diffuse authority	Top-down decision making
Decentralized decision making	
Speedy results—short-term perspective	**Patience—long-term view**
(Rush to failure)	(Cautious deliberative action)
Direct communication	**Indirect communication**
Straightforward—"all cards on the table"	Reticence
Confrontational	Harmony, face saving
Human agency as primary causality	Role of fate, karma
Truth is fixed, permanent	Truth is strongly contextual

American Tendency	Vietnamese Tendency
Contract terms are binding	Contract terms are circumstantial and subject to change
Overstatement of achievements	Self-effacing
Universalization of American experiences (others should imitate American ways)	Particularistic outlook

Additionally, the adviser, in this case, Colonel Miller, was lower in rank than his advisee, General Hưng. For a lower-ranking adviser to suggest removing a high-level officer was an act rarely seen, unless the advisee was a really bad person. This was not the case with General Hưng who was not a womanizer, did not take bribes, and did not shy away from his military duties. In fact, he was a straightforward and capable officer who during this An Lộc battle was fighting alongside his troops in the trenches. He had endured the terrible shelling of the town with all his troops and suffered through highs and lows throughout the duration of the battle in the forefront of the battlefield. As a matter of fact, on two occasions, the NVA came within 50 yards of his bunker. Had the enemy proceeded forward, they would have neutralized the commanding post and captured all the officers, and the battle would have been lost.

An Lộc Field Commander and U.S. Adviser

After the first attack on An Lộc, part of the northern side of the city fell into enemy hands, especially the area around the Đồng Long Airfield, which prevented resupply and evacuation of wounded troops. General Minh's decision was to drop the 1st Airborne Brigade—which included the 5th, 6th, and 8th Battalions; the 3rd Airborne Artillery Battalion; and a reconnaissance company under the command of Colonel Lê Quang Lưỡng (later promoted to brigadier general, the last commander of the Airborne Division)—on two dry fields close to Highway 13 north of town and at mid-distance between the Cần Lê Bridge and the Đồng Long Airfield. From there, the troops would march south and attack enemy troops stationed at the airport and the northern end of the town. Lieutenant Colonel Nguyễn Văn Biết along with Lieutenant Colonel Lý Đức Quân's 7th Regiment would attack the enemy from the south. Of course, the VNAF and U.S. Air Force would drop bombs before the airborne, rangers and infantrymen mounted their attacks.

This strategy, when presented to the ARVN 5th Division leadership, was approved by Colonel Miller, although General Hưng decided to first meet with Colonel Lê Quang Lưỡng, the Airborne Brigade commander, the following

VII. A Clash of Personalities

day, 14 April, to discuss the plan. On that day, in the early morning mist, a helicopter flying low above tree tops dropped Colonel Lưỡng at the Military Sector headquarters of Colonel Trần Văn Nhựt. And I was ordered to meet and pick up Colonel Lưỡng and drive him back to the divisional headquarters.

When I arrived at the underground headquarters of the Bình Long Military Sector, I understood why U.S. advisers fell backward and overwhelmingly praised Colonel Trần Văn Nhựt, province chief and commander of the Military Sector. The underground bunker, named B-15, previously housing the ARVN Special Forces, was recently built by the U.S. forces. It was deep, sturdy, and three times larger than the small, cramped, somewhat moldy, and darkly lit divisional bunker. There was no starker contrast between the more than two-decade-old divisional bunker and the recently built B-15 bunker. The latter was brightly lit, large enough for Vietnamese and U.S. officers to sit and work in an orderly manner around an operation table, which was filled with up-to-date maps of the town and the battlefield. There was no lack of cigarettes, tea, coffee, and other food products dispensed around. Compared to the divisional bunker, the B-15 bunker appeared in the midst of the confrontation like a vacation home.

As mentioned above, Colonel Nhựt was a warrior and a politician. Almost all the U.S. advisers in An Lộc were housed at the B-15 bunker, except for Colonel Miller and two of his subordinates. The total number of U.S. advisers from the military zone and other units during this whole battle could have been as high as 10 or more, from lieutenant colonel down in rank. They all had been well treated by Colonel Nhựt who displayed a natural smartness or "emotional intelligence" as previously mentioned. On the other hand, it was thanks to this handful of advisers who contacted the U.S. Tactical Air Command and the Strategic Air Command to drop bombs on enemy forces that the defenders were able to hold on to An Lộc. Later, it was only natural that this group would praise Colonel Nhựt for his close collaboration as well as his demeanor.

However, Colonel Nhựt only commanded a small number of troops, maybe less than a battalion of RF and SDF or roughly 600 soldiers, in An Lộc itself. Although the advisers had suggested that he commanded a regiment of 1,000 troops, that number was somewhat high. Colonel Nhựt also did not make any major tactical battlefield decision at An Lộc; that military role belonged to General Hưng. One of the advisers of the TF-52 unit was then 1st Lieutenant James H. Willbanks who arrived at An Lộc on 12 April—one day before the An Lộc battle began, but more than one week after the battle of Lộc Ninh—and had to be evacuated on 9 July because of a shrapnel wound. On his return to the U.S., he took a post-graduate course and was later promoted to lieutenant colonel. Based on Colonel Miller's documents, he decided to write as part of his master's degree on the battle of An Lộc where he effusively praised Colonel Nhựt while downsizing General Lê Văn Hưng's role in the battle. Being located in another bunker, he was not aware of, nor did appreciate, the huge cultural and military differences as well as thinking processes between Colonel Miller and General Hưng before and during the An Lộc battle.

Willbanks noted that General Hưng was a "demoralized" man, "totally indecisive and unable to handle the stress of high-intensity combat."[3] In the same vein, Andrade reported that "Colonel Miller thought that Hưng would probably be happy as long as he could sit and do nothing, even if the entire country burned around him in the meantime." All these assessments could only come from Colonel Miller, because neither Willbanks nor Andrade was in close contact with General Hưng. The scornful language Willbanks used in his 1995 book—two decades after General Hưng's death—suggested the deep distaste Colonel Miller had for the general.[4]

When Colonel Miller first came to the ARVN 5th Division in the summer of 1971, he reported to TRAC (Third Regional Assistance Command) that "Hưng displays outstanding leadership, is aggressive, organized, and forceful. He appears extremely knowledgeable, has confidence in himself, and is quickly gaining the confidence of his subordinates." No one knew why Miller had diametrically changed his opinion a few months later. Either he was not candid about his earlier observations or he had badly misread his counterpart. Andrade further wrote that although "he respected Miller, Hưng rarely sought out his advice and often did not inform him of tactical decisions."[5] Therefore, the problem with Miller was that he felt disrespected by Hưng.

General Thi commented that Hưng, like many South Vietnamese as detailed in the first chapter, was a "rather taciturn and independent man [who] ... liked to act on his own and was not eager to listen to the advice of his counterparts."[6] Andrade pointed to the fact that he "disliked overbearing Americans who wanted the war fought according to American rules. This resentment colored Hưng's relations with U.S. officers since the early 1960s, garnering him a reputation as being "anti–American."[7] This reasoning was not correct for two reasons. First, General Hưng had never displayed any overt anti–American stance. On the contrary, he deeply appreciated the help of U.S. advisers who called for air support day in and day out for him. Second, he had an excellent working relationship with Colonel Ulmer, Miller's replacement. Colonel Ulmer did not experience any burst of anger or any major verbal argument toward General Hưng; nor did he threaten to pull the adviser group out of An Lộc like Miller did.

VII. A Clash of Personalities

The other argument rested on the difference of opinion regarding the strategic defense of Lộc Ninh. Colonel Nguyễn Công Vĩnh, commander of the ARVN 9th Regiment at Lộc Ninh was an old and weak officer who needed to be transferred to a desk office or to simply retire. What was holding him in Lộc Ninh was unknown to Hưng, although Miller speculated that it was because of Vĩnh's relationship with Hưng. But when Miller asked Hưng about replacing Vĩnh, Hưng responded that he "would incur the wrath of someone in Saigon with political ties to Vĩnh if he did that."[8] That alone would suggest that Hưng had nothing to do with keeping Vĩnh in his position in Lộc Ninh. Besides, according to ARVN rules, a division commander could only make a recommendation but could not fire or demote his regimental commander. Only the Corps commander could. Either way, replacing him would take time and could not be done while a major enemy attack was threatening.

Although Colonel Miller thought that Lộc Ninh could be reasonably defended,[9] the location of the town on the northern end of the province and close to the Cambodian border made the task extremely difficult, if not impossible. The huge NVA forces stationing in Cambodia could relentlessly attack this outpost until it fell and then withdraw safely into their sanctuaries without worrying about reprisal from a stretched ARVN force. For the ARVN, bringing reinforcement troops to An Lộc was already a huge task, let alone taking them all the way to Lộc Ninh. Since that outpost was very small in size and could barely accommodate three small compounds, positioning the reinforcing troops there would present a huge safety problem. The outpost would be massively shelled like An Lộc and would surrender faster; otherwise it would be destroyed in no time. Lộc Ninh with its flat terrain and lack of natural defenses was, therefore, not a defendable place.

As mentioned above, Colonel Miller had suggested that General Hưng relinquish his command to Colonel Nhựt, Bình Long province chief.[10] This in-your-face suggestion from a colonel to a general, from a foreigner to a native, from an adviser to a commanding officer, reeked of arrogance because it was not only insulting, but was also a major break of military protocol and common sense. Colonel Miller would have been wiser to report his recommendation to his superior, General Hollingsworth, who would communicate with General Minh, the Corps commander; the latter in turn would have made the final decision.[11] Or the matter could go higher from General Hollingsworth to General Abrams then to General Cao Văn Viên, chairman of the JGS. When an American adviser reported via his superior to General Viên about a Vietnamese officer whom he considered ineffective, inept or otherwise unsuited for command, General Viên and his counterpart General

Abrams would travel together on field inspections, and General Abrams "would comment tersely on the state of the command and the ability of the commanders as he saw it. But he never suggested either the promotion or the relief of anyone."[12] If even General Abrams would not suggest any promotion or relief of anyone, why would Colonel Miller continue to attack and disparage General Hưng through the writings of then Lieutenant Willbanks?

Frances Fitzgerald was probably close when she wrote about U.S. military advisers, especially Colonel Miller.

> Covered with righteous platitudes, theirs was an essential colonialist vision, borne out of the same insecurity and desire for domination that had motivated many of the French. When their counterparts did not take their instructions, these advisers treated the Vietnamese like bad pupils, accusing them of corruption and laziness, and attempted to impose authority over them.[13]

Prior to the battle, General Hưng commended Colonel Miller for being a brave and resilient officer who had come through U.S. Army ranks, from a private to colonel, which was a respectable and worthwhile achievement indeed. The French have this nice expression *"un très respectueux officier sorti du rang."* He also felt that although Colonel Miller was a fine commander in the Korean War and other battlefields, he had not had enough experience in the war in Vietnam to lecture a Vietnamese general, commander of a division. Besides, in a military organization, whether Vietnamese or American, a general is a general, and a colonel is a colonel, and the gulf between the two is sometimes as wide as the Grand Canyon.

Colonel Miller, on the other hand, considered General Hưng as a "young" general or a "Delta-Clan general," a derisory and belittling term, which equated to being "green." The American press at that time reserved this appellation to senior members of the ARVN 21st Division who were staunch supporters of President Thiệu. However, only a few of them were eventually rewarded with good positions in the army or administration. By extension, it designated young military personnel who rose rapidly through the ranks because of suspected political ties to Thiệu.[14] This was not the case of General Hưng who rose in ranks through his own merits. He was a seasoned fighter and a well-regarded regiment commander in the IV Corps before becoming the commander of the 5th ARVN Division; he also had received more combat medals than any other Vietnamese counterpart of his rank.

The two fighters disparaged each other and subconsciously became enemies. But their attitudes were totally different. Colonel Miller violently argued with General Hưng right in the tiny bunker at An Lộc. As a southern gentleman, General Hưng was an easygoing person who forgot everything even after a heated discussion. Colonel Miller, on the other hand, brought his grudge back to the U.S. and during each presentation, discussion, conference he made about the An Lộc battle, he continued to belittle General Hưng.

Tactical Disagreements

The other event had to do with what happened inside the underground bunker. On 7 April 1972, for security reasons, the divisional operational headquarters was moved to the bunker located close to the administrative building of the village. This was an old bunker built by the Japanese some two decades earlier and refurbished to house the Forward Operations Center of the III Corps commander, General Minh, for the An Lộc battle. Since General Minh decided not to come to An Lộc, the bunker was turned over to General Hưng.

From the ground through the opening of the bunker and down 10 steps, one would immediately face the main room of the bunker or the division's TOC where all the sleeping cots were located. Five steps toward the left was the communication section with all its electronic devices. This was the nerve center of the 5th Division. Twenty steps toward the right was located a private room reserved for the commander with its iron bed, a small refrigerator, a small table and a chair. General Hưng, however, had relinquished his private room to Colonel Mạch Văn Trường who was recovering from a shrapnel injury to his shoulder sustained prior to the first enemy attack. He would only reoccupy his room by the last week of April. During that interval period, he slept in the bunker's main room where two cots placed side by side were reserved for the two most important officers at An Lộc, General Hưng, field commander, and Colonel Miller, U.S. adviser. The two cots were separated by a small coffee table. Close to Colonel Miller's cot were those of the two other advisers, Lieutenant Colonel Ed Benedict, assistant to Miller, and Major Alan Borsdorf, operations assistant of the adviser group. At the coffee table where the two main officers often discussed the strategy of the day, many loud confrontations had occurred during that April month.

Colonel Miller, seeing An Lộc being reinforced with the 1st Airborne Brigade and the 81st Airborne Commando Group, suggested launching an immediate attack to reoccupy the commercial center on the north end of the town as well as the Đồng Long Airfield. These areas had been occupied by enemy troops during the first attack from 13 to 16 April. If such a counterattack were to occur, Colonel Miller mentioned that he would request Strategic and Tactical Air Force to provide maximal support for General Hưng's troops. He also suggested using the 1st Airborne Brigade, the 81st Airborne Commando Group and the 3rd Ranger TF during the main attack while the other units would be ready to fight from their positions. He estimated that General Hưng could mobilize 3,000 troops for that endeavor and the Đồng Long Airfield, once recovered from the enemy, would be useful to the resupply and evacuation operations; it would provide a more stable and economical supply route than the daily airdrop. Without the Đồng Long Airfield, Vietnamese and U.S. helicopters flying in and out of the LZ were in constant danger of being shot down by enemy forces. Although Colonel Miller's suggestion was correct, it was premature.

According to prisoners' statements—an NVA officer who was caught by the ARVN 3/7 Battalion during the first attack on 17 April and another NVA *hồi chánh*[15]—the fact that the 271st Regiment of the VC 9th Division had been wiped out by B-52 boxes at Phú Lố and Phú Bình hamlets a few days earlier suggested the NVA 5th Division had failed in its attack in the northwest section of the town. Enemy troops—the VC 272nd Regiment—were only holding the Đồng Long Airfield and the northern section of An Lộc. The prisoners also reported that COSVN would prepare for a bigger attack on An Lộc from the northeast by the 5th Div/VC. Another smaller attack from the southwest would be spearheaded by the 9th Div/VC. Tanks, artillery, and anti-aircraft guns would support the above two divisions. The 7th Div/NVA would send a regiment to attack the southeast side of An Lộc where the airborne brigade was stationed. Facing these potential dangers and the possibility of a larger and more dangerous conflict, General Hưng became leery about launching a counterattack at that time. This difference in strategic assessment increased the level of antagonism between the two officers. The confrontation took place over a period of many days, even as the second phase of enemy attack had ended (18–21 April).

The situation, which had become tense with every passing day, forced me to step into General Hưng's private quarters and discuss the matter with him. He told me earlier that he regarded Colonel Miller as an experienced soldier who did not know a lot about warfare in Vietnam. He explained that he only needed Miller for the strategic air support and tactical resupply, but not for his tactical point of view. Sometimes, Hưng responded nicely to Miller; but on many occasions, he kept quiet and left the operational bunker. Colonel Miller also told me, "Your 'young' general is good for keeping his silence rather than for speaking and acting." "Yes, Sir. His 'silence' means that he would stand firm and fight; his soldiers would look to him to stand firm and fight. He is young, but he is the best and a very experienced warrior in our army," I politely replied.[16]

VII. A Clash of Personalities 127

Hưng had also told Miller that in case of another attack in the future, COSVN would be able to mobilize more than 20,000 NVA troops as well as other infantry, artillery, tank, and special units with a total force of more than three divisions. Had the ARVN at the time of the discussion counterattacked to take back the Đồng Long Airfield and part of the northern section of the town as Miller had suggested, the losses would have been high. Even in case of success, ARVN forces, whose numbers stood at 7,000 prior to the first attack, would have to spread thin to take control of all the new positions, thereby weakening the line of defense. Therefore, although a counterattack at that time might temporarily be successful, ARVN forces would be annihilated by a stronger NVA counterattack.

The argument about "tactics" increased the divide between these two leaders. General Hưng naturally had reported all details to his superior, General Minh, and so did Colonel Miller with General Hollingsworth. Colonel Miller's animosity against General Hưng, although hidden by the western way of reporting, could not be controlled at that time or later when he returned to the U.S. He continued to discredit General Hưng with terms like "almost paralyzed,"[17] "indecisive and unable to handle the stress of high-intensity combat,"[18] and "he looses [sic] all his composure."[19] He also provided personal documents to 1st Lieutenant James H. Willbanks, who once served as an adviser for the TF-52 of the ARVN 18th Infantry Division. Lieutenant Willbanks, after returning to the U.S., used these documents[20] to write his master's report, which was later expanded into a book entitled *The Battle of An Lộc*, published by the Indiana University Press in 2005.

Looking at the events at the time, one could see that Colonel Miller's assessment of the battlefield was narrow. The 5th Div/NVA was keeping its 174th Regiment in the area of the rubber plantation and the Quản Lợi airfield as a reserve unit in case the ARVN suddenly decided to retake this important position five to six kilometers northeast of An Lộc. Facing this gathering of NVA forces in the east and southeast of An Lộc in addition to other factors mentioned above, General Hưng could not approve Colonel Miller's plan to retake the northern end of An Lộc and Đồng Long Airfield at that time. Basically, the ARVN did not have enough reserves left to throw into the battlefield in case the counterattack failed.

Besides, as the battlefield situation in the southeast sector remained unstable, pulling the airborne troops out of their crucial positions to spearhead an attack on the Đồng Long Airfield and the northern end of the town as suggested by Colonel Miller would not be a smart strategy. One wonders why he kept on pushing for an counterattack on the northern sector of the town until the end of April. Willbanks wrote, "Colonel Miller had once again become frustrated with General Hưng. After the jubilation of blunting the attack on 19–20 April had faded, Miller urged Hưng to put his troops on the offensive to retake the northern part of the city. However, no amount of pleading was able to force Hưng to give such an order."[21]

Was Willbanks aware that on 19–20 April the NVA had violently attacked the 6th Airborne Battalion forcing it and its artillery company to withdraw from Hill 169 to An Lộc's military zone? Did he know that the airborne brigade had lost a third of its force in these two days and was therefore unable to lead any new attack? If he did, why did he not mention it in his book? Or did he just want to protect the tactical opinion of Colonel Miller and forget about this important event?

Although General Hưng appreciated the work and support of Colonel Miller and the other advisers, the final decision rested on him, the commander of the battlefield from the ARVN side. Colonel Miller as an adviser and a guest, by pressing and nagging the general constantly, came out not as a friendly adviser, but as a bully. General Hưng had behaved more than courteously toward Colonel Miller during these difficult times as Willbanks had remarked when he wrote, "Hưng no doubt resented Miller's pushing and overbearing attitude, feeling that the American was overstepping his bounds and meddling in South Vietnamese affairs."[22]

As to the report that "the general sat in his bunker, with only limited contact with his regimental commanders, and waited for U.S. airpower to save the day,"[23] this was another example of a one-sided statement professed by Colonel Miller. If General Hưng did not have daily contact with his commanders, how could he oversee the ever-changing battlefield, give daily reports to General Minh, and lead his troops to success?

When these communication problems occurred, the adviser could not only talk to his counterpart, but also to his U.S. superior. The latter would tell his Vietnamese counterpart who would relay the message to his subordinate.[24] Colonel Miller apparently had made multiple reports to his superior, General Hollingsworth. Whether the latter had communicated them to General Minh was not known. It was probably this failure by Generals Hollingsworth and Minh to act in response to Miller's requests that increased the latter's bitterness toward General Hưng. Failure basically meant ignoring/not acting on Miller's claims.

The Adviser's Role

Being an adviser, like being a teacher, is not an easy task to fulfill or role to play. The task is further complicated by cultural, ethnic, and training differences. It is not all about experience or professional competence; strangely many experienced officers turn out to be not good advisers—although these qualities do help. It is not about flooding the advisee with data, suggestions, and advice to the point of drowning him and leaving him feeling incapable of performing his duty. It is not about passively waiting for the advisee to come to him as the last resort, because by then it may be too late to change anything. It is above all an art: that of counseling, that of teaching. It is about growing an individual, cultivating him, making him a competent individual who would be able to handle adversity. If the adviser's role is similar to that of a teacher, the adviser is more than a teacher.

To accomplish his duty, the adviser not only has to understand his advisee, know him and his needs, but he also wants to improve himself. He is teaching an adult person, a grown-up man who has a position and a place in society, which in this case is his unit and the army he serves. If the adviser is technologically advanced and can call on B-52 bombers or any other type of air support, the advisee has years of war experience in his country. If the adviser knows where to call for material supplies, the advisee knows which of his units he can rely on to deal with a certain situation. If the adviser knows how to deal with the U.S. Army, the advisee knows how to deal with the Vietnamese public, the local people: in the end, it is a war for "the hearts of the people."

Besides, the advisee has his "face" to protect: he does not want to appear ignorant or weak in front of his unit to the point of being dependent on his adviser for everything. If he does appear weak or incompetent, he would not be able to lead his troops any longer; his men would not want to serve or put their lives under his command. This is a battle for the advisee to shine and to win and time for the adviser to fade away. The role of the adviser is to prop his advisee up, to support him, to make him feel competent and comfortable to assume his position. This is where many advisers have made a mistake: they want to shine instead of letting their advisee shine. The focus should be on the advisee: this is his unit, his country, and his war, and he should be able to shine. It requires a lot of maturity, control, and self-confidence for the adviser to know when to back out and let his advisee take the credit. But by backing out, both advisee and adviser will shine because by giving credit to his advisee, the adviser has won the confidence and trust of his advisee who will from then on turn to him for more advice. On the other hand, berating the advisee, using the adviser's position of strength and influence to force him to do something, would only harden the man, convince him to stay away from the adviser. This is why being an adviser is an art that is based on true human relationship. As such, it requires time; a one-year tenure is too short to produce connection and generate influence.

Vietnamese officers in their evaluation of the American military effort stress the tendency of U.S. advisers "to overtake and patronize" the South Vietnamese, a practice that "seemed to edge ARVN commanders toward a passive role, especially since modern warfare required so much skill in the employment of U.S. controlled combat support assets."[25]

Besides, to do a good job of advising or "coaching" a person, whether in a public or military field, requires a good if not an intimate knowledge of that person. Since each adviser would stay in ARVN combat units only six months at most, the rapid manpower rotation forced each tactical commander to deal with as many as 20 to 30 different advisers over the war years[26]; such rapid turnover, sadly, was not conducive to steady progress and improvement of the units.

Besides language and cultural differences, the advisers' good life did not make interaction between tactical commanders and U.S. advisers easy.

> It seemed that no American could survive without his PX, his compound, and his daily bath. In time American compounds and PX's became monumental institutions of American culture in Vietnam. To the underprivileged Vietnamese, these constituted a whole world apart, a world so distant that Vietnamese seldom really felt close to Americans in a cultural sense.... An ARVN officer, if criticized for not keeping pace with American drive, was usually heard retorting, "If I lived that kind of life, I could do the same."[27]

Exposure to the "unattainable good life" of the Americans created in ARVN soldiers a "complex of inferiority and sometimes bitterness, which accounted for the distance they always tried to keep from American advisers in order not to be hurt."

In addition, U.S. advisers knew that their service would be limited to one year, unless they renewed it; they knew that no matter how difficult the hardship would be, there was light at the end of the tunnel. Therefore, they either could behave aggressively like Rambo[28] because that would be the only time for them to shine on the battlefield or bide their time until their service ended. On the other end, ARVN troops knew that once enrolled in the ARVN, they would be in for the duration. They were trapped, for nothing was more restrictive and emotionally depressing for their young minds, no matter how enthusiastic they were in the beginning about performing their duty, than to realize that they were stuck forever in an unending war unless they were severely disabled or had reached retirement age.

In general, the South Vietnamese were grateful to U.S. advisers for sacrificing their lives and for helping them attain remarkable achievements in terms of combat readiness and technical and managerial skills.

VII. A Clash of Personalities   131

The majority of U.S. Army advisers came out of their tour of duty with a better, more sober understanding of the problem the RVNAF had to face in the war. More importantly, they invariably came away with profound compassion and a heartfelt affection for their counterparts with whom they had shared the hazards and spartan conditions of combat. Many such relationships had developed into lasting personal friendships.[29]

One night toward the end of April 1972 around midnight while I was sitting at the square operations table—that replaced the old short table—Colonel Miller came and told me he needed to talk to General Hưng. The latter had retired into his private quarters, which had been vacated by Colonel Mạch Văn Trường who had been sent back to his unit. Colonel Miller told me that he would call TRAC to "rescue" the divisional combat assistance team out of An Lộc. He showed me his letter which was written on a yellow operations form. I read the short sentence—although I do not remember the exact wording—and asked him a simple question: "Colonel, do you have any feeling toward the troops in this division?" "Yes, I do have respect for them, but I have to leave," he answered. I requested that he please sit down and went to General Hưng's private quarters to present the yellow memo. The latter just laughed at it, but he could not hide his anger. "Let him go," he said. "This is not possible. You have to see him," I answered.

I left the room and went to the refrigerator, cut a few pieces of *chã lụa* (pork roll), and placed them on a plate before setting them along with a few beer cans on the operations table. I told Colonel Miller that General Hưng would be out in a minute and returned to my cot. A few minutes later, General Hưng walked out properly dressed in his fatigues with a general star sewn on his shirt collar. He smiled and shook Colonel Miller's hand, and the two sat down and talked normally like nothing important had happened. They talked about things that no one dared to come close by to listen to, but they did not argue like the days before.

After that night, from morning until the next day, the 2nd and 3rd Bureaus of the Operations Command headquarters did not receive any order from General Hưng to counterattack on the Đồng Long Airfield and the northern section of the town. I only knew that in the area of responsibility of the 81st Airborne Commando of Lieutenant Colonel Phan Văn Huấn with his unusual working tactic, he was able to reoccupy each house, each row of houses, and destroy each enemy group at a time. His control area, therefore, had been widening toward the north end of town. U.S. Spectres kept coming every night over the town and the peripheral area to destroy enemy tanks and army trucks.

One day in early May 1972, I don't remember which one, one parachute that did not open in time sent a supply pallet crashing through the roof of a brick building belonging to the 2nd Bureau operational office where more than two dozen NCOs and officers were working. It created a four-meter-deep hole in the basement, although the walls remained intact; only the roof and floor of the house had disappeared out of our view. No one was hurt because my two captains and I were in the bunker of the administrative building working on the operations log, and the other officers and troops were in their foxholes outside the building. That unavoidable hole was still useful to us for it became our safe working place in the future.

About a week or 10 days later, after I finished lunch with colleagues in that pallet-induced hole and was about to walk to my administrative bunker, I saw a U.S. colonel standing by Colonel Bùi Đức Điềm, the operational chief of staff, outside the door looking with a surprised look at the gaping deep hole. I climbed out of it to greet him. He told me he was the new adviser replacing Colonel Miller and would like to talk to me about enemy troops and get a report on the prisoner who was caught a few days earlier. I met with him in the operations room for about 10 minutes. That was the day we were preparing for another round of enemy attack in May. His name was Colonel Walter F. Ulmer. He was in his forties, not very tall but well proportioned and good looking. He seemed to be quiet, reserved, although he was very knowledgeable. He was definitely different from Colonel Miller who wanted to talk all the time. It struck me that Colonel Miller had quietly left town the night before, although his associates had remained in An Lộc to work with Colonel Ulmer.

The new adviser and the division commander appeared to work in sync. The support of the U.S. Air Force was fast and effective in the violent new round of attack. As to Colonel Miller, I did not know where he was transferred. Even if he had sent his request for "evacuation" of the whole assistance team out of An Lộc, his superiors would only rescue him because Washington was not about to abandon An Lộc right in the middle of a fight. Which U.S. commander in Vietnam would have the gall to remove the whole team out of An Lộc? Naturally, only Colonel Miller suffered from the backlash. Before the battle of An Lộc, he was slated to become commander of a U.S. brigade with the possibility of becoming general. But after returning to the U.S. until his retirement, he remained a colonel although had the chance of becoming a potential commander. This may have been the source of his growing hate toward General Hưng. We have to be happy for him, for one of his sons who graduated from a well-known U.S. military school later fought bravely in Iraq and was promoted to lieutenant general. That was his best consolation.

VII. A Clash of Personalities

Colonel Ulmer was different than his predecessor. While Miller was passionate and deeply involved in the details of his relationship with General Hưng, Ulmer was detached and observant. While Miller was emotional and moody, Ulmer was calm and coldly calculating.

But Ulmer was concerned about the overall situation when he saw the chaos that greeted him when he first landed in An Lộc. The scene of dead and dying lying around in the corridors of the forward command post and the moans of men in agony struck him deeply and made him think about a possible extraction. Ulmer later recounted how Hưng seemed "weary and cautious, but he was clearly in command." He was fatigued and nervous for having carried alone the responsibility for the defense of An Lộc since early April. Ulmer recalled, "Hưng never buckled, though he was clearly concerned."[30]

VIII

The Siege

Once the first attack failed on 16 April 1972, the NVA/VC began tightening their siege on the town using "strangulation and starvation tactics" before attacking in force.[1]

All of Humanity Died in An Lộc

Even before the battle began, Colonel Miller, senior adviser to the 5th ARVN Division, while driving around town observed, "The message was written on all the faces of the civilians and the military. The civilians were arriving from surrounding areas, yet An Lộc was still a ghost town."[2] Among the evacuees was Pastor Diệu Huỳnh who led 500 Montagnards (minority highlanders) from neighboring villages to seek shelter at the railroad station on the east side of the city.[3] For a town that barely topped 15,000 people, the final tally showed that 36,179 people had been evacuated to Bình Dương and 7,723 to Chơn Thành.[4] These numbers depicted the extent of the displacement of people. Once they relocated to An Lộc and realized that the town was the primary target of the attack, they moved to other towns further south.

The remaining people who did not have friends or relatives in other towns or could not afford to move for any other reason just stayed where they were until they could not stand it any longer and tried to escape one way or another. Others remained in bomb shelters, no matter how flimsy they were. Some of them consisted of just a few pieces of wood, a table, a layer of sandbags placed on top of a shallow burrow. Villagers who were not able to dig a tunnel joined the soldiers in their foxholes.

The communists did not spare civilians and targeted them, not only in town, but also when they tried to escape from it. On 8 April even before the main attack took place, hearing civilians' voices over loudspeakers, Captain

VIII. The Siege

Nguyễn Ngọc Khuê, assistant S3, climbed on the roof of the 3rd Ranger Group forward center to observe the situation. He noticed a large number of civilians waving white flags walking out of the town toward Highway 13 and heading south. Led by two Buddhist monks, they used loudspeakers to warn both warring sides to hold their fire to let civilians safely get out of town. As they moved past the southern sector held by the provincial forces, Khuê heard heavy artillery explosions in that area. He realized that the column was fired on by enemy artillery round after round. Children's cries were heard all the way to where Khuê was standing. After the first few shots and following guidance from forward observers, the enemy aimed their mortar guns directly at the middle of the column of civilians, sending bodies flying in the air. Arms and legs could be seen hanging from the trees alongside the road. People sought shelter behind tree trunks, leaving injured and bloodied bodies of relatives and friends on the highway pavement and the area nearby. After the shelling stopped, realizing with horror the evil intention of the communists, priests, bonzes and civilians returned to their homes or shelters in town.

When Major Khuê was sent to a communist reeducation camp in the North after the war ended in 1975, he mentioned this incident in a self-criticism statement. The political officer then explained,

> The revolution shelled this civilian crowd because this was a crowd of puppet civilians, filled with reactionaries and counterrevolutionaries. We could not exclude them and we had to teach them a lesson.[5]

Enemy guns aimed toward town proved to be accurate and deadly. They destroyed everything of material value to the defenders. They shelled the hospital, first-aid units, schools, administrative buildings, towers, artillery guns, defensive units, trucks, and so on. They fired on any moving target, causing people to hide further underground or behind any still standing walls. They completely leveled the initial divisional forward command post early in the battle as they definitely knew of its location. Had the divisional staff not moved to the new bunker or had the new bunker not been available, they would have been wiped out. When ARVN gun crews tried to confuse enemy gunners by shifting their positions after firing, the new positions were soon spotted and shelled. Hostile troops on rooftops in the northern part of town relayed information to VC/NVA firing units. Within the defensive parameter, six young women were found with radio transmitters concealed in their brassieres. Accused of relaying information to enemy gun crews, they were tied up and left in "an impact area where NVA artillery subsequently killed them."[6]

Along with the encirclement and isolation, the continuous shelling, and the repeated attacks with infantry and armor on An Lộc, the lack of food, water, blood, medications and sanitation supplies gradually worsened the suffering of the common people and the soldiers. One officer turned writer described the situation:

> the suffering was as long as Highway 13 from An Lộc to Chơn Thành.... Highway 13, a road of white bones on red earth the color of blood, a road with anonymous graves scattered along Tàu Ô and Tân Khải, streams turned red from the earth and human blood.[7]

War was brutal, and the communists were more inhumane than most: they never wanted to make the distinction between civilians and soldiers. This was not the first nor the last time that civilians were shelled or shot at. The action was intentional and premeditated, for this inhumane behavior had happened before, if not condoned by their leaders, during any armed encounter involving communist soldiers. They either hid behind civilians using them as shields or just gunned them down if they tried to escape.[8] Far from being the people's defenders, they shot them point blank without pity.

During the first attack on An Lộc, an enemy T-54 tank rolled into town, stopped in front of the Catholic Church and opened fire with its cannon and guns on women and children attending a prayer service, killing 100 people. Running out of ammunition, it then withdrew to the city square where the tank crew put up a white flag.[9]

The North Vietnamese made no attempt to win the hearts and minds of the South Vietnamese civilians. On the contrary, they just wanted to punish them for not supporting the revolution. They showed a callous disregard for the plight of civilians running away from them; their goal was to terrorize the population and to force them back into the besieged cities where they would become additional burden for ARVN defenders.[10]

In the face of violent and repeated shelling and in despair, townspeople just dug deeper and buried themselves into tunnels deeper in the ground. They had returned to a kind of prehistoric life living in tunnels and burrows, scared, hungry, starving, and eating whatever they could put their hands on: some rice, canned food, whatever soldiers would share with them. And the town was no better than its citizens; it was smashed by bombs and mortars and pulverized into pieces. It lay breathless and lifeless. Not even a cat or dog dared running around. Even birds somehow avoided flying across town. Did they instinctively know something? There was no noise, except for that of bombs, artillery shells, and crew-served or individual guns.

> No trace of human life was left on the face of earth. Like a giant termite that lives under a layer of dirt, the town was buried in bunkers deep in the earth, the deeper the better.... The shelling so filled the sky that death was every-

where, the dead bodies scattered like weeds. Death became something natural.... People died in An Lộc. All of humanity died in An Lộc.[11]

Aerial Resupply

With Highway 13 blocked by units of the NVA 7th Division south of An Lộc and the loss of Quản Lợi airstrip, the town was cut off from the rest of the country and left without a fixed-wing airstrip. Besides, the NVA, having gained control of the high ground overlooking An Lộc, could deliver with precision shells and mortars into the town or aim at incoming aircraft. There would be no more supplies or reinforcements brought in by land until Highway 13, the lifeblood of the province, was reopened and secured. With a population of 15,000, the town would need 200 tons of supplies a day including 140 tons of ammunition, 36 tons of rice and 20 tons of water. The requirement would increase as the siege progressed and as nearby refugees poured into An Lộc. The resupply mission became the critical element for the defense and survival of the town.

Since the center of town was subjected to a rain of fire from the north and west, the resupply zone was moved to the open field on the south side of the town. Between 7 and 12 April, all supply missions were flown by Vietnamese Air Force Chinook CH-47 helicopters, which were greeted by mortars and crew-served machine guns. The helicopters hovered over the field long enough to drop their cargo. The use of helicopters ended on 12 April when one VNAF CH-47 Chinook helicopter was shot down by enemy antiaircraft fire. The aircraft was piloted by Major Nguyễn Hữu Nhân, deputy squadron commander; all five crew members were killed. Overall, the VNAF 237th Helicopter squadron lost 10 Chinooks in a two-month period. From 12 to 19 April, supplies were dropped by fixed-wing cargo plane C-123s, which to be accurate had to fly at low altitude. On the 40th of such sorties, a VNAF C-123 was shot down, putting an end to the C-123 mission.[12]

The U.S. then tried to deliver supplies with C-130 planes using the computerized aerial drop system (CARP) at low altitude. Pilots circling over the town were given the go-ahead to descend toward the town by following Highway 13 from the south. Near the soccer field, the computer took over and released the supplies at a prearranged point. The first aircraft sustained minimal damage as it climbed back into the sky. Fifteen minutes later, the second aircraft began its dangerous descent run; by that time, the NVA gunners were ready. As the plane approached its drop point, the gunners fired into the sky in front of the plane, which shuddered under the impact of dozens of bullets. The flight engineer was killed, the navigator and co-pilot wounded. Fire broke out in the cargo when incendiary rounds ignited some of the pallets. While the crew were busy controlling the fire, the automatic release devices failed, and the loadmaster had to step in to cut the ropes by hand. The crates fell to earth, and the wind extinguished the flames. The C-130 climbed upward and returned safely home. After two more sorties, it was realized that the cost of continuing this type of resupply was too high. The Air Force had lost one C-130 and damaged four others. Although the bravery of the pilots was exceptional, it was time to change the plan.[13]

As the resupply efforts failed, the defenders suffered from shortage of food, water, and ammunition. The NVA used the occasion to call ARVN troops to desert. But the Air Force continued their drops at low altitude with a poor delivery rate. Of 845 tons delivered, only 45 tons fell inside the South Vietnamese perimeter. The Air Force then tried to drop supplies at high altitude using the HALO (high altitude, low opening) method that allowed a precise delivery of goods with minimal losses. However, the chutes failed to open in time, causing pallets to smash into the ground or to drift to the enemy side. Malfunctions were traced to Vietnamese packers who did not have the technical experience to handle the sophisticated packing technique. The Air Force had to revert to low-altitude delivery on 23 April during daytime, then nighttime on 26 April to avoid anti-aircraft artillery.

At night, delivery was difficult because the many signal lights and fires confused the crews looking for a small drop zone under intense enemy fire. Putting up huge signal lights could only invite enemy ground fire as well as anti-aircraft fire. Besides, any type of signal light, no matter how short a period it was used, attracted enemy ordnance. Also, during night drops, ARVN recovery teams had difficulty locating the pallets once they landed on the ground. If signal lights were attached to the pallets to allow for easy detection, they attracted defenders as well as enemies, causing wild firefights in the middle of the night.[14] If defenders needed the supplies, so did their enemies. Besides, the less-than-optimal resupply program caused some troops to fear for shortage. The frightened individuals tended to believe that relief would never come, and "personal survival became a dominant thought in a confused situation with deteriorating discipline." Once they recovered the supply pallets, some of them acting out of desperation and indiscipline refused to turn over the supplies to the central authorities. The ground situation was resolved only once the resupply problem was solved and discipline was reestablished.[15]

The resupply mission was not only difficult; it was risky and dangerous despite the many brave efforts of the Air Force and the ground recovery teams. Colonel Miller in his bunker wrote sarcastically in his daily journal,

VIII. The Siege

"At the close of this writing, the Air force just dropped a C-130 load one kilometer north of my location in the lap of Charlie." General Hollingsworth complained, "Less than thirty percent was recoverable by friendly forces.... The system seems to be going from bad to worse."[16] Frustration was everywhere—in the air and on the ground. As the resupply team intensified its effort, it seemed to harm rather than help the defenders' cause. This was exemplified by the story of a VC officer who during the interrogation process after being caught on the east side of the town requested a can of fruit cocktail. He explained that he had been dining on fruit cocktail since American drops had been recovered from his unit. A U.S. adviser who was present during the interrogation and was subsisting on brackish water, canned fish and rice found the request extremely depressing.[17]

The savior of An Lộc defenders turned out to be the U.S. 347 Tactical Airlift Wing, which used C-130 airplanes that flew over 10,000 feet to avoid the dense and precise anti-aircraft artillery. They also developed and perfected the HALO system during which parachutes were partially deployed in the beginning to slow the fall rate to 130 feet per second. A timing mechanism deployed the chutes fully at 10 or 20 meters above ground. The Army sent 76 packers from the 549th Quartermasters Aerial Resupply Company in Okinawa who corrected major problems and instigated new procedures, which rapidly improved the quality of aerial resupply.

Results were not always pretty (rice bags and cans of fruit broke open), but the hungry soldiers scooped them off the ground and ate them. On one occasion, a one-ton pallet of fruit landed on top of one of the few operational jeeps in town, crushing it completely. Luckily no one was hurt. General Hưng's troops later received 90 percent of all the airdrops (2,735 out of 2,984 tons of supplies) from 4 May until 25 June when aircraft could finally land. With a normal airdrop, less than one-third of the pallets delivered arrived at destination: the rest was either lost to the enemy or damaged. High explosives and medical supplies could not adapt to this technique. The violent impact with the ground could cause ammunition to explode and fragile medical supplies to break apart.[18]

Besides, these airdrops were dangerous to the defenders. The force of each pallet of ammunition or food reaching the ground could exceed two to four tons. The drop, which began as a tiny dot in the sky, could reach the ground in 30 seconds and crush a couple of defensive sites and bury defenders in their own foxholes if the chutes failed to open in time before the pallet hit the ground.

By 8 May, the resupply problem seemed to have been solved: of the 88 tons dropped, 68 were recovered, 19 tons lost to malfunctions, and only one ton fell into the enemy's hands. The TRAC commander finally could turn his attention to other matters.

In the beginning, each unit dispatched its own soldiers to collect its share of food and ammunitions. Some troops came early, others late, resulting in an uneven collection and distribution of food and supplies, which in turn led to arguments and fights. Colonel Bùi Đức Điềm had to step in and supervise the distribution of supplies because he was the only high-ranking officer available around the drop site. His rank of colonel gave him enough clout to prevent fights between representatives of the different units. In spite of his efforts and because the supply situation had become desperate during the weeks of 16 April and 8 May, firefights had broken out between ARVN units competing for the available pallets. In the end, Colonel Lưỡng from the Airborne Brigade was given the unenviable task of calming down the "hotheads" and reinstituting discipline because his unit was the closest to the drop site and no one would dare to argue or fight against a paratrooper. To supervise the collection and distribution of supplies also meant being exposed and the risk of being killed by incoming enemy shells or crushed by a fast-falling pallet of food or ammunition.

People congratulated each other for one feat or another. One could congratulate oneself, although at that battlefield, I had witnessed people who, pretending to be mute and deaf, kept working in the midst of falling bombs or whizzing shells, like Colonel Điềm or a certain communication corporal named Lê Văn Sáu. One could see the latter, whether day or night, throughout the duration of the An Lộc battle, and right after a bout of shelling had ceased, climbing over this or that electricity pole to reattach a telephone line severed by a shell or a blast. Without his admirable dedication, it would have been impossible for the different units to communicate with and support each other during the critical moments leading to enemy attacks.

It was regrettable that no person of authority had slipped into President Thiệu's hand a National Order Medal to hang on Colonel Bùi Đức Điềm's shoulders or a Medal of Valor for Corporal Lê Văn Sáu's shoulders. These unselfish men truly deserved these medals. This is not to say that the others did not: they all deserved it for the simple fact of having hung on in their foxholes and tunnels during the worst shelling and brutal attacks in Vietnam War history.

The Second Attack

On 18 April, COSVN launched its second attack on An Lộc with tanks and infantry, during which its troops, while suffering greatly from stubborn

VIII. The Siege

ARVN ground resistance and air attacks, also caused some setback to the ARVN airborne units. The arrival of ARVN elite troops having raised defenders' hope made them better fighters. The establishment of a safe LZ not only allowed the evacuation of the wounded, but also brought in a stream of supplies and reinforcement troops. The latter, whether large or small, changed the prospect of the battlefield. There was nothing more stimulating and comforting than seeing fresh troops arriving, wounded friends being evacuated and ammunition and food rolling in. Troops from all units felt reenergized and stronger in their fighting positions.[19]

On 19 April, the second day of the second COSVN attack on An Lộc, the NVA/VC massively shelled An Lộc and the positions occupied by the 3rd Airborne Artillery unit and the 6th ARVN Airborne Battalion on Windy Hill, Hill 169, and Srok Ton Cui Hill. The brunt of the attacks came from the 275th Regiment of the VC 5th Division and the 141st Regiment of the NVA 7th Division.

Once the NVA artillery had stopped firing, infantry and enemy tanks stormed Windy Hill from the north and northeast. They were determined to destroy the last artillery guns on Windy Hill that had provided fire support to the besieged town since all other artillery pieces in An Lộc and Quản Lợi Airfield had been destroyed by NVA attacks. Second Lieutenant Trần Đại Chiên opened fire when the tanks arrived within 50-meter range. Two tanks were destroyed, and the enemy retreated in panic. The enemy resumed artillery fire on the hill, then attacked again supported by the two remaining tanks. The paratroopers destroyed these tanks but had to disperse under heavy fire. That night, all six 105 mm howitzers belonging to the airborne unit on Windy Hill were annihilated, and the artillery ammunition store—close to 1,000 shells—was hit and blew up, sending up flames and sparks that lit up the night.

The NVA during this attack on Bình Long Province had progressively neutralized all ARVN artillery guns. They first seized the firebase protecting Lộc Ninh in early April, then destroyed the artillery unit at Hùng Tâm and at Quản Lợi Airfield. The attack on An Lộc on 13–14 April caused the destruction of all the town's artillery units. On 16 April, an ammunition storage area at Lai Khê was indirectly hit, causing the destruction of 8,000 rounds of ammunition for 105 mm and 155 mm howitzers as well as many artillery batteries. The destruction of the last six artillery tubes on Windy Hill on 19 April left the defenders with no artillery unit for a potential counterattack. This was about the time that Colonel Miller had an argument with General Hung about launching a counteroffensive on the north end of the town.[20]

Attacks continued into the night with infantry and tanks after the 150-

meter-high Windy Hill was almost flattened by multiple rounds of NVA shelling. Although the troops of the 6th Airborne Battalion fought back valiantly and repulsed many waves of infantry attacks, by early morning their stronghold was overwhelmed. Lieutenant Chiên, heavily wounded, remained behind to cover the retreat of his platoon. He threw his last grenade toward them but died under a hail of enemy bullets. His brother, a battalion commander, was also killed in Quảng Trị that same year.

Major Phạm Kim Bằng, deputy commander of the battalion, along with his remaining troops pulled back and were able to reassemble at the forward commanding post of Lieutenant Colonel Lê Văn Ngọc, deputy commander of the airborne brigade on Hill 169. As enemy turned their artillery guns toward Hill 169, Colonel Lưỡng ordered troops on Hill 169 to withdraw to An Lộc.

The second wing of the 6th Airborne Battalion under the command of Lieutenant Colonel Nguyễn Văn Đỉnh at Srok Ton Cui Hill fared even worse. Attacked by overwhelming forces, it had to open a blood road to pull back to the southeast on the left side of the Bé River. After suffering from multiple ambushes and attacks on their withdrawal path, the remaining 106 men including Lieutenant Colonel Đỉnh, the battalion commander, and 14 artillery men were picked up and ferried to Lai Khê. Small groups of stragglers and survivors were later able to stream back to friendly lines in An Lộc and further south to Chơn Thành and Lai Khê.[21] The 6th Airborne Battalion suffered greatly as it lost half of its forces, more than 200 troops dead or lost in action and hundreds wounded.

On the night of 20–21 April, under attack by two NVA regiments, the wing under Lieutenant Colonel Lê Văn Ngọc on Hill 169 was also attacked and with 150 troops remaining was ordered to pull back to An Lộc along the same path the 8th Battalion took a few days earlier.

Thus all the high elevations southeast of An Lộc were again under communist control. However, the NVA units were not strong enough to dislodge the whole airborne brigade out of the highway south of town. Under the bright and experienced command of Colonel Lê Quang Lưỡng, and leaders like Lieutenant Colonels Lê Văn Ngọc, Văn Bá Ninh, and Nguyễn Chí Hiếu, the brigade was able to protect the highway-turned-runway for U.S. Chinooks and VNAF helicopters to supply and evacuate the wounded until the end of the battle, albeit with some interruptions.

The NVA 7th Division, although still holding on to the area around Tàu Ô Falls, was ordered to send its 141st Regiment to the southeast of An Lộc to put pressure on the airborne units in the area. What worried General Hưng most was the news from the Technical Company of the 5th ARVN Division advising him that the F-6 and 275th Regiments of the NVA 5th Division after being reinforced in the highland area had returned to An Lộc; besides, the NVA 469th Sapper and the 208th Artillery and 271st Anti-aircraft Regiment/COSVN from the Quản Lợi Airfield had also moved down to Sóc Trào and Hương Thanh Hamlets about five to six kilometers northeast of Windy Hill.

As civilian casualties kept mounting and the devastation and misery of the people in An Lộc were laid bare, the International Red Cross on 20 April asked for a 24-hour cease-fire to evacuate the wounded. The communists, true to their un-humanitarian and criminal behavior, refused. Not only had they destroyed the town and killed civilians and soldiers indiscriminately, but they also refused to allow the evacuation of the wounded and critically ill civilians. Madame Nguyễn Thị Bình, chief VC negotiator at Paris, declared that no truce was possible and that the attack would go on.

By nightfall of 20 April, the attacks had subsided. While the attack against the airborne went well for the NVA, for three full days the 9th NVA/VC Division had thrown everything they had against the besieged town and its tired defenders—shells, mortars, tanks, and repeated infantry assaults—without major success. The defenders held firm. Not only was it a brutal and bloody physical battle, but it was also a deadly one: wounded soldiers and civilians had nowhere to go, medications and hospital supplies were limited, surgeons could only control the bleeding and perform amputations before evacuating the sick ones to major military centers. But the hardened resistance turned out to be a great moral victory for the defenders. By setting a 20 April deadline to conquer the town, the NVA forced the defenders to fight, and they did. They gave everything they had; relentlessly and almost without any break, they came back to their positions and repulsed one brutal attack after another. When the deadline passed and the defenders still held the town, the enemy seemed less invincible. Another prediction had failed to come true. For the attackers, it was a true letdown. For the second time in a row, they had failed in their job.[22]

On 21 April, the communists continued their daily deadly shelling, concentrating on the southern sector held by the 1st Airborne Brigade.

On 22 April, troops supported by two T-54 and two PT-76 tanks attacked the 8th Airborne Battalion on the southwestern sector of An Lộc. ARVN troops destroyed all four tanks. They also guided a C-130 Spectre to attack a column of five tanks approaching from the south. All tanks were destroyed. Another column of three tanks attacked the 5th Airborne Battalion in the southwest sector with infantry support. ARVN troops again destroyed these three tanks.

After the 20 April deadline had passed, the communists declared they would control the town by 1 May. They decided to launch another violent attack on the night of 30 April in an effort to celebrate the 1 May International Labor Day in town. They must have been desperate to wage a major attack at night. After a powerful artillery preparation, enemy troops launched deadly attacks against the northern and western sectors. Again the defenders bravely fought back without giving away any inch of the terrain and finally forced the attackers to withdraw by 11:00 hours on 1 May.[23]

Every day and night, enemy shells and mortars kept exploding without a break at a rate of more than 1,000 units a day causing injuries to troops and civilians and further damaging the town. Everyone knew that a relief wing would be coming from the south and another attack would be coming shortly, and that their lives were hanging on a thread, for anyone could be hit by a fragment of mortars or shells or an errant bullet, or a pallet of supplies coming down from the sky without a deployed parachute. But they were still willing to die while defending An Lộc as their commander had asked them. With a leader willing to die protecting the town, they too were willing to sacrifice themselves. How could foreigners understand South Vietnamese troops fighting in Vietnamese battlefields? It is sad to know that some uninformed foreigners had written falsehoods about the Vietnam War. Some of them later retracted and apologized for their writings or sayings about Vietnam. These people at least still have a sense of right and wrong.

Another facet of the war had been exposed during this battle. Western and local newspapers had reported NVA/VC soldiers being chained to their weapons or inside their tanks. Even General Hollingsworth had personally observed the remains of one NVA soldier whose "hands were tied to his .51 caliber machine gun." The western world had reacted in horror to these stories.[24] They realized that on one side ARVN soldiers freely fought for their freedom while the NVA/VC were fighting for a war imposed and dictated by the communists in Hanoi. Whether the individual NVA soldiers volunteered to be chained or whether NVA/VC officers found it necessary to chain their men to force them to fight, they knew they would face a stubborn resistance from ARVN soldiers.

Shell Shocked

During the three weeks from 18 April to 5 May—when the third attack against An Lộc began—two events that eventually affected the aura and the future of General Lê Văn Hưng's military career occurred. They have been brushed upon briefly above and are worth mentioning in detail here.

VIII. The Siege

The first event related to the LZ, which had been established and secured by the 8th Airborne Battalion under Lieutenant Colonel Văn Bá Ninh. It was an effective way of transferring out wounded troops and receiving fresh troops and thus had brought hope to many defenders.

While they were bracing for the next round of enemy attack, one day toward the end of April 1972, one officer wearing the rank of colonel with a mild injury that had already been treated and healed and an artillery major showed up at the LZ to try to get onto one of the evacuation helicopters. Security troops guarding the LZ seeing a colonel dared not intervene, although they contacted Lieutenant Colonel Văn Bá Ninh who then reported to Colonel Lê Quang Lưỡng. The latter drove right away to the LZ and inquired about the officer's rank and wound condition. The wounded officer stated that he was Colonel Mạch Văn Trường, commander of the ARVN 8th Regiment/5th Division. Then Colonel Lê Quang Lưỡng gently asked the officer, realizing the nature of the wound, "Do you really want to be evacuated for such a small wound?"

He immediately called General Hưng to inform him about the situation, following which I was ordered to go to the LZ to receive the "wounded" colonel and major and take them back to the divisional forward command post. Of course, General Hưng gave them hell. It just happened that a day earlier, he had ordered Colonel Trường back to work after he had convalesced more than a week for a minor shoulder injury. Colonel Trường, who apparently had developed "cold feet" after witnessing the barrage of enemy rockets and mortars, after returning to his unit had decided to get out of the front. But Trường turned out to be General Minh's protégé. By doing his duty and preventing him from flying out, General Hưng accidentally stepped on the toes of General Minh. That first incident of "pretending to be sick to escape from the front line" was well known to many people, especially Lieutenant Colonel Văn Bá Ninh (later promoted to colonel).

A second incident linked to that same protégé would later land General Hưng in the hot seat with General Minh. The latter would deal him many blows later that ultimately affected his overall career.

IX

The War Game in Chơn Thành

Besides Lộc Ninh and An Lộc, a third battlefield took place at Chơn Thành that summer of 1972; although not a lot of people had paid attention to it, that battle was to some degree as crucial as the one in An Lộc. Chơn Thành was located at equal distance (30 kilometers) between An Lộc in the north and Lai Khê, the 5th ARVN Divisional Headquarters, in the south. All these three provincial towns were connected by Highway 13.

The sideshow battle in Chơn Thành allowed General Minh to battle in wits against VC General Trần Văn Trà for the purpose of decreasing the enemy's pressure on An Lộc. Not recognizing this is failing to understand the dynamics of the An Lộc battle.

The Tàu Ô and Bàu Bàng Choke Points

In the three weeks between the first attack on An Lộc on 13 April 1972 and the replacement of Colonel Miller by Colonel Ulmer, the ARVN 21st Infantry Division under Major General Nguyễn Vĩnh Nghi had moved from the Mekong Delta to relieve the 1st Airborne Brigade of Colonel Lê Quang Lưỡng, which had been sent to An Lộc. The 21st Division with its three regiments, the 31st, 32nd and 33rd, along with the 9th Cavalry Battalion had been assigned the job of removing the blockade on Highway 13 north of Chơn Thành initiated by the NVA 7th Division. The blockade was made of many smaller choke points from different units of this large division. The choke point consisted of a system of foxholes and tunnels connected together for better support and protection—troops called it a tripod—in this case a system of three foxhole units and tunnels blocking the highway and both

IX. The War Game in Chơn Thành

sides along the highway for over 10 to 20 kilometers in length. In principle, an ARVN "entrenched fortification" or the NVA choke point, if protected by a sturdy fortification, would require a three times larger force to uproot it. General Minh was using the case of An Lộc as an example where attacking forces were three times larger than defending forces.

The entire ARVN 21st Infantry Division arrived at the III Corps and MR3 on 10 April 1972 before completing its move two days later. Major General Nguyễn Vĩnh Nghi placed his forward command post at the Lai Khê base along with the Forward Command Post of the III Corps. He moved his 31st Regiment to Suối Tre six kilometers northwest of Lai Khê and kept the 33rd Regiment at Lai Khê for reserve. He then moved his 32nd Regiment to Chơn Thành on 11 April. The choke points on Highway 13 from Lai Khê to Chơn Thành had been removed by the 1st Airborne Brigade dislodging the 141st and 209th Regiments of the NVA 7th Division, which had been augmented by the independent 101st Regiment and anti-tank and anti-aircraft artillery units located at Bàu Bàng from 9 to 12 April. Later, General Nghi was told to improve highway safety from Bình Dương to Bến Cát District and from Lai Khê to base Vân Đồn, six kilometers north of Lai Khê within 10 days from 14 to 24 April, but to leave alone the section between Vân Đồn and Chơn Thành. General Minh theorized that within 10 days, the COSVN would set up a new system of choke points on that unchecked stretch of Highway 13.

Sure enough, that stretch on Highway 13 was cut off on 24 April when the VC shot a civilian bus with a B-40 rocket, killing and injuring many passengers, and established a choke point for the second time at Bàu Bàng, 10 kilometers north of Lai Khê and six kilometers north of Vân Đồn base, where a battalion of the ARVN 33rd Regiment was located. The choke point was strong and manned by the NVA 101st Regiment, air artillery and anti-tank units, and two battalions of the NVA 209 and 165 Regiments. General Minh knew that the ARVN 21st Division with its three regiments, even after dislodging the choke point at Bàu Bàng, would not be strong enough to free the whole Highway 13 from Chơn Thành to An Lộc. Being a cautious general, he asked for reinforcement from the JGS/RVNAF, which latter gave him the 3rd Airborne Brigade. A new strategy was used by the airborne unit to dislodge these choke points.

Size-wise, the airborne forces sent to free the check points were only one-third of the size of the enemy forces. It was only later that one could understand General Nguyễn Văn Minh's strategy. His goal was to hold down with a small elite force the bulk of enemy forces in order to annihilate them with artillery while pretending to fight in order to assess enemy strength and to pull in more enemy forces to Chơn Thành to relieve the pressure on An Lộc.

The new offensive, called "Toàn Thắng 72-D," began on 24 April with the 1st, 2nd, and 3rd Battalions of the ARVN 3rd Airborne Brigade under the command of Lieutenant Colonel Trương Vĩnh Phước (shortly thereafter promoted to colonel) and the support of the 31st Infantry Regiment, a reconnaissance company of the ARVN 21st Division and the 5th Armored Cavalry. This was the second attack on Tàu-Ô stream by an airborne brigade, but the first to go to Tân Khai hamlet. In reality, in both cases, the first attack using the 1st Airborne Brigade by Colonel Lê Quang Lưỡng and the second using the 3rd Airborne Brigade by Colonel Trương Vĩnh Phước, the goal was not to uproot enemy forces at Tàu-Ô stream but to hold them in check. Or, to put it in simpler terms, it was a reconnaissance operation into the lion's den at the brigade level. If this operation could dislodge the checkpoint, it would be good; if not, General Minh could still figure out the strength of enemy forces in the area.

It should be remembered that General Nguyễn Văn Minh upon graduating from the Dalat Military Academy—the Vietnamese equivalent of West Point—went into the Airborne Group and remained there until he became captain before being appointed head of the Operations Bureau in the Saigon-Cholon Sub-Zone under Colonel Dương Văn Minh (who later became general and caused the collapse of the Republic of Vietnam twice). The latter had pacified the Bình Xuyên of Bảy Viễn in the Cho Lon and Rừng Sát area (1954–1955). To leaders like Colonel Lê Quang Lưỡng and Trương Vĩnh Phước, General Nguyễn Văn Minh was their elder; and to sacrifice their lives for their elder was no big deal. That was the noble tradition of airborne officers.

With two brigades in action (1st Brigade in An Lộc and 3rd on Highway 13), the ARVN Airborne Division had to set up a forward command post for Brigadier General Hồ Trung Hậu, deputy commander of the Airborne Division, at the headquarters of the 32nd Regiment at Chơn Thành to direct and support. In principle, General Nguyễn Vĩnh Nghi would be the commander of the forces designed to uproot the blockade on Highway 13. But in the Toàn Thắng 72-D offensive, the forward command post controlled and directed the 3rd Airborne Brigade and the 5th Cavalry Battalion. The commander of the cavalry battalion was Colonel Trương Hữu Đức, who died in action during the uprooting of the first blockade with the 1st Airborne Brigade and was promoted general on 13 April.[1]

On 24 April, the 31st Infantry Regiment, after being pulled out of a highland battlefield, was airlifted from Suối Tre to three kilometers southeast of Tàu-Ô Creek on the side of Highway 13 to support the 3rd Airborne Brigade in its attack. The following day, the 2nd Airborne Battalion was airlifted to the eastern side of Highway 13 between Tàu-Ô Creek and Tân Khai hamlet to conduct an attack on these two targets. As soon as helicopters landed, the battalion under the command of Lieutenant Colonel Lê Văn Mạnh was met by enemy mortars and anti-aircraft shells but proceeded in its attack.

On 26 April, the 1st Airborne Battalion under Major Lê Hồng was dropped on the western side of Highway 13 to attack and occupy Đức Vinh Hamlet, five kilometers north of Tân Khai. At that time, the NVA thought that General Nghi's forces would attack Tàu-Ô Creek instead of north of it at Đức Vinh. Therefore, their blockade at Tàu-Ô Creek and Tân Khai was sturdy and manned by the 209th and 165th Regiments of the NVA 7th Division along with anti-aircraft and anti-tank artillery units. They left Đức Vinh Hamlet without defense. The encounter at Tàu-Ô Creek and Tân Khai was strong, while it was only mild at Đức Vinh. The 2nd Airborne Battalion had to set up a temporary base in the area of operation with a few 105 mm howitzers.

For many days, the 2nd Airborne Battalion conducted many attacks on enemy positions but failed to displace them despite aggressive support from VNAF and USAF airstrikes, including B-52 bombing. Although the NVA suffered major losses, it held tight in its positions. At the Đức Vinh Hamlet, the 1st Airborne Battalion encountered minimal resistance until 2 May, when the enemy launched a full attack with mortars first, followed by infantry attack. According to intelligence reports, the 271st Regiment of the VC 9th Division, which had been reinforced after its losses at An Lộc on 13 April, had been sent to the northwest of Đức Vinh. The 141st Regiment of the NVA 7th Division after collaborating with the F6 and 275 Regiments of the VC 5th Division to attack the ARVN 6th Airborne Battalion at Windy Hill, Hill 169 and Srock Ton Cui from 18 to 21 April, had been returned to the NVA 7th Division and moved to assist the 271st Regiment to attack and destroy the 1st Airborne Battalion. What General Minh had predicted turned out to be true: attack south of An Lộc so that enemy troops were forced to shift its troops south, thereby decreasing the pressure on An Lộc.

With danger looming at Đức Vinh, General Minh ordered Major General Nghi to move his 31st Regiment from the northwest of Chơn Thành to Đức Vinh and at the same time to airlift the 21st Reconnaissance Company to Đức Vinh to support the 2nd Airborne Battalion.

One has to admit that the NVA 7th Division was an elite unit. Not only did it benefit from the sturdiness of the defense system built by the U.S. years ago on both sides of the highway at Tàu-Ô, but it also improved it so that it could withstand the severe bombing of South Vietnamese and U.S. air forces. It also improvised its mobile defense: for example, it organized counterattacks at the levels of companies and battalions and sent its reconnaissance units to closely follow ARVN units, to order artillery bombing on enemy positions, and to ambush and counterattack them. Therefore, the 2nd Airborne Battalion had difficulty in getting close to the blockade area. These events gave General Minh an idea of the strength of the enemy: he knew that his forces were too few to dislodge the NVA, although he believed that the elite airborne unit with the assistance of the air force would be able to uproot enemy forces. However, having only one battalion to fight each target might be too little and too risky. The Tàu-Ô area was held by the 209th Regiment of the NVA 7th Division, plus an anti-aircraft artillery unit with surface-to-air missiles with infrared homing device SA-7, and an anti-tank unit with AT-3 Sagger anti-tank missiles, while the ARVN had only two companies of the 2nd Airborne Battalion with four 105 mm howitzers. At Tân Khai hamlet, the 165th Regiment of the NVA 7th Division and the 271st Regiment of the VC 9th Division faced the two companies of the 2nd Battalion. In each area, NVA forces were three to four times larger than ARVN forces.

War Game

One could see the unconventional or unscripted way General Nguyễn Văn Minh was shifting his troops, only to realize later that a chess game was going on between Generals Minh and Trà along the 60-kilometer axis between Lai Khê and An Lộc, with Chơn Thành being the crucial center. Everyone knew that the destruction of the ARVN 5th Infantry Division of the III Corps stationed at An Lộc required a cutting off of supplies and reinforcement to this division or, more exactly, of its lifeblood: Highway 13. And the ideal place to set up a choke point would be at Tàu-Ô Creek up to Tân Khai hamlet from 15 to 20 kilometers north of Chơn Thành. The town of Chơn Thành controlling the crossroads of Highway 13 that led to An Lộc and Highway 14 leading to the province of Phước Long and Quảng Đức was considered to be the strategic point south of An Lộc.

Both Generals Minh and Trà knew that Chơn Thành was important to the survival or loss of An Lộc. General Minh had always stationed a regiment there to protect the springboard from which to send liberating forces to free An Lộc and to act as a "magnet" for NVA forces to gather so that they could be easily disposed of by artillery and airstrikes. The more they came, the better it would be for the defending forces to neutralize them. But General

IX. The War Game in Chơn Thành 151

Trà did not want to "roast" his troops there. General Minh knew it too; therefore he left the area between Lai Khê and Chơn Thành unguarded from 14 April 1972 onward after the 32nd Regiment of the ARVN 21st Division had moved to Chơn Thành to replace the 1st Airborne Brigade. He only stationed a battalion of the 33rd Regiment at Vân Đồn base six kilometers north of Lai Khê and patiently waited for enemy troops to jump in. COSVN commander General Trần Văn Trà had to act, for he could not leave that section of Highway 13 open for the ARVN 21st Division to use to uproot his blockade at Tàu-Ô Creek and to bring reinforcements to the besieged An Lộc.

When COSVN initiated its first attack on An Lộc from 13 to 16 April as planned, it caught the ARVN off guard, leading to the loss at Lộc Ninh; but soon the attack fizzled because of General Hưng's decisive actions at the Cần Lê Bridge. The second attack on An Lộc from 18 to 21 April was also underwhelming because of General Minh's decisive actions at Chơn Thành as mentioned above. Although COSVN's two consecutive attacks did not secure any major victory, Radio Hanoi still proclaimed that An Lộc had been taken on 18 April. The desire of Hanoi's Military Central Committee was therefore obvious: An Lộc was the main target of the Total Offensive in the summer of 1972, not Kontum or Quảng Trị. And COSVN should not be underestimated.

COSVN was then forced to take over An Lộc at all cost in subsequent attacks even if it had to use its last unit. Therefore, besides reinforcing their units, perfecting their attacks and blocking ARVN reinforcement from Chơn Thành to An Lộc, COSVN mobilized its sapper and artillery units with the intent of destroying the forward command post of the ARVN 5th Division as well as the support center of all the III Corps units at Lai Khê. It also sent a regiment to attack the Tống Lê Chân and Minh Thạnh bases on the Saigon River, held by ranger units about 18 to 25 kilometers southwest of An Lộc so that they could send reinforcement and supplies between the secret zone Dương Minh Châu in Tây Ninh and Zone D at the border of Biên Hòa and Bình Dương Provinces. If in some areas COSVN had achieved some degree of success, the overall plan was no longer well coordinated, causing COSVN to lose the initiative in the Bình Long battlefield from An Lộc to Chơn Thành. It no longer could execute the policies of the Politburo of the Communist Party because of the unorthodox way General Minh shuffled his units.

General Minh, by leaving the section between Vân Đồn Base to Chơn Thành open, forced COSVN to make a choice, and it made the wrong move. Twice, it sent forces to block south of Chơn Thành; twice they had been uprooted. The first time on 4 April, when the NVA launched its first attack on An Lộc, due to strategic need, COSVN had no choice but to block Highway

13 in order to prevent ARVN reinforcement from coming to the rescue from the south. The blockade had been uprooted by the 1st Airborne Brigade from 9 to 11 April from two fronts, one from Lai Khê moving northward and the other from Chơn Thành moving southward. Sandwiched between these two attacks, the NVA 7th Division, the independent 101st Regiment and other supporting units left 200 dead and moved away. On the second occasion, the NVA was forced to settle at Bàu Bàng from 22 April onward. The ARVN 21st Division uprooted them with two frontal attacks like the 1st Airborne Brigade did two weeks earlier. The ARVN 33rd Regiment and the 9th Armored Cavalry attacked from Lai Khê northward, and the 32nd Regiment with a subunit of the 9th Cavalry Battalion attacked from Chơn Thành southward with air force assistance. The ARVN took five days to do the uprooting, causing communist forces to take on major casualties. As a result, COSVN had no more forces to set up another blockade.

The fast and decisive way General Minh maneuvered his troops caught the COSVN by surprise, which resulted in attackers losing their initiative. General Trà was unable to beat General Minh's troop maneuverability, which did not follow the usual ways an army would react when it was being attacked. The first example was the case of the ARVN 21st Division. When it moved from the Mekong Delta to Lai Khê and Chơn Thành on 12 April, General Minh did not use that division to uproot the Tàu-Ô blockade north of Chơn Thành. He instead used the 1st Airborne Brigade to uproot Bàu Bàng (9–11 April) then the Tàu-Ô blockade on 12 April. While the NVA 7th Division was fighting for survival, he pulled the airborne brigade out (13 April) to reinforce An Lộc on 14–15 April. The sudden pullout of the airborne brigade forced the COSVN to move the NVA 141st Regiment of the NVA 7th Division from Tân Khai to An Lộc to join the VC 5th and 9th Divisions in the second attack against An Lộc on 18 April.

In the second example, once the COSVN could not take over An Lộc after two attacks despite controlling Windy Hill and Hill 169, General Minh who was worried that An Lộc could remain endangered sent the 3rd Airborne Brigade to Tàu-Ô and Tân Khai, more importantly to the Đức Vinh Hamlet, south of An Lộc, forcing the COSVN to move the 271st Regiment of the VC 9th Division and the 141st Regiment of the NVA 7th Division, then encircling An Lộc, to Đức Vinh to prevent the airborne brigade from advancing to An Lộc. The pressure exerted by the NVA on An Lộc as a result lessened after the second attack, although the town was still pounded by a thousand mortars and missiles of all kinds each day.

These two examples illustrate General Minh's expert strategy and skill in moving troops. On the An Lộc battlefield, General Trần Văn Trà had been sidestepped by General Nguyễn Văn Minh. Although the battle had been going on for three weeks from 22 April to 11 May, General Minh had not thrown his reserve forces into the battlefield. Why? First, because he trusted General Lê Văn Hưng's and Colonel Lê Quang Lưỡng's skill and ability to hold An Lộc with the air support of U.S. and Vietnamese Air Forces. Second, after sending the 3rd Airborne Brigade into the enemy's den at Tàu-Ô stream then to Tân Khai hamlet to have an idea of the overall strength of enemy forces, he was ready to commit the 21st ARVN Division to relieve the pressure on and to free An Lộc. He might wait for a few days to receive additional elite troops to reinforce the 21st Division before making the final move toward An Lộc.

Up to now, one has been able to visualize the Bình Long battlefield as seen by two combat veterans, the III Corps and MR3 and COSVN commanders. General Trần Văn Trà, having by then come to know his main opponent on this battlefield, General Nguyễn Văn Minh, had become more circumspect and calculative and did not launch any rush attack like the first two times, except for using the NVA 7th Division to block the 3rd Airborne Brigade from Tàu-Ô stream to Tân Khai and Đức Vinh.

In An Lộc, there were small firefights as defenders slowly pushed back attackers who, unable to withdraw, had hung on closely to defendants' positions in order to avoid air attacks. Enemy tanks that had not been destroyed in the previous attack had melted into the occupied neighborhood, hiding by being well camouflaged behind destroyed houses or large vacant units. They knew well not to move around unless necessary; otherwise they would be destroyed by AC-130 Spectre gunships.

It was understood that COSVN had used this lull time to reinforce its troops, stabilize its positions, and move ammunition to get ready for the final stage of taking down An Lộc.

X

Breaking the Siege

The battles were brutal and deadly in all three fronts in the Fiery Red Summer of 1972: Quảng Trị, Kontum, and An Lộc. General Abrams said,

> What you've got here, in my opinion, is a go-for-broke thing by the North Vietnamese. And they've thrown everything they've got in it.... It's just an all-out onslaught, and the losses on both sides—I mean, *he's* [the NVA] losing tanks like he didn't care about having any more, *and* people, *and* artillery, *and* equipment. The level of violence, and the level of brutality, in this whole thing right now is [*sic*] on a scale not before achieved in the war in Vietnam.[1]

The LAW Rocket Launcher

In An Lộc, General Hưng and Colonel Ulmer who had come to the same conclusion had requested the U.S. Air Force to strike some Arc Light boxes on secret locations and relay stations along previously known communist infiltration routes from the Cambodian border. They also included bridges built by truckers to haul tree trunks from the forests between north of Bình Long and Kratie. Spectre gunships were requested every night, while during the daytime, Vietnamese aircraft continuously patrolled the area.

The makeshift helicopter landing path on Highway 13 south of town had been well protected by the 8th Airborne Battalion. Vietnamese and U.S. helicopters continued to evacuate wounded troops—usually from shrapnel fragments—or deliver needed supplies. Aircraft hit by missiles or shells, although not significant in numbers, could occur with each arrival or departure from An Lộc. Yet, supplies came in everyday, and wounded soldiers were evacuated almost daily.

Of course, one should congratulate Colonel Lê Quang Lưỡng and his troops, but also the brave pilots, Vietnamese and American, who, unselfishly forgetting their own lives, came in and out of hell like taking their daily meals. They were brave—very brave. How about the rest of the troops—main and special forces, rangers, PF and RF? Everyone was waiting for an attack to come from the south although the timing was not known. Each personal foxhole was dug deeper and became better protected by the addition of newer sandbags. There was nothing sophisticated about the defensive front: no steel, no concrete—just these old, cheap sandbags to defend against the million-ruble artillery pieces, tanks, and sophisticated shells and mortars. They each carried a jug of water and a few bags of rice, although dry U.S. rations, whenever available, would be much better because each of these rations contained four cigarettes. Each puff of cigarette they inhaled would inflate their lungs, brighten up their faces, and render them more alert, energized; they then clutched their guns ready to stand guard, day and night, or take a swipe at their enemies. That alone would not be enough until they were able to secure an M-72 rocket launcher, which was widely provided to An Lộc defenders at that time. Then, once a tank was detected coming toward them and pushed by an irresistible force, they sprung out of their foxholes to take a shot at it: hit or miss, alive or dead, they did not care. If they could just shoot at a tank, death would be soothing. That was the spirit of the An Lộc defenders.

The warhead of the LAW (light anti-tank weapon) contained an explosive charge shaped to direct a jet of high-velocity molten copper capable of burning through inches of steel plate. It had become a fairy tale or a rare truth in the history of the battle against tanks by the people and troops of An Lộc. One is talking about the people and troops because the military sector—under the order of Colonel Trần Văn Nhựt—during that period of time had set up a recruitment center for popular and regional forces. People within drafting age could sign up for recruitment while youths were also willing to bear arms against the enemy. That was the golden point for Colonel Trần Văn Nhựt. As for the tale of the M-72 launcher, not only had troops used this weapon to destroy tanks, but popular forces and even laypeople had also run behind troops to shoot tanks.

General Hưng, after the first attack, had ordered the creation and training of "tank-destroying teams," which roamed every corner, dead end, and back alley within the town and chose the most propitious ambush sites to destroy enemy tanks.[2] Even I was addicted to the M-72 launcher. On 18 April during the second attack wave, one tank just happened to drive right in front of the divisional forward command center. As the latter was unmarked, the enemy was not aware of it. And when it tried to turn around, General Hưng took a grenade and threw it at the tank, barely denting it. Colonel Lê Nguyên Vỹ who was running behind took his M-72 launcher, aimed, and shot it, half destroying it; as it limped forward for a few more yards, a ranger shot it the second time causing it to burn.

As I ran behind and lost the chance to take a shot, I picked up the launcher Colonel Vỹ had just used—whatever metal it was made of, I did not know, but it was white—brought it home and, like the troops, whenever I was idle, sawed the launcher into nice, thin bracelet-shaped rings that were smoothed and inscribed with words to be used for a souvenir. Hundreds of soldiers wore these bracelets and later gave them to their girlfriends as war bracelets. As for me, I kept them for myself. They are priceless because they were fashioned out of the M-72 launcher Colonel Vỹ used to shoot the above tank; I carried them with me for the last four decades through thick and thin.

What I have written above depicts the indomitable spirit of the troops of all units of the army, policemen, local people and regional forces who were willing to defend An Lộc against the communists. That spirit soared to the highest level due to two main reasons: General Hưng's declaration to defend An Lộc to death and the efficacy of the M-72 rocket launcher that had been introduced to An Lộc. ARVN troops refused to run away from the battlefield because if their general stood there to defend the town, they too had to spring out of their foxholes to shoot tanks. It should be remembered that if the fanciest armaments fell into the hands of feeble or weak officers or soldiers, they would become useless tools, whereas in the hand of willing and dedicated men, they could be deadly weapons. Whether U.S. authorities and the press were aware of these factors or not is not known.

As mentioned earlier, the M-72 launcher had not been found to be effective in Lang Vei, Bến Hét, during Lâm Sơn 719, and in Lộc Ninh. But when used at short-range, and if aimed at the sides or rear of the tanks where the armor was thinner and not sloped, the launcher was extremely effective, especially in An Lộc. Even in the case of the tank shot by Colonel Vỹ as described above, it required two shots fired from the rear to destroy a T-54 tank. This means that the M-72 launcher was not 100 percent effective and that troops needed to remain composed and persistent in order to destroy a tank.

The morale of ARVN troops combined with the use of U.S. guns and bombs had brought victory to An Lộc, a small town without good and modern fortifications where less than 8,000 defenders had won the battle against a three-times-bigger elite army. This victory had even surprised top world strategists like Sir Thomas Thompson of England and General Moshe Dayan of Israel. And naturally, General Trần Văn Trà could not even predict that the third communist attack on An Lộc—that he had planned and was the commanding officer of—would eventually fail.

The Third Attack

The decisive battle was so brutal and vicious that no defenders of any city anywhere in the world from World War I to World War II had ever suffered like the troops and people of An Lộc during this third wave of attack that began on 11 May 1972. This includes the city of Guernica of Spain[3] that was bombed by German and Italian air forces during World War II and became Picasso's immortal painting in the previous century. The exception may be Nagasaki and Hiroshima.

On 9 May, just a few days after the 3rd Airborne Brigade pulled out of Đức Vinh, Tân Khai and Tàu-Ô, although enemy troops were still holding the blockade points in these areas and reinforced the artillery and anti-aircraft guns at the An Lộc battlefield, a Chinook transporting reinforcement troops to 2/8 Battalion was shot down during landing. Reinforcement was thus interrupted. All day long, the airfield was shelled continuously preventing any aircraft from landing. The emergency crisis worsened because the town was also shelled twice as usual.

On 10 May, General Cao Văn Viên, general chief of staff of the JGS/RVNAF (general chief of staff of the Joint General Staff of the Republic of Vietnam Armed Forces) flew to Lai Khê—the main base of the ARVN 5th Infantry Division and the forward command post of the III Corps and MR3—to meet with General Nguyễn Văn Minh and U.S. adviser General James G. Hollingsworth of the Third Regional Assistance Command or TRAC. Reasons for this meeting included the situation noted above and news extracted from an important POW who was an officer of the reconnaissance battalion of the VC 5th Division and was caught by the 3rd Ranger Brigade of Lieutenant Colonel Nguyễn Văn Biệt at Quản Lợi, east of An Lộc on 6 May. This POW revealed that on 20 and 21 April, the COSVN held several meetings to criticize the various units previously attacking An Lộc and to set up a new attack plan. In the past, because the NVA 9th Division had done poorly and without coordination with the NVA 202nd and 203rd Tank Regiments, the COSVN had lost during these attacks. Therefore, a new attack plan had been drawn up to conquer An Lộc and destroy the ARVN 5th Infantry Division of General Hưng at all costs. The brunt of the attack would be carried by the VC 5th Division with tank units, the 469th Sapper Regiment as well as artillery and anti-aircraft units of the 70th Artillery Division from the north and northeast sides of town. The VC 9th Division along with tanks and artillery units would attack from the west and southwest sides of town. The forces would be positioned as follows:

Main forces:
- 174th Regiment/5th VC Division with one tank unit and a unit of the 429th Sapper Regiment would attack from the north.
- E6th Regiment/5th VC Division with one tank unit and a unit of the 429th Sapper Regiment would attack from the northeast.
- 275th Regiment/5th VC Division would be the reserve troops for this group.

Secondary forces:
- 271st Regiment/9th VC Division with one tank unit from the south at Cổng Xã Cam.
- 272nd Regiment/9th VC Division with one tank unit from the west at Cổng Phú Lố.
- 95C Regiment/9th VC Division as reserve troops.

One should not forget the sophisticated AAA the NVA had brought to the An Lộc battlefield. It began appearing in strength on 16–17 April, and by nightfall on 17 April, the town was ringed on three sides. There were .51 caliber, 23 mm and 37 mm weapons in evidence. On 9 May, the first SA-7 was observed, and several were fired against An Lộc on 11–15 May. At the height of the battle, there were about a dozen weapons in use around the town.

All this AAA significantly affected air support available to the defenders by:
- reducing forward air controllers' (FAC) effectiveness; FAC had to move to higher altitude, causing visual reconnaissance to be less effective;
- reducing close air support effectiveness;
- complicating aerial support resupply; and
- complicating airspace coordination.[4]

Although these hurdles were eliminated on time, resupply to and reinforcement of the troops and evacuation of the wounded decreased in volume for a period of time.

At the 10 May meeting as mentioned above, although ARVN generals did not know the exact time and date of the attack, they had decided to fight against time to bring reinforcement troops to An Lộc. But how? The ARVN had approximately 4,000 troops left to fight against almost two enemy divisions. An attempt to fly in reinforcements by Major Nguyễn Tấn Trọng turned into a disaster as his Chinook plane was hit by dense anti-aircraft fire. The plane burst into flames killing three crew members. The pilot Nguyễn Tấn Trọng and co-pilot were captured by the enemy and released after the 1973 Paris Agreements were signed.[5]

X. Breaking the Siege

Many Arc Light boxes were planned and aimed at the periphery of the town at the time the attack began. Other boxes would be dropped on the enemy's secret zones and on their transportation routes in the surrounding province. The elite 15th Regiment of the ARVN 9th Infantry Division under the command of one of the five best fighters in the southwest Mekong Delta—Lieutenant Colonel Hồ Ngọc Cẩn—with a tank battalion and a 105 mm artillery unit was ordered to move to An Lộc to reinforce it on 11 May 1972.

Although 11 May was recorded as the critical time either to save or destroy An Lộc between the III Corps and MR3 and the COSVN, the final decision about the fate of the town rested in the hands of General Lê Văn Hưng and Colonel Lê Quang Lưỡng, for the simple reason that the arrival of reinforcement troops under the command of Lieutenant Colonel Cẩn and the taking of other measures to relieve the pressure on An Lộc were made two days after the beginning of the attack. On the other hand, General Trà's decision to take An Lộc at all costs and to destroy the ARVN 5th Infantry Division was laid in ruins two days after the communist assault began.

On the night of 10 to 11 May, although it was late and I was not on duty, I did not understand why I could not sleep. I just thrashed and rolled from one side to another in my cot; part of it may be due to the loneliness I had perceived in the night and partly due to the cool air that made me feel afraid. Strangely, I could not hear any rocket or mortar falling down on the perimeter like any previous night. Everything became unusually *quiet*. The quietness before the doom.

Suddenly I woke up because I knew it. I rushed to the communication center of the division and requested the on-duty soldier to give me a hotline to the private residence of Colonel Hoàng Ngọc Lung in Saigon, the chief of staff for intelligence of the JGS/RVNAF (J-2/JGS/RVNAF). From 1958 to 1963, Colonel Lung, then a captain, was the deputy commander of the Intelligence School Cây Mai where I was a 1st lieutenant trainer. Our commanders were consecutively Major Phạm Văn Sơn and Major Hồ Văn Lời. Mr. Hoàng Ngọc Lung presently lives in Virginia, USA. To wake Colonel Lung up at this untimely hour must be an important matter. When I heard his voice over the phone, I immediately said, "Colonel, tonight is the crucial night for An Lộc," and proceeded to give him details of the event, statements of the POW, as well as personal vibes about the frightening silence from midnight until then, exactly 02:35.

He immediately registered the report, agreed with my assessment and told me, "I'll immediately report to the general chief of staff of JGS, Dưỡng. Take it easy, everything will be all right. I wish you a lot of luck."

I felt relieved because Saigon had been advised. I walked up to the opening of our underground bunker and saw a soldier from the 5th Reconnaissance Company and two squads of soldiers protecting the division's commander standing on guard while other soldiers lay on the floor of an isolated house or in the operation room with their guns close by, under their heads or by their sides. The sky was clear with a few rare stars; the moon was barely visible. The ground, which looked dim with flickering lights from a faraway fire, appeared like a desolate and ghostly area. A dark and chilly feeling ran down my spine.

I came back to the mouth of the underground bunker and asked the sentinel, "Anything new, soldier?" "No," he answered, "although I feel that a big battle is looming." "You are correct," I answered. "Be brave."

I just finished my sentence when I heard the *whoosh* sound of a rocket getting out of the mouth of the gun. An explosion in the north and northeast side of town was followed right after by a series of explosions all over the city; it sounded terrible. The earth shook and shook. I walked down to the underground bunker and noticed that everyone had been awakened by the sound of explosions that was one hundred times worse than the worst explosion in the past. Some officers sat on their cots while others lay down on the ground. I sat on the ground leaning against my cot following my natural fear because the explosions sounded so terrible that one wondered whether it was the end of world.

One has to imagine that the sound of explosions was similar to that of 50 or 70 large drums beating in unison by a band of crazy drummers without interruption for almost three hours from 02:45 until early in the morning. It was estimated that 10,000 to 12,000 rounds must have fallen on An Lộc that morning. The earth shook and shook and the operations room was thought to have crumbled but did not. It was like a miracle. Although hundreds of shells fell all around us, none fell on the opening of the bunker of the divisional headquarters, which was not very thick. Only one shell was needed to obliterate the whole bunker and kill the operational staff, including General Hưng and Colonel Ulmer, and the battle of An Lộc would have ended right there. It took less than five minutes of shelling before the two leaders picked up their phones to call their units. Stunned, I did not know what to do. All around, the other officers acted the same way. Apparently they could not think of anything else but wait for something. Someone probably prayed.

Major Ingram said the barrage was so heavy that to leave your bunker was "certain death." Captain Moffett said "the noise was going up to a crescendo.... It sounded like somebody was popping popcorn—shaking it all over the city."[6]

The terrible sound of explosions continued without interruption. Suddenly,

X. Breaking the Siege

I saw Colonel Vỹ who was sitting on his cot stand up and go to the communication table; Colonel Điềm put his helmet on and got out of the bunker to check the perimeter. Lieutenant Colonel Đăng, chief of staff S-3 for Operations, and I immediately went to the communication table, put on our headphones to register reports from individual units, and forgot all the rest. I was stunned and almost paralyzed because of the fear—one that I had never experienced before. I felt ashamed. Hưng, the general, an old classmate, during the terrible pounding of shells and missiles just took it easy and called each unit to ask for information and give orders as if nothing had happened. In retrospect, I was way behind him. He had more than 50 Medals of Valor, of which 26 were palm leaves—the highest type of medal for soldiers who had brilliantly and bravely won victories on the battlefield—which were given in front of the Armed Forces of Vietnam. I had counted them on his jacket after a military ceremony. That means that he had been commended for his valor 26 times before the Armed Forces. As for me, I had no more than two of them. Nothing was more humbling than being an officer with the lowest combat citations.

Hours later, although the sound of explosions had ceased and the sky was not clear yet, it was about 05:30 hours when the perimeter forces reported attacks by enemy tanks and infantry. Early reports revealed that in all directions, defenders had destroyed tanks suggesting a major battle was being fought. However, Lieutenant Colonel Lý Đức Quân, commander of the ARVN 7th Regiment, reported that he had lost contact with the battalion chief of the 3/7 Battalion, except for the two company commanders of the battalion; that the western defense perimeter at Phú Lô gate had been trounced; and that enemy forces controlled the provincial jail and the Public Works Office. From there, they began attacking the 5th Reconnaissance Company of 1st Lieutenant Lê Văn Chánh who was protecting the western side of the divisional headquarters; it was then realized that enemy forces were just one street away from the headquarters.

On the northeastern front, the 52nd Ranger Battalion, which was heavily attacked, was trounced in the middle and split into two separate wings. In the northwest, enemy troops, after taking over the area around the provincial "Open Arms" Branch Office and the nearby high school, attacked the 5th Reconnaissance Company, one street away from the headquarters. Therefore, the divisional operational headquarters was being attacked from the northwest at about 150 meters and from the northeast at about 100 meters from General Hưng's bunker. Without hesitation, General Hưng immediately got out of his bunker with the communication group, 2nd Lieutenant Tùng, his aide, followed behind with Colonel Ulmer. The protection squad that was stationed in the nearby villa rapidly gathered around General Hưng and Colonel Ulmer who were standing close to the flag pole yard communicating with leaders of different units.

At that time, Lieutenant Colonel Vỹ and all the officers and personnel in the bunker went to the front of the defensive line of the headquarters, which was facing Nguyễn Huệ Street. The line was serviced by two reconnaissance squads protecting the operation staff and personnel of the 1st, 2nd, 3rd, and 4th Bureaus of the division totaling almost 40 guns including Colonels Bùi Đức Điềm and Lê Nguyên Vỹ. Staying in the bunker were Captain Cường, Triệu from the 2nd Bureau, communication officers and personnel. Of course, all the unit leaders were in direct contact with General Hưng, although their staff continuously reported to the Tactical Operations Center (TOC) which was then transcribed by the two captains and communication personnel.

As mentioned above, General Hưng had the ability to remember the coordinates of specific locations; to direct the bombing of fighter planes on specific targets, sometimes as close as one street away; and to remember names and communication frequencies of all the company leaders of all units under his direction. Not every commander had this ability, which was not simple memorizing but having the ability to devise a way to memorize all these numbers. I was standing on the inside of the protection line surrounding the headquarters and listening to the noises of gunfire. I then realized that I was not staying there to shoot at someone, but to be around my commander to make him aware of what he needed to know about the enemy. Not seeing Lieutenant Colonel Đăng, chief of the S-3 Operations, anywhere, I returned to the flag pole yard where General Hưng stood and approached his aide, 2nd Lieutenant Tùng. It was then that I realized that General Hưng was talking to 1st Lieutenant Chánh; Lieutenant Colonel Quân, commander of the 7th Regiment; and Lieutenant Colonel Biết, commander of the 3rd Ranger Battle Group while at the same time directing VNAF pilots to strike specific targets for these officers. Occasionally he read coordinates for Lieutenant Tùng to give to Colonel Ulmer, who stood about 40 feet away and was also directing armed Cobra helicopters to strike at targets requested by General Hưng. Later as the south and southeast areas requested air support, he let Colonel Lê Quang Lưỡng and Trần Văn Nhựt coordinate air support with their U.S. advisers. The eastern side was coordinated by Lieutenant Colonel Nguyễn Văn Biết, commander of the 3rd Ranger Battle Group, and the northern side by Lieutenant Colonel Phan Văn Huấn, commander of the 81st Airborne Commando Group. General Hưng coordinated air attacks on the northwest side for the 8th Regiment.

X. Breaking the Siege

The northern and northwestern fronts of the 81st Airborne Commando Group and the 8th Regiment, although having destroyed many tanks, had been weakened because their lines had been trounced and pulled back a little bit. Each time General Hưng communicated to the 8th Regiment, he either talked to the deputy commander, Major Huỳnh Văn Tâm, or called directly the battalion chiefs instead of the "absent" regiment commander Mạch Văn Trường.

From early morning until 09:30, 180 aircraft missions by VNAF and USAF had been flown and more than 10 B-52 boxes dropped around the perimeters of the defensive lines, although the situation got worse with time. For the whole day, there would be more than 90 B-52 sorties supporting An Lộc alone. One commando detailed the effects of the B-52 strikes:

> The earth vibrated violently, the compressed air caused me to have difficulty breathing. I didn't know if the two sorties were finished because I had not recovered my consciousness. The city darkened as the cloud of dust had risen and covered the sun light ... many children still had bleeding in their ears and noses.[7]

For this attack, the enemy had installed and used new AAA batteries. A U.S. captain on the ground stated that he "had never heard so much 37 mm and 23 mm firing" in his life.[8] For the first time in An Lộc, the use by the NVA of the SA-7 heat-seeking surface-to-air missile—known as Strela—had been confirmed. Any aircraft flying above 10,000 feet would be safe; otherwise, pilots had to carefully dodge any missile that left a telltale trail of white smoke as it moved toward its intended victim.[9]

In the midst of the battle, a distress call from General Hưng's command bunker was received by TACAIR. An enemy tank was aiming directly at the bunker ready to fire its gun. Lieutenant Colonel Gordo Weed answered the call with his A-37. On the first pass, his 250-pound bomb scored a hit at the tank, but the bomb was a dud. Although the tank stopped firing at the bunker, it continued to move forward. On the second pass, the bomb destroyed the tank and routed its supporting infantry troops.[10]

The 5th Reconnaissance Company besides the two squads assigned to the divisional staff, one close to him and the other along the Nguyễn Huệ Street, had 40 remaining troops; half of them were either wounded or killed. This was a critical and dangerous moment for General Hưng, for these troops, despite their courage and valiance, would not be able by themselves to protect the forward command post against the attacks of enemy forces. In the end realizing that the south and southeast sections had been under the control of the airborne units, he asked Colonel Lưỡng to send the 63rd Company to reinforce the 8th Airborne Battalion of Lieutenant Colonel Văn Bá Ninh that was occupying the northern end of the temporary runway all the way down to Xã Cam Gate where six enemy tanks had been shot early in the morning.

The 5th Airborne Battalion

The most important decision was to move the 5th Airborne Battalion of Lieutenant Colonel Nguyễn Chí Hiếu from the southeast to the northern end of An Lộc in order to recover positions taken by the enemy in the morning and to move the Reconnaissance Company of the 1st Airborne Brigade to protect the ARVN 5th Infantry Division's forward command post that had been covered by the 5th Reconnaissance Company for more than four hours. That was an important decision; although it lightened the defense in the south and southeast of An Lộc, it would protect the survival of An Lộc by shielding the 5th Division's headquarters. General Hưng and Colonel Lưỡng had made a fateful decision for An Lộc above the other decisions taken by the III Corps and MR3, the TRAC Headquarters, the JGS/RVNAF, the MACV, Saigon or Washington. That was clear.

The half-strength 5th Airborne Battalion moved into An Lộc in two wings. The men were filthy from living in the ground, and they were hungry and anemic from skimpy rations. One in every three or four soldiers was bandaged. As they moved into town or what remained of the town, the degree of devastation became apparent. One U.S. soldier embedded in the airborne battalion wrote,

> [An Lộc] had been wrecked, knocked apart, and abandoned. Roofs were torn off buildings, walls were blasted apart, and tumbled, burned out cars and trucks lay in scorched spots on the streets.... Dead soldiers, civilians, cows, pigs, chickens, and things I couldn't identify were lying in the street or partially buried in the rubble. The thick cloying green stink of the decaying dead permeated everything.... One destroyed T-54 tank was burned out and a broken track had run off into the street.... The crew was still aboard and the rotting bodies, the burned vehicle, and the oil and grease on the shattered pavement combined to produce a gagging stink.... A wrecked jeep had been blown onto the roof of a partially destroyed two-story building. It was upside down and embedded in the shattered rafters.[11]

The first wing in a counterattack recovered the provincial high school and the Open Arms Branch's area and connected the two wings of the 52nd Ranger Battalion. The second wing recovered the Public Works Office on the west side of the division's headquarters while an airborne company arrived to strengthen the defensive line of the headquarters. The enemy was not prepared to face the ferocity of the 5th Airborne Battalion.

By 14:00, the outcome of the battlefield of that day had been settled. The 5th Airborne Battalion, the Reconnaissance Company of the 1st Airborne Brigade, had become the saviors of the 5th Infantry Division's forward command post, and the 5th Reconnaissance Company was the elite unit that protected its commander. With only 40 troops left, it had repulsed wave after wave of communist attacks from 06:00 to 10:00 hours before the airborne unit came to the rescue. Within one year after the battle of An Lộc, 1st Lieutenant Chánh of the 5th Reconnaissance Company was promoted to major and district chief of Định Quán District, province of Tuyên Đức.

Thanks to the airborne units and the bombing of enemy positions by Cobra helicopters, although the presence of SA-7 Strela missiles and 23 mm, 37 mm, and 57 mm anti-aircraft guns made air attacks dangerous at the northern end of the town, the ARVN 8th Regiment was able to recover its lost positions, and the 81st Airborne Commando Group also counterattacked and recovered the police station and the new market, which were lost early in the morning along with the early-morning defensive lines. From the afternoon until evening, strategic air force called by Generals Hưng and Hollingsworth, TRAC commander, dropped 10 more Arc Light boxes outside of An Lộc, especially on the northern, eastern and western sides, giving support to the 81st Airborne, the 3rd Ranger Battle Groups and the 7th Regiment in their reconquest of lost positions; many of these boxes fell 800 meters from the defensive line. All the positions had been recovered although the lines of the 52nd Ranger Battalion still had a hole in its mid-part as enemy troops tried to stay close to the ARVN rangers in order to avoid the bombing. On the western side, they still occupied the jailhouse.

One of the airborne command posts was a house that fronted directly onto the street on the northeastern corner of An Lộc. The enemy was hiding in the buildings across the street less than 30 meters away. As gunfire exchanges were frequent, they moved to a concrete cellar with a low ceiling and crumbling walls. The place was dark, odorous and divided into two rooms, which they shared with civilians. A few elderly, a dozen children and a pregnant woman occupied one of the rooms and the paratroopers the other.

Early in the morning, a seriously wounded soldier was brought to the command post. Although he had been hit in the lower arm, he had decided to stay back and fight until he was too sick to do anything. His arm was swollen with redness streaking upward. Pus was oozing from the wound. Although his friends knew that the battalion's physician had passed away a few days earlier from shrapnel wounds, they brought him to the command post to see if Colonel Hiếu could do anything for him. It was obvious to everyone that an amputation was needed soon; otherwise he would die. As no one was medically qualified, without training, anesthesia or sterilization, they took off his left arm at the elbow level with a heavy-bladed Ka-Bar knife after placing a tourniquet on the upper arm. The patient screamed and kicked, but his buddies held him down and he lapsed into unconsciousness. The stump was wrapped in a wad of cotton and a length of bandage, and the soldier was taken to first aid for further care.[12]

The shelling of the town continued day and night. One morning, a loud explosion rocked the house. The basement was filled with dust, and no one could hear anything. After a few minutes of shock, it was realized that a shell had penetrated into the house and exploded in the upper level killing a few soldiers. The concrete floor was sturdy enough to protect the people living in the basement. Except for the concussion, they were all fine, although the civilians were screaming and moaning.

The explosion had a marked effect on the pregnant woman and her baby. The latter decided to come out, causing the mother-to-be to scream and yell. As the yelling and screaming intensified, the paratrooper decided to see whether he could do anything to help. The lady was on her back with her knees up while holding her belly. The elderly women around her appeared confused, not knowing how to react. The slicked-black hairs were visible followed by the face of the child. The paratrooper held the head and pulled gently, causing the whole baby to slide out easily. There was a gush of blood and water that filled the basement. The baby, who was crying, was given to the mother, who by then had stopped crying.[13]

The experience with the Airborne Brigade was certainly unique, even for a veteran U.S. paratrooper.

> An Lộc was an unhealthy place in every respect and the psychological stresses served to underscore the physical dangers and discomforts. Considering the length of time the men were engaged in that do-or-die fight, I marveled at how well they held up.
>
> Vietnamese paratroopers were aggressive beyond belief at every level from squad to brigade. Assaults were ordered with little or no fire support, albeit often by necessity, and soldiers and officers routinely attacked with very little consideration for the personal costs involved.... They attacked upright with single-minded focus; they simply concentrated on killing the enemy while ignoring danger.... They understood about dying and were not afraid of it.[14]

Resist Until Death

Communist units suffered major losses including personnel, and the number of tanks that were destroyed rose to 40 on 11 May. The rest of their

X. Breaking the Siege 167

troops hung on to the outer edge of the defensive lines because VNAF and USAF had been bombing their attacking lines heavily. However, almost all the tanks used in May were PT-76 light amphibious models suggesting that all the T-54 tanks had been destroyed in previous attacks.[15] On that day, more than 300 air sorties had been registered, and strategic air force had dropped 30 B-52 boxes on enemy concentration points and communication axes, including 20 Arc Light boxes on the periphery of the defensive lines. Because of their "hanging" on defensive parameters, the shelling of An Lộc was not heavy: only about 1,000 shells. Besides, gunships from Utapao Air Base had been destroying many cannons and tanks around An Lộc.

At night when General Hưng called me to his special room to evaluate the battle events, we realized that the POWs' statements differed somewhat from the day's events. The VC 5th Division—the main force in this third attack—only used the following:

- The 174th Regiment to attack from the north the positions of the ARVN 8th Regiment and the 81st Airborne Commando Group.
- The NVA E-6 Regiment to attack the 3rd Ranger Battle Group from the northeast and east.
- The NVA 275th Regiment overpowered the Windy Hill and Hill 169. It was also known that the headquarters of this regiment was at Srok Ton Cui as reported by electronic monitoring by the Technical Company of the ARVN 5th Infantry Division.
- In the meantime, the NVA 95C Regiment of the NVA 9th Division attacked the northwest.
- The 272 Regiment attacked the ARVN 7th Regiment of the 5th Division from the west.
- As to the south, the 271st Regiment/NVA 9th Division divided into two wings attacked a unit of the provincial PF and moved to Huỳnh Thúc Kháng Street along the western side of the Bình Long Military Sector headquarters while the second wing attacked the Xa Cam Gate manned by the 1/48 Battalion of the 52 TF—then under the command of the 1st Airborne Brigade—about two kilometers from the positions of the 8th Airborne Battalion south of the temporary landing zone.

From early morning, Colonel Lê Quang Lưỡng ordered the 8th Airborne Battalion of Lieutenant Colonel Văn Bá Ninh to counterattack; it destroyed six tanks and recovered the western section of town. Therefore, there had been five points of attack, not four, and at each of these points at the regimental level, eight to 10 tanks from the NVA 202nd and 203rd Tank Regiments participated in the attack. As this coordination was loose, tanks arrived to the defensive lines first but did not know where to go and therefore were easily destroyed by defenders. The infantry would show up only after most of the tanks had been disabled.

What was surprising was that the southeast where the headquarters of the 1st Airborne Brigade, the Reconnaissance Company, and the 5th Airborne Battalion of Lieutenant Colonel Nguyễn Chí Hiếu were stationed had never been attacked, while the VC 5th Division and the accompanying 209th Regiment along with other specialized units were stationed on hills in the southeast region about three to four kilometers from the 1st Airborne Brigade. Why? It had been speculated that the COSVN did not want to fight against this elite unit and waste forces unnecessarily, except for an incursion into the southern end of the landing zone. Had they attacked the 7th and 8th Regiments/ARVN of the 5th Division and overwhelmed their headquarters, the battlefield would have been leveled because the airborne units located in the south and southeast would have been isolated and easily defeated. This third offensive on An Lộc had failed because of the mishandling of this situation. Since the NVA did not want to attack the southeast positions, General Hưng and Colonel Lưỡng felt confident enough to move the 5th Airborne Battalion and the 1st Airborne Recon Company to counterattack on the western and northwestern sides allowing the defensive forces to regain their lost positions.

Later, I saw documents stating that the 275th Regiment of the VC 5th Division, not the 271st Regiment/VC 9th Division, had attacked Xa Cam Gate—position held by the 1st/48th Battalion of the 52nd TF.[16] This must have been a misstatement or printing error because the 275th Regiment belonged to the VC 5th Division. The VC 5th Division had, therefore, spent all its forces and had nothing left to fight against the 1st Airborne Brigade. This statement may be correct. Despite being correct, it was also a strategic error in this third phase of the attack. As for Willbanks, he did not list any force in this attack. He must have followed the JGS/RVNAF Military History Branch's document in writing that the 274th Regiment/VC 5th Division attacked the positions of the 81st Airborne Commando Group. This unit did not participate in the offensive because it belonged to none of the above divisions. The VC 5th Division was comprised of the 174th, E-6, and 275th Regiments; the VC 9th Division had the 271st, 272nd and 95C Regiments. Because northern communists failed to disclose information about their units, misstatements are bound to occur.

Back to the night of 11 May, General Hưng had inquired about how enemy forces got all those artillery rounds. I told him they not only used the guns the COSVN 69th Artillery Division had, although they had received lots of guns and ammunition from their bases on Chhlong River in Kratié, but also the 105 mm and 155 mm howitzers and the 60 mm and 81 mm mortars the ARVN 74th Ranger Battalion left at base Alpha; the artillery units at Lộc Tấn from the ARVN 1st Cavalry TF; those from the 53rd Artillery Battalion at Lộc Ninh; and those from the ARVN 52nd TF at Hùng Tâm bases. Overall, they had collected more than 40 howitzers and 8,000 rounds of ammunition, which they moved to An Lộc along with their own guns.

In sum, units of the COSVN 69th or 70th Artillery Division had used all available guns from large to small, 60 mm, 61 mm, 81 mm, and 82 mm mortars; 120 mm and 160 mm Soviet guns; 122 mm, 105 mm, and 155 mm howitzers; the mobile 8 to 10 tubes of 75 mm guns, without recoil, placed on trucks; and finally the 130 mm guns with delayed firing, which perforated the target before exploding. A few documents denied the NVA had used these guns. The particular characteristics of the 130 mm gun were as follows: it emitted a sound when it emerged out of the mouth of the gun and when it hit the target. Once the latter was penetrated, the explosion was followed by an 8 to 10 meter smoke plume. Only one such missile would destroy a large bunker. The sequence, thud, thud, boom, followed by a plume of smoke is characteristic of the 130 mm gun the Soviets had given to the NVA. The gun was first used during Lam Son 719 and the following summer as they shelled and overran FSB Fuller. The NVA had used it in Corps I at the onset of the offensive and for the first time in III Corps at An Lộc, although two units were available at that time. The NVA therefore had used the largest arsenal of guns possible at An Lộc in order to destroy the defending forces and capture it even if it had been turned into a no man's land. It was estimated that each person, civilian or soldier, had received five or six artillery rounds at the frequency of 9,000 to 11,000 rounds being shelled into An Lộc. No one knew the correct number, probably not even the gunners, although they failed to take the town.

On 12 May 1972, to solve some supply issues, the NVA firing on the defensive perimeters lessened to about 2,000 rounds. Tanks, however, kept coming. Rangers attached to the 5th ARVN Division saw several T-54 tanks moving from the east through Route 303. As the latter crossed a stream by way of a narrow concrete bridge to get to An Lộc, the rangers positioned themselves on both sides of the road about 30 meters from the bridge with the goal of knocking off the lead tank right on the bridge, thereby blocking it off. As the lead tank reached the middle of the bridge, six M-72s hit it. The vehicle was destroyed at the right spot.

At noon on 15 May, Sergeant 1st Class Cao Tấn Tài was credited for destroying two T-54s. Perched on the roof of a building, he hit his first target from a distance of 10 meters. The M-72 round hit the front part of the turret and ignited ammunition inside the tank. He immobilized the second tank by targeting its front road wheel then proceeded to fire two more shots at the turret from a range of 20 to 30 meters. One round detonated the tank ammunition.[17]

On 12 May at sunset, the NVA troops began attacking ... at nighttime.

- On the western side, the 272nd Regiment/VC 9th Division augmented by tanks attacked the ARVN 7th Regiment.
- In the northeast, the 174th Regiment/VC 5th Division attacked the 52nd Ranger Battalion.
- the E-6 Regiment/VC 5th Division moved against the 36th Ranger Battalion in the east.

On all defensive lines, tanks were destroyed and attacking forces were pushed back with heavy enemy losses. Twenty-eight NVA tanks had been destroyed in town including six others at Xa Cam Gate by the 8th Airborne Battalion, bringing the total to 34 kills; they were of all kinds: T-54, PT-76, BTR-50 and ZSU.

On the morning of 13 May, the NVA had no units left to launch any attack. From that date onward, sporadic gunshots occurred in all areas where the NVA still had some strongholds: west, north, and northeast. They still rained mortars and missiles indiscriminately on the town and its perimeters, although they did not have enough strength to launch any major attack until General Hưng launched his counterattack in June.

Probably because of major losses or a change in tactics, General Trần Văn Trà ordered the VC 5th Division to pull out of the battlefield the following week to open new battlefields that General Nguyễn Văn Minh had predicted and spared units to deal with.

The VC 9th Division hung around the defensive parameters or just encircled the town. The artillery units of the COSVN 69th Artillery Division were still firing on the town while their anti-aircraft guns aimed at VNAF and USAF aircraft. The number of shells/mortars had decreased from the thousands to a few hundred, then a dozen a day. An Lộc could be considered safe and the defending units victorious in this wild red earth battlefield. However, the generals were still cautious and reserved like General Nguyễn Văn Minh who would not declare victory until his troops had arrived in An Lộc. He had new plans for An Lộc while General Trà had other plans elsewhere in the B-2 battlefield, which comprised RVNAF MR3 and MR4.

For the defenders, the fatigue, the lack of sleep, the uninterrupted fighting, the hunger, the unbearable stench of unburied dead, the confinement into a narrow location, the fear, the constant barrage of shelling, and the mounting number of unevacuated casualties began to sink in; the morale of the troops by that time had almost reached the breaking point.[18] By mid–May, they had held on for almost a month and a half, subsisting on whatever food and drink they could get their hands on, taking a nap here and there, fighting the enemy, their own fear, and demons, and trying to survive another day.

Of course Washington, the Pentagon, TRAC and especially the RVN and the ARVN had shared responsibilities for and worries about the survival and loss of An Lộc. As for the worries, they could only send in more reinforcements or increase the bombing, but the fighting on the ground had to be done by the defenders in An Lộc. The latter would either win or lose; this did not mean having in hands the best armaments, but also a courageous fighting spirit besides receiving the support of the U.S. and Saigon.

How could one fully explain the loneliness of the fighters on the battlefield as they waited for incoming enemies on the perimeter? It was while they waited that they would feel lonely the most. They only had their resolve and a gun when the enemy launched their attacks. They had to be at the perimeter to fight back or wait for the metallic birds to come from Guam or Utapao to save them. One moment of loneliness was enough to decide a victory or defeat. Wait and shoot. Live or die. Only they could understand their loneliness. No one could understand them. If they were coward, they would have run away, and then who would save Washington or Saigon?

Not many people understood the loneliness and sacrifice of the An Lộc defenders. Nixon or Kissinger, Colonel Miller, Dr. Willbanks, who would save them? We, the troops defending An Lộc? I am talking in place of my fellow soldiers who had fought at An Lộc. Of course, we will never forget the U.S. pilots who courageously flew dangerous missions to bomb enemy positions or to supply us with ammunition and food as well as the U.S. advisers who worked in other units close by to protect An Lộc.

But each country has its own pride. Yes, we only asked for the means and support so that we could fight; but do not tell us how to fight. At An Lộc, not a few advisers made comments that we had lost our fighting spirit. I told them, then and now, that they were wrong, and the result of the battlefield had more than proven it.

XI

Releasing the Pressure on An Lộc

The Counterattack

It was probably early in the morning of 11 May when General Hưng told General Minh that the NVA had massively shelled the town and would attack it once the shelling had stopped. General Minh and his staff immediately made plans to save An Lộc the next day. According to my own assessment, the plan had two parts separated by a few days.

First, attack strongly to uproot the blockade at Tàu-Ô stream, although in reality to hold the NVA 7th Division in place and prevent it from sending any reinforcement northward either to An Lộc or to take down the 3rd Airborne Brigade.

Second, during the third attack on An Lộc in the two hamlets of Đức Vinh and Tân Khai about 10 kilometers south of An Lộc, the NVA 7th Division had two regiments, the 165th and 141st, along with the 271st of the VC 9th Division. Of course it had to return this latter regiment which would participate in the An Lộc attack. The two remaining regiments which had been battling against the ARVN 3rd Airborne Brigade must have suffered major damage under air attacks from VNAF and USAF. Then General Minh would send in a fresh unit, not only to decrease the pressure on the Airborne 3rd Brigade, but also to reinforce General Hưng's forces in An Lộc.

The first part of the strategy began early on 11 May 1972.

The 32nd Regiment/ARVN 21st Infantry Division augmented by two tank units, the 1/5 and the 1/2 Cavalry Companies divided into wings and originating from Chơn Thành, moved along Highway 13 to attack the three-kilometer-long blockade area at Tàu-Ô stream. The district of Chơn Thanh was protected by the 9th Regiment/ARVN 5th Division—newly formed from the combination of two battalions temporarily under the operative command of the ARVN 21st Division, which was covering Highway 13 from Lai Khê to Chơn Thanh. At the Tàu-Ô battlefield, a violent confrontation ensued. When the 32nd Regiment moved in, enemy forces included the 209th Regiment of the NVA 7th Division augmented by the 101st Regiment, the C-41 Anti-tank Company, a reconnaissance company/NVA 7th Division, and an anti-aircraft artillery company—roughly about 1,200 troops. The units that holed up in fortified shelters built by U.S. forces on both sides of the highway and connected together by a thick maze of fortified tunnels had been bombed by Vietnamese and U.S. planes for some time and probably suffered no small losses. They probably received small reinforcements and supplies at night, although the blockade persisted. They naturally could not move anywhere in order to reinforce other units. Therefore, General Minh was able to accomplish part of his strategy, although he had to reinforce the 32nd Regiment with three ranger battalions, the 65th, 73rd, and 84th.

The second part of his strategy was activated on 14 May 1972. On 11 May when the 15th Regiment/ARVN 9th Infantry Division arrived at Lai Khê, General Minh thought about airlifting it directly to An Lộc as reinforcement. However, because of the massive shelling of the town in the early hours of the day and knowing that the NVA would subsequently attack with tanks and infantry, he changed his strategy by moving the unit on land. After many days of preparation, although the intensity of attacks against An Lộc was decreasing and the defensive forces were holding on their own, the strategy proceeded as planned. Two wings had been designed to introduce the unit to the battlefield.

The first wing, consisting of the 15-TF, which included the 1st, 2nd, and 3rd Battalions and the 15th Reconnaissance Company; the 9th Armored Cavalry; and the 93rd Artillery Company under the command of Lieutenant Colonel Hồ Ngọc Cẩn, moved into Tân Khai in three phases. From there, they headed toward An Lộc.

In the first phase the 9th Armored Cavalry, the 1/15 Battalion, and the 93rd Artillery Company originating from Chơn Thành moved north to the Ngọc Lầu intersection about two kilometers north of Chơn Thành, then swung around the west side of Highway 13 and by 15 May would arrive at the Tân Khai hamlet and establish the Long Phi Firebase.

In the second phase, the 2/15 Battalion was airlifted to about one kilometer west of the hamlet and moved into the hamlet on 16 May. Then the headquarters of the 15-TF would be dropped into the firebase before moving into the hamlet. In the third phase, the 3/15 Battalion and the 15th Reconnaissance Company would be airlifted west of Tân Khai. All the units moved to the hamlet without problem.

The second wing, comprising the 33rd Regiment/21st Infantry Division with its infantry battalions under the command of Lieutenant Colonel Nguyễn Viết Cần, would also head to Tân Khai, from where it moved to An Lộc in a parallel fashion to the first wing.

On 17 May, one battalion of the 33rd Regiment would be airlifted to the Long Phi firebase to protect the artillery unit and replace the 2/15 Battalion, which would move out to follow the 3/15.

On 18 May, the 33rd Regiment (-) originating from a firebase three kilometers north of Chơn Thành would move east of Highway 13 along the path of the 9th Armored Cavalry and the 1/15 Battalion a few days earlier to move to Tân Khai that day. Therefore by 18 May, the two wings to be used to liberate An Lộc had arrived at the assembly area and attack position, which was about 10 kilometers south of An Lộc.

But these 10 kilometers were the "life and death" course, especially dangerous for both wings if there had not been another friendly wing that would join in and change the complexion of the course and the An Lộc battlefield.

On 18 May when the 33rd Regiment (-)/21st Division arrived at Tân Khai, the 15-TF of Lieutenant Colonel Hồ Ngọc Cẩn began its move to An Lộc with three battalions, a reconnaissance company, and the 9th Armored Cavalry; it left the TF-15 deputy commander to direct the Long Phi firebase along with four 105 mm howitzers and two 155 mm howitzers and a battalion of the 33rd Regiment to support and protect the base the day before. Therefore, when moving to An Lộc from Tân Khai, the 33rd Regiment (-) of Lieutenant Colonel Nguyễn Viết Cần had only two battalions, a reconnaissance company and no cavalry unit. It should be remembered that the two wings were moving to free and shake hands with the defending units at An Lộc, although they did not have a unified higher-rank commanding officer—e.g., a full colonel—to coordinate the work of the leaders of the two different wings moving toward the same goal.

Naturally, General Nguyễn Vĩnh Nghi who was the commander of the ARVN 21st Infantry Division oversaw all these units; but, being at Lai Khê, he was also directing other units and therefore needed to designate a leader whose staff would coordinate the advance of the TF-15 and 33rd Regiment. The other question related to the imbalance of forces: a TF with a lot of troops and a regiment that was missing a battalion while the two units were moving toward the same goal, the TF on the west and the regiment on the east side? First, there was a lack of unified command as well as an imbalance of forces; second, the operational strategy was loose without close coordination and support. The on-site decision of a unified command would greatly facilitate the operational activity of two different units. Based on logic, the above assessment may be correct, although a close look at the battlefield may explain the configuration of the two units as designed by either General Minh or Nghi. In fact, the western wing of Lieutenant Colonel Hồ Ngọc Cẩn encountered a twice-stronger force than that of Lieutenant Colonel Nguyễn Viết Cần.

On the night of 18 May, enemy forces began shelling the Long Phi firebase, forcing Lieutenant Colonel Hồ Ngọc Cẩn to leave behind the 1/15 Battalion to coordinate with the battalion of the 33rd Regiment in order to expand the range of control around the firebase and decrease enemy firing.

The TF-15 from the time it got out of Tân Khai sustained many attacks and was harassed continuously with mortar shells on 19, 20, and 21 May like the airborne units in the past. The heaviest fight occurred at Đức Vinh hamlet, which was the battlefield area of the 141st Regiment/NVA 7th Division. In spite of this on the morning of 22 May, that wing had moved to about one kilometer south of Thanh Bình Hamlet, which lay outside the defensive perimeters about two kilometers southwest of An Lộc. It was, therefore, very close to the town, although the NVA 141st Regiment prevented it from reaching the town. The 2/15 and 3/15 Battalions and the 15th Reconnaissance Company were heavily shelled and attacked by infantry supported by tanks, which were all repulsed. But it could not move forward or backward and was surrounded from 23 May onward. Troops that were killed were buried in place while wounded ones could not be evacuated. For many days, supplies and ammunition were dropped by parachutes. Helicopters could not drop in, and only a few dozen air missions had been successful. The 9th Armored Cavalry moved on Highway 13 unimpeded from Tân Khai to Đức Vinh following the path of the TF. On the evening of 23 May, Lieutenant Colonel Cẩn decided to open a blood road with his armored unit to evacuate about 100 wounded to Tân Khai. It was successful. The following day, when they tried to return to the TF base, they were ambushed by a battalion and an anti-tank unit; losses were high, many dozens of troops were killed, dozens were lost in action, close to 80 were wounded, and 22 M-113 armored cars were shot with B-40 and B-41 shells and AT-3 Sagger missiles. The TF had to send a unit to support and protect the cavalry to return to firebase Long Phi at Tân Khai. After that event, the remaining troops gathered in an area outside Thanh Bình hamlet to reorganize the unit. Only 350 troops were able to fight. On 25 May, the TF tried to push toward An Lộc but was unsuccessful. Air support was vital as ever.

The second wing, the 33rd Regiment (-) of Lieutenant Colonel Cẩn connected with the 31st Regiment/21st Division, which was brought in as reinforcement for the 1st Airborne Battalion in the Đức Vinh hamlet. When the airborne moved, the 31st remained in the Đức Vinh area. The following day, the 33rd Regiment moved north, but the 31st was ordered to remain put. Once out of Đức Vinh, the 33rd Regiment was attacked by the 165th Regiment/NVA 7th Division. On 31 May, it tried to move north but was checked in place again. Enemy losses were high because of air strikes. Losses on the 33rd Regiment were due to injuries from 61 mm and 82 mm mortars and 122 mm rockets. There were more than 200 wounded.

In the next four to five days, the two wings were assaulted on various occasions by the NVA 141st and 165th Regiments. Losses mounted although wounded could not be evacuated; helicopters could not land because of effective and deadly anti-air defense.

Lieutenant Colonel Nguyễn Văn Đỉnh

In these difficult times, as the two "liberating wings" were pinned down a few miles from An Lộc, a savior came out in the form of the 6th Airborne Battalion/1st Brigade under the command of Lieutenant Colonel Nguyễn Văn Đỉnh.

"Try to help me with this," said General Minh. "You're the only one who can do it. How old are you? Are you an acting or permanent lieutenant colonel?"

"General, I'm thirty three," said Lieutenant Colonel Đỉnh. "I've been an acting lieutenant colonel for a year. I assumed command of the battalion after the operation in Laos."

"I'll ask General Đống to make you deputy commander of an infantry division. Lưỡng (chief of staff for Military Region III), take Đỉnh's name, rank, serial number and immediately make him a permanent lieutenant colonel."

"Thank you, General. I'll try hard."

With that, General Nguyễn Văn Minh, III Corps commander, sent Lieutenant Colonel Đỉnh to try to link up with the forces in An Lộc. If successful, the NVA encirclement of An Lộc would be broken up after a two-month-long siege, thus freeing the town and closing a chapter in the brutal Bình Long attack; if not, the battle would rage on, no one knows for how long. There was no other option. Wounded troops needed to be evacuated, reinforcements brought in to replace the dazed and tired soldiers, and food and medications supplied to citizens and soldiers. Especially, dead bodies needed to be buried to prevent potential health hazards from spreading.

He then congratulated Đinh for being able to make it back from Windy Hill. General Minh stood and saluted Đinh, a person five ranks below him and very inferior to him in position. Đinh saluted the general back. This event, which occurred quickly at the Lai Khê's III Corps forward command center, contradicted all the rules related to command procedures, rank, and military regulations.[1]

The 6th Airborne Battalion was thus sent back into action at An Lộc with a huge and important mission: to link up with the 1st Airborne Brigade. It also had to liberate the ARVN 15th and 33rd Regiments, which had been bogged down by enemy forces while trying to connect with An Lộc defenders. In addition, it would bring with it 300 reinforcement troops for the beleaguered 15th Regiment of Lieutenant Colonel Hồ Ngọc Cẩn.

Two months earlier on 17 April 1972, Lieutenant Colonel Nguyễn Văn Đinh, commander of the 6th Airborne Battalion, was flown in with his troops to reinforce An Lộc. He rapidly recovered Windy Hill and Hill 169 after a well-conducted attack. While stationing at Srok Ton Cui, his unit was mauled by the 141st and 165th Regiments/NVA 7th Division and the 209th Regiment/VC 5th Division in the early hours of 21 April. He had to open a blood road to get to the Bé River before being picked up by helicopters with the remaining 125 troops. The attacking force was six times stronger than his (2,400 vs. 400). Phạm Kim Bằng, the battalion executive officer, was seriously wounded. Cao Hoàng Tuấn, the most outstanding company commander, was dead, and every soldier was worn out.

That was the lowest point of Đinh's military career. This was the first time since it was formed 18 years earlier that the 6th Airborne Battalion had been torn apart. In Lai Khê where the remnant of the battalion recovered and picked up new recruits—excesses from other airborne units, wounded troops who had recovered, including many seasoned officers—as well as eager new personnel, Đinh and his company commanders tried and tried again with all their hearts. "Try hard" was the Airborne's motto. For one month, they drilled and drilled the freshly minted crew whose other duty was to guard the highway and the base in "maneuvers under fire."

Of the 412 men, three-fourths were new troops. For one month Đinh had the new recruits drilled daily, although everything had been about theory. None of them had fired live ammunition, but the combat spirit was high. The battalion was finally ready with its 61st, 62nd, 63rd, and 64th Companies. On 3 June, as it rained, recruits were taught the fundamentals of grenade throwing and basic hand signals.

Đinh convened his company commanders for a final meeting. On the map, he showed them the plan,

On the left of the highway is the 15th Regiment; on the right, the 33rd Regiment. They have been pinned down for one month and cannot evacuate their wounded; they don't have enough food. And up there in the north is the 8th Regiment close to An Lộc that has been waiting for one month for the link-up. Our job is to make the link-up happen.

The new recruits were enthralled; they were ready and could smell the smoke of the fire and the thrill of the action. At 10:00 on 4 June, the 61st Company was lifted by helicopter to Đồng Lô, eight kilometers west of Highway 13. They were met by anti-aircraft fire on arrival. The rest of the battalion landed one kilometer away. At 12:30, the battalion reassembled and moved northward to Đức Vinh 1 to receive the three companies of the 15th Regiment. They then moved to Đức Vinh 2 where they camped for the night. On 5 June, they continued northward passing Xa Cát stream close to Highway 13. On the road lay nylon bags of dried rice, clothes, and head scarves belonging to civilians who tried to escape from An Lộc a few weeks earlier. The black and rigid bodies were lying here and there. The stench was overpowering. The battalion soldiers vomited all night.

On 6 June, Đinh talked to his commanders:

> Today is 6/6. A day of destiny. At Normandy this was the longest day. Our battalion is the 6th battalion. Three times six equals 18. Add the two digits of 18 and you get a 9, a lucky number. Within a 6 lies the potential to be a 9. Potential is better than full development, which always precedes decline. So this is a lucky day for us. I hope we'll meet the enemy and we'll defang them.[2]

Traveling north, they suddenly hit the flank of the 165th Regiment/NVA 7th Division that was engaging with the 33rd Regiment of Lieutenant Colonel Nguyễn Viết Cần. Charging and firing at the same time, they overwhelmed the enemy, forcing them to move northward toward Windy Hill and Hill 169. Being under no pressure, Lieutenant Colonel Cần's units set up a landing zone to evacuate about 200 wounded, and the units then crossed the rubber plantation Xa Trạch to reach Đồng Phát hamlet about four kilometers south of An Lộc.

That same day, the 6th Airborne unit crossed to the west side of the highway, hit the 141st Regiment/NVA 7th Division broadside, freed and connected with TF-15 and gave 300 fresh troops to Lieutenant Colonel Hồ Ngọc Cẩn. The latter unit also established an LZ to evacuate 150 wounded. The 6th Airborne Battalion became the savior of two wings from the southwest on the battlefield south of An Lộc. The hero, Lieutenant Colonel Nguyễn Văn Đinh, commander of the 6th Airborne Battalion, had established a record by beating badly both the 141st and the 165th Regiments/NVA 7th Division

XI. Releasing the Pressure on An Lộc

in critical battles, taking revenge on the same units that had mauled his troops two months earlier at Srok Ton Cui and Windy Hill.

By evening, the 6th Battalion positioned itself east of Highway 13, with the 15th Regiment on its left and the 33rd behind them. About one kilometer ahead was the ARVN 8th Battalion, and beyond the 8th laid An Lộc with its red-tile roofed administrative building. The solution of the Bình Long Battle rested in that one kilometer. On 7 June, there was one last objective, an enemy position on the right side of the road between the 6th and 8th Battalions. The 6th Battalion halted momentarily to evacuate wounded and receive supplies.

On 8 June, as the battalion got ready for the final fight, they realized that during the night the enemy had dug out new communication trenches 500 meters from their positions. At 08:45 they began their assault: they ran and fired at the enemy. In two hours, they had decimated two enemy companies with the exception of a POW who was so paralyzed by fear that he could not talk. They then continued their march northward to the Xa Cam plantation. Following another attack, the enemy scattered to the west.

At 17:45, Ngô Xuân Vĩnh, nicknamed "Vĩnh the Kid"—he was only 23, the youngest 62nd Company commander of the 6th Airborne Battalion—shook hands with Nguyễn Trọng Ni of the 81st Company/8th Battalion at a spot 100 meters north of the Xa Cam Plantation sign. Both company commanders belonged to the same company at the Thủ Đức Infantry School. As tears of pride and happiness flowed freely on their cheeks, an American adviser took the picture as they clasped their hands. The linkup had been accomplished. The siege of An Lộc had been broken. An Lộc was free again. In front of them, smoke was rising from the cooking fires in An Lộc as people prepared for the evening meal.[3]

The ARVN 33rd Regiment moved through Đồng Phát 1 hamlet without problem until it exchanged heavy fire with enemy troops midway between Đồng Phát 1 and 2. Regretfully, after pushing back enemy forces and settling at Đồng Phát 2 hamlet, on 9 June the regiment commander, Lieutenant Colonel Nguyễn Viết Cần, died from an incoming gun shell. He was posthumously promoted to full colonel.

If in the southeast there were two sons who sacrificed for the country, General Đỗ Cao Trí, commander of III Corps and MR3, and his brother Lieutenant Colonel Đỗ Cao Luận, in the southwest, the Nguyễn Viết family also had two brothers sacrificing for the country, General Nguyễn Viết Thanh, commander of the IV Corps and MR4, and his brother Colonel Nguyễn Viết Cần. How many other families have two or three sons who had sacrificed their lives for a free Vietnam? Loving sorrows to them.

From 8 June onward, the complexion of the battlefield had changed completely. In the city, General Hưng ordered all units to counterattack and recover all positions taken by enemy forces in the past.

On the west side, the 7th Regiment/ARVN 5th Division recovered the area around the jailhouse all the way to Phú Lố Gate and the Hoàng Hoa Thám Street that went around the west side of town.

In the north, the 81st Airborne Commando Group recovered the business area north of town and the Đồng Long Airfield. Pursuing their operation, they discovered a deep bunker in a neighboring forest. Hearing noises, they called the suspected NVA soldiers to surrender, only to find two little girls, very emaciated, dazed, and too weak to climb out of the bunker, with their clothing in tatters. They took the girls to the headquarters and realized they were Hà Thị Loan and Hà Thị Lộ, age eight and nine respectively. Their father was an RF soldier defending Đồng Long. When the airfield was overrun, their mother tried to take them and a brother to town but was killed by a mortar. Their brother was also killed. The two girls survived for two months in the bunker with vegetables and water from rain. They were later reunited with their father.[4]

During mopping operations, ARVN soldiers found the hulks of burned-out tanks scattered all over the battlefield, including a dozen tanks abandoned inside B-52–fashioned craters. Obviously the latter constituted unexpected obstacles to the movement of armored vehicles. They found one enemy headquarters that had been destroyed by C-130 gunships; inside the command post were destroyed communication equipment and many skeletons.

In the east, the 3rd Ranger Battle Group recovered its former position on Nguyễn Du Boulevard all the way to the railroad track to the Quản Lợi Gate. By midday 12 June, the remaining enemy troops that could not get away on time were killed.

South of town where the 1st Airborne Brigade had control all the time, the temporary LZ at the end of the highway reopened in early June when the units from Tân Khai moved in. Since the 6th Airborne Battalion and the ARVN TF-15/9th Infantry Division had arrived at An Lộc perimeters and connected with the 8th Airborne Battalion, many types of helicopters flew in troops, evacuating wounded on a regular basis, although occasionally a few rockets sill fell on the LZ.

On 13 June, General Nguyễn Văn Minh ordered the 18th Infantry Division to ship the 48th Regiment to An Lộc, replace the battered troops of the 5th Division, and take back Windy Hill and Hill 169. The replaced soldiers out appeared to be "in very rough shape"; malnourished with their uniforms in tatters. Some were "barefoot, some were dazed and some were too exhausted to do more than shuffle."⁵ The constant fighting, the pounding of the bombs and mortars, the exhaustion, and the fatigue had stressed these fighters beyond their limits and sapped their physical reserves.

An Lộc Liberated

From 13 June onward, the town of An Lộc and the province of Bình Long were considered to be liberated, and Saigon and Washington felt much better. Hanoi could not control An Lộc as it had claimed earlier. The political and military strategies of the communists had failed.

On 14 June, President Nguyễn văn Thiệu sent congratulations to the commanders of the III Corps and MR3, the 5th Division, the 21st Division, and all units and soldiers of all ranks who had fought at An Lộc or helped open Highway 13.

In reality, the section between Chơn Thành and Tân Khai had not been reopened. The ARVN 32nd Regiment/21st Infantry Division which suffered major casualties in the blockaded area at Tàu-Ô stream had been returned to the ARVN 21th Infantry Division for reinforcement and replaced by the 46th Regiment. The 141st and 165th/NVA 7th Division, after facing many battles against the TF-15, 33rd Regiment, and 6th Airborne Battalion the week before, although having suffered huge losses, gathered on 17 June outside Tân Khai and set up dozens of anti-aircraft guns and mortars with the goal of erasing the Phi Long firebase of the TF15. General Nghi, commander of the ARVN 21st Infantry Division, had to send in the 31st Regiment from outside Đức Vinh hamlet along with two infantry battalions and the 9th Armored Cavalry TF (-) to protect the firebase.

On 18 June, the 1st Airborne Brigade of Colonel Lê Quang Lưỡng had been ordered to separate from the ARVN 5th Infantry Division, move to Tân Khai and engage the above two NVA regiments. They killed close to 600 troops and confiscated more than 70 guns including anti-aircraft batteries. That was the last major battle that this savior unit achieved on the Bình Long battlefield. After that, all airborne units were ferried to Chơn Thành and returned to Saigon to reinforce the I Corps and MR1. Remnants of the two NVA regiments pulled back to Tàu-Ô Stream. Apparently the NVA 7th Division had lost three-quarters of its troops and half of its guns south of An Lộc and on Highway 13, although they still controlled the blockade at Tàu-Ô while their COSVN leaders had lost one of the biggest battles of this period.

The Bình Long victory had been affirmed by the generals, unit commanders and defensive and supportive troops of An Lộc. But above all, it was the spirit of "holding on till death" from the general to the unnamed troops like an RF soldier, a PF soldier, a policeman, a civilian villager, a teenager named Đoàn Văn Bình who once asked Colonel Trần Văn Nhựt for a gun to take down a tank, or a secretary that saved An Lộc.

That secretary who fled the war zone sought refuge in an area protected by the 81st Airborne Commando Group; by writing a couplet to congratulate troops of this elite unit, she had in her own way contributed to the protection of An Lộc.

> An Lộc địa sử ghi chiến tích
> Biệt cách dù vì quốc vong thân
> *An Lộc history records this feat:*
> *Airborne commandos sacrificing their lives for the country.*

After the war, the appreciative An Lộc people erected a stele on which were inscribed the above words to honor the fallen soldiers of the 81st Airborne Commando Group. The stele was taken down by the communists after their takeover of South Vietnam in 1975. Besides the commando cemetery, which was the largest military cemetery in An Lộc, the paratroopers being spread to different sectors had two smaller cemeteries, one near the An Lộc hospital and the other one close to the vicinity of the helicopter pad.

One former resident of An Lộc who had returned to her native city after the war wrote,

> The old cemetery, that served as the symbol of loyalty and heroism, had become an urban center. Those vengeful "atheists" had dug out the remains of our brothers and dumped them outside Xa Cam gate. With a heavy heart, I found my way to Xa Cam gate, but in front of me, there was a sad and quiet rubber tree forest and the dusty red soil routes on which I used to play with my friends, kicking up the red dust, those same roads on which the frightened residents of An Lộc had fled away, those roads that were soaked up with the blood of my brothers and of the enemy; I whispered a prayer for your spirit—our national heroes—for the spirit of all Vietnamese who had died during this atrocious war, for the early liberation of the Fatherland from this incarcerated life.[6]

All the towns and villages of the southwest, southeast, and even Saigon rejoiced at the news of victory. Merchants at the central Bến Thành market and other Saigon markets knew that "General Hưng had defended An Lộc to death and won." Apparently few people knew that holding An Lộc and defeating General Trần Văn Trà were the major feat of the smart-thinking General Nguyễn Văn Minh, Commander of the III Corps and MR3. And it was the widespread aura of General Hưng and another factor to be told later that would adversely affect his future military career. In reality, it is hard to

XI. Releasing the Pressure on An Lộc

have won a major battle and to remain in the army under the same commander.

First, the leaders of the COSVN were pretty upset, especially General Trần Văn Trà, who knew he would lose at An Lộc; however, since the Fiery Summer Offensive was drafted and directed by the Politburo and the Central Committee had not concluded defeat yet in the I and II Corps, they, like high-class boxers who even hit in the face, would not fall and lie down without reacting. Therefore from the end of May to mid–June, they opened new battlefields in Phước Long, Xuyên Mộc, Đất Đỏ District of Phước Tuy, Đức Huệ District of Hậu Nghĩa, Cái Bè, Cay Lậy District of Định Tường, and Mộc Hóa District of Kiến Tường, Provinces of IV Corps. In III Corps regions, General Minh knew about it and had defensive forces set up. The reason why General Trà reached down into the IV Corps was because according to communist designation, the NVA B-2 Front (or the communist 2nd Military Region) comprised not only the ARVN III, but also the IV Corps.

Although General Trà tried to enlarge the battlefield, that summer was not easy for him for the simple reason that the COSVN had only a few principal divisions like the 5th, 7th, 9th and the newly formed C30B along with a few local units at the regimental or battalion levels. The local units were not good, and that summer, only the NVA 7th Division and the 69th Artillery Division were units that hung around for a long time. The battlefields could be considered like huge ovens ready to "roast or burn" their new recruits. The huge ovens moved everywhere, north, south, east, west, where generations after generations of those "born in the north and died in the south" were fed into them without break. If they died, new ones would replace them. The more they were fed with new recruits, the more people died. That was why the Communist Party of Vietnam advised northerners to be patriotic to "fight against Americans and save the country" and "liberate the people of South Vietnam."

Next, one has to talk about the struggle of the ARVN soldiers in An Lộc who gave so much hope to people of all ranks not only in South Vietnam, but also in the world. Major John Howard wrote in his paper,

> The circumstances of desperation forced the ARVN to stand up to the enemy's impressive war machine and neutralize its effectiveness. In doing so, the Vietnamese soldier vindicated the less than resolute actions of former comrades in other campaigns. Often maligned by the world press prior to the offensive, he renewed his faith in himself, his leaders, and in the human frailties of the enemy.[7]

Well-known strategists like Moshe Dayan of Israel came to South Vietnam to try to understand how defenders of a small town could vanquish the elite troops of General Võ Nguyên Giáp, and Sir Robert Thompson, the British strategist—then special adviser to President Nixon—had been given a special tour of An Lộc by General Hollingsworth on 15 June 1972 and shown by General Hưng the almost complete devastation of the town as well as remnants of communist tanks strewn all over the defensive lines. Sir Thompson had been surprised by the fighting spirit, courage and resilience of the defenders of An Lộc. He mentioned that the defenders' feat at An Lộc was much bigger than that at Điện Biên Phủ and admired the generals, commanding officers and troops. There probably was no battlefield where officers and troops ran after tanks to take a shot at them. General Paul Vanuxem, a French veteran of the Indochina War, called An Lộc "the Verdun of Vietnam,"[8] and Sir Robert Thompson mentioned it as "the greatest military victory of the Free World against Communism in the post World War II era."[9]

The repercussion of the An Lộc victory spread to South Korea, Formosa, and the Philippines, forcing the chairman of the GCOS/JGS/RVNAF to form a delegation comprised of fighters to visit and talk about "the Battle of An Lộc" in Taipei and South Korea.

On 16 June, General Nguyễn Văn Minh came to visit and congratulate the defending troops. He was wildly cheered, especially by troops of the 8th Regiment of Colonel Mạch Văn Trường, one of Minh's protégés. That night, whoever listened to the Voice of the Army could hear Mạch Văn Trường relate that General Minh flew over the An Lộc sky to direct, encourage, and congratulate soldiers in order to raise troops' spirit and to drop down barbecued pork and *bánh hỏi*[10] to defending soldiers.

On 18 June 1972, General Minh declared that An Lộc was liberated.

On that same day, General Hưng was hit with an additional misfortune, this one worse than anything before: General Minh sent a message to General Hưng to return Colonel Mạch Văn Trường to the Operational Headquarters III Corps and MR3 so that he could prepare all documents related to the battle of An Lộc. He had also been chosen and designated by the III Corps and MR3 to the GCOS/JGS/RVNAF as the delegation leader of all "heroes of An Lộc" to spread the good news to other countries. Probably without thinking, General Hưng refused. The next day, General Minh himself called General Hưng who then suggested to him to designate another person because Colonel Mạch Văn Trường was unfit. This was the first time General Hưng disobeyed his superior's order. For many days, Major General Đào Duy Ân, deputy commander, and Colonel Phan Huy Lương, operational chief of staff of III Corps and MR3, called General Hưng to listen to General Minh's order but the latter refused. The following night, General Ân also called me because he trusted me when I worked at J-2/III Corps and MR3 and knew I was friendly with General Hưng. He advised me to tell him to listen to the corps and region's commander. I saw General Hưng and told him about General Ân's advice.

"That is not possible. Why not designate Colonel Vỹ, Colonel Lưởng or Colonel Nhựt? To designate Colonel Nhựt would be most appropriate because he is a local to this region," General Hưng answered with this sentence and turned to another subject.

"Do you think they still have troops, Dưỡng?" he asked

"No. They only have artillery left," I responded.

In truth, after defending forces counterattacked and recovered all positions lost and once the 81st Airborne Commando Group raised the national flag on the hill over the Đồng Long Airfield the afternoon of 12 June, COSVN infantry units had pulled out of An Lộc after suffering major losses twice or three times those of the defending forces. According to my own account, their losses could amount to 8,000, most of them related to bombing by VNAF or USAF. That number does not include the number of wounded, which could be twice or thrice as high. Their total losses at the Bình Long battlefield could be as high as 20,000, along with hundreds of tanks and armored cars, hundreds of artillery guns, and a few thousand crew-served and personal guns.

The 1st Airborne Brigade left An Lộc on 16 and 17 June for Tân Khai where it fought its last battle at Bình Long before returning to Saigon. They took a few days of rest before being shipped to the Quảng Trị battlefield. On 24 June, the 81st Airborne Commando Group was returned to the JGS/RVNAF. They had performed magnificently in An Lộc but also paid a heavy price: 68 KIA and close to 300 WIA. These numbers luckily were lower than those predicted by Colonel Huấn, their commander. He told them before the maneuver he intended to take 550 men and predicted that about 300 of them would not return. He then asked for volunteers; all 1,000 men or so raised their hands.[11]

The defensive lines that were turned over to the ARVN 5th Infantry Division and the PF units of the military area were much thinner. But enemy units had no more troops to wage a new battle; they had moved to Cambodia to be reinforced before opening new battlefields as mentioned above. But they still shelled the town for many more days: a dozen or two a day. These were mobile artillery units pulled by trucks that were difficult to eradicate. There were still some deaths, although rare; those who died once the raging battle was over really had bad karma. Therefore, those who had cold feet could feel worse than before. Those like Mr. Mạch Văn Trường who "feasted" on "barbecued pork and *bánh hỏi*" during the battle had managed to get out of An Lộc early and play the role of heroes. The straight talkers like General Hưng who refused to speak of absurdities or comply with their superiors' requests were classified as insubordinate. The fact that this event was known to many other people made the commander madder. Although he could not retaliate then, he would do it later. There was no rush.

Phú Đức Village

The price of war was borne by everyone, from troops to civilians and the town itself. In a poor country that was fighting to defend itself against an invading army, having survived the battle was by itself a blessing compared to the thousands of others who had died or were dying around them. For the people of An Lộc, whatever they had—a thatched hut, a small house or a garden plot—no longer existed. Almost everything they had built up and saved for years or decades had been destroyed, turned into ruins by those who brought in the war in order to take over the place to form the seat of the revolutionary government.

Almost everyone had left An Lộc as soon as they could: they were not used to that type of shelling and not prepared to deal with the deadly projectiles. In early July, the town that once was the home to 15,000 civilians or more had only 1,000 left. The month before, more than a thousand civilians had died from the abominable shelling. Many thousands of them had taken refuge in the nearby Phú Đức village, on the southeast side of the town that had been spared because of its lack of strategic value. Most of the wounded had been taken to the Phú Đức pagoda, which had a yard large enough to serve as a reception area after the provincial hospital had been blown apart. The pagoda itself was small with minimal facilities. They then lay on the dirt floor in the pagoda courtyard with almost no medical care. At least they were safe from the shelling. One army physician wrote about the village,

> Two flamboyant flower trees laden with bright red blossoms stood at the entrance. One might blame Nature for being so insensitive. In the courtyard, lay at random refugees deep in their pain and sadness while up above, the flamboyant flowers displayed their radiant beauty. Maybe I was the only person to have noticed the gorgeous blooms. No one else cared to look up at the top of the trees. Despite the contrast between the misery of the refugees and the splendor of the flowers, at least in this hell on earth, something sparkling fresh existed like a ray of hope to make life less depressing.[12]

After evacuating the last patient from the destroyed An Lộc hospital to Phú Đức, Corporal Nguyễn Văn Tiến did not return to the provincial hospital.

Convinced by two friends who lived in Phú Đức, he decided to remain there. The place was definitely safer than An Lộc, and he could spend all his time looking after the patients who needed any help they could find. He started caring for those who had infected wounds that had not been treated and cared for in a long time, using the bandages and antiseptic solutions that were in his possession. By word of mouth, people kept coming, transforming the pagoda yard into an outdoor first-aid station.

Then from spitefulness at their inability to capture An Lộc or because of a change in strategy, the enemy began raining down bombs and mortars on Phú Đức, disrupting the peace and tranquility and killing hundreds of innocent and unprotected people. War had followed these poor civilians to this peaceful abode. And the vicious cycle began churning. The ephemeral peace became a hell on earth in Phú Đức also. The home of Buddha was not even spared.

An Lộc in Ruins

The place called An Lộc was still there, although the town itself had almost disappeared from the map. Any careful observer could only count five or six still standing houses, although none of them had a complete roof. How could a town survive a barrage of a thousand rounds or more a day for more than two months in a row? Although the shelling continued for one more month, it was not as intense as before; but people continued to be scared of getting out into the open and refused to show their faces and look at the blue sky. They, however, could not look at the sky without looking down and seeing all the miserable devastations inflicted on their beloved town. Some, therefore, decided not to look at all. The reality was far worse than the ignorance of reality.

In the beginning people huddled in the school hoping its sturdy walls would protect them at least from the shells. When the enemy did not even spare the school, the survivors scurried to the nearby bunkers to live close to the soldiers. They cooked and slept in the soldiers' bunkers or in basements, makeshift bunkers, or wherever they could find a safe place; many who were too scared to go outside relieved themselves in tins which they threw out of the bunkers. They all had gone underground, the deeper the better, hoping to survive through the battle. They ate whatever they could put their hands on or whatever troops would share with them.

Many did not even have a family left. Children had become orphans, women became widows, and parents lost their sons and daughters. One civilian all of a sudden had to face the death of his wife and five children after a mortar fell on their dwelling. The reinforcement he had put up was not strong enough to withstand the blow of the projectile. Glad to be alive, he helped people put together the mangled pieces of flesh and bones for the final burial, trying to make sure they fit together. How could he be sure? All these pieces looked alike. But in his agony, he did his best to try to send them away as a whole instead of in pieces. That was his final gift to his loved ones. He did not even cry; he was stunned and had no tears left to shed. Around him, people were more or less in the same situation.

When they finally emerged on the ground, emaciated, weak, and wobbly, with barely skin on bones and with dirty rags on them—they did not have a shower for many weeks, if not months—they faced a devastated town that bore ill resemblance to the one they had lived in three months earlier. Theirs was a poor country town that once had houses standing, lights, cars, trucks, trees, and colors.

Now there was nothing left, just a uniform grayish black monotony among crumbled houses and buildings. Even the red soil had turned into a greyish color that resulted from the more than 78,000 rounds that fell on the town. The ground was pockmarked by innumerable craters large and small. Streets were littered with immobile, charred masses of steel, which represented former tanks. The few military vehicles were also covered with a greyish layer of dust over flat tires and broken windshields. The stench of garbage and death permeated the air. Bodies of enemy soldiers that had turned into skeletons lay here and there. Then there were the mass graves. From a lively town, An Lộc had become a ghost city and in certain places a cemetery where dead and living co-existed and shared two square kilometers of land. There were no cats, dogs, or animals running around; the birds had even deserted the area. There was no running water or electricity. Nights were dark as caves. It was surprising that no epidemics had broken out in this situation. The town was quiet except for occasional rounds that fell here and there. There were no cars on the streets except for occasional wrecks that still managed to run in the middle of a desolated war zone. The sky, however, was still blue and the sun bright. There was still hope in the air.

There was no official death toll, and numbers are variable. One does not know the exact number of civilian deaths because so many people had come in and left town in between. ARVN defenders sustained 5,400 casualties and 2,300 KIA or MIA. One battalion of the 5th ARVN had 26 troops left from a strength of 300. The NVA had never released their numbers, although they were estimated at 10,000 KIA and 20,000 WIA. The three NVA divisions were decimated. There were more than 80 burned-out enemy tanks and other vehicles in and around the town.

President Thiệu's Visit to An Lộc

On 7 July 1972, President Nguyễn Văn Thiệu, accompanied by a few ministers, Generals Cao Văn Viên, GCOS/JGS/RVNAF, and Nguyễn Văn Minh, came to An Lộc to congratulate defenders. General Hưng ordered troops to expand their range of control because he feared short- and long-range shelling. The president and the delegation which dropped by on the LZ south of An Lộc were received by General Lê Văn Hưng and Colonel Trần Văn Nhựt and escorted to a villa located above the bunker of the headquarters of the 5th Division. Neither the villa nor the bunker was hit by any of the 70,000 shells that fell over the town during the previous three months.

Inside the villa were piles of maps to be presented to the president should he ask, but he said he came not to ask questions but to reward the meritorious officers of the courageous Bình Long Province, to proclaim that the victory of An Lộc was that of the free world and to elevate the troops to one rank higher. President Thiệu declared,

> An Lộc held—and held. Where Điện Biên Phủ lasted 56 days before collapse, An Lộc held on for 70 days before driving the communists out leaving the town strewn with the wreckage of field guns and derelict Soviet T54s....
> [The] An Lộc victory was not only that of the Republic of Vietnam Armed Forces over three enemy divisions, but also the victory of the Free World's democracy over communist totalitarianism.

Since officers of the airborne and ranger units had left An Lộc, they would be elevated later: Colonel Lê Quang Lưỡng was made brigadier general and commander of the ARVN Airborne Division. Then, the president hung some promotional ranks and medals symbolically on a few officers.

President Thiệu read the commendation promoting General Hưng to the rank of full brigadier general officially and awarded him the National Order, Third Class—the highest medal of the nation—with Gallantry Cross and Palm for his glorious victory. Colonel Trần Văn Nhựt was officially promoted to full colonel officially and awarded a National Order Medal, Third Class, with Gallantry Cross and Palm, and Colonel Mạch Văn Trường was officially promoted to full colonel. As he finished reading, President Thiệu proceeded to go to the next person, Lieutenant Colonel Lý Đức Quân, commander of the 7th Regiment, when suddenly General Minh walked to him and explained, while thrusting into his hands a National Order Medal, Third

Class, that the National Order Medals, First and Second Class, were usually reserved for foreign dignitaries and chiefs of state.

"Mr. President, please pin on Colonel Trường the…"

"Does Colonel Trường have a Fourth Class National Order Medal yet?" the president interrupted.

"Yes…. I have already suggested … in an official proposition to the JGS … pretty soon," General Minh responded.

The president hesitated but walked to Colonel Trường and pinned on him a National Order Medal, Third Class, with Gallantry Cross and Palm.

Beautiful scheme. Well choreographed. After that, the president pinned the colonel insignia to Lieutenant Colonel Lý Đức Quân and Lieutenant Colonel Trịnh Đình Đăng, 3rd Bureau chief of the division. Next he pinned the Lieutenant Colonel insignia on me and Major Huỳnh Văn Tâm, deputy commander of the 8th Regiment, the person who truly commanded the 8th Regiment throughout the An Lộc battlefield. A few sub-officers and troops were given new insignia.

After the ceremony, the president and his delegation were given a visit to all the fighting sites of the An Lộc battlefield. President Thiệu stopped at the charred hulls of five T-54s that were lying around the command post of the 8th Regiment and had pictures taken with soldiers. He stopped and knelt in prayer before the Savior's Statue that had remained intact despite two months of continuous shelling. He visited the 81st Airborne Commando Group cemetery and knelt in front of its memorial monument to commemorate the fallen commandos as well as the residents who had lost their lives during the battle.

General Hưng presented to President Thiệu the helmet he wore during the siege in appreciation for his visit. The president tapped Hưng's shoulder, shook his hands, and then boarded the departing plane. He must have treasured the gift because he kept the helmet on his desk at the Independence Palace.[13]

The delegation stayed in An Lộc for two hours during which no shell fell on the city. The president indeed was very lucky. A lot of happiness, but also a lot of misfortune. Later, after he immigrated to the U.S., he did not speak or write a word for many years. Silence is golden.

During this ceremony, obvious injustice was visible. Colonel Lê Nguyên Vỹ was not present at this ceremony and was not promoted to brigadier general; he did not receive any commendation. It was only two years later when General Phạm Quốc Thuần became commander of the III Corps and MR3 that he was promoted to commander of the 5th Division in place of Brigadier General Trần Quốc Lịch. Another person who had performed the most deeds in An Lộc under the most difficult circumstances was Colonel Bùi Đức Điềm; as mentioned earlier, he was old oak left somewhere in the forest of Bình Long; he did not receive any promotion or commendation until South Vietnam was lost.

One sad note is worth mentioning. Just a few days after President Thiệu visited An Lộc, on 7 July 1972, Brigadier General Richard J. Tallman, deputy commander of TRAC, along with a few staff officers flew in to visit An Lộc. As his helicopter landed on the provincial runway, it was shelled; the first shell missed him, although the second one fell in the middle of the delegation as they ran for cover. Three officers were immediately killed. General Tallman was evacuated to 3rd Field Hospital and operated on. Due to the severity of his injuries, he died on the operating table. During the Bình Long battle, from Lộc Ninh to An Lộc and the blockade of Tàu-Ô stream, many U.S. advisers had either died or were lost in action. I do not know how many. We, the fighters of An Lộc, pay tribute to you and share our grief with your families. We thank troops from the USAF and other units for having participated in this battle and saved us.

Reassignment

On 11 July 1972, the 18th ARVN Infantry Division under the command of Colonel Lê Minh Đảo moved in to replace the 5th Infantry Division, which was transferred back to its base in Lai Khê. The 25th Infantry Division moved to Chơn Thành replacing the 21st Infantry Division to continue the job of uprooting the blockade at Tàu-Ô stream. Overall, the losses by the 21st Infantry Division were worse than those of the 5th Infantry Division, but the division was able to pin down the NVA 7th Division—with a total loss of probably 7,000 troops—preventing it from reinforcing any friendly unit. Major General Nguyễn Vĩnh Nghi, after returning to the southwest, was pinned a third star and promoted to commander of the IV Corps and MR4.

I returned to Lai Khê with a lot of sadness. I was promoted to lieutenant colonel on the battlefield on 7 July 1972, five years after wearing the major rank—three years on temporary basis, two as a full grade—that was the last reward of my military career. I felt a sadness I did not find any cause for. Maybe because I had seen the heat in a battle—this time it was a real battle—life and death, blood and flesh all over as well as common graves for innocent people. I had seen the suffering of troops with pictures of sublime sacrifice, as well as the sordidness in the military system.

Yes, the indomitable ARVN—I love that corps like my own life, more than anything in life. And because of it, after my immigration to the U.S., I left everything to go back to school and do what I once called "*lật đất*," or unearthing documents to learn more about the truth and to defend our colors. I have achieved my goal by writing the story of that war in English—a few-hundred-page-long book that I felt was as complete as it could be—to answer our critics. But the truth that needs to be unearthed cannot be kept hidden forever; therefore, I need to expand somewhat to bring justice to those who had passed away.

Apparently General Hưng had also done some thinking on his return from An Lộc. Maybe he had been more aware of and thought more about the sentence "a successful general, thousands of dead troops." He did not want it that way. For a general who has directed a battle, life and death, victory or failure, are just normal events. No leader would want to sacrifice too many of his troops. I know that losing troops at the Lộc Ninh battle has made him think a lot. Maybe he felt guilty for having let down his teacher. In truth, he has not. General Minh had supported him from 1st lieutenant to general, as he told me. General Hưng wanted to use his life to thank his teacher. But he also had brought honor to himself and General Minh over a long period. As to his judgments in An Lộc, although they did not coincide with those of General Minh, he had saved An Lộc in its moment of distress.

Once dining together sometime after the An Lộc battle in a nice and quiet restaurant in Saigon, General Hưng asked me, "Do you like to read philosophy books, Dưỡng? Are you a practicing any religion or following any doctrine?" "No," I answered. "I hate philosophy and do not like any doctrine or anyone who wants to tell me about morals. I am not knowledgeable in these fields." "So do I," he said. "But there are a lot of things that make us think about religion in life, and life and death."

I think and know that General Hưng was not only an officer who knew how to wage battles on the battlefield, but he also has thought more than those who have just enjoyed perks in life or have not valued the lives of their troops. He has followed what was right and acted by it. He was a progressive and bright mind with many solid and concrete thoughts, a love for soldiers, national colors, and the country. Only people like him could think about shooting themselves in the heart and brain to destroy what was precious in them before others could do it to him. I knew that in An Lộc, he was mum, and willing to accept the injustice of those whom he had considered as his benefactors and owed respect. Why did people want to destroy the prestige of these noble and truthful spirits? Until today, more than four decades after his self-sacrifice, the plan to denigrate him still affects some

XI. Releasing the Pressure on An Lộc

people living abroad, including fellows who had worked with him in the past. I understand and know him more than anyone who has loved him. I am sorry for having written those words.

I thought that because of having made a correct and just decision to deny letting Colonel Mạch Văn Trường return to Lai Khê to lead the delegation "Brave Bình Long," General Hưng had been called "disloyal to his master." Was it just because this was the additional drop that caused the water to overflow or because the prestige of General Hưng has spread far and near around the country? The word "disloyal," which has been used in front of me, has been witnessed by Colonel Mạch Văn Trường who is presently living in California. The two generals (Minh and Hưng) having passed away a long time ago, I, as a person who has the responsibility to "overturn the soil," want to relate the truth because the living are still here.

Just about a week after my return to Lai Khê from An Lộc, General Minh through an intermediary invited me to have lunch with him at his Biên Hoà headquarters. Although the invitation surprised me, I accepted it; I do not remember the exact date, but just that afternoon after I arrived at General Minh's residence overlooking a river, I was led to the commander's trailer. There I found him in company with Colonel Mạch Văn Trường. I saluted him and was led to the dining room. Throughout lunch, he was pleasant to Trường and me. When he finished his meal and while sipping coffee and smoking, he gravely explained to me why he had invited me to have lunch with him:

> Dưỡng has been working with me and knows me. I hate those who are disloyal to me. Go back and tell Hưng not to be disloyal to his master. I have saved his neck on many occasions not only at An Lộc but also on many occasions at the 21st Division. I have supported Hưng from the time he was a captain to general. Why did he turn his back on me?

These words so surprised me that I remained quiet, not daring to breathe for a few minutes. Even Colonel Trường did not say anything. I flew back to Lai Khê in a very pensive mood. Thus General Minh had used me as an intermediary to transmit his feelings and words to my friend and immediate superior. After thinking for a few days, I met General Hưng in his office and repeated General Minh's words. General Hưng smiled softly—a forced and sad smile—but like his usual self, he did not say anything. He did not show any anger or emotion. From that time on, he looked at me in a friendlier manner. He understood the reason why I refused to return to Lai Khê to stay with him in An Lộc to fight against the enemy. He did not give me any favor, only a truthful heart feeling from one man to another.

Not long after that, General Hưng was ordered to transfer his position of commander of the 5th ARVN Division to airborne Colonel Trần Quốc Lịch and to return to Biên Hoà to become head of operations to General Minh. And not long after, I heard people joking about General Hưng's blinking eyes and rampant rumor that since he had never left his bunker at An Lộc, he was afraid of sunlight and blinked his eyes all the time. I had mentioned earlier that General Hưng used to blink his eyes a long time ago since his years as a cadet. More than that, using that tic as proof, people surreptitiously reported to the highest level of the government and the ARVN and blamed his incompetency for the huge losses at Lộc Ninh. When he returned to Biên Hoà, I knew he would stop at that rank.

Before Colonel Trần Quốc Lịch was assigned to replace General Hưng, Colonel Trường was made province chief and head of the military section of Long Khánh. As for Colonel Lê Nguyên Vỹ and Colonel Bùi Đức Điềm, I had lost track of them. Assistant operation chief III Corps and MR3 was the post Colonel Lê Nguyên Vỹ held when he destroyed a tank at An Lộc, and each night, he, Trịnh Đình Đăng and I slept in cots in the bunker close together for almost three months.

On another occasion after the Biên Hòa episode, I met an army news officer from the RVNAF Political Warfare Directorate in Lai Khê. He had asked Colonel Trịnh Đình Đăng for a copy of operations log of the 5th Infantry Division at An Lộc in order to write a personal biography of General Minh. Colonel Đăng referred him to me because when the six officers of the 3rd Bureau of the headquarters were killed by a 122 mm rocket while they were lunching, no one had kept the operations log, except Colonel Đăng, me and two captains, Dương Tấn Triệu and Nguyễn Chí Cường of my 2nd Bureau (they both were promoted to major and still worked for me after An Lộc). Therefore, that document had been retyped and kept by me during that period. The drawbacks of the report included the lack of documentation of the positions of friendly units in An Lộc and the air missions of VNAF and USAF because the latter two captains were intelligence, not logistics officers. After the visitor explained the reason for his request, I turned him down and told him in a sentence that I still remember today, "If you ask these documents for the Press Section of the Political Warfare Directorate, I'll give them to you right away; but for writing a personal biography for General Minh, I refuse."

The visitor simply left without saying anything. I knew that my career path would be shut down also and stop there.

A few days later, I brought a copy of the records to the History Branch/JGS/RVNAF to turn it over to Colonel Phạm Văn Sơn for documentation, but he was away. I gave it to a major in this division. Later, I was told that the history of the An Lộc Bình Long battle was written by Lieutenant Colonel Lê Văn Dương, the new chief of History Branch/5th Bureau/RVNAF, with the assistance of Major Lê Văn Ban and Captain Tạ Chí Đại Trường. Occasionally they had made reference to the operations log of the 5th Division written by Captains Triệu and Cường during their stay in An Lộc.

Later, he and I settled in Honolulu and met each other occasionally.

XII

Besieged Towns

Although there were many sieges of towns and encampments throughout the whole Vietnam War, three of them stood out because of their impact on the outcome of the war. These were the sieges of Điện Biên Phủ, Khe Sanh, and An Lộc. In this chapter, we will look at how these sieges were won or lost and how they were waged as well as their impact on the war.

Điện Biên Phủ (13 March–7 May 1954)

General Henri Navarre, commander of the French Forces in Indochina in 1953, decided to set up a fortified airhead in the village of Điện Biên Phủ to prevent the communists from reinforcing and supplying their troops in neighboring Laos. He thought that without further reinforcements, the communist forces would withdraw from Laos. Điện Biên Phủ was a 6-by-18-kilometer-wide valley surrounded by hills in northwest North Vietnam close to the Laotian border. It was the seat of a village that was displaced by the war and lay about 300 kilometers from the Chinese border where the North Vietnamese communists received their Chinese armaments and supplies and about the same distance from Hanoi, the headquarters of French troops in North Vietnam.

Stuck in a mountainous jungle area, it therefore could not be easily supplied or reinforced by roads, which were primitive at best, or by air because it was at the extreme operating range of transport aircraft or fighters of the time. It was considered safe from artillery fire from the surrounding hills, which were about 12 kilometers from the local airstrip on maps. In reality, the latter airstrip was only five kilometers from the closest hill line. Navarre's experts also estimated that the operation at Điện Biên Phủ would carry little or no risk.[1] The overly optimistic intelligence estimates, which turned out not to be correct, eventually led to the downfall of the French forces. While reviewing the report, Navarre then thought it was a "mediocre solution," but the only one available.

General Giáp had never revealed the strength of his troops nor the calibers of his artillery guns, although it was estimated at between 30,000 to 50,000 men and 20 to 24 105 mm howitzers, 15 to 20 75 mm howitzers, 20 120 mm mortars, 40 82 mm mortars, 80 37 mm anti-aircraft guns, 100 anti-aircraft guns, and 12 Katyusha six-tube rocket launchers.[2] The communists held the high ground three to four kilometers from the airstrip and two kilometers from the French entrenchments.

The French had 10,800 men holding eight strongpoints scattered throughout the valley and named alphabetically with female names: Anne-Marie, Beatrice, Claudine, Dominique, Eliane, Gabrielle, Huguette, and Isabelle. They had 24 105 mm howitzers, four 122 mm mortars, four 155 mm howitzers, 10 light tanks, six fighter aircraft and six observation planes. The quality of their forces, which were multi-national, varied. The paratroopers, legionnaires, and some African units were good while the local T'ai units were definitely inadequate. Many of the latter soon deserted the battlefield, leaving 3,000 to 4,000 troops out of a garrison of 10,000. The fortifications were frail due to lack of building materials: due to distance and road inadequacy, the French failed to move enough materials for the defense. The artillery support was inadequate; the lack of camouflage and concealment and the poor planning and organization of counterattacks rounded up the deficiencies of execution. Colonel Christian de Castries, the French commander at Điện Biên Phủ, was a talented and aggressive commander of light armor, but unsuitable for the trench warfare that soon unfolded at this battlefield. He had no appetite for the defense and no experience or skill in its tactics and techniques.[3]

Since the French positions were spread out over a large area (Isabelle was seven kilometers south of the village, Gabrielle three kilometers north), the communists used trench warfare to knock down one outpost after another before concentrating on the airstrip and attacking the four main ones: Dominique, Eliane, Claudine, and Huguette. Outnumbered and with scattered and weak defensive positions, the French units failed to assist one another during the three-month-long attack.

Phase I: 13–30 March. The first attack began on 13 March 1954 at 17:00 hours with Việt Minh bombardment of Gabrielle and Beatrice outposts, both exposed but defended by an Algerian battalion and a Legionnaire battalion respectively. That night's attack was focused on Beatrice, which was poorly fortified. The Việt Minh's artillery struck the airfield where planes, fuel, ammunition burned and exploded. A round hit the command post killing the Legionnaire commander and his staff. Another artillery shell killed the commander's immediate superior, leaving the three companies without central coordination. At 00:15 on 14 March, Beatrice was overrun and the French lost 400 out of 500 defenders. The Việt Minh lost 600 KIA and 1,200 seriously wounded. A counterattack was ordered but put on hold to accommodate for a four-hour truce.

The defenders reorganized their defenses and received the 5th Vietnamese Parachute Battalion (BPVN), which dug in on Eliane at 18:00 hours. At 17:00 on 14 March, Gabrielle was shelled then attacked, but the French held. At 03:30 on 15 March, the Việt Minh shelled and attacked again. At 04:00, Gabrielle lost its command leadership following a shell burst. Colonel Castries ordered Colonel Langlais to mount a tank-led counterattack; but of all the available forces, he chose for the attack the 5th BPVN, which had just parachuted into the camp the night before. They were exhausted and unfamiliar with the barbed-wire entanglements of Điện Biên Phủ. Located at the southeast side of the central camp, they had to traverse the whole encampment to get into position. They also did not have the energy and experience of the other available units.

The counterattack began at 05:30 hours. Halfway toward Beatrice, they were hit with heavy mortars and shells. Part of the battalion escaped harm by moving forward while the rest froze and lay there taking heavy casualties. The counterattack having stalled, the remaining Algerian defenders of Beatrice left the compound with the rescuing unit and returned to the main camp by 09:00. Losses were heavy on both sides: 1,000 KIA for the French and somewhere between 1,000 and 2,000 KIA for the Việt Minh with double that number wounded.

The fall of Gabrielle and Beatrice left only the Anne Marie fortification held by the 3rd T'ai Battalion standing on the northern semicircle of outposts. Demoralized by the fall of the other outposts and undermined by communist propaganda that warned them that this was not their war but that of foreigners, the bulk of the T'ais slipped away on the night of 15–16 March. The remaining T'ais and French pulled back to Huguette strongpoint. The rest of the month marked a lull period during which the two sides prepared for new battles. On 28 March, the French mounted a surprise counterattack destroying 17 anti-aircraft guns and killing 350 Việt Minh troops.[4]

Phase II: 30 March–30 April. The Việt Minh attacked the five eastern hills Eliane 1 and 2, Dominique 1 and 2 and a small hill between Dominique 1 and 2; and the three western hills Huguette 1, 6 and 7. The attacks were brutal and intense and were followed by counterattacks that were no less intense. Positions changed hands many times with heavy losses on both sides. By 12 April, the morale of the Việt Minh soldiers broke. Giap's losses amounted to 16,000 to 19,000: 6,000 KIA, 8,000 to 10,000 seriously wounded and 2,500 captured. The Việt Minh and the French lived in the mud and filth of the trenches, which were flooded by monsoon rains. The medical conditions were terrible: the Việt Minh 50,000-man army had only *one* surgeon and six "assistant doctors," who in essence were simple medics. Injured soldiers usually died from infections and gangrene.[5]

The French were in no better shape because they had received only minimal supplies and reinforcements due to active Việt Minh artillery guns. The strong southern position Isabelle was completely isolated and ripe to fall.

Phase III: 1–7 May. By 2 May, Eliane 1 and Dominique 3 had fallen; Eliane 3 and Huguette 5 were under attack. Both sides fought in water, often waist deep, and the battlefield was then an epic of agony and courage. On 6 May, the Việt Minh 102nd Regiment went on the attack on Eliane 2. It was met with a TOT (time-on-target) firing in which various artillery units fired at different times so that the rounds arrived on target at the same time. When the smoke disappeared, the French had won the first round. General Giáp then employed a rarely used stratagem: he had a mine shaft burrowed under Eliane 2, loaded it with 3,000 pounds of TNT, and blew up Eliane 2. By 05:00 on 7 May, the position was overrun. A final assault on the center of the camp began at 15:00 hours, and the garrison surrendered at 17:30 hours on 7 May 1954.[6]

The intensity and violence of the enemy artillery attack on the tiny town of An Lộc had never been witnessed before even at the 1954 Điên Biên Phủ or the 1968 Khe Sanh battlefields. At Điện Biên Phủ, General Võ Nguyên Giáp's troops had to systematically take over each French outpost and communication trench day by day in order to reach the headquarters of De Castries on Hill A-1. There, the communists later built a museum to the feat of arms that divided Vietnam into two states courtesy of communist troops. Phạm Tiến Duật wrote a beautiful poem about the museum on the hill. That poem could be considered as "reactionary" although the communists did not realize it or just disregarded it. Giáp's artillery positions on the adjoining hills dropped bombs on perimeter troops, although the intensity, accuracy, and power of destruction was neither fierce nor strong.

In the prisoner exchange, only 3,290 were alive out of the 10,863 taken prisoner at Điên Biên Phủ. At camps like Dachau or Buchenwald, 80 percent had died; among the Điện Biên Phủ prisoners, 70 percent had perished.[7]

The French commission of inquiry, which convened in 1955 to find out what went wrong at the battlefield, found a plethora of mistakes. General Navarre had underestimated the strength of the Việt Minh who were armed and advised by the Chinese army. Điện Biên Phủ could not be defended because it was accessible only by air and should have been evacuated back in December. General Cogny shared the blame for failing to advise Castries about changing his passive defense tactics and about the Viet Minh tactics of hiding their artillery. General Castries did not improve the defensive dispositions of the base. Being a tank commander, he was found to be unsuited for the defense of a base supplied by air.[8]

Khe Sanh (21 January–8 April 1968)

Khe Sanh was a well-fortified U.S. Marine position (III Marine Amphibious Force IIIMAF) located at the Vietnamese-Laotian border west of Cam Lộ, province of Quảng Trị, on Route 9 leading to the strategic town of Tchepone—an important provincial Laotian transportation hub for communist troops dispatched from Hanoi to infiltrate into South Vietnam. The town was the focus of the 719 Lam Sơn offensive in 1971 by the ARVN. Khe Sanh, which was protected by 5,500 U.S. Marine troops and reinforced by 1,100 ARVN Rangers, was under the command of Colonel Davis Lounds.

Although road communication was interrupted between Khe Sanh and the eastern U.S. artillery base of Calu about 35 kilometers from Cam Lộ and Khe Sanh was surrounded by large units of the NVA Route 9 Front's forces, which consisted of three infantry divisions—325 C, 304th, and 320th—and a regiment of the 324th, one artillery division and other special units, Khe Sanh was protected by an advanced electronic barrier and surrounded by heavy fortifications. Few people had heard about the electronic barrier, which was invisible, ran over many kilometers in length and surrounded the perimeter defenses. It was an anti-infiltration barrier complete with new technologic anti-personnel and anti-tank sensors. The latter were as small as a grenade or as large as an anti-tank mine, while others were tubes a few meters long. All these devices were dropped from U.S. aircraft and landed on the ground undetected among grass, trees, or rocks. Infiltrating troops or tanks were detected by these sensors, which triggered signals to the central command. The latter then ordered the suspicious area bombed.

According to various sources at that time, General Westmoreland had also devised the so-called Niagara Operation, which used B-52 bombers to protect the base and to eliminate as many enemy troops as possible. However, many U.S. strategists thought that such a trap could backfire into another

Điên Biên Phủ, which meant losing the war. Therefore, the Khe Sanh battlefield became the talk of every politician, military personnel, and especially newspapers, which eventually raised fears in every U.S. family and institution. President Johnson had even uttered these famous words, showing his dislike for the area: "I don't want any damn Dinbinphoo."[9]

The NVA Route 9 Front's troops, having surrounded Khe Sanh for months, attacked surrounding hills controlled by U.S. troops and shelled the base with a few hundred mortars daily. However, these mortars were launched from afar and over a long period of time; the lone infantry assault that was aimed at the southern perimeter location held by the ARVN Rangers was quickly repulsed. Each time enemy troops tried to infiltrate other areas, like the north, northwest and east, which were flooded with sensors, they were destroyed by either the 175 mm howitzers located at Calu base or by B-52 boxes. Besides, every day, U.S. Air Force SAC (Strategic Air Command) would send B-52 bombers to drop bombs on enemy positions causing thousands of them to die before they even set out to attack Khe Sanh. Overall, U.S. Air Force bombers delivered 14,223 tons of bombs and rockets while the U.S. Marine Air Wing dropped 17,015 tons of ordnance.[10]

The decision to take a stand at Khe Sanh was Westmoreland's[11]: Khe Sanh was a useful observation post, a platform for launching special operation forays into Laos and controlling the traffic on the nearby Ho Chi Minh Trail. However, the North Vietnamese had other ideas. General Trần Công Mẫn, editor of the newspaper *Nhân Dân Quân Đội* (People's Army) once told an American journalist,

> Westmoreland thought Khe Sanh was Điện Biên Phủ. But Điện Biên Phủ was the strategic battle for us. We mobilized everything for it. At last we had a chance to have a favorable balance of forces…. We never had that at Khe Sanh; the situation would not allow it. Our true aim was to lure your forces away from the cities, to decoy them to the frontiers, to prepare for our great Tết Offensive.[12]

The above comment could be self-serving because the NVA would not mass three divisions, or a total of 22,000 troops according to the CIA,[13] around Khe Sanh just to try to divert attention away from the cities. They themselves badly needed these three divisions to prepare an attack somewhere else. Second, if they did not intend to attack Khe Sanh, why would they launch that many attacks against the nearby hills and overpower the village of Lang Vei on 7 February? Why would they dig that many trenches toward the Khe Sanh base? Why would they build two new roads parallel to Route 9 to the north and south and extend them to Laos if there was no purpose to them?[14] As mentioned above, one of the reasons they could not muster enough manpower to overrun the base was simply because too many troops had been killed by the B-52 bombing.

The high number of U.S. losses was estimated at 1,000 KIA, 4,500 WIA.[15] How large were the communist losses (estimated at 10,000–12,000), only northern leaders would know the exact number, although they were as mute as the old forests of the region or robots that did not have any feeling or fear. No one dared to reveal the truth. However, on the political side, the potential attack on Khe Sanh had caused fear among U.S. political and military authorities and news agencies to the point that they forgot the terrible murders caused by the communists in Huế during the Tết Offensive.

The decision was made to eventually abandon Khe Sanh. Once abandoned, the marine positions were bulldozed flat, the airstrip was removed, and the bunkers were destroyed. No physical presence remained for fear the communists would use it for propaganda purpose. Both sides claimed victory, although Khe Sanh provided neither a clear victory nor a definite defeat for either adversary.[16]

An Lộc (7 April–7 July)

An Lộc was attacked by the COSVN 5th, 7th, and 9th Divisions (previously VC, but gradually replaced by NVA troops) which had been hiding respectively in base areas (BA) BA 712, BA 714, and BA 711 in Cambodia. The VC 5th Division attacked Lộc Ninh first on 4 and 5 April with artillery and tanks and overwhelmed the village on 6 April. Things could have gone better for a while had the age-old commander of Lộc Ninh been replaced by one of his younger and more aggressive assistants; the end result, however, would not have been different because of the presence of overwhelming enemy forces.

A forward regiment of the VC 5th Division took over Quản Lợi airstrip northeast of An Lộc on 7 April while the NVA 7th Division blocked Highway 13 south of An Lộc. The NVA attacked the town from 13 to 15 April with artillery and tanks but were repulsed. They attacked again on 19 April but made no further progress.

On 11 May came the third attack on An Lộc with heavy artillery and tanks. Again no progress was made. The punch was gone as the NVA was pounded by B-52 strikes. The battle of An Lộc was won by the valor of the ARVN troops and attacks by U.S. and VNAF fighter-bombers. Highway 13, however, was only freed for civilian and army traffic in July.

Critique

Although the communists had used overwhelming troops to defeat the French forces, the loss of the Điện Biên Phủ battle was General Navarre's own doing.

First, he chose the wrong place to fight: a remote mountainous jungle area that was difficult to resupply and reinforce. Although Điện Biên Phủ was, according to Navarre, a "marginally defendable place" because of its inaccessibility by land or by air, he made up his mind to take a stand right there. It was a brave tactic that, if successful, would not only prevent the communists from spreading the war into Laos, but would localize them into North Vietnam where they would be more easily controlled. But he then failed to adjust his objectives to his means. The survival of the garrison hinged on keeping the airfield intact and the airspace above Điện Biên Phủ open so that airdrops could be made; otherwise the place was condemned.[17]

Second, the French's selection of Castries as the commander of the garrison turned out not to be the correct one: the latter was not aggressive enough to prepare for the attack, to beef up the defensive sites, and to wage a tough battle, although his troops fought courageously against overwhelming forces. As a matter of fact, they revolted against him and downgraded him as an emeritus commander while Lieutenant Colonel Langlais took over the command and sharpened the later phase of the defense.[18] Castries underestimated his enemy and failed to make forays to neutralize the enemy's artillery guns. He did order one single expedition, which although successful came too late to reverse the tide. Had there been another leader since the beginning of the battle, history could have been different.

Third, the failure of Navarre to bring in supplies and reinforcements doomed the defense: while Giáp could bring in two fresh divisions, Castries had to rely on his worn-out and decimated troops. Still the understrength French forces were able to inflict on the communist forces a morale breakdown, although in the end, the French had to surrender.

General Giáp adapted well to the siege. He cornered Navarre into taking a stand in a "mediocre" place from which the latter could not get out. He had his artillery guns well positioned to disable the airstrip and prevent aircraft from bringing in reinforcements. He rallied his troops when they broke down and brought in enough reinforcements to drown out the French. There were, however, a few occasions when the French could have overwhelmed their attackers had they received reinforcements. Of course, Giáp paid dearly for all these efforts as he lost more than two of his five divisions in this battle and barely mentioned these astronomic losses in his book. He did not care to throw new troops after new troops into the battlefield and was oblivious to the pain and suffering of these soldiers. The Vietnamese call this desperate act "roasting" the troops or unnecessarily wasting them until he became victorious. About Giáp, Safer wrote,

> Utterly brainwashed by ambition. Sending so many young men to die is never a matter of moral hesitation. It is, and especially in Giáp's case, only a question of the strategy of the moment.... Brave men are the tools for carving one's initials in the pantheon.[19]

When the reporter Safer asked whether he had any regret about sending so many people to a certain death, Giáp answered, "Never. Not a single moment."[20]

The veterans, however, were no dupe of the general's intentions. One of the crippled veterans at the Thuận Thanh Field Hospital north of the DMZ said, "Please ask the heroic general [Giáp] if the General Offensive (Tet Offensive) was worth it ... tell him one of his soldiers, a lot of his soldiers aren't sure."[21]

As for Khe Sanh, the way the NVA had waged the battle was incoherent to American eyes. Giáp, or whoever was in charge, simply would not expose three divisions just for show and tell or for the B-52 bombers to target them. There must be another reason for it. The best one advanced by Davidson was that General Giáp was in the vicinity—one of the caves—of Khe Sanh directing the attack himself.

Giáp mobilized three divisions to the Khe Sanh area in December 1967 and January 1968. The 304th and 325C Divisions were supported by tanks and artillery with the decision as of 20 January to overrun Khe Sanh.

From 21 January to 10 February, he made five battalion-size assaults against the outposts including Lang Vei and Khe Sanh village to occupy the high positions over the Khe Sanh garrison. From there, his forces could easily fire on Khe Sanh.

Then, in mid–February, he changed his mind, probably on the account of the resolute defense of the marines or on the possible use of atomic bombs by the U.S. On 23 February, the NVA launched a record number of shells and mortars at the camp—1,307. On 29 February, he launched a regiment assault on the perimeter held by the ARVN 37th Ranger Battalion and used the occasion to get out of the battle zone.[22]

Thus Westmoreland won a colossal gamble, not so much by his own brilliance as by Giáp's ineptitude and vacillation.[23] General Westmoreland had once asked Colonel Argo, a military historian to give a general assessment of Khe Sanh against classic sieges. Argo found a total of thirty-nine sieges going all the way back to the siege of Constantinople in 1453. Although medieval fortresses held fairly well against sieges, the advent of gunpowder changed the outcome of the sieges. Of the 15 sieges identified in the 20th century, defenders were successful in only two instances: the Soviets at Leningrad in 1941–1944 and the Americans at Bastogne in 1944. Success was often due to the effective dispatch of relief forces and the withdrawal of attackers.[24]

During a meeting of the National Security Council on 27 March 1968, General Earl Wheeler, chairman of the JCS, suggested that Hanoi had achieved its goal, which was to pull away U.S. forces from Huế and Saigon, their main objectives during the Tết Offensive. General Westmoreland, the former MACV commander, on the other hand, contended that it was a U.S. victory because the U.S. had inflicted a lot of casualties on the NVA.

But from a strategic point of view, the abandonment of Khe Sanh on 12 June 1968, the day after Westmoreland relinquished his MACV command under pressure by President Johnson and his adviser General Maxwell Taylor, defeated its original purposes. The latter were to: (1) protect the DMZ, (2) cut off enemy infiltration to the South, and (3) support a potential invasion of Laos.[25] The abandonment of Khe Sanh laid bare the northeast corner of South Vietnam allowing the NVA free access to this area and continuing troop reinforcement in the I Corps and MR1.

The An Lộc defenders suffered from a massive shelling never experienced before by defenders at any other battlefield, including Khe Sanh and Điện Biên Phủ. Just in one day, they had received more than 10,000 rounds—15 percent of the shelling fired by the NVA during the whole siege at Khe Sanh. They were also attacked by tanks, not once but on multiple occasions—one of the rare times the NVA used tanks in their attacks on South Vietnamese soil. The combination artillery/tanks/infantry attack was deadly as the NVA troops were able on two occasions to control half of the town. They were within 100 meters—barely two blocks—from the divisional command post.

In spite of the deteriorating situation, General Hưng fought on even when enemy forces were converging on his bunker. He was weary and cautious, but still in command. "Hưng never buckled, though he was clearly concerned."[26] Troops had confidence in him because he had mentioned to them that he would resist until death and would not be taken alive should he fail. He instilled in them the will and determination to hang in the battle and fight on. He remained in the destroyed town suffering through all the enemy's shelling and mortaring like any infantry troop. He suffered from the same deprivation of food, sleep, and rest like any other combatant at An Lộc. For more than two long months, he shared the same pain, pressure, and suffering as his soldiers.

In a war as in law, possession is nine-tenths of ownership, and after the smoke has cleared, An Lộc still remained in Saigon's hands. As one anonymous American adviser observed, "The only way to approach the battle of An Lộc is to remember that the ARVN are there and the North Vietnamese aren't. To view it in any other way is to do an injustice to the Vietnamese people."[27] The An Lộc victory was a permanent one as Saigon still controlled the town until the end of the war in 1975.

Although overwhelmed by NVA artillery and manpower, defenders benefited from the effective airpower of the U.S. and VNAF. The NVA used the same pattern of attack-lull, attack-lull, which the ARVN used to their advantage to bring in fresh troops. The failure of the enemy to coordinate infantry and tanks favored the defenders who hunted down and killed all the tanks. Giáp strategically erred in trying to overrun a rubble-strewn town instead of bypassing it and driving down Highway 13 to Saigon.[28] At that stage, he was still longing to possess a South Vietnamese town to prop up the National Liberation Front.

If at each phase of the Vietnam War a major battle did have an important political impact, Điện Biên Phủ and Khe Sanh carried an important strategic and political message for solving the conflict, while the fiery summer of 1972 at An Lộc also had its own important political implication. The loss of An Lộc would be much worse than that of Điện Biên Phủ or Khe Sanh. If the loss of Điên Biên Phủ led to the loss of half of the nation's territory to the communists, that of Khe Sanh and the Tết Offensive could cause the U.S. president to lose his self-confidence. On the other hand, the loss of An Lộc would lead to an earlier loss of South Vietnam, a Republican candidate overwhelming a Democratic opponent in the presidential election, or a loss of prestige for the U.S. forces.

The potential differences and similarities between the three battlefields are listed in the following table.

Table II. Characteristics of the Three Battlefields Waged During the Vietnam War

	An Lộc	*Khe Sanh*	*Điện Biên Phủ*
Year	*1972*	*1968*	*1954*
Location (Vietnam)	South	Center	North
Topography	Open, hills	Valley, hills	Valley
Perimeters (km)	1.5 × 1.5	16 × 9	
Siege (length, days)	94	77	56
Defense			
Forces	7,500	5,500	10,000
Civilians	10,000	0	0

XII. Besieged Towns

	An Lộc	*Khe Sanh*	*Điện Biên Phủ*
Year	1972	1968	1954
Artillery (def)	None	Yes	105 mm (24), 155 mm (4)
Tanks (def)	None	Yes	Yes
Air support	Yes	Yes	No
Losses	5,000	1,000 KIA	2,200 KIA
Offense			
Forces	21,000	22,000	30,000
Tanks	Yes	Not used	No
Losses	10,000	10,000 est.	8,000 KIA, 10,000 WIA

XIII

Return to the Mekong Delta

In August or September 1974, I do not remember exactly when, Colonel Lê Nguyên Vỹ was promoted to commander of the 5th Infantry Division replacing Brigadier General Trần Quốc Lịch, who was transferred to the position of chief inspector IV Corps and MR4. Colonel Vỹ earned the promotion thanks to Lieutenant General Phạm Quốc Thuần who had replaced Lieutenant General Nguyễn Văn Minh as commander of III Corps and MR3. General Thuần was commander of the ARVN 5th Infantry Division when Colonel Vỹ was commander of the 8th Regiment. It was at that time that I decided to request a transfer to the J-2/JGS/RVNAF (Joint Staff Intelligence of the Joint General Staff of the Republic of Vietnam Armed Forces), which was luckily approved.

At the end of 1974, the J-2/JGS/RVNAF, realizing that the instability had gotten worse following the signing of the Paris Accords in January 1973, where all the clauses pointed to a surrender of Nixon-Kissinger to the communists (all the political commentators had used similar terminology), the RVNAF began waging a "poor man's war," solo this time, as mentioned by President Thiệu. The situation got worse with time, and the RVNAF soldier ended up fighting a war with old armaments and limited ammunitions. This occurred in all units throughout the four military regions. The U.S. were not withdrawing "with honor," but by signing the above Accords, Kissinger knew he had already lost to northern communist Lê Đức Thọ. Accordingly, the U.S. had to withdraw within a time frame troops as well as all the advisory groups to all RVNAF units with the exception of a few technical specialists and embassy employees. MACV, the huge U.S. assistance command in South Vietnam, became the Defense Attaché Office (DAO) under the direction of a two-star general to communicate and support the RVNAF. In the military regions, the huge MACV system like FRAC, SRAC, TRAC and DRAC (1st, 2nd, 3rd, and Delta Regional Assistance Command) was dissolved; all the support reverted to the consulates of cities of the regions.

The huge NVA forces that had been waging war inside South Vietnam were allowed to remain in the regions they controlled as well as in Cambodia and Laos. Although officially the U.S. had estimated there were 150,000 NVA troops in South Vietnam, the real number was more than 250,000 troops. NVA support units in Cambodia and Laos had been actively repairing and upgrading the Hồ Chí Minh Trail in order to bring in additional troops and ammunition to the South Vietnamese battlefield. The latter trail thus had become the "Sullivan Boulevard," a wide open highway to South Vietnam.[1]

In conformity with the Paris Accords, the USAF had ceased all support activities on the trail such as reconnaissance, spying, and bombing with CBU bombs or B-52 bombers. Therefore, the communists were not only free to enlarge the Western Trường Sơn Route (aka, the Hồ Chí Minh Trail), but also to build the duplicate Eastern Trường Sơn Route on the eastern border of the Annamite Chain (or Trường Sơn in Vietnamese), from west of Cam Lộ, Quảng Trị, in the North to Đôn Luân, province of Phước Long, in the South after they took over this province in January 1974. While the new highway allowed thousands of Molotova trucks to bring troops and ammunition to the southwest region of South Vietnam to begin the biggest southern offensive ever, it also brought war to the highlands, especially Ban Mê Thuột.

Forced to defend a new front with cut-off support from the U.S., President Thiệu decided to abandon the highlands. This resulted in a South Vietnamese calamity earlier than the Communist Party had even expected. But this catastrophe would not have happened had the U.S. not been willing to leave Vietnam as the clauses in the Accords had suggested. The U.S., who had to retrieve all the mines dropped to blockade the port of Hải Phòng at the end of 1972 under President Nixon's order, could refuse to do it. They could also bomb North Vietnam anywhere—Hanoi, Hải Phòng, railroads used to transport ammunitions, military supplies from China to North Vietnam—to retaliate for the NVA launching the 1972 Summer Offensive in violation of the Paris Accords.

On the other hand, the removal of all the mines around Hải Phòng meant that Hanoi could receive thousands of tons of military supplies—tanks, cannons, the newest models of guns and ammunition from the Soviet Union through two fleets of 150 huge transport ships coming from the two navy seaports of Odysey and Vladivostok that berthed in Hải Phòng every day. The failure for the U.S. to "attack North Vietnam, Laos, and Cambodia by sea, air or land" meant that railroad trains could transport military gear from China to North Vietnam without impediment. Total mobilization of youths aged 16 and above along with the massive infusion of armaments and ammunitions from China and Russia made North Vietnam the fourth-largest army in the world behind the U.S., Russia and China. However, South Vietnam was only allowed to trade in "one for one," which meant that the U.S. would exchange one broken tank for another, one damaged canon for another one. Therefore, the ARVN suffered from hundreds of inconveniences and losses. Rockets could not be used like in the past in an unlimited fashion; in fact, after the Accords, each unit could only fire three shells a day for each 105 mm or 155 mm howitzer, while the NVA continued to receive an unlimited supply of ammunition provided by their Chinese and Russian comrades. Additionally, the U.S. had cut off military aid to South Vietnam. As the battles raged worse after the Accords, with dwindling supplies, South Vietnam could not fight against a well-armed opponent, resulting in huge human losses especially on the battlefields and along the borders with Laos and Cambodia.

In that critical situation, especially after the NVA took over the province of Phước Long on 1 January 1974 in full violation of the Paris Accords, Washington, instead of helping, turned a blind eye to Saigon, although the Ford administration did request Congress to give $300 million to South Vietnam. The supplemental aid was voted down after a year of discussion. In December 1974, the NVA planned to cut off South Vietnam at the level south of Đà Nẵng by taking over the provinces of Nông Sơn, Dục Đức and Thường Đức and fighting all the way to Hội An when they were stopped at the district of Đại Lộc. The Airborne Division of Brigadier General Lê Quang Lưỡng was pulled out of Quảng Trị by Lieutenant General Ngô Quang Trưởng, I Corps and MR1 commander, to fight against the NVA 304th and 308th Divisions north of Thường Đức, especially on Hill 1062 from August until December 1974, although the U.S. continued to ignore the violation. President Nguyễn Văn Thiệu and his cabinet knew the U.S. had abandoned South Vietnam.

The J-2/JGS/RVNAF had been informed of communist plans to launch a total offensive during the spring of 1975. Two colonels had been assigned by Colonel Hoàng Ngọc Lung, chief of J-2/JGS/RVNAF, to the 2nd Bureau of the headquarters of I Corps and MRI and II Corps and MRII to serve as liaison officers. As for me, I was assigned as liaison officer to the 2nd Bureau/ IV Corps and MR4. The role of these liaison officers was to follow up and send news of battle fights and enemy positions from one region to another, one locality to another, and vice versa.

At that time, Brigadier General Lê Văn Hưng had been assigned by Major General Nguyễn Khoa Nam, commander of the IV Corps and MR4, to serve as his deputy. Prior to that, General Hưng served as operations deputy to Lieutenant General Nguyễn Văn Minh III Corps and MR3. Around July or August 1972, Major General Nguyễn Vĩnh Nghi, who had been promoted

XIII. Return to the Mekong Delta 211

to commander of IV Corps and MR4 (replacing Lieutenant General Ngô Quang Trưởng who was sent to Danang as commander to replace Lieutenant General Hoàng Xuân Lãm to open a counterattack to retake Quảng Trị after the Fiery Summer Offensive), had suggested to name General Hưng as commander of the 21st Division. When General Nguyễn Khoa Nam replaced General Nguyễn Vĩnh Nghi, he made General Hưng his deputy and the second most important military figure of the Mekong Delta region. In reality, Generals Nghi and Nam held high esteem of General Hưng, although the smear campaign against him had reached the highest levels of the administration a long time ago.

When I arrived at Cần Thơ after meeting the 2nd Bureau/IV Corps and MR4, I came to meet the deputy commander, General Hưng. He shook my hands and asked what I was doing in Cần Thơ. I told him of my new assignment.

"Where do you stay?" he asked.

"Wherever, with your help," I answered.

"Come and stay with me," he said.

My only belonging was a green iron trunk from the time I was a cadet. It contained a few sets of military garb, civilian clothes, books and a pair of tennis racquets. From the end of 1974, I stayed at General Hưng's residence and had dinner with the couple every day. Work was not difficult: in the IV Corps and MR4 2nd Bureau's office, I called the hotline to the J-2/JGS/RVNAF to get information about other military regions and to report intelligence and battlefield news to General Hưng. Although the number of conflicts overall rose in all regions of South Vietnam, my role was to report them to him. If he needed important information at night, I just used the hotline in the operation room in General Hưng's residence to call Saigon. The quiet southwest allowed me to play tennis a few evenings a week and to play chess games on Sunday with the provincial tribunal president, Judge Đỗ Nam Kỳ, whom I met at the Ngọc Lợi tennis court. Although he was a northerner, his name was Nam (south). The Hưngs had two children at that time: a six-year-old son and a two-year-old daughter whose grandmother helped to care for them.

General Hưng allowed me to move freely and never asked about my whereabouts. Whenever I had dinner with them at home and after we were done, he and I sat on the front porch to look at the park across the street where the arrow of a triangle pointed to the north of Cần Thơ. We then talked about war and people in general during these evenings. Questions and answers were simple and short like in a conversation. Each question, however, carried a special meaning, which forced us to think, although we did not have a definite answer. For example,

"Why did they attack Thường Đức, Đại Lộc? To cut the South in half and isolate Danang?"

"No. Not exactly. Had they taken over Hội An, we would lose Danang, Huế, Quảng Trị. And if the U.S. stayed quiet, they would attack Highway 19."

"And then?"

"They would take the north of Nha Trang and bring in the Provisionary Government of South Vietnam and set up a neutral government over the controlled area."

"But General Lưỡng had beaten them there."

"They would fight another day. Without General Trưởng and Lưỡng, we would have lost Central Vietnam, but it would be better for the rest of South Vietnam."

"Why?"

No answer.

"We do not lack talented men, heroes."

When he said these words, General Hưng admitted the military talents of General Ngô Quang Trưởng, commander of the I Corps and MR1, and General Lê Quang Lưỡng, commander of the Airborne Division who had saved and preserved An Lộc. But did he know and realize he was one of these heroic men?

And it was at General Hưng's residence that I met one night Colonel Mạch Văn Trường, whom General Hưng had invited for dinner to celebrate his appointment as the commander of the 21st Infantry Division. From the time he arrived in Cần Thơ, I had the chance to know more about him because if a good reputation spread far, a bad one spread further. Rumors suggested that Colonel Mạch Văn Trường, when he was chief of Long Khánh Province, was investigated by the inspector general for graft and abuse of power with the final recommendation that he be removed from his post, not be assigned any leadership position for five years, and demoted. While waiting for sentencing by the Military Court, he was assigned to the position of chief inspector of the 21st Infantry Division. Suddenly, officers in the Mekong Delta were surprised to hear that he was promoted to commander of the 21st Infantry Division, bypassing many senior officers, including Colonel Nguyễn Văn Kiểm, interim commander of the 21st Division, and Colonel Lâm Chánh Ngôn, COS, who was Mạch Văn Trường's superior. Rumors also had it that Trường was at odds with his old master, General Nguyễn Văn Minh, who was at the time the commander of the Military Region of Saigon replacing Admiral Chung Tấn Cang who had returned to the post of commander of the navy. Since Mr. Trường had a few new masters who controlled the fate of the country and the army, the recommendation of the inspector general was trashed in the garbage can.

That night, at General Hưng's residence and after he retired to his room, Colonel Trường and I sat on the front porch looking at the park. I did not even have time to talk when he began,

"I know you did well in school, but in the army if you are too earnest, you would not move very far. You need advisers like I do. This is how I got here."

He then explained how he won over General Minh and other leaders at the time. As a Chinese-Vietnamese, he strongly believed in astrology. His horoscope showed that although he did not have any principal star, he had three other stars that carried the word "No." If that combination were successful, he would be made general in no time. True enough, a few weeks later, he was promoted general. I congratulated him and told him he was a man of strong will and purpose, for while he was at the 5th Infantry Division, he always carried with him a self-help book entitled *How to Be a General*—I do not remember who the author was—whenever I saw him. I believe that had South Vietnam survived, he would have been further promoted to two- or three-star general and would hold a major position either in the army or the government. As for Generals Hưng and Lưỡng, they were hidden behind and taken down by huge stars like Greed and Destroyer of the Army. I did not know whether General Hưng knew about it, but General Lưỡng did. Decades later, after he immigrated to the States and while still alive, I had the fortune to talk to him a couple of times. He told me once why he was doubted and slighted at that time but still useful—because there was no one to replace him. Young generals who were trusted at the time were Generals Lân, Đảo, Nhựt, Vỹ and Trường.

After the communists took over Ban Mê Thuột, General Hưng and I discussed the reason why they targeted that city and speculated that they would attack along Route 19 from Ban Mê Thuột to Ninh Hoà to form a neutral government north of Nha Trang to the DMZ. That turned out not to be correct. Maybe they did not finish the Eastern Trường Sơn Route because they were stuck at Đức Lập District, province of Quảng Đức, which prevented them from bringing supplies from Khe Sanh to Phước Long and Lộc Ninh and then directly to Saigon. Therefore, they had to attack Ban Mê Thuột and control Quảng Đức like they had overpowered the province of Phước Long in 1974, as suggested by Colonel Trịnh Tiếu, 2nd Bureau chief II Corps and MR2.

Events then occurred very fast, surprising a lot of people, including the NVA, because of fatal decisions made by President Thiệu. The communists had planned to control South Vietnam only in 1977. Kissinger thought that South Vietnam would be lost following a decent interval, a term suggested by Frank Snepp, a CIA officer in Saigon, in his book entitled *Decent Interval*, so that the U.S. would not be called "traitors" for letting Saigon down.

From 20 April 1975, General Hưng wanted me to return to Saigon to learn more about the political and military situation after General Nguyễn Vĩnh Nghi, commander III Corps and MR3 Operational Advanced Command, and Brigadier General Phạm Ngọc Sang, commander of the VNAF 6th Division, got lost at the Ninh Thuận Airfield and Brigadier General Lê Minh Đảo was fighting ferociously against and held back the NVA at Long Khánh. But the land route was cut off at Tân Trụ, province of Long An, by many NVA divisions belonging to the newly formed Tactical Unit 232 of Lê Đức Anh, so I could not return to Saigon. The ARVN 7th Infantry Division could not dislodge them. I was waiting all week long without success. Finally, on 27 April, while General Hưng and I were sitting on the front porch after our dinner, Saigon changed masters from President Thiệu to Vice President Trần Văn Hương and soon to General Dương Văn Minh. General Hưng told me that after he visited troops the next morning, he would let me use his command helicopter to go back to Saigon. At that time, he asked his aide to bring two automatic Czechoslovakian firearms that were given to him by a unit commander at An Lộc. This type of gun when folded over was as small as a handgun but fired 79 bullets singly or automatically. He pointed to the gun and said, "You can have one, Dưỡng. If the communists show up at the gate, fire until the last bullet. As for me, I will save four bullets."

I understood immediately and told him, "No. You have the right to keep only one bullet." Silence. I did not know whether 1st Lieutenant Tùng heard me.

The next morning, 28 April 1975, I took the helicopter to Saigon and landed at the flag courtyard of Trần Hưng Đạo Camp. At that time, General Dương Văn Minh had been bestowed the historic role of guiding the downfall of South Vietnam.

Only a few days after, on 30 April, I heard that General Lê Văn Hưng had killed himself. Probably not with the Czechoslovakian firearm, but whatever it was, he had become a god to his soldiers and many people in South Vietnam.

XIV

Hell in a Very Insignificant Place

Insignificant Place

To a cerebral westerner like Andrade, An Lộc may look like "Hell in a Very Insignificant Place." He could not understand why both sides fought for a few-square-kilometer area of red soil that did not hold any strategic or military value: "a small insignificant patch of ground"?[1] Bernard Fall had written the same thing about Điện Biên Phủ decades earlier in his *Hell in a Very Small Place*. This seems to echo the lack of interest on this topic by the U.S. media and people at a time when Washington had disengaged itself from the war in Vietnam.

However, the Joint Chiefs of Staff did not feel the same way because it continued to give the green light or at least did not prevent General Hollingsworth, the TRAC commander, from supporting the ARVN during the An Lộc battle.

For the Vietnamese, An Lộc was a big event, a die-for battle. They had to defend the last square meter of land from falling into the hands of the communists; they had to protect the integrity of their territory. If they did not, where would they live? Where would their descendants live? That was their homeland, the sacred land that was bequeathed to them by their ancestors; the land they later would bequeath to their offspring.

The irony of the statement made by Andrade and Fall may reflect the fact that they did not care about the "insignificant patch of ground" as long as it was on Vietnamese soil, but would they care about it if it were on U.S. soil? Would they fight for it if it involved their land, their houses?

And yes, it was hell out there; there was no question about it. To witness the hundreds of people who died day after day under continuing rains of mortars and rockets was a sad and tragic feeling. To see civilians, women and children, hiding in the few square meters of bunkers for more than two months was really painful. To witness civilians being slaughtered as they tried to escape from the battle zone was tragic in itself. To see the hundreds of troops who died on the battlefield because they could not be evacuated or treated adequately definitely hurt. War was definitely inhumane. We do not write to condone the 21-year-long war, but we must accuse the aggressors of this conflict. They were the ones who had destroyed the nation of Vietnam.

This is where many westerners had strayed. They had never asked themselves why the North Vietnamese were in Cambodia to begin with. This was a true violation of Cambodian sovereignty. Why did they bring their tanks and troops all the way down there to invade and attack the South Vietnamese on South Vietnamese soil? An Lộc and Lộc Ninh were both South Vietnamese towns. Why did the NVA infringe upon South Vietnamese soil? Why did they violate the 1954 Geneva Agreements and the 1973 Paris Accords, which they had signed and which stipulated that they should not use force against the South Vietnamese? They were the real aggressors in this conflict. They were the ones who sowed pain, terror, and killing on South Vietnamese soil. The Vietnam War from the U.S. and South Vietnamese sides was thus a war against communist aggression.

This is where the Hagels come into play. In 1968, 21-year-old Chuck Hagel was riding shotgun on a U.S. armored carrier with his brother Tom when the VC detonated a land mine under the carrier. Both were wounded, and Chuck pulled his brother out of the burning turret before the carrier exploded. They survived the incident and Chuck returned from Vietnam with two purple hearts and Tom with three purple hearts and a bronze star. Tom became a liberal Democrat and a law professor who called the war rotten and immoral. Chuck became a Republican senator who is presently secretary of defense under President Obama.[2] These are two brothers who went to war and ended having two different opinions about the war. Tom Hagel and many Americans like Jane Fonda, who have embraced the lies and propaganda of the Hanoi communists, have failed to understand that the communists were the real aggressors and the cause of the Vietnam War. The North Vietnamese only wanted to establish a communist regime in Vietnam by stealing the government from the southern nationalists. Forty years after the end of the war, they still want to hold on to power, refusing to accept democracy and a multi-party system for Vietnam.

Self-Killing

When Saigon surrendered at 10:00 on 30 April 1975, in the Mekong Delta the generals continued to debate the future of the IV Corps. They

XIV. Hell in a Very Insignificant Place

finally gathered their staff and saluted the South Vietnamese flag one last time in the headquarters' court. They then bid farewell to the staff and to each other. General Nguyễn Khoa Nam, the IV Corps commander, went to the Phan Thanh Giản Military Hospital in downtown Cần Thơ to comfort and bid farewell to the hospitalized soldiers there. General Hưng returned to his office.

By 16:00 in the city of Cần Thơ, home of the IV Corps and MR4, General Lê Văn Hưng (1933–1975) was still proclaiming that he would not surrender to the communists. How could he? He had waged war against them all his life and had heroically resisted them during the violent siege at An Lộc. He had no other choice because he had dedicated his life to defending the Republic of Vietnam. As a man of honor, he could not dishonor himself by surrendering to them. He had made his choice when he was in An Lộc three years earlier.

He met with a delegation of the Cần Thơ city councilmen who urged him not resist lest the city be shelled by the VC with devastating results. He told them he would bring the matter up to General Nam, although both were committed to defend the lives of Cần Thơ's citizens. He later met his wife and son and advised her to be brave and to raise his son as a man. He then gathered his soldiers and told them,

> I will not abandon you in order to evacuate my family. I cannot surrender in this shameful situation. If I have yelled at you on occasion, when mistakes were made, please forgive me.

He shook their hands and drove them out of his office, after which he locked himself in. A gunshot was later heard. His family and staff broke into the office and found the general, his arms outstretched, still convulsing with blood all over his uniform. He had shot himself in his heart at 20:45 on 30 April 1975.

General Nguyễn Khoa Nam (1927–1975), born in Đà Nẵng, central Vietnam, graduated from the Thủ Đức Military Academy in 1953 as an Airborne officer. As a company commander of the 7th Airborne Battalion, he fought the Bình Xuyên in Saigon in 1955. He fought the VC around Saigon during the 1968 Tết Offensive. He was one of the few generals who earned their ranks through hard work. During his career, he had molded the 7th Division into one of the most efficient in the ARVN. His last assignment was that of a three-star general and commander of the ARVN IV Military Region (MR4) which comprised the whole Mekong Delta. Well liked by his soldiers, he used to drop by to see them during their military operations. A vegetarian, he led a simple life and followed Buddhist rules closely. As a bachelor, he was not susceptible to bribery which in Vietnam was usually channeled through officers' wives.

With the imminent fall of Xuân Lộc, the last bastion of resistance before Saigon, he had discussed plans with his deputy, General Hưng, about withdrawing their troops to a secret place in the delta in order to continue the fight. Until the end, he requested every officer and soldier to remain at their post. When he became aware that the provincial chief of Kiên Giang Province had left his post on a boat, he ordered pilots to sink it with rocket and machine gun.[3] On Monday, 28 April, General Nam met with Ambassador Francis McNamara, U.S. consul general of the Mekong Delta, for the last time. After thanking him for the U.S. help over the years, he told the consul not to take with him any military, particularly officers, if he were to evacuate out of Cần Thơ.[4]

Things were quiet in the MR4 as there was no imminent danger of being overrun by the enemy. When President Minh went on the radio on 30 April to announce his surrender to the communists, General Nam became obviously upset. He even refused President Minh's pleas to order his soldiers to lay down their arms. He could not understand why Saigon had to surrender without putting up a fight. After conferring with General Hưng, he reluctantly went along with the president's decision.

In the evening after having visited his soldiers at the hospital, he returned to the headquarters and was told that General Hưng had taken his life. At 23:00, he called Mrs. Hưng to offer his condolences. As a man of war, he did not believe in surrendering to people he did not like and thought he could defeat. He locked himself in his office, put on his official white uniform along with all his medals, sat at his desk and shot himself in the head. That incident occurred in the early hours of 1 May 1975. His body was taken to the morgue and buried at the Cần Thơ military cemetery among his peers. In 1994, his remains were exhumed and cremated. His ashes were stored at the Gia Lam Pagoda in Gia Định.

General Lê Nguyên Vỹ (1933–1975), born in Sơn Tây, North Vietnam, graduated from the Officers Candidate Course at the Regional Military School, MRII, at Phú Bài near Huế, class of 1951. He was a colonel at the battle of An Lộc in 1972. As the attack raged on and as the enemy got closer, he single-handedly took an M-72 anti-tank gun to blast away a communist T-54 tank. He became deputy commander of the ARVN 21st Division and in 1974 went to the U.S. for military training. On his return, he became commander of the ARVN 5th Division. When Saigon surrendered, he gathered his staff and bid them farewell. He locked himself in his office and shot himself with a Beretta 6.35. When the VC officer came to take over the military office, he calmly saluted the general and said, "This is how a general should behave."⁵

General Trần Văn Hai (1925–1975), when he was a colonel, parachuted at the famous battle of Khe Sanh in 1968. He became commander of the ARVN 7th Division in 1974 and was known as a brave and clean officer who also cared about his soldiers. In April 1975, President Thiệu offered to take him out of the country, but he refused. He remained at his post and was notified of a heavy concentration of enemy troops across the border in Cambodia. He called the CIA person requesting air support to blow them away. "We have them in the open. Now is the time to get them.... I need help. Help me, CIA man." But the agent could not do anything and the general later watched hopelessly as the enemy crossed the border and overran his troops. General Hai committed suicide instead of surrendering to the enemy.

General Phạm Văn Phú born in Hà Đông, North Vietnam, graduated from the Dalat Military Academy, Class 8. He was the man who ordered the withdrawal from the II Corps under President Thiệu's insistence. Back in 1954, then Captain Phú parachuted with his company into Điện Biên Phủ to reinforce the French troops. When Điện Biên Phủ fell, the Việt Minh held him prisoner although they later released him. He vowed never to become prisoner of the communists again. He committed suicide on 30 April 1975.

There are many more officers who committed suicide in the last days of the war. Colonel Nguyễn Hữu Thông, commander of the 42nd Regiment, 22nd Division, took his own life instead of surrendering. Colonel Hồ Ngọc Cẩn, commander of the 15th Regiment, 9th Infantry Division, province chief and commander of Chương Thiện Province & Sector, refused to surrender to the enemy. He and his men fought until the end, when he was captured before he could kill himself. He asked the VC to salute his flag the last time before being shot to death by the enemy. Former Prime Minister Trần Chánh Thành, fearing a fall into the hands of the communists he had deserted decades earlier, took a poison.

To die for one's country is not only an act of bravery; it is *the* act of bravery. For soldiers, it is just an extension of their military career, a part of their duty. As war was seen as a noble act, *tuẫn tiết*, or self-sacrifice/war suicide, serves as redemption in case of defeat. It is also a way to tell the enemy they might have won the battle/war, but they do not deserve it because they do not have *chính nghĩa* or just cause. It is not only just cause; it is the belief that the cause they are fighting for deserves their total sacrifice.

Although *tuẫn tiết* means "war suicide," there is no good corresponding word in English because the act itself is not practiced in the Christian West. Secondly, the words "self-sacrifice" or "war suicide" do not convey the moral and courageous implication of the act. It is a closer equivalent of the Japanese hara-kiri or seppuku.[6] Although *tuấn tiết* and seppuku are technically different, the end result is the same: the death of the victim by himself or at the hands of the assistant. Vietnam and Japan are two of the few countries in the world whose leaders killed themselves to wash away the ignominy of war loss.

Westerners do not believe in taking their own lives when they lose the ultimate battle, although it is a known fact that ship captains would go down with their sinking ships. South Vietnamese Captain Nguyễn Văn Tha indeed went down with his disabled destroyer *HQ10* during the battle of the Paracel Islands[7] against the communist Chinese in 1974. Easterners, on the other hand, are willing to die following crucial battle losses in order to preserve their honor. They do not want to surrender, to be caught and have to go through the shame of being held prisoner. By taking their own lives, they still feel they have control of their lives or have redeemed their honor.

One soldier prefers to die with their honor intact. The other is willing to suffer from the humiliation of defeat. There is no intention to belittle those who have surrendered. They have done it in order to save their troops and the civilian population; they have done it because their commander in chief, President Dương Văn Minh—no matter how undeserving he was—has ordered them to surrender.

These people have a very high sense of morality. They are ashamed of handing over the troops under their command to the enemy for they feel they would betray "not their emperor, but a sovereign state that had ceased to exist long before, whose ideals they, as military officers, still respected."[8] Although South Vietnam lost the war, the fact that five generals and scores of colonels and other officers took their own lives at the end of the war shows that there is something bigger and larger than defeat or victory. There is pride and belief that what they have fought for—freedom, heroism, and dignity of human life—is worth more than life itself. By sacrificing themselves, they freeze in history the bravery and courage of the RVNAF.

Epilogue

The Vietnam War was a war of ideologies, although it may not seem that way to some in the U.S., who saw the war as a waste and at some points even supported Hanoi.

But to the South Vietnamese, it was a war of ideologies, of common sense, chivalry, *chính nghĩa* (just cause) and justice, not a brutal war of aggression, intrigues, double-crossing, wickedness, and cowardice as played by the North Vietnamese.

Why then did the South Vietnamese lose the war?

Of all the causes, the main one was related to the weaknesses inherent in democracy itself—the incapacity to sustain a long, unfocused, inconclusive, and bloody war. This applies to the U.S. as well as South Vietnam.[1]

First, Saigon never understood the concept of Vietnamization until it was too late. Or rather, they trusted the U.S. too much to the point of letting Kissinger bargain away the fate of South Vietnam. Vietnamization was a strategy that would clear the way for the U.S. to leave South Vietnam whether the latter was ready or not[2]; it was not simply a modernization or expansion of the RVNAF. Since even President Thiệu believed until the end that Washington would come back and assist them, the South Vietnamese were not ready to take charge and assume all the costs of supplies and ammunition which were prohibitive by Vietnamese standards. Without support and assistance, Saigon simply fell apart.

> The strength of South Vietnam and its armed forces had been built primarily on foreign aid, not on its national resources. The fate of South Vietnam therefore depended on its American friends.[3]

Second, the revolutionary war was a political war in its totality. Saigon, as a fairly democratic society by Asian standards of the time, was waging a halfhearted war because it was also trying to build its country, its economy and administrative systems. While the NVA was heavily indoctrinated, tightly organized, and grossly exploited to support the revolutionary war effort, there was minimal indoctrination of the ARVN in its political role or requirement for it to support the South Vietnamese people.[4] There was no unity of effort between the U.S. and the Republic of Vietnam to wage combined political, economic, military, diplomatic, and psychological war fronts.

Third, while Hanoi waged a protracted war, the U.S. pursued a "limited" war, limited not only in geography but also in length. "Limited war" was the brainchild of a group of academic theorists who believe that force can be applied "skillfully along a continuous spectrum … in which adversaries would bargain with each other through the medium of graduated military responses."[5] The problem is that communists were not gentlemen warriors and would not deal with honor and respect. Therefore, using that strategy was simply playing into the hands of Giáp who would use it to erode the morale and resolution of his enemy. Besides, when the U.S. felt it had done enough, it just withdrew whether the job was done or not. While the South Vietnamese were indebted to the U.S. for their help, they were shocked by the "limited" commitment of their partners.

One ARVN officer wrote,

… Go ahead and leave Vietnam, my friends,
if you are exhausted,
if you are ashamed,
for not being honest with yourself before you came…
We pray that those pages [of history] do not make you troubled and bitter.[6]

Fourth, South Vietnamese soldiers when ably led performed well, such as at An Lộc in 1972 and Xuân Lộc in 1975. However, the combat leadership and tactical competency of the generals were often lacking. Major Thomas Bibby wrote,

It [the leadership] lacked the competence to do the job when the crisis arose; the aggressiveness to take and gain the initiative from the enemy; and ultimately the credibility to maintain the loyal support of its soldiers and the South Vietnamese people.[7]

Where do we go from here?

In this war of ideologies, the South Vietnamese may be afraid of the communists because their cruelty, but they have no respect for them who just prove to be vile aggressors and extremists. The NVA combatants are neither chivalrous fighters, nor innovators. They have no code of honor. If they do not kill people, they just throw them in reeducation camps like a "consignment of pigs to the market."[8] After 1975, they even sent poets to jail: Nguyễn Tú was incarcerated for 13 years, Trần Dạ Từ 12 years, Nhã Ca more than a year.⁹ They just duplicated the things taught to them by the Russian and Chinese communists and waged the war in a monstrous and inhumane way. That is why four decades after the war, the North Vietnamese still have failed to rally the overseas South Vietnamese, also known as the Việt Kiều to their side. How could they when they engaged in such a lowly, unchivalrous way of fighting, when they killed people right and left, and when they lied through their teeth?

- They stole the government in August 1945 out from under the nose of the nationalists.[10] The goal was to seize the power from the hands of the Japanese and the legal Vietnamese government before the arrival of the allied troops.
- They set up a coalition government and then eliminated all nationalists from the government.[11]
- They dealt in secrecy with the French they had fought against before siding with them to purge all the nationalist parties.[12]
- They violated the 1954 Geneva Agreements and the 1973 Paris Accords, which stipulated that no force should be used to invade the other side in order to reunify the country.

The overriding theme of the communist culture, which is foreign to Vietnam, is hatred. While adults are taught "criticism and self-criticism," children learn to sing revolutionary songs, to hate their parents and report them if necessary.[13] This culture is very different from the Vietnamese culture, which espouses respect of elders and love for their parents. Therefore, the South Vietnamese in no way could accept this communist concept.

THE DAY VIETNAM IS FREE

The Vietnamese dream about the day
when they will be free again,
free from oppression and repression,
from communism,
free to act out,
and to speak out their own thoughts.

It has been a long journey,
from antiquity until today.
The Vietnamese
were not free under the Chinese,
they were not free under the French,
they are not free under the communists.

The Chinese forced them
to bow to China,
The French forced them

to bow to France,
The communists forced them
to bow to Marx and Lenin,
They all have enslaved them
one way or another.

Of all evils, the communists are the worst,
They force the people to serve
one party and its leaders,
to obey the Cong An,
and to bribe their minions.

The Vietnamese were born free.
Then came the Chinese, the French,
and the communists
who told them what to do,
where to sit, what to believe.
They have enslaved, demeaned,
and corrupted them.

The Vietnamese wish to be free again,
free to talk, to walk tall, and to act,
free from all oppression and foreign ideologies,
free to be Vietnamese.
If it took them one thousand years
to free themselves from the Chinese,
if it took them one hundred years
to free themselves from the French,
they will set aside, if need be,
another thousand years
to get rid of the communists
for they were born FREE
and free they will remain.
  Nghia M. Vo

Safer once remarked, "The Vietnamese have no sense of time the way we understand it ... their mental and body clocks are tuned more to history than to the ticking urgencies of ordinary life."[14]

The Vietnam War is a war of ideologies: of nationalism and justice against communism, of freedom against subservience, of nationhood and self-determination against internationalist communism, of humanity against cruelty and barbarism. It is a fight for justice and *chính nghĩa*/just cause.

That is why there will always be TWO VIETNAMS, for the divide between northerners and southerners, more exactly communists and nationalists, is as wide as the Grand Canyon.

Appendix I:
War Self-Immolation in Vietnam
Nghia M. Vo

To die for one's country is not only an act of bravery, it is *the* act of bravery. For soldiers, it is just an extension of their military career, a part of their duty. As leaders have asked their soldiers to sacrifice themselves for the good of the society, it is only right for leaders to go through the same motion and practice what they have preached.

As war is seen as a noble act, *tuấn tiết* (self-immolation) serves as redemption in case of defeat. It is also a way to tell the enemy, "You might have won the battle/war, but you don't deserve it because you don't have *chính nghĩa* (just cause)." It is not only just cause; it is also the belief that the cause they are fighting for deserves their total sacrifice.

Although *tuấn tiết* means "war suicide," there is no good corresponding word in English because the act itself is not practiced in the Christian West. Secondly, the word "suicide" does not convey the moral and courageous implication of the act itself. It is a closer equivalent of hara-kiri or seppuku.[1] Although hara-kiri is practically a disembowelment, its practice varies from person to person. If the blade is inserted deeply enough, it could cause an immediate death through intra-abdominal bleeding. If inserted superficially, the still-alive victim would be beheaded by the assistant. While *tuấn tiết* and hara-kiri can be technically different, the end result is the same: the death of the person through his own hand or the hands of his assistant.

Vietnam is one of the rare countries in the world where leaders killed themselves when they lose a war. We will review these cases of *tuấn tiết* during the pre- and anti-colonial wars and the anti-communist war.

Past Self-Immolation

At least seven leaders are known to have killed themselves for their country during the anti-colonial war: Võ Tánh, Ngô Tùng Châu, Võ Duy Ninh, Trương Công Định, Phan Thanh Giản, Nguyễn Hữu Huân, and Hoàng Diệu. Many more officials could have committed suicide throughout history, although their deeds may not have been recorded.

Võ Tánh and Ngô Tùng Châu

Võ Tánh was one of the military warlords from Gò Công in the Mekong Delta who had defeated the Tây Sơn around Gia Định-Saigon in 1783.[2] Nguyễn Ánh, the scion of the Nguyễn dynasty, realized he needed this valiant free spirit's assistance if he wanted to defeat the Tây Sơn. It was only in 1787 that he was able to lure and recruit him into his army by giving him his sister as concubine. From that time onward, Võ Tánh participated in most of Nguyễn Ánh's battles against the Tây Sơn and proved to be one of his best generals.

In March 1799, Võ Tánh's troops besieged Qui Nhơn—a port city in central Vietnam—which after four months of resistance surrendered. Nguyễn Ánh changed the city's name to Bình Định (Pacified). He left Võ Tánh and Ngô Tùng Châu in charge of the city that sat in a rebel-controlled area and returned to his base in Saigon.

Nguyễn Ánh at that time was waging a seasonal or "monsoon" war against the Tây Sơn by attempting to retake rebel-controlled regions from south to north. In the spring, when the winds blew away from the Indochinese Peninsula, he loaded his crack troops onto his sailboats and headed toward a military target in the Vietnamese central coastal area. He dropped them off close to the target area where he met the rest of his troops that had arrived by land. The combined army then attacked the target, which was decisively taken. In the fall, he left troops to guard the newly conquered region and headed home with the monsoon winds, which in November blew back toward the peninsula. Each year, he had about a six- to eight-month window to wage war as the winds shifted biannually.[3]

Realizing the strategic loss of Bình Định, which controlled access to Phú Xuân (Huế)—the Tây Sơn headquarters—Tây Sơn general Trần Quang Diệu decided to retake the city and its surroundings. In early 1800, Diệu had his troops guard all land exits of Bình Định while a Tây Sơn naval fleet blocked the sea approach. Nguyễn Ánh in early April came to the rescue of Võ Tánh who was holed up inside the besieged Bình Định. It was a tough battle, which lasted until February 1801 (10 months) before the Tây Sơn fleet was destroyed after a bloody 28-hour sea battle. With the sea approach cleared, Nguyễn Ánh ordered Võ Tánh to get out of town: the latter refused to leave without his soldiers.

Nguyễn Ánh at that time realized that the bulk of the Tây Sơn troops were encamped in front of Bình Định leaving the capital Phú Xuân almost defenseless. Leaving Võ Tánh to hold the Tây Sơn army in place, he moved with his fleet to Phú Xuân and up the Hương River where as expected he found minimal resistance. His troops took over the city on 15 June 1801—26 years after the day he was forced to leave town.

Bình Định in the meantime was still besieged by the Tây Sơn. For the last 17 months, the defenders had put up a valiant resistance. Running out of food supplies, they finally decided to kill their animals (horses and elephants) for their meat. Võ Tánh, knowing the end had arrived, discussed the surrender with General Diệu: his only request was that his soldiers would be spared. He then had a scaffolding built on which he stacked the remaining gunpowder. Dressed in full military regalia, he got up on the scaffolding and lit the powder, which blew him into pieces. That was the signal for his men to open the garrison's gates for the Tây Sơn to take over. Ngô Tùng Châu had preceded him in death by taking poison. When General Diệu entered the citadel, he realized the braveness of his adversaries and had their remains buried with honors.[4]

Võ Duy Ninh

A combined Franco-Spanish force (2,500 French troops aboard 13 warships and 450 Spanish troops on a warship) attacked Danang on 1 September 1858. It met with severe resistance from the Huế imperial troops, led by General Nguyễn Tri Phương. After five months of fierce combat, the invaders could only control an inhabited stretch of shore. Frustrated, the French commander Rigault de Genouilly took two-thirds of his troops and ships and sailed on 10 February 1859 toward Vũng Tàu where he thought he would face lesser resistance. He blasted his way along the Saigon River before taking the Gia Định citadel on 17 February 1859.[5]

Aware of the Danang attack by the French, General Võ Duy Ninh, the military commander of Gia Định-Saigon citadel, thought his troops would need some retraining to keep abreast of new tactical maneuvers. The Vietnamese used breech-loading muskets, and each soldier was able to practice shooting one single round each year. He unfortunately chose the wrong time for the exercise: he did it when the French came to town. The remaining troops that guarded the citadel were unable to hold against the French. Frightened by the massive shelling, they ran away. General Ninh, when aware of the defeat, committed suicide rather than surrender the Gia Định citadel to the French.[6]

Trương Công Định (1820–1863)

Định, born in 1820 in central Vietnam, moved with his father—a colonel—to Saigon. He later married a wealthy Định Tường landowner's daughter and used his wife's financial resources to build a *don dien* (plantation). He enrolled impoverished workers and soldiers to assist him in his agricultural business. After Võ Duy Ninh committed suicide in February 1859, Định rallied around him imperial troops that had fled in disarray. With about 1,000 troops, he began a guerrilla war against the French. His initial military successes led the king to grant him the title of deputy commander of the southern forces.

By 1861, his army of 6,000 men gave him many battle successes. The following year, he was promoted commander of all the southern *nghia quan* (volunteer soldiers for a cause). The French were frustrated at not being able to crush the rebels as they "were everywhere and nowhere." He then moved his troops to Gò Công where he continued his guerrilla movement.

When the 1862 Saigon treaty was signed,[7] the Huế court cut off its support to Định and his *nghĩa quân*, being fearful that the French would use the insurrection as an excuse to expand their conquest in the South. The court even ordered Phan Thanh Giản to pressure Định to lay down his arms. Định not only lost the logistical support of the imperial court, but the French were free to focus their effort solely on fighting the rebels. Local people who collaborated with the French gave the rebels new problems. Định, however, refused to comply with the court's pressure, arguing that his mandate came not from Huế, but from the will of the people in the occupied territories. He gave himself the title of "Great General for the Pacification of the Westerners" and asked for the financial and moral support of the local people now that he had lost the court's support.

In February 1863, Admiral Bonard encircled Định in his stronghold of Gò Công from which he escaped after sustaining heavy casualties. On 19 August 1863, betrayed by a former rebel, he was ambushed and wounded. Facing imminent capture, he took his own life.[8]

Years later, Định's wife returned to her hometown much impoverished. King Tự Đức felt that Định was a righteous man who deserved praise. He felt that he needed to support his widow who was alone, poor, sick and miserable. He granted her a monthly allowance of 20 *quan* of cash and two *phường* of rice. This was more than a mandarin could expect for his pay.⁹

Phan Thanh Giản (1796–1867)

Gian was the first southerner to pass the mandarinate exam—which would qualify him for an administrative or military position in the king's government—with honors at the very young age of 30. Many qualified candidates could not pass the exam until their mid-forties. In 1831, he was appointed province chief of Quảng Nam. The troops he sent to quell a Cham rebellion were defeated and caused him to be removed from his post. Although he was given another position, he learned to accept failures and successes in a dignified and stoic, almost fatalistic, way.

The Huế court at the time of the French invasion was divided between the *chủ chiến* (hawks, led by Nguyễn Tri Phương, Hoàng Diệu, Tôn Thất Thuyết, and Hoàng Tả Viêm) and the *chủ hòa* (doves, led by Phan Thanh Giản, Lâm Duy Hiệp, Nguyễn Bá Nghi, and Trương Đăng Quế).

Despite being hawkish, the *chủ chiến* were unable to think of any strategy to oppose the French. They did not contemplate mass resistance probably because the court had in the past so antagonized the South that any thought in that direction would prove futile. They had taken down the Lê Văn Khôi rebellion, sentenced the leaders to death, and massacred about 2,000 people. They had desecrated Lê Văn Duyệt's tomb and put three generations of his family to death. They had placed the South under direct court control and sent all southern generals and lettered men away from the South, the upper leadership of which was no longer native. Southerners no longer felt like trusting the government. The *chủ hòa*, on the other hand, felt that they could no longer resist the overwhelming firepower and military force of the foreigners.

The court sent Phan Thanh Giản and Lâm Duy Hiệp to negotiate the Saigon treaty, which was signed on 5 June 1862. Besides the loss of three eastern provinces, freedom for Catholic priests to proselytize was granted throughout Vietnam. King Tự Đức flew into a rage when he heard the news. By performing a necessary but unpleasant duty, Giản and his colleagues were not only vilified by the court, but also rebuked by Tự Đức, who called them "criminals."¹⁰

Tự Đức, however, did not take any sanction against them; on the contrary, he elevated Giản to viceroy of the Southern Region and resident grand dignitary and plenipotentiary (Chánh Sứ Toàn Quyền Đại Thần). Giản, being 67 at that time, requested permission to retire, but his request was denied.

He was sent to France to negotiate the return of the three eastern provinces, although he was not successful. He became aware of France's technical and military advances. He saw trains running faster than horses, ports crowded with ships armed with powerful guns, and gas lamps burning brighter than oil lamps.

When he told Tự Đức about his assessments, the latter brushed away Giản's apprehensions by saying that if people were faithful and sincere, tigers would pass by without hurting them, crocodiles would swim away and everyone would listen to them.

Tự Đức—as the top Confucian man in the country—implied that the foreigners, French included, would respect a man of a high level of rectitude like Phan Thanh Giản if the latter fully believed in the Confucian doctrine. Having seen his powers slipping away from him—loss of territorial integrity to the French, civilian unrest in northern and central Vietnam, internal division between the chủ chiến and chủ hòa, and powerlessness against the French—Tự Đức could not help but ask himself why everything was falling apart under his feet. He probably wanted to reassure himself first. Akin to Montezuma who tried to stop the advance of the Spanish conquistadors with arrows and human sacrifices, akin to Nguyễn Văn Thiệu who in 1975 tried to stop the advancing communists with the magic words of the Paris Accords, Tự Đức attempted to repel the French with sharpened staves, swords and righteousness. He lived in an ancient Confucian world and belatedly realized that the French did not believe in righteousness, but only in guns and cannons.

There were, however, heroism and self-righteousness in abundance in the Mekong Delta. Nguyễn Đình Chiểu (1822–1888), who was legally blind at that time, heaped scorn on those who collaborated with the French. He would not touch anything that was western in origin like soap powder or perfume.

The Vietnamese, however, did not have the economic and technological means to build up a strong military response. The Huế government, as a Confucian state, did not have a foreign ministry and was not able to keep up with news and advances of the western world. The ministers at the court locked in their gilded ivory tower and their thousand-year-old Confucian leaning did not care about what was happening in the modern world. The few who had traveled abroad like Nguyễn Trường Tộ and Phan Thanh Giản and talked about western technological advances were simply laughed at.

The French, using another pretext, conquered three southwestern provinces and forced Giản to sign the 1867 treaty granting France control over the whole of South Vietnam or Cochinchina. He returned home dejected and declared that the French flag would not be allowed to fly above the fortress as long as he was alive.

He returned to the king all badges of office and the 23 royal awards he had acquired during a lifetime of distinguished service and intended to fast until he died. In contrast to other officials, he did not have a big estate or retinue to serve him. Being still alive two weeks later, he took additional poison that killed him.[11]

The *chủ chiến* sprang into action. They declared him guilty of the loss of the six provinces. Having killed himself, they thought he should be spared posthumous decapitation. Tự Đức, however, revoked all his titles, positions and grades; had his name removed from the stele of the *tiến sĩ* degree holders; and ordered his body exhumed and decapitated (*trâm hầu*).[12]

We leave for a thousand generations the sentence of *trâm hầu*. Thus we execute those who are already dead in order to warn those who are still living.[13]

Thus died in infamy one of Vietnam's greatest civil servants and patriots. As an abiding Confucian and a victim of the Nguyễns' failed policies of neo-Confucianism and self-isolation,[14] he took the blame for the loss of the six provinces with equanimity.

The thousand-generation sentence did not even last one generation. King Đồng Khánh rehabilitated him 19 years later (1886) and returned to his family his titles and medals.

Nguyễn Hữu Huân (?–1875)

Also known as Thủ Khoa Huấn,[15] he was one of the leaders of the resistance movement in the South. Caught by the French, he was forced to wear a *cangue*—a wooden framework—around the neck as a portable pillory. It was a sign of infamy. He bit his tongue and died before being executed by the French. He left a few verses that forever immortalized him. Forced to wear a *cangue*, although stooping under the weight of the device, he, like a hero, held his head high and straight.[16]

Hoàng Diệu (1829–1882)

Peasant unrest, tribal rebellions, Catholics, pirates, and the Lê restoration movements contributed to the chaos in the North, which remained an unsettled region under the Nguyễn regime. When the southern Nguyễn conquered North Vietnam, which had been under the Lê for more than four centuries, and after reunifying the country following a complete North–South division for two centuries (1600–1602), northerners were as expected not happy to submit to the Nguyễn and demonstrated for the restoration of the northern Lê.

A French merchant trying to find a way to get to China using the Red River fought verbally with officials in Hanoi. In 1873, French officials in Saigon dispatched Captain Francis Garnier to solve the problem. The 200-man French force backed by powerful artillery, using this excuse, overran the Hanoi citadel, which was defended by 7,000 men. They suffered only one casualty and two wounded. They soon controlled four provinces in the Red River delta. Garnier was ambushed by the Black Flag river bandits and killed. A treaty was signed the following year with the Hue court allowing the French to trade and proselytize Catholicism all over Vietnam.[17]

Chaos resulted as the *nghĩa quân* joined the battle against the French. Tự Đức had to call on China for help. In 1882, French troops led by Captain Henri Riviere attacked the Hanoi citadel for the second time. Although the defense had improved this time, Vietnamese soldiers could not withstand the shelling of the naval artillery. The ammunition depot was hit and blew up. Soldiers scrambled for their lives. The commanding officer, General Hoàng Diệu, calmly wrote the report and hung himself from a tree amidst the burning city. His body was brought back to his hometown of Quảng Nam for burial. Riviere went further but again was ambushed and killed by the Black Flags.

It is interesting to note that while Tự Đức could not do anything against the French, the river brigands were able to kill two French officers and hold off their offense.

Modern Self-Immolation

In 1975 as the fall of Saigon was taking place, many high-level officers and Saigon officials who refused to surrender took their own lives.

General **Nguyễn Khoa Nam** (1927–1975) graduated from the Thủ Đức Military Academy in 1953 as an airborne officer. He fought against the Bình Xuyên in Saigon in 1955 and the Viet Cong around Saigon during the 1968 Tet Offensive. He molded the 7th ARVN Division into one of the most efficient South Vietnamese units. As a three-star general and commander of the IV Corps and Military Region, he used to drop by to see and support his soldiers during their military operations. A vegetarian, he led a simple life and followed Buddhist rules closely.

Until the end, he requested every officer and soldier to remain at their posts. When designated President Minh announced his surrender to the communists, he reluctantly went along with the decision. He and General Hưng gathered their staff and saluted the South Vietnamese flag one last time at the Corps headquarters court. They then bid farewell to the staff and to each other. He went to the Phan Thanh Giản Military Hospital in downtown Cần Thơ to comfort and bid farewell to the hospitalized soldiers.

When he returned to the headquarters, he was told that General Hưng had taken his life. At 23:00 hours, he called Mrs. Hưng to offer his condolences. As a man of war, he did not believe in surrendering to people he thought he could defeat. Alone in his office, he put on his white uniform along with his medals, sat at his desk and shot himself in the head in the early hours of 1 May 1975. His body was taken to the morgue and he was later buried at the Cần Thơ Military Cemetery among his peers. In 1994, his remains were exhumed and cremated. His ashes were stored at the Gia Lâm Pagoda in Gia Định, Vietnam.

Two-star General **Lê Văn Hưng** (1933–1975) graduated from the Class 5 Thủ Đức Reserve Officers School and was known as one of the five "Tiger Officers" of the ARVN. He was made general and commander of the 5th ARVN Division in 1972 when North Vietnamese General Giáp unleashed a three-pronged attack on Quảng Trị (I Corps), Kontum (II Corps) and An Lộc (III Corps). General Hưng and his soldiers defended An Lộc for 95 days and defeated an overwhelming enemy force. He was later promoted to the post of deputy to General Nam. In late April 1975, these two generals were offered evacuation thrice, but they flatly declined.

By 16:00 hours on 30 April 1975, General Hưng was still proclaiming he would not surrender to the Viet Cong. He later met with his wife and son and told her to be brave and to raise his son as a man. He gathered his staff and told them,

> I will not abandon you in order to evacuate my family. I cannot surrender in this shameful situation. If I have yelled at you on occasion, when mistakes were made, please forgive me.

He shook their hands and drove them out of his office, after which he locked himself in. Not even his wife was allowed to remain in his office. A gunshot was later heard. His family and staff broke into the room and found the general, his arms outstretched, still convulsing with blood all over his uniform. He had shot himself in the head at 20:45 hours on 30 April 1975.[18]

General **Lê Nguyên Vỹ** (1933–1975) graduated from the Officers Candidate Course at the Regional Military School, MRII, at Phú Bài near

Huế, class of 1951. He was a colonel at the An Lộc battle in 1972. As the attack raged on and as the enemy got closer, he single-handedly took an M-72 anti-tank gun and shot a communist T-54 tank. He became deputy commander of the 21st ARVN Division before going to the U.S. in 1974 for military training. On his return, he became commander of the 5th ARVN Division. When Saigon surrendered, he gathered his staff and bid them farewell. He locked himself in his office and shot himself with a Baretta 6.35 mm. When the VC officer came to take over the military office, he calmly saluted the general and said, "This is how a general should behave."[19]

General **Trần Văn Hai** (1925–1975), then a colonel, had parachuted himself into the famous battle of Khe Sanh in 1968. He became commander of the 7th ARVN Division in 1974 and was known as a brave and clean officer who also cared for his soldiers. In April 1975, President Thiệu offered to take him out of the country, but he refused.

He remained at his post and was notified of a heavy concentration of enemy troops across the border in Cambodia. He called the CIA representative to request air support, "We have them on the open. Now it's the time to get them. I need help. Help me, CIA man."

But the agent could not do anything and the general watched hopelessly as the enemy crossed the border and overran his troops. General Hai committed suicide instead of surrendering to the enemy.[20]

General **Phạm Văn Phú** graduated from the Dalat Military Academy, Class 8. He ordered the withdrawal from the II Corps under Thiệu's insistence. The Việt Minh held him prisoner after the fall of Điện Biên Phủ, although they later released him. He had vowed never to become prisoner of the communists. He committed suicide on 30 April 1975.

Many more officers had committed suicide during the last days of the war, although most of these cases have not been fully reported. This should not come as a surprise because many of them had spent their youths fighting the communists, and the end result was heart and dream shattering. Colonel Nguyễn Hữu Thông, commander of the 42nd Regiment of the 22nd Division also took his own life instead of surrendering.[21] Colonel Hồ Ngọc Cẩn, commander of the 15th Regiment, 9th Infantry Division, refused to surrender to the enemy. He and his men fought until the end and he was captured before he could kill himself. He asked to salute his flag the last time before being executed by firing squad. Lieutenant Colonel Nguyễn Văn Thông saluted the Soldier Statue in central downtown Saigon before pulling the trigger on himself. Around 14:00 hours on 30 April, after a decent meal, Major Đặng Sĩ Vinh had his wife and seven children drink some medicine before killing them and himself. His last note read like this, "Forgive us. We do not want to live under a communist regime." Former Prime Minister Trần Chánh Thành, fearing a fall into the hands of the communists he had deserted before 1954, ended his life by taking a poison.

This was a mass self-immolation never seen before in Vietnamese history. At least five generals, three colonels, a major and a politician took their own lives in various places throughout Vietnam.

Courage and Sacrifice, East and West

Southerners have always put up resistance against invaders and foreigners: they fought against the Chams, the Khmers, the French, and then the communists. This is not to say that they are xenophobic. Far from that, they have welcomed foreigners and were open to commerce and industry. Their history of mingling with the Chams, Khmers, and Chinese was notorious, especially during the period of southern migration.[22] However, the French who landed in Saigon in 1859 forced the southerners to bear arms against them.[23] In the 20th century, they fought against the communists who took over power in North Vietnam in 1945.

Võ Tánh and Ngô Tùng Châu fought for the South. They sacrificed themselves to preserve their honor and not to fall into the hands of their enemies, the Tây Sơn. They at the same time tried to preserve their moral purity.

All these heroes lived for their *nghĩa* (righteousness): duty to the king and country. As Phan Thanh Giản was 67, he no longer wanted to work and had asked the king to simply retire; however, under the insistence of the king, he took on the position of viceroy of the South. This was a losing proposition because there was no way anyone could defend the South against the French who were mighty militarily as well as eager to conquer Vietnam. Giản had asked Tự Đức on various occasions to reorganize the army, buy new guns and artillery pieces, but to no avail. The end result was almost foreordained. Despite these facts, he tried to deflect the blame away from the king by assuming all the blame himself.

Trương Định wanted to fight on, but the king told him to lay down his arms. He decided to carry on the insurgency warfare anyway, making sure to deflect the blame away from the king.

During the anti-communist war, 300,000 South Vietnamese soldiers lost their lives to defend South Vietnam against the Hanoi government. They were great, courageous men who had dedicated their lives to their country. When the latter sank, some killed themselves rather than surrender. Instead of flying out, they preferred to die in their country. Despite being offered to be flown away, Generals Nam and Hưng refused and killed themselves. General Lê Minh Đảo, commander of the Xuân Lộc region—the last bastion of resistance against the North Vietnamese during the Vietnam War—also declined to be airlifted by the U.S.; he ended up being confined to concentration camps for the next 18 years during which he almost lost his life. There was no greater dedication and self-sacrifice than this.

These people had a high sense of responsibility and morality. They were ashamed of handing over the troops under their command to the enemy or of turning themselves in. They felt they were betraying "not their emperor, but a sovereign state that had ceased to exist long before, whose ideals, they as military officers, still respected."[24] Although South Vietnam had lost the war, the fact that five generals, scores of colonels and officers of various ranks, and even civilians took their own lives at the end of the war showed that there was something bigger than defeat or victory. There was pride and belief that what they were fighting for—freedom and dignity of human life—was worth more than life itself. By sacrificing themselves, they implied that life without freedom was not worth living. By dying, they made a mockery of communism, a theory they fought against and died to resist.

Westerners do not believe in taking their own lives when they lose the ultimate battle, although it is a known fact that ship captains would go down with their sinking ships. South Vietnamese Captain Nguyễn Văn Thà did indeed go down with his disabled corvette *HQ10* during the Paracels battle against the Chinese in 1974.[25] Easterners, on the other hand, were willing to die following crucial battle losses to preserve their honor. They did not want to surrender, to be caught and have to go through the shame of being held prisoner. By taking their own lives, they still felt they had control of their lives or had redeemed their honor. This is an expression of extreme courage and nationalism.

One soldier prefers to die with his glory intact. The other is willing to suffer from the humiliation of defeat. There is no intention to belittle those who surrendered. They did it in order to save their troops or the civilian population; they did it because the commander in chief, President Dương Văn Minh, ordered them to surrender.

Each man chose his version of glory, each man his pain and suffering. There is no right or wrong solution to the problem. Each person was the master of his own life. What is unique about the Vietnamese (at least the South Vietnamese) culture is that over the centuries, *tuẫn tiết* has been a part of the tradition. The Japanese shared the same tradition. Great numbers of officers, soldiers, and even civilians killed themselves when faced with defeat and the prospect of being captured. They felt a man of honor would not allow himself to be captured by his enemy. Only hara-kiri could erase shame, express ultimate devotion, or register a protest.

It should be noted that South Vietnam has been in existence since 1600 while communism has been present only for the last seven decades. While southern nationalists believe in *tuấn tiết*, northern leaders who demanded that soldiers sacrifice themselves for the party did not. Although General Giáp, who had sacrificed—in Vietnamese, the word *nuong* or "roast" is used—tens of thousands of North Vietnamese soldiers during the Tet Offensive and lost many more during the 1972 Eastern Offensive, had been demoted from his position of commander of the People's Army, he still held on to power and did not believe in killing himself.

Conclusion

This study reveals a fairly high number of *tuấn tiết* throughout Vietnamese history. *Tuấn Tiết* seems to be a unique southern nationalistic Vietnamese tradition akin to the Japanese hara-kiri or seppuku.

Chapter Notes

Introduction

1. This was one of the few times that the North Vietnamese used their most advanced Soviet-made T-54 tanks on the battlefield in South Vietnam. These tanks were so huge and clunky that they caused fear in the defenders.

2. ARVN or Army of the Republic of Vietnam in its early years was composed of infantry regiments (main forces). Later, it expanded to include navy, air force, artillery, and other territorial units (RF and PF: regional and popular forces) and was designated as the Republic of Vietnam Armed Forces or RVNAF. To avoid switching back and forth we will use interchangeably ARVN and RVNAF.

3. The NVA offensive began on or about 1 April with attacks on surrounding posts, although the attack on An Lộc did not materialize until the night of 11 April. The NVA wanted to attack earlier, but the move was delayed because of poor coordination. General Hung declared the town liberated on 12 June, and the president visited An Lộc on 7 July. By day 60, the town had been freed, e.g., no major engagement had occurred; however the roadblock south of An Lộc was not cleared until day 90 plus. Therefore, we and some others have used the "94-day siege" to be accurate.

4. Vietnamization of the war was a term coined by the Nixon administration in 1968 to designate the shifting U.S. policy of replacing U.S. ground troops in Vietnam by ARVN troops, thus facilitating the U.S. withdrawal out of Vietnam.

5. Dale Andrade, *Trial by Fire*, 371.

6. Two years later, the NVA came back and used the same pattern of attack to "liberate" Phước Long—a town north of An Lộc—from where they assaulted Ban Mê Thuột and took over the II Corps. In this regard, the battle of An Lộc has become similar to the battle of Bastogne during World War II where the Germans desperately needed to capture a vital road intersection so that they could continue their westward attack and movement of their supplies.

7. "Viets on Way to Victory at An Loc—Top Adviser," *Pacific Stars and Stripes*, April 23, 1972.

8. Highway 13 has also been called Route 13 because in some areas, the four-lane highway became a two-lane country road. For the sake of simplicity, from here on, we will call it Highway 13.

Chapter I

1. NVA: North Vietnamese Army, which was a given name to the units of the Hanoi Communist Party's Popular Army of Vietnam—PAVN—fighting in South Vietnam by MACV authorities. We will use the NVA terminology in this book. DMZ: demilitarized zone dividing North and South Vietnam.

2. Ngo Quang Truong, *The 1972 Easter Offensive*, 106. General Trưởng became the I Corps and MR1 commander following the Quảng Trị defeat to the communists.

3. Andrade, 373.

4. Norman Hannah, *The Key to Failure*, 298. Laos was not a neutral buffer as intended in Geneva, but a partitioned state whose southeastern sub-sector was a pistol aimed by Hanoi at South Vietnam.

5. The French like the word "Indianized"

238

as it relates to India, while U.S. authors recently use "Hinduize" as it relates to the Hindu faith of these people.

6. Michael Freeman and Warner Roger, *Angkor*, 63–67. The first king of Cambodia was Jayavarman II. One inscription reads, "His Majesty came from Java to reign in the city of Indrapura."

7. Henry Kamm, *Cambodia*, 18–21.

8. Ibid., 23.

9. Nghia M. Vo, *Saigon: A History*, 51. Since the king of Vietnam lived in Huê, some 500 miles away, the ceremony in Saigon was simply a ritual: a few bows in front of an altar. As he arrived to the ceremony late one year, he had to pay a fine of 3,000 taels of silver before being released.

10. Arthur Dommen, *The Indochinese Experience*, 441. President Diem received Harriman at Independence Palace together with General Lyman Lemnitzer, chairman of the Joint Chiefs of Staff.

11. Ibid., 438–442.

12. Ibid., 455–465. The flaws of the Geneva Accords concerned the mode of operation of the ICC or International Control Commission. The ICC worked well from 1954 to 1958 because decisions were made in unanimity with a majority report and a minority report submitted. Harriman in 1961–1962 under pressure from the communist bloc allowed the ICC to operate on a majority basis rather than unanimity, which would give a commissioner veto over ICC actions. Article 14 could not only prevent the initiation and carrying out investigations; it also allowed the accused party to never be indicted. Hannah, 46; John Prados, *The Blood Road*, 53. After the Accords were signed, foreign forces must withdraw from Laos within 75 days.

13. Prados, 56.

14. Hannah, 62–63, 72.

15. Hannah, 76. The Vietnamese communists flagrantly violated the Geneva Accords by failing to withdraw from Laos, driving the Laotian neutralists off the Plain of Jars, partitioning Laos into three sections, and infiltrating into Vietnam.

16. Guenter Lewy, *America in Vietnam*, 24.

17. Prados, 69.

18. Hannah, 217.

19. Richard Nixon, *No More Vietnams*, 47.

20. Prados, 70.

21. Ibid., 78–80.

22. Lewy, 50.

23. Lewy, 84. In December 1964, total enemy strength was estimated at 180,700; by December 1967, it stood at 261,500.

24. Ibid., 133.

25. Lewis Sorley, *Westmoreland*, 91.

26. Van Nguyen Duong, 106–107. Sullivan simply did not want anyone to interfere with his area of influence. This turf war limited President Johnson's choice of options.

27. Sorley, *Westmoreland*, 92. He was not imaginative enough strategically to circumvent the rules until at the end of his tenure as MACV commander when he used the Khe Sanh outpost, which was only a few miles from the Vietnamese-Laotian border, to deploy SOG teams and make forays into Laos.

28. Lewis Sorley, *A Better War*, 4.

29. Alexander Haig, *Inner Circles*, 161.

30. Việt Cộng, short for Việt Nam Cộng Sản, or Vietnamese communist, is used to designate the local communist insurgents in opposition to the NVA or northern communists. After the 1968 Tết Offensive, since most of the VC had died, they were replaced by NVA troops. Therefore we are using VC and NVA interchangeably.

31. Sorley, 122–123.

32. Ibid., 98.

33. Sorley, 91; Lewy, 89. In fiscal year 1968, almost 14 billion were spent for bombing and offensive operations but only 850 million for pacifications and various aid programs.

34. A. J. Langguth, *Our Vietnam*, 63.

35. Quoted by Sorley, 95.

36. Bruce Palmer, Jr., *The 25 Year War*, 28.

37. Stephen Hosmer, *The Fall of South Vietnam*, 61.

38. Phillip Davidson, *Vietnam at War*, 338–339. The strategy of *gradualism* calls for *not* applying maximum force to defeat the adversary, but to employ a continuous spectrum—from diplomacy, to crises short of war, to an overt clash of arms—in order to exert the desired effect upon the adversary's will. Inherent in this doctrine is a distrust of the military's desire to win a war as fast as possible.

39. Thomas Ahern, *Vietnam Declassified*, 364.

40. Rufus Phillips, *Why Vietnam Matters*, xiv.
41. Dommen, 252.
42. Vo, *Saigon*, 219.
43. Hosmer, 133–134.
44. Sorley, *A Better War*, 164.
45. Palmer, 37. The Vietnamese were constantly outgunned, with predictable results in battlefield outcomes and morale, not to mention reputation.
46. Thomas McKenna, *Kontum*, 32–33.
47. Hosmer, 131–133.
48. Ibid., 134–137.
49. Ibid., 137–142.
50. Palmer, 43.
51. Tran Van Don, *Our Endless War Inside Vietnam*, 6.
52. Henry Kamm, *Dragon Ascending*, 58, 168–169.
53. Dommen, 339–343. "The basis of this land reform was hate; it was hate that would regenerate the vital energy of the peasants, make them a fundamental revolutionary force"; Stephane Courtois, *Black Book of Communism*, 568–569; Robert Turner, *Vietnamese Communism*, 132–146. More than 50,000 people were executed during the campaign; this does not include collateral damage, especially family members of victims.
54. Thomas Edsall, *New York Times*, October 28, 2012.
55. John Shaw, *The Cambodian Campaign*, 3.
56. Edward Miller, *Misalliance*, 89–113. The newly elected French prime minister pursued contradictory policies. He sought an agreement with northern communists to preserve French influence in North Vietnam and at the same time kept French troops in Saigon and other parts of Indochina for an indefinite period. The Binh Xuyen, a mafia-type armed gang, controlled the Saigon police and ran brothels and casinos in Saigon; they paid Bảo Đại a monthly stipend of 1.5 million piasters (U.S. $43,000). The Hoa Hao and Cao Dai sects were heterodox armed religious groups that controlled swaths of territories in South Vietnam. Besides, there were the VC and nationalist groups like the Đại Việt who also vied for power; Mark Moyar, *The Vietnam War*, 34.
57. Tran Van Don, 22–23, 29; Turner, 53, 58–60, 63. Hanoi eliminated much of the nationalist opposition: hundreds of Đại Việt and Việt Nam Quốc Dân Đảng (VNQDD) were executed in 1946.
58. Turner, 143–146.
59. Philip Catton, *Diem's Final Failure*, 202. "Lodge played a very different role in late 1963; it was a calculated, self-righteous and, in the end, deadly performance."
60. Shaw, 4.
61. Catton, 210. Diệm expressed the nationalism that was spearheaded by two well-known non-communist nationalists, Phan Bội Châu and Phan Châu Trinh in 1910–1920. The two Phan fought the French colonialists using two different strategies: violence and cooperation, respectively.
62. Dommen, 298. Hồ Chí Minh was never voted in as a president by popular vote and remained president for life until his death.
63. "Achievements of the Campaign of Denunciation of Communist Subversive Activities (First Phase)" (Republic of Vietnam: The People's Committee for the CDCSA, May 1956), 51.
64. Vo, *Saigon*, 13–19.
65. Moyar, xiv, 36; Miller, 43–46, 138–139. Personalism, a concept proposed by the French philosopher Mounier, addressed the economic as well as spiritual needs of the person, thus becoming an antidote to the materialistic excesses of capitalism and communism. It had much in common with Confucianism and implied moral duties: a spirit of sacrifice and social responsibility in order to foster respect for one's fellow man and respect for one's self.
66. Turner, 53, 58–60, 63.
67. Dommen, 505.
68. Miller, 324–326.
69. Moyar, 2; Moyar suggested that the Vietnamese fought each other out of a desire for power or freedom from the central authority. Over the centuries, one clan or faction had always fought against another clan or faction. Vanity and cruelty prevailed in these contests. This is confirmed by a well-known saying that if one puts two Vietnamese together, they would work well together; but if one adds a third Vietnamese, discord and disarray would ensue.
70. Dommen, 410, 503.
71. *mò tôm*: basically catching shrimp at the bottom of the river.
72. Van Nguyen Duong, *The Tragedy of the Vietnam War*, 1–5.

73. Ahern, *Vietnam Declassified*, 367.
74. Moyar, xiv, 92–94.
75. Nguyen Long and Harry Kendall, *After Saigon Fell*, xiii.
76. The Vietnamese communists placed the VCP above the State of Vietnam. Thus they, and Hồ Chí Minh included, could not be called patriots because they were always internationalists before being Vietnamese patriots.
77. Merle Pribbenow, *Victory in Vietnam*, 5.
78. Tom Wells, *The War Within*, 83. After the war ended, it was revealed that the Chinese had more than 170,000 troops in Vietnam during the war.
79. http://www.militaryhistoryonline.com/20thcentury/articles/chinesesupport.aspx.
80. Wells, 575.
81. Ibid., 579.
82. Francis Winters, *The Year of the Hare*, 177–189. Prochnau wrote about how he and Halberstam used "the Buddhist story to bring down Diệm." Halberstam did not hesitate to reiterate misrepresentations of easily verifiable facts. When Kennedy became aware of the conspiratorial spirit of Halberstam, he attempted to have him transferred, but the publisher of the *New York Times*, Arthur Ochs, refused. Sheehan provided a national and international forum for a cashiered officer, Colonel John Paul Vann. Bigart was another correspondent who suggested ditching Diệm and sending troops to support a military junta. Prochnau suggested that the "destruction of a government is within the legitimate framework of journalistic enterprise." Malcolm Brown was the reporter who published the photo of the burning monk. Although the decisive role of the *Times* in the Vietnam tragedy cannot be overlooked, Kennedy "bore the responsibility of being intimidated by the crusading press."
83. Tom Polgar, "We Were a Defeated Army," http://lde421.blogspot.com/2013_01_01_archive.html (accessed 7 June 2013).
84. Howard Jones, *Death of a Generation*, 18, 73, 103, 141. In 1961, when the VC hit the capital of Phước Thành Province, they brazenly executed its chief, his assistant, and 10 civil servants and inhabitants, including a woman and a child. There were pictures of beheadings of women and children along with government officials. They blocked roads with barricades in which were concealed grenades. Bui Diem and David Chanoff, *In the Jaws of History*, 43, 52. They assassinated their political non-communist rivals, Huỳnh Phú Sổ, Tạ Thu Thâu, Ngô Đình Khôi, Phạm Quỳnh.
85. Palmer, 29.
86. Pribbinow, 27.
87. Ibid., 51–52.
88. Prados, 15.
89. Ibid., xiv.
90. bộ đội: communist infantry troop.
91. Prados, 45.
92. Hannah, 5: He confirmed on French TV on February 16, 1984; *The Economist*, 25 February 1984.
93. Lewy, 66.
94. Prados, 372.
95. Lien Hang Nguyen, *Hanoi's War*, 45–47.
96. Ibid., 64–65.
97. Prados, 18.
98. Prados, 298. North Vietnam contracted Chinese ships or even used its own ships disguised as Chinese vessels.
99. Sorley, 101.
100. Moyar, 96–97. This explains how they were able to send so many recruits through the trail to the South, most of whom would die from war wounds or diseases, malnutrition, or lack of medicine. The system, however, was not completely foolproof as soldiers would continue to desert: more than 200,000 would surrender to South Vietnamese authorities. Others were chained to their guns or tanks to prevent them from running away.
101. Kamm, *Dragon Ascending*, 152.
102. Prados, 132–133: Russians manned SAM air defense systems, piloted jet fighters.
103. Duiker in Pribbinow, xvi.
104. Bob Seals, *Chinese Support for North Vietnam*, MilitaryHistoryonline.com.
105. Lewis Sorley, *Chronicles*, 820–821; McKenna, 59–61.
106. Shaw, 7.
107. Prados, 16.
108. Kamm, 33–34.
109. MACV Command History, C-1.
110. Shaw, 9.
111. Palmer, 104.
112. Henry Kissinger, *White House Years*, 240.

113. Palmer, 97.
114. Leslie Gelb, *Power Rules*, 55.
115. Langguth, 562; Palmer, 100.
116. Palmer, 101.
117. Sorley, *A Better War*, 204, 208.

Chapter II

1. James Collins, *The Development and Training of the South Vietnamese Army*, 1–9.
2. Ibid., 9–10.
3. Ibid., 139.
4. Clarke, *Advice and Support*, 29.
5. Collins, 132–135.
6. Arthur Dommen, *Indochinese Experience*, 922–924; Vo, *Saigon*, 195–198. Major General Nguyen Khoa Nam and General Le Van Hung committed suicide on the night of 30 April and 1 May in Can Tho. General Tran Van Hai, commander of the 7th Division; General Le Nguyen Vy, commander of the 5th Division; General Pham Van Phu; and former Foreign Minister Tran Chanh Thanh also committed suicide.
7. Ronald Frankum, *Operation Passage to Freedom*, 205; Vo, *Saigon*, 130–133. There were more than 800,000 people who were evacuated by various ships. Many others flew aboard French planes and others either walked through the DMZ or Laos and Cambodia. Many of the refugees would leave Vietnam a second time in 1975 when they lost their country.
8. This arrangement is typical of the Vietnamese family, in which a wage-earning person contributes to the welfare of the extended family since the state welfare system was inexistent.
9. This generation of officers trained under the French system was still conversing in French during the war period.
10. See Chapter XIII.

Chapter III

1. Dale Andrade, *Trial by Fire*, 373. Much of the 1st Aviation Brigade had already been redeployed to the U.S., and that portion of the brigade that remained in South Vietnam was spread over all four military regions. The squadron of the 11th ACR was redeployed to the U.S. on April 6, 1972, and was not a factor during the An Lộc battle.
2. Phan Nhat Nam, "An Lộc: The Unquiet East," 80. The number 13 is considered to be an unlucky number for the Vietnamese. Highway 13 was probably named by the French who do not believe in this superstition.
3. Lam Quang Thi, *Hell in An Loc*, 27.
4. McKenna, *Kontum*, 32–33.
5. There were 200,000 communist troops who abandoned their army and switched to the Government of Vietnam's side by the end of the war. This was the biggest win for Saigon despite the heavy indoctrination by the political commissars on the communist side. There were very few ARVN troops who switched to the communist side; when ARVN troops went AWOL, they usually returned to their villages to do farming.
6. Lewis Sorley, *Vietnam Chronicles*, 821–822. The difference between U.S. and ARVN intelligence estimates could be explained by the factors mentioned in the text. The enemy had simply pushed back its strike date because they did not have all their units and tanks in place. They just wanted to surprise the ARVN by using at the same time attacks by infantry and tanks, which ARVN intelligence had not been able to locate.
7. Lam Quang Thi, 59.
8. Cao Đài is a syncretistic and monotheistic religion officially founded in Cholon, South Vietnam, then officially established in the city of Tây Ninh in 1926. Adherents engage in prayer, veneration of ancestors, non-violence, and vegetarianism.
9. Andrade, 385.
10. Ha Mai Viet, *Steel and Blood*, 152.
11. Since U.S. advisers felt that this bunker was not safe, they wanted to leave An Lộc. They, however, agreed to stay back when the headquarters were moved to the Japanese bunker.
12. Use diversionary attacks in other places, but concentrate on An Lộc.

Chapter IV

1. Dale Andrade, *Trial by Fire*, 395–396.
2. Lam Quang Thi, *Hell in An Loc*, 55–57.
3. James Willbanks, *The Battle of An Lộc*, 51.
4. Ibid., 52–54.

5. Ibid., 193n24.
6. Nghia M. Vo, *The Bamboo Gulag*, 114–116. Northern camps staffed and controlled by the Cong An or secret police imposed a stricter discipline on prisoners than southern camps run by the North Vietnamese Army. High-level officers and high-ranking officials, members of the police department, were sent to the North where they spent 10 to 20 years in the camps while the usual stay in southern camps was 2 to 5 years. Northern camp prisoners were older and had more medical problems than those in southern camps. The hard work, the harsh treatment, the long incarceration, the lack of medication and medical care, the cold and unpleasant weather, the lack of heating systems, and the poor food and nutrition contributed to a higher mortality rate in northern camps compared to southern camps. Sending a person to a northern camp was equivalent to signing his death certificate. Families were usually left in the dark and advised three to six months or sometimes years later that a certain inmate had passed away. If they could afford it, they would travel to the North to collect the dry bones of their relatives.
7. Lam Quang Thi, 58–60.
8. Ibid., 61.
9. Ibid., 62.
10. Andrade, 418–419.
11. Colonel Stephen W. Bachinski, *Province Report, Kontum Province, Period Ending 30 April 1972* (May 1, 1972), 2–3, RG 472, National Archives.
12. Message from General Creighton Abrams to Secretary of Defense Melvin Laird, 1601Z, May 1, 1972, Center of Military History, Fort Leslie J. McNair, Washington, DC.

Chapter V

1. McDermott, *Year of the Hare*, 77–78.
2. Ha Mai Viet, *Steel and Blood*, 404n88. Colonel Lê Nguyên Vỹ had also suggested to Colonel Nhựt on another occasion to have division combat engineers place anti-tank mines on Highway 13 north of town. Colonel Nhựt disagreed, saying that anti-tank mines would be obstacles for vehicles from the rubber plantation leaving the city.
3. Tom Wells, *The War Within*, 536.

4. Lam Quang Thi, *Hell in An Loc*, 88. Nguyen Cau, a TV reporter who stayed in An Lộc during the entire siege, recalled that statement.
5. Ibid., 142.
6. Quoted in CHECO Southeast Asia Report, *The Battle for An Lộc*, 16.
7. Interview by CHECO, 16.
8. Lam Quang Thi, 82.

Chapter VI

1. CHECO, 15.
2. The U.S. and their allies used the 81 mm mortars while the Russians and their communist partners preferred the 82 mm mortars.
3. Lam Quang Thi, *Hell in An Loc*, 87–88. ARVN soldiers had never seen such huge tanks, which although documented at a few other battles, had been first seen in the III Corps. The M-72 rocket launcher, used in other battles, was also released to III Corps soldiers at this battle.
4. James Willbanks, 76.
5. Private communication.
6. Tran Van Nhut, *An Loc*, 117. North Vietnamese soldiers were brainwashed to the point of believing that An Loc had been liberated and that local people would welcome them in. The same propaganda worked for the VC during the 1968 Tết Offensive.
7. Walter Ulmer, *Armor*, January–February 1973, 14–20.
8. Willbanks, 11–12.
9. McDermott, *True Faith and Alliance*, 129.
10. CHECO, 19–20.
11. Andrade, *Trial by Fire*, 438–439.
12. Ibid., 440–441.
13. Andrade, 446.
14. Ha Mai Viet, *Steel and Blood*, 157. The date of the destruction of the local hospital by shelling was April 16 for Ha Mai Viet.
15. Andrade, 449–450.
16. Lam Quang Thi, 110–112.
17. Andrade, 492–493.
18. Ha Mai Viet, 406n99.
19. Nguyen V. Quy, "War Fortune and Misfortune," in Chat V. Dang, et al., *The Vietnamese Mayflowers of 1975*, 371.
20. Willbanks, 148.
21. An T Than, "In the Eyes of the Storm: Binh Long District Hospital," in Chat V.

Dang et al., *The Vietnamese Mayflowers of 1975*, 201–204.
22. Khue Ngoc Nguyen, *Ranger Magazine*, 2003, 10–12. The Group was assigned the northern sector of An Lộc and Quản Lợi Hill.
23. Ibid., 22–24.
24. Ibid., 28–29. The Ranger Group was later commended for having retaken the Open Arms Office and retrieving important communication documents from the enemy.
25. McDermott, 55–58.
26. Ibid., 63–64. This was the personal experience of an American GI who was imbedded in a Vietnamese airborne unit.
27. Ibid., 94–95.
28. Lam Quang Thi, 126–127.
29. McDermott, 75–76.
30. Lam Quang Thi, 128.
31. Khue Ngoc Nguyen, *Ranger Magazine*, 2003, 36–37.
32. Lam Quang Thi, 130–133.
33. Tran Van Nhut, 131, 137.
34. Lam Quang Thi, 136.

Chapter VII

1. James Willbanks, *The Battle of An Loc*, 67. "Miller suggested to the clearly demoralized Hung that he relinquish command to Colonel Nhut, the province chief."
2. James Bruton, "Analyzing Vietnamese Culture" in Nghia Vo, et al., *The Women of Vietnam*, 127–170.
3. Willbanks, *The Battle of An Loc*, 62.
4. Andrade, *Trial by Fire*, 391.
5. Ibid., 390. In Cao Van Vien, et al., *The U.S. Adviser*, 66–73, ARVN generals argue that the relationship between the U.S. adviser and the Vietnamese commander is fraught with misunderstandings because of their culture, upbringing, way of life, technical abilities, leadership, and so on. Unless the parties want to subordinate their personal desires to the good of the unit, there is no way to foster a true working relationship. The adviser is usually more junior than his counterpart and has minimal war experience, although he is well trained and could offer theoretical and material support to the commander. The adviser sometimes wants to have things done immediately because of his short tour of duty; but if he keeps on harassing the commander with ideas and uninterrupted suggestions regardless of substance, his effectiveness as an adviser will be greatly diminished.
6. Lam Quang Thi, *Hell in An Loc*, 30.
7. Andrade, 389.
8. Ibid., 393–394.
9. Ibid., 391.
10. Willbanks, *The Battle of An Loc*, 67.
11. Cao Van Vien. *The U.S. Adviser*, 38–40. During the Westmoreland years, once the same report reached General Vien, an investigation would be ordered by General Vien who would act based on the conclusion of the investigation.
12. Lam Quang Thi, 31.
13. Frances Fitzgerald, *Fire in the Lake*, 369.
14. Lam Quang Thi, 28.
15. *hồi chánh*, or returnee, is an enemy soldier who has surrendered and rallied to the South Vietnamese side. During the war, more than 200,000 VC switched sides; they were never heard from again after the communists took power in 1975. It was feared many were executed for having betrayed the revolution.
16. Van Nguyen Duong, *The Tragedy of the Vietnam War*, 153.
17. Willbanks, *The Battle of An Loc*, 41.
18. Ibid., 62. Willbanks wrote, "Miller saw Hưng as totally indecisive and unable to handle the stress of high intensity combat."
19. Ibid., 91. Willbanks wrote, "When the chips are down he looses [sic] all of his composure."
20. Ibid., xv.
21. Ibid., 112.
22. Ibid., 62.
23. Ibid., 112.
24. Thomas McKenna, *Kontum*, 10.
25. Cao Van Vien, *The U.S. Adviser*, 190.
26. Ibid., 73–74. The fact that advisers rotated every six months seemed to curtail the effectiveness of the advisory effort. A good working relationship requires better understanding, mutual trust and harmony between adviser and his counterpart, which could only be obtained through a long association.
27. Cao Van Vien, *The U.S. Adviser*, 197.
28. John Rambo is the archetype of a troubled Vietnam War veteran and former Green Beret in David Morrell's novel *First Blood*. Rambo is skilled in survival tactics, weaponry, hand-to-hand combat, and guerrilla warfare.

29. Cao Van Vien, *The U.S. Adviser*, 198.
30. Andrade, 473–474.

Chapter VIII

1. CHECO, 21.
2. CHECO, 15–16.
3. Lam Quang Thi, *Hell in An Loc*, 84.
4. Lam Quang Thi, 190.
5. Khue Ngoc Nguyen, *Ranger Magazine*, 2003. This was also reported by Phan Nhat Nam (see below) and Major Raymond Haney, U.S. adviser to the 5th ARVN Division at An Loc (see CHECO, 24). Fallen refugees "laying in ditches like cordwood."
6. CHECO, 25–26.
7. Phan Nhat Nam, "An Loc: The Unquiet East," 78. When a few hundred civilians attempted to escape from the town by walking south on Highway 13, they were gunned down by the VC who did not care whether they were civilians or soldiers.
8. In May 1972, civilians poured out of the besieged Quảng Trị city in the northern part of Central Vietnam on buses, scooters, bicycles, or on foot. Artillery observers intentionally adjusted the fire of NVA guns onto the column of refugees. On 9 May, President Thiệu denounced this butchery, which killed and injured thousands of innocent civilians. (See Ian Ward, "Why Giap Did It," 6.) A long section of National Highway 1 was thus littered with charred bodies and burned civilian vehicles. The scenery was so horrifying that the section of highway was later called "the Highway of Horror." On another occasion, in March 1975, while trying to get out of Ban Mê Thuột behind the II Corps convoy, they were shelled and gunned down on Route 7B during which tens of thousands of civilians lost their lives. The convoy was dubbed the "Convoy of Tears." (See Dommen, *The Indochinese Experience*, 903; Englemann, 230. The number of dead civilians and soldiers was unknown but estimated to be in the tens of thousands.)
9. James Willbanks, 81.
10. McKenna, *Kontum*, 93.
11. Phan Nhat Nam, 94–95.
12. Ngo Quang Truong, *The 1972 Easter Offensive*, 118–119. An Lộc had survived thanks to airdrops by dedicated and courageous pilots and airmen who risked their lives to save the population of the town.
13. Andrade, *Trial by Fire*, 452–456.
14. CHECO, 32–33.
15. Ibid., 33–34.
16. Andrade, 460.
17. CHECO, 34.
18. Andrade, 461.
19. Willbanks, 94; Lam Quang Thi, 100. Thi somehow placed the second attack on 15 April, which was followed by a lull the following day, 16 April, that lasted until 21 April. One wonders why Thi uses that date because the first attack lasted from 13 to 15 April. Willbanks, on the other hand, placed it on April 19. Our date of April 18 is close to Willbanks's date.
20. CHECO, 22–23.
21. Lam Quang Thi, 135–136.
22. Andrade, 446–447.
23. Lam Quang Thi, 137–138.
24. CHECO, 40–41.

Chapter IX

1. An Lộc Chiến Sử Phan Nhật Nam, 1972—The Battle of An Lộc by War Reporter, Airborne Captain Phan Nhật Nam, 1972.

Chapter X

1. Lewis Sorley, *Vietnam Chronicles*, 834, emphasis in original.
2. Lam Quang Thi, *Hell in An Loc*, 101.
3. Guernica is a Basque country village that was bombed by German and Italian airplanes during the war at the behest of the Spanish Nationalist forces in 1937 during the Spanish Civil War.
4. Walter Ulmer, *Armor*, May–June 1974, 23–25.
5. Lam Quang Thi, 144.
6. CHECO, 42.
7. Lam Quang Thi, 146; Andrade, *Trial by Fire*, 477.
8. CHECO, 44.
9. Andrade, 475.
10. CHECO, 43.
11. McDermott, *True Faith and Alliance*, 106–108.
12. Ibid., 114–116.
13. Ibid., 117–118.
14. Ibid., 135, 145.
15. CHECO, 47.
16. Document from the Military History Branch of the GCOS/JGS/RVNAF recorded "275th Regiment/VC 9th Division."

17. Walter Ulmer, *Armor*, January–February 1973, 17.
18. Lam Quang Thi, 154.

Chapter XI

1. Phan Nhat Nam, *Crossroads*, 83.
2. Ibid., 87.
3. Ibid., 82, 93.
4. Lam Quang Thi, *Hell in An Loc*, 178–179.
5. James Willbanks, 142.
6. Lam Quang Thi, 242–243.
7. John Howard, "The War We Came to Fight," 19.
8. Verdun was one of the major battles between Germans and French in the First World War. It resulted in more than 700,000 casualties, half from each side.
9. Lam Quang Thi, 2.
10. *Bánh hỏi* is rice vermicelli woven into intricate bundles and often topped with chopped scallions and garlic chives to be consumed with barbecue pork. This is a fancy dish that is expensive, best served hot, time consuming to prepare, and therefore cannot be made in large quantities to be dropped to thousands of soldiers.
11. Lam Quang Thi, 183.
12. Nguyen V. Quy, in Chat V. Dang, et al., *The Vietnamese Mayflowers of 1975*, 374.
13. Lam Quang Thi, 185–186. General Hưng's steel helmet had a camouflaged cloth cover. On the front was embroidered a black star with black thread. Across was Hưng's signature written with a black marker, with a dedication to President Thiệu.

Chapter XII

1. Davidson, *Vietnam War*, 188–189.
2. Ibid., 223–224.
3. Ibid., 233–234. He was not aggressive enough to promote the defense of the embattled area.
4. Ibid., 235–245.
5. Ibid., 256–258.
6. Ibid., 261–262.
7. Morgan, *Valley of Defeat*, 634.
8. Ibid., 639–640.
9. Prados, *Valley of Decision*, 289.
10. Ibid., 297.
11. Ibid., 285. It was made in December 1967.
12. Ibid., 8–9. The comment, however, could be totally self-serving.
13. Ibid., 271.
14. Ibid., 268–269.
15. Ibid., 454.
16. Brush, in Marc Gilbert, *The Tet Offensive*, 208. Ironically, the communists built a monument at Khe Sanh to commemorate the battle. Among the words inscribed on the monument are "112,000 U.S. and puppet troops killed and captured. 197 airplanes shot down. Much war material was captured and destroyed. Khe Sanh another Điện Biên Phủ for the U.S."
17. Davidson, 275.
18. Ibid., 243.
19. Safer, *Flashbacks*, 19.
20. Ibid., 26.
21. Ibid., 20.
22. Davidson, 562–567.
23. Ibid., 571.
24. Prados, *The Blood Road*, 350.
25. Lam Quang Thi, *Hell in An Loc*, 207.
26. Andrade, *Trial by Fire*, 474.
27. Ibid., 502.
28. Davidson, 701.

Chapter XIII

1. William H. Sullivan was ambassador to Laos during the 404 project—U.S. Air Force covert operation in Laos—and as a former gunnery officer, he personally directed the bombing of the Hồ Chí Minh Trail in order to minimize civilian losses. This civilian control and the restriction of operations rankled the military and allowed the NVA to almost run freely on the trail.

Chapter XIV

1. Andrade, *Trial by Fire*, 371.
2. Myra McPherson, "Chuck Hagel," *New York Times*, 13 January 2013.
3. Alan Dawson, *55 Days*, 8.
4. Francis McNamara, *Escape with Honor*, 136. When the U.S. consul in Cần Thơ decided to evacuate Americans and some Vietnamese workers on 30 April, he took with him 300 locals; his boat was stopped by the riverine area command navy but allowed to proceed by Commodore Thắng.
5. Nghia M. Vo, *The Bamboo Gulag*, 18–21.

6. "Seppuku" is the correct term while "hara-kiri" is the commonly used word. The person disemboweled himself with his own sword and was beheaded by his assistant who in a sense completed the victim's work.
7. The Paracel Islands are a group of islands located in the South China Sea and claimed by Vietnam, the Philippines, and China. These islands were part of South Vietnam until 1974 when China came in and occupied them after sinking a South Vietnamese battleship during the battle of the Paracels. http://www.sacei07.org/Newsletter65.pdf.
8. Arthur Dommen, *The Indochinese Experience*, 923.

Chapter XV

1. Davidson, *Vietnam at War*, 798–799.
2. Davidson, 604.
3. Cao Van Vien, Dong Van Khuyen, *Reflections on the Vietnam War*, 135.
4. Davidson, 800–801.
5. Osgood, *Limited War*, 10–11.
6. Cao The Dung, *Contemporary Literature*, 306–309.
7. Quoted in Willbanks, *Abandoning Vietnam*, 284.
8. Neil Jamieson, *Understanding Vietnam*, 364–365.
9. Nhã Ca is a poetess whose only crime was to have written a book about the terror, killings, and mayhem inflicted by the communists when they took over the city of Huế in 1968. The book has been translated into English in 2014.
10. Turner, *Vietnamese Communism*, 37–38. Back then, they proclaimed human rights, rights to ownership, and civil rights. Everything sounded great until they took power. Then people realized they got nothing: no human rights, no ownership rights.
11. Turner, 47–51. Opposition candidates were eliminated on grounds that they were "collaborators," corrupt, or suspect elements. In Hanoi, Ho Chi Minh received 169,222 votes although the population at the time was only 116,000.
12. Turner, 57–59.
13. Turner, 122.
14. Morley Safer, *Flashbacks*, 4.

Appendix

1. "Seppuku" is the correct term, while "hara-kiri" is the commonly used term. The person disemboweled himself with his own sword and was then beheaded by an assistant, who in a sense completed the work.
2. The South (*đàng trong*) seceded from the North (*đàng ngoài*) in 1600; this was followed by the first full scale north-south war from 1627 to 1672. During the revolutionary period (1771–1802), there was no central government in the South because the southern Nguyen had been toppled by the Tây Sơn rebels. The latter had expanded their control over the present-day central Vietnam while the Nguyen scion—Nguyen Anh—barely had control of the Mekong Delta. In the North, the Trinh lords controlled the House of Le. Warlords roamed freely. They raised their own armies and fought for whomever they liked.
3. Nghia M. Vo, *Saigon*, 38–39, 43–44; Taylor, *History*, 300–302, Nguyễn Ánh took 26 years to recover his ancestors' throne. He was a methodical, conscientious, and careful fighter. Part of this had to do with the fact that he had to rebuild his government infrastructure to raise funds to continue the war. Secondly, he wanted his army to have sufficient supplies and food without having recourse to stealing from peasants and villagers. Everywhere his army went, he had new granaries built for their needs. Third, having lost many battles to the Tây Sơn in the beginning had made him more cautious than usual.
4. Le Thanh Khoi, *Le Vietnam*, Editions de Minuit, 1955, 318–321.
5. Mark McLeod, *The Vietnamese Response to French Intervention*, 43–44.
6. Ibid., 52.
7. The three provinces of Biên Hòa, Gia Định, and Định Tường were ceded to the French with a few commercial ports. The Catholic religion could be practiced freely throughout Vietnam.
8. McLeod, 63–65.
9. Ibid., 74.
10. Ibid., 50–54.
11. See Chapter I.
12. The names and birthplaces of the graduates of the triennial examination are chiseled in stone steles that sat on stone tortoises housed at the Văn Miếu (Temple of

Literature). How anyone could decapitate a skeleton is anyone's guess. But the king's ruling had to be carried out, and decapitation had to be done.

13. McLeod, 55–56.

14. Vo, *Saigon*, 43–45. When Gia Long recovered his throne in 1802, his biggest mistake was to return to the old Confucian system to prop up his regime. Locked in this mentality, he and his descendants completely sealed off their country to modernization and trade. This process weakened their regime so much that it could not put up any resistance against westerners. A few thousand soldiers armed with guns and artillery were able to take over the whole country in a few years.

15. A *cử nhân* (licentiate) graduate of the regional examinations of 1852.

16. Translated by Huynh Sanh Thong, *An Anthology of Vietnamese Poems*, 84.

17. Neil Jamieson, *Understanding Vietnam*, 47–48.

18. A. J. Dommen, *The Indochinese Experience*, 921–924. Generals Nguyen Khoa Nam and Le Van Hung had thrice been offered evacuation by their American adviser before he departed and each time refused.

19. Nghia M. Vo, *The Bamboo Gulag*, 18–21.

20. Dommen, 923.

21. Dommen, 921–922.

22. Vo, *Saigon*, 16–19, 54–55. By immersing and melting into the culture of the local Chams, Khmers, by interbreeding with them and the Chinese, the southerners have created a new way of being Vietnamese. They adopted Mahayana Buddhism, culture, food, and clothing of the Chams, Khmers.

23. See Truong Cong Dinh above.

24. Shannon French, *Code of the Warrior*, 220–223.

25. http://en.wikipedia.org/wiki/Battle_of_the_Paracel_Islands.

Bibliography

Ahern, Thomas L. *Vietnam Declassified: The CIA and Counterinsurgency*. Lexington: University Press of Kentucky Press, 2010.
Andrade, Dale. *Trial by Fire: The 1972 Easter Offensive, America's Last Battle in Vietnam*. New York: Hippocrene Books, 1995.
Blair, Anne. *Lodge in Vietnam: A Patriot Abroad*. New Haven, CT: Yale University Press, 1995.
Bui Diem and David Chanoff. *In the Jaws of History*. Bloomington: Indiana University Press, 1999.
Cao The Dung. *Van Hoc Hien Dai: Thi Ca va Thi Nhan*. Contemporary Literature: Poetry and Poets. Saigon: Quan Chung, 1969.
Catton, Philip E. *Diem's Final Failure: Prelude to America's War in Vietnam*. Lawrence: University Press of Kansas, 2002.
Clarke, Jeffrey. *Advice and Support: The Final Years, 1965–1973*. Washington, DC: U.S. Army Center for Military History, 1988.
Collins, James Lawton. *The Development and Training of the South Vietnamese Army, 1950–1972*. Washington, DC: Department of the Army, 1975.
Courtois, Stephane, Nicolas Werth, Jean-Louis Panne, et al. *The Black Book of Communism*. Boston, MA: Harvard University Press, 1999.
Dang, Chat V., Hien V. Ho, and Nghia M. Vo. *The Vietnamese Mayflowers of 1975*. Charleston, SC: Book Surge, 2009.
Davidson, Phillip B. *Vietnam at War: The History 1946–1975*. Novato, CA: Presidio, 1988.
Dawson, Alan. *55 Days: The Fall of South Vietnam*. New York: Prentice Hall, 1977.
Dommen, Arthur J. *The Indochinese Experience of the French and the Americans: Nationalism and Communism in Cambodia, Laos, and Vietnam*. Bloomington: Indiana University Press, 2001.
Engelmann, Larry. *Tear before the Rain: An Oral History of the Fall of South Vietnam*. New York: Oxford University Press, 1990.
Fitzgerald, Frances. *Fire in the Lake: The Vietnamese and the Americans in Vietnam*. New York: Little, Brown, 2002.
Frankum, Ronald B. *Operation Passage to Freedom. The United States Navy in Vietnam*. Lubbock: Texas Tech University, 2007.
Freeman, Michael, and Roger Warner. *Angkor: The Hidden Glories*. New York: Houghton Mifflin, 1990.
French, Shannon E. *The Code of the Warrior: Exploring Warrior Values Past and Present*. Lanham, MD: Rowman & Littlefield, 2003.
Gelb, Leslie H. *Power Rules: How Common Sense Can Rescue American Foreign Policy*. New York: HarperCollins, 2009.

Gilbert, Marc J., and William Head. *The Tet Offensive.* Westport, CT: Praeger, 1996.
Ha Mai Viet. *Steel and Blood: South Vietnamese Armor and the War for Southeast Asia.* Annapolis, MD: Naval Institute Press, 2008.
Haig, Alexander M., with Charles McCarry. *Inner Circles. How America Changed the World: A Memoir.* New York: Warner Books, 1992.
Hannah, Norman B. *The Key to Failure: Laos and the Vietnam War.* Lanham, MD: Madison Books, 1987.
Higgins, Marguerite. *Our Vietnam Nightmare. The Story of U.S. Involvement in the Vietnamese Tragedy, with Thought on a future Policy.* New York: Harper & Row, 1965.
Hosmer, Stephen T., Konrad Kellen, and Brian Jenkins. *The Fall of South Vietnam: Statements by South Vietnamese Military and Civilian Leaders.* New York: Crane, Russak, 1980.
Jamieson, Neil L. *Understanding Vietnam.* Berkeley: University of California Press, 1993.
Jones, Howard. *Death of a Generation: How the Assassination of Diem and JFK Prolonged the Vietnam War.* New York: Oxford University Press, 2003.
Kamm, Henry. *Cambodia: Report from a Stricken Land.* New York: Arcade, 1998.
_____. *Dragon Ascending: Vietnam and the Vietnamese.* New York: Arcade, 1996.
Kissinger, Henry. *White House Years.* Boston, MA: Little, Brown, 1979.
Lam Quang Thi. *Hell in An Loc: The 1972 Eastern Invasion and the Battle That Saved South Vietnam.* Denton: University of North Texas Press, 2009.
Langguth, A. J. *Our Vietnam: The War, 1954–1975.* New York: Simon & Schuster, 2000.
Lewy, Guenter. *America in Vietnam.* New York: Oxford University Press, 1977.
McDermott, Mike. *True Faith and Allegiance: An American Paratrooper and the 1972 Battle for An Loc.* Tuscaloosa: University of Alabama Press, 2012.
McKenna, Thomas P. *Kontum: The Battle to Save South Vietnam.* Lexington: University Press of Kentucky, 2011.
McLeod, Mark W. *The Vietnamese Response to French Intervention, 1862–1874.* New York: Praeger, 1991.
McNamara, Francis. *Escape with Honor: My Last Hours in Vietnam.* Dulles, VA: Brassey's, 1997.
Miller, Edward. *Misalliance: Ngo Dinh Diem, the United States, and the Fate of South Vietnam.* Boston, MA: Harvard University Press, 2013.
Morgan, Ted. *Valley of Death: The Tragedy of Dien Bien Phu that Led America into the Vietnam War.* New York: Random House, 2010.
Moyar, Mark. *Triumph Forsaken: The Vietnam War, 1954–1965.* New York: Cambridge University Press, 2006.
Ngo Quang Truong. *The 1972 Easter Offensive.* Indochina Monograph. Washington, DC: U.S. Army Center of Military History. bnpham@foxinternet.net (accessed 28 December 2012).
Nguyen, Lien Hang. *Hanoi's War: An International History of the War for Peace in Vietnam.* Chapel Hill: University of North Carolina Press, 2012.
Nguyen Long, and Harry Kendall. *After Saigon Fell: Daily Life under the Vietnamese Communists.* Berkeley: University of California, Institute of East Asian Studies, 1981.
Nixon, Richard. *No More Vietnams.* New York: Arbor House, 1985.
Osgood, Robert E. *Limited War Revisited.* Boulder, CO: Westview Press, 1979.
Palmer, Bruce, Jr. *The 25 Year War: America's Military Role in Vietnam.* Lexington: University Press of Kentucky, 1984.
Phillips, Rufus. *Why Vietnam Matters: An Eyewitness Account of Lessons not Learned.* Annapolis, MD: Naval Institute Press, 2008.

Prados, John. *The Blood Road: The Ho Chi Minh Trail and the Vietnam War*. New York: Wiley, 1999.
_____, and Ray W. Stubbe. *Valley of Decision: The Siege of Khe Sanh*. New York: Houghton Mifflin, 1991.
Pribbenow, Merle L. *Victory in Vietnam: The Official History of the People's Army of Vietnam, 1954–1975*. Lawrence: University of Kansas Press, 2002.
Safer, Morley. *Flashbacks: On Returning to Vietnam*. New York: St Martin's, 1990.
Seals, Bob. *Chinese Support for North Vietnam during the Vietnam War: The Decisive Edge*. MilitaryHistoryonline.com. http://www.militaryhistoryonline.com/20thcentury/articles/chinesesupport.aspx (accessed 22 December 2012).
Shaw, John M. *The Cambodian Campaign: The 1970 Offensive and America's Vietnam War*. Lawrence: University Press of Kansas, 2005.
Sorley, Lewis. *A Better War: The Unexamined Victories and Final Tragedy of America's Last Years in Vietnam*. New York: Harcourt Brace, 1999.
_____. *Vietnam Chronicles: The Abrams Tapes, 1968–1972*. Lubbock: Texas Tech University Press, 2004.
_____. *Westmoreland: The General Who Lost Vietnam*. New York: Houghton Mifflin Harcourt, 2011.
Thich Nhat Hanh. *Vietnam: Lotus in a Sea of Fire*. New York: Hill & Wang, 1967.
Tran Van Don. *Our Endless War inside Vietnam*. Novato, CA: Presidio, 1978.
Tran Van Nhut. *An Loc: The Unfinished War*. Lubbock: Texas Tech University, 2009.
Turner, Robert. *Vietnamese Communism: Its Origin and Development*. Stanford, CA: Hoover Institution Press, 1975.
Van Nguyen Duong. *The Tragedy of the Vietnam War: A South Vietnamese Officer's Analysis*. Jefferson, NC: McFarland, 2008.
Vo, Nghia M. *The Bamboo Gulag. Political Imprisonment in Communist Vietnam*. Jefferson, NC: McFarland, 2004.
_____. *Saigon: A History*. Jefferson, NC: McFarland, 2011.
_____, Chat V. Dang, and Hien V. Ho, eds. *The Women of Vietnam*. Denver, CO: Outskirts Press, 2008.
Ward, Ian. "Why Giap Did It: Report from Saigon." In *North Vietnam's Blitzkrieg: An Interim Assessment*, edited by Brian Crozier, 1–10. London: Institute for Study of Conflict, October 1972.
Wells, Tom. *The War Within: America's Battle Over Vietnam*. Berkeley: University of California Press, 1994.
Willbanks, James H. *Abandoning Vietnam: How America Left and South Vietnam Lost Its War*. Lawrence: University of Kansas Press, 2004.
_____. *The Battle of An Loc*. Bloomington, IN: Indiana University Press, 2005.
Winters, Francis X. *The Year of the Hare: America in Vietnam, January 25, 1963–February 15, 1964*. Athens: University of Georgia Press, 1997.

Monographs and Journals

"Achievements of the Campaign of Denunciation of Communist Subversive Activities (First Phase)." Republic of Vietnam: The People's Committee for the CDCSA, May 1956.
Cao Van Vien and General and Lieutenant General Dong Van Khuyen. *Reflections on the Vietnam War*. Indochina Monographs. Washington, DC: U.S. Army Center of Military History, 1980.
Chu Xuan Vien. "Observations and Conclusions." In *The U.S. Adviser*. Indochina Monographs. Washington, DC: U.S. Center of Military History, 1980.
Edsall, Thomas B. "Billionaires Going Rogue." *New York Times*, October 28, 2012.

http://campaignstops.blogs.nytimes.com/2012/10/28/billionaires-going-rogue/?src=me&ref=general.

Howard, John. "The War We Came to Fight. A Study of the Battle of An Loc, April–June 1972." Student research paper, 1974 (on file).

Khue Ngoc Nguyen. "The Battle of An Loc, Binh Long." *Tap San Biet Dong Quan (Ranger Magazine)*, no. 7 (2003).

McPherson, Myra. "Chuck Hagel, Under Attack Again." *New York Times*, January 13, 2013. http://www.nytimes.com/2013/01/09/opinion/chuck-hagel-under-attack-in-vietnam-and-on-capitol-hill.html?hp&_r=0.

Phan Nhat Nam. "An Loc: The Unquiet East." *Crossroads* 13, no. 2 (1999): 77–102.

Polgar, Tom. "We Were a Defeated Army." http://lde421.blogspot.com/2013_01_01_archive.html.

Schafer, John C. "Phan Nhat Nam and the Battle of An Loc." *Crossroads* 13, no. 2 (1999): 53–75.

Ulmer, Walter F. "Anti-Aircraft Employment on a Battlefield in South Vietnam." *Armor*, May–June 1974, 23–25.

———. "Notes on Enemy Armor." *Armor*, January–February 1973, 14–20.

Index

abandon 89, 106, 110, 132, 164, 180, 202, 205, 209–210, 217
Abrams, Creighton 15, 76, 93, 123–124, 154
advisee 120, 129
advisory 30, 36
aggressiveness 222
airborne 5–6, 18, 32, 36, 49, 53, 55, 61, 68, 93–94, 100, 107–113, 115, 141–143, 164–168, 175–180
Algerian 197–198
Andrade, Dale 215
Anne-Marie 197–198
anti-communism 23
anti-war movement 25
arc light 79–80, 110, 154, 159
ARVN 4–7, 17, 25, 34, 43, 59, 64, 75=76, 83, 94, 114, 123, 127, 141, 150, 200, 222, 232
atrocities 76

B-52 9, 28, 30, 55, 76–77, 80, 86, 98, 110, 126, 149, 163, 167, 200–202
Bạc Liêu 23, 38
Ban Mê Thuột 50, 209, 213
Base Charlie 52
Bàu Bàng 146–147, 152
Bé River 49, 51, 56–57, 77, 82, 142, 177
Beatrice 197–198
Bến Cát 49, 57, 147
Bến Hãi River 26
Bến Hét 72, 97, 156
Bến Thành Market 182
Benedict, Ed 125
Bibby, Thomas 222
Biên Hoà 33, 40, 42, 62–63, 92, 151, 194
Bình Định 226–227
Bình Dương 49–50, 52–53, 84, 92, 107, 116, 134, 147, 151

Bình Long 31, 34, 48–52, 57–58, 63, 73, 87, 91, 94–95, 102, 109, 116, 123, 151, 154, 167, 179, 181, 193
Bình Xuyên 20, 148, 217, 232
Black April 47
border war 5, 9, 29, 34
bracelet 156
bravery 113, 138, 219–220
Browne, Malcolm 25
Bùi Diễm 16
Bùi Đức Điềm 46, 78, 88, 105, 132, 140, 162, 191, 194
bunker 3, 6, 58–59, 72, 74, 97, 102, 105–106, 114–115, 120–121, 124–126, 132, 135–136, 138, 160–163, 180, 187, 189, 194, 202
Bunker, Ellsworth 12

Cà Mau 23, 38
callous 136
Calu 200–201
Cam Lộ 200, 209
Cambodia 4–6, 9–11, 15–16, 26, 29–34, 37, 48–50, 55–57, 71, 75, 90, 97, 123, 154, 185, 202, 209, 216, 219, 234
Cần Lê River 5, 51–52, 60, 73–74, 77–79, 81–83, 87, 104, 108, 120, 151
Cần Thơ 33, 40, 43, 123, 211–212, 217, 233
Cao Đài 20, 58
Cao Phú Quốc 104
Cao Tấn Tài 169
Cao Văn Viên 36, 123, 157, 189
CARP 137
Castries, Christian de 197–200, 203
casualties 17, 63, 68, 70, 77, 84, 95, 102, 105, 108–109, 143, 152, 171, 181, 188, 198, 205, 228
China 184, 209–210, 230

253

Chinese 10, 13, 18, 24, 27–29, 61, 67, 72, 87, 97, 196, 200, 210, 220
Chính nghĩa 219, 221, 224
Chinook CH-47 100, 112–113, 137, 142, 157–158
Choke point 146–147, 150
Chơn Thành 50–52, 57, 60, 89, 91, 95, 99, 109, 113, 116, 134, 142, 146–152, 172–174, 181, 191
Chou En Lai 85
Chùm Bao 66, 69
cigarette 105, 121, 155
Claudine 197
collective outlook 119
Communism 1–5, 9–15, 20–22, 28–29, 49, 53, 57–60, 76, 86, 90–91, 105, 116, 134–136, 143, 184, 189, 200, 202, 206, 209, 216, 218, 223
concentration attack 59, 61, 92
Confucius 10, 230–231
Cong An 224
COSVN 31, 34, 53, 55, 60, 63, 71, 84, 90–91, 109–110, 127, 141, 151–153, 168, 181, 183
counterattack 6, 92, 108, 114–115, 126–127, 131, 141, 164–165, 168, 172, 197
Củ Chi 49, 92

Đại Việt 20
Dak To 76
Đàng Ngoài 21, 247
Đàng Trong 21, 247
Đặng Văn Sung 17
DAO 208
Đào Duy Ân 184
Dầu Tiếng 53, 84
Davidson, Philip 29, 204
Dayan, Moshe 156, 183
defend to death 87
delivery 138
Delta clan 124
democracy 16, 19, 22, 25, 189, 216, 221
detachment-left-in-contact 112
devastation 2, 143, 164, 184, 187
Diệm *see* Ngo Dinh Diệm
Điện Biên Phủ 112, 116, 189, 196–199
Diệu Huỳnh 134
dispersion attack 60
diversionary attack 62, 64
DMZ 9, 29, 87, 204–205
Đỗ Cao Luận 179
Đỗ Cao Trí 29, 33, 36, 49, 58, 179
Dominique 197–199
Đồng Văn Khuyến 18
Đồng Xoài 49

Dương Tấn Triệu 79, 100
Dương Thu Hương 28
Dương Văn Minh 28, 148, 214, 220, 236

Easterner 117, 119, 236
electronic barrier 200
Eliane 197–198
entrenched fortification 147
extrovert 119

face 67, 227
Fall, Bernard 215
Fan Muong 31–32
FANK 31–32
Fiery Summer 54, 183, 206, 211
Fitzgerald, Frances 25, 124
Fonda, Jane 216
forward air controller 158
France 184, 189, 196–199, 208, 219
free world 184–189
FSB Alpha 50, 64–65

Gabrielle 197
gallant 104, 115, 189
general offensive 204
Geneva Accords 29, 35, 38
Gia Định 37, 40, 49, 92, 218, 226
Gia Lam 218, 233
Gianh River 27
Gò Công 226, 228

Hagel, Chuck 216
Hai Bà Trưng 39
Hải Phòng 86, 209
Hải Vân pass 27
Haig, Alexander 13
Halberstam, David 25
HALO 138–139
Hanoi 2, 4, 9, 16, 18, 23, 29, 61, 86, 90, 114, 151, 181, 232, 235
Harriman, Averell 200
hero 37, 46–47, 62, 114, 178, 182, 184, 186, 204, 212, 217, 220, 230, 235
Highway 13 77
Hiroshima 157
Hồ Chí Minh 23, 25, 90
Hồ Chí Minh Trail 3–4, 12, 26, 56, 201, 209
Hồ Ngọc Cẩn 159, 173–175, 219, 234
Hồ Trung Hậu 148
Hồ Văn Lời 39, 159
Hoà Hảo 20
Hoàng Diệu 20, 229, 231
Hoàng Ngọc Lung 159, 210
Hoàng Thông 51

Index

Hoàng Xuân Lãm 211
Hóc Môn 211
Hồi chánh 54, 126
Hollings, Fritz 15
Hollingsworth, James 4, 93, 123, 127, 139, 144, 157, 184, 215
Hồ's bộ đội 115
Huế 9, 10, 36, 202, 205
Huguette 197–198
Hùng Tâm 52, 58, 64, 73, 83, 141, 169
Huỳnh Tấn Phát 57, 90
Huỳnh Văn Tâm 44, 88, 114, 163, 190

Indianized 10
individualism 119
Indochina 9, 35, 90, 184, 196
indoctrination 28, 221
infighting 11, 22
inhumanity 22, 136, 216, 223
International Red Cross 184
introvert 117, 119
invasion 12, 25–26, 61, 205, 229
Isabelle 197, 199

Johnson, Lyndon B. 13, 15, 201

Kampong Cham 30–31
Kennedy, John F. 11–12
Khe Sanh 11, 200–202, 204, 206
King Savang 11
King Sihanouk 11
Kissinger, Henry 57, 62, 83, 85, 171, 208, 221
Kontum 9, 46, 61, 76, 87, 151, 233
Korea 12, 124

Lai Khê 41, 44, 49, 52, 60, 78, 88, 109, 141, 147, 152, 173
Laird, Melvin 30, 76
Lâm Quang Thi 74
Lâm Quang Thơ 33
land reform 20
Lang Vei 72, 97, 156, 201
Lansdale 17
Laos 10–15, 18, 26, 29, 72, 196, 201
LAW 72, 96, 154
Lê Đạt Công 32–33, 41
Lê Duẩn 26, 57, 86
Lê Đức Thọ 26, 57, 85–86, 208
Lê Hồng 149
Lê Minh Đảo 33, 36, 191, 214, 236
Lê Nguyên Vỹ 36, 45–46, 58, 71, 78, 88, 155, 162, 190, 194, 208, 218
Lê Quang Lưỡng 108, 111, 120, 142, 145, 148, 153, 159, 167, 181, 189, 210

Lê Quang Tín 104
Lê Quý Dậu 104
Lê Thọ Trung 40, 42–44, 81
Lê Văn Chánh 79, 161
Lê Văn Hưng 4, 6, 33, 35–37, 109, 116, 122, 144, 153, 159, 189, 210, 214, 217, 233
Lê Văn Mạnh 149
Lê Văn Ngọc 108, 111, 113, 142
legionnaire 197
Leningrad 90, 205
limited war 16, 29, 34, 222
literary reform 22
Lộc Ninh 4–5, 50–51, 53–54, 57, 62, 64–73, 75–76, 97, 121, 123, 156, 192
Lộc Tấn 50, 54, 59–60, 66, 68–69
Lodge, Cabot 29
loneliness 21, 159, 171
loud mouthing 27
Lounds, Davis 200
Lưu Yểm 50
Lý Đức Quân 44, 79, 82, 120, 161, 189–190

M-72 rocket launcher 72, 96, 115, 155–156
Mạch Văn Trường 41, 44, 88, 163, 184, 189
Malaysia 10
mass burial 103, 105
McNamara, Francis 218
McNamara, Robert 12–13
meddling 128
Mekong Delta 10, 19, 29, 31, 50, 55, 146, 152, 159, 208
MENU 30
Miller, William 65–67, 72, 77, 82, 107, 118, 120–125
misery 4, 143, 186
Montagnard 64, 113, 134
murder 3, 22, 26, 76, 202

Nagasaki 157
nam tiến 10
National Military Academy 36
nationalism 21–22, 224, 236
Navarre, Henri 196–197, 200, 203
neutralization 11–12
Ngô Dinh Diệm 11, 20–22, 24–26, 39
Ngô Quang Trưởng 210–212
Ngô Tùng Châu 226–227, 235
Ngô Xuân Vĩnh 179
Nguyễn Ánh 21, 226
Nguyễn Bá Long 46
Nguyễn Bá Thịnh 74
Nguyễn Cao Kỳ 90

Nguyễn Chí Hiếu 109, 111, 142, 164, 168
Nguyễn Chí Thanh 90
Nguyễn Công Vĩnh 44, 50, 64, 70, 72
Nguyễn Đình Chiểu 230
Nguyễn Đức Dương 44, 50, 65–66, 77
Nguyễn Đức Trạch 79
Nguyễn Hoàng 21
Nguyễn Huệ campaign 60, 83, 91
Nguyễn Hưng Chiêu 37–38
Nguyễn Hữu Huấn 226, 231
Nguyễn Hữu Nhân 137
Nguyễn Hữu Thọ 57, 90
Nguyễn Hữu Thông 219, 234
Nguyễn Khoa Nam 36, 210–211, 217, 232
Nguyễn Ngọc Khuê 135
Nguyễn Quang Nghi 69–70
Nguyễn Tấn Trọng 158
Nguyễn Thị Bình 143
Nguyễn Tri Phương 227–229
Nguyễn Trọng Ni 179
Nguyễn Tú 222
Nguyễn Văn Biết 79, 88, 105, 120, 157, 162
Nguyễn Văn Của 50
Nguyễn Văn Đinh 109, 142, 176–178
Nguyễn Văn Hiếu 33, 49
Nguyễn Văn Hòa 52, 73, 77, 83, 88
Nguyễn Văn Linh 90
Nguyễn Văn Minh 90–91, 93–94, 109, 113, 147–148, 150, 153, 157, 170, 176, 180, 182, 184, 189, 208, 210, 212
Nguyễn Văn Quý 102
Nguyễn Văn Tha 220, 236
Nguyễn Văn Thiệu 36, 86, 93, 181, 189, 210, 230
Nguyễn Văn Thịnh 51
Nguyễn Văn Tiến 186
Nguyễn Viết Cần 174–175, 178–179
Nguyễn Viết Thanh 179
Nguyễn Vĩnh Nghi 146–148, 174, 191, 210, 214
Nhã Ca 222
Niagara Operation 200
Nixon, Richard 12, 30, 62, 80, 83, 85–86, 171, 184
Nùng 44

Olympic wounded 102
onslaught 116, 154
open arms 97, 106–107, 161, 164
orphan 39, 187
overbearing 122, 128

pacification 14, 228
pallet 107, 132, 138–140, 144
Pantheon 204
Paracel Islands 220
paratrooper 6, 104, 111–113, 115, 140–141, 165–166, 182, 197
Paris Accords 25, 27, 74, 208–210, 216, 223, 230, 252
Pathet Lao 11–12
patronization 130
people's court 76
Phạm Hùng 86, 90
Phạm Kim Hoàng 42
Phạm Quốc Thuần 190, 208
Phạm Tiến Duật 199
Phạm Trọng Phùng 65
Phạm Văn Phú 219, 234
Phạm Văn Sơn 159, 194, 199
Phan Huy Lương 184
Phan Nhật Nam 50
Phan Thanh Giản 217, 226, 228–230, 233
Phan Văn Huấn 113, 131, 162
Phú Đức 6, 103, 186–187
Phú Lô 81, 110, 126, 158, 161, 180, 198
Phú Xuân 226–227
Phước Long 49–51, 56–57, 91, 150, 183, 209–210
POL 28
Polgar, Tom 25
political war 221
poor man's war 208
possession 187, 206
Prey Nokor 10
Prochnau, William 25
protracted war 222

Quản Lợi airstrip 52, 60, 81, 91, 94, 137, 141, 143
Quản Long airfield 79
Quảng Nam 27, 229, 232
Quảng Trị 209–212
Qui Nhơn 226

Rambo 130
ranger 18, 49–51, 54, 59–61, 65, 68, 79, 87–88, 94, 105–107, 165, 180
reality 90
redemption 219, 225
Regional Force 36, 51, 60
regroupee 26
Resolution 15 26
ruin 3, 114, 159, 186–187
Rusk, Dean 12

Saigon 28, 34, 41, 62, 75, 83, 89, 92, 171, 181, 206
SALT 85
Savior's Statue 190

Index

SDS 24
self-immolation 225–235
Seppuku 220, 225
Sharplen, Bob 25
Sheehan, Neil 25
shelling 2, 58, 68, 70, 75, 101–104, 116, 135, 140, 143, 160, 166, 186, 228
shuffle 181
Sihanoukville 27, 29–30
Snepp, Frank 214
Soviet Union 11–12, 14–16, 18, 24, 28, 51, 85–86, 97, 209
Spectre gunship 99, 106, 153–154
Srok Ton Cui 109–111, 113, 141–142, 167, 177, 179
Stieng 57, 82
Sullivan, Ambassador 13, 209
Suối Máu 71
survival 15, 25, 87, 137–138, 150, 152, 171, 203
Sway Rieng 31–32, 57

T-54 1, 3, 59, 61, 71–72, 85, 95–97, 100, 110–111, 136, 143, 156, 164, 169–170, 190, 218
tactical operations center 42, 45, 58, 65, 73, 78, 114, 125, 162
tactics 23, 48, 127, 134, 170, 197, 200
Tallman, Richard J. 191
tank destroying team 155
Tàu-Ô Stream 5, 89, 91, 93, 148, 153, 172, 181, 191
Tây Ninh 14, 30–31, 33–34, 48–49, 51–52, 56–58, 64, 87, 91, 151
Tây Sơn 226–227, 235
Tchepone 33, 200
Thailand 10–12, 98
Thiệu 25, 36, 86, 89–90, 93–94, 124, 140, 181, 189–191, 208, 210, 214; *see also* Nguyễn Văn Thiệu
Thompson, Thomas 156, 184
Thủ Đức 34–38, 40, 65, 107, 179, 217, 232–233
Thuận Thanh 204
time on target 199
Tống Viết Lạc 106
TRAC 191, 208, 215
Trâm hầu 231
Trần Chánh Thành 219, 235
Trần Công Mẫn 201
Trần Dạ Từ 222
Trần Đăng Khoa 44, 72, 75
Trần Quang Diệu 226
Trần Quang Khôi 48, 92
Trần Quốc Lịch 190, 194, 208

Trần Văn Bé 71
Trần Văn Bình 41, 58, 62–63
Trần Văn Hai 219, 232
Trần Văn Hương 214
Trần Văn Nhựt 50, 52, 79, 87, 121, 155, 162, 182
Trần Văn Trà 90–93, 109, 146, 151–153, 170, 182–183
Trị Thiên 87
Trinh Đình Đăng 45, 65, 88, 100, 190, 194
Truman, Harry S 35
Trương Công Định 226, 228
Trương Hữu Đức 148
Trương Khánh 106
Trường Sơn 26, 49, 56, 209
Trương Vĩnh Phước 148
Tự Đức 228–232, 235
tuẫn tiết 219–220, 235; *see also* self-immolation
Two Vietnams 224

Ulmer, Walter 98, 122, 132–133, 146, 154, 160
underground 13, 58–59, 70–73, 81, 103, 121

Văn Bá Ninh 109, 111, 142, 145, 163, 167
Văn Tiến Dũng 61
Vanuxem, Paul 184
Verdun 184
Việt Cộng (VC) 11, 13, 70, 118, 232
Việt Minh 197–198, 200, 219, 234
Việt Nam Quốc Dân Đảng 20
Vietnamization 2, 13–14, 62, 83, 85, 221
vindicate 14, 183
Võ Bẩm 26
Võ Duy Ninh 226–228
Võ Nguyên Giáp 61, 184, 199
Võ Tánh 226–227, 235
Võ Trung Thứ 44

Washington 10, 15, 29, 34, 62–63, 83, 85, 132, 164, 171, 181, 210
Weed, Gordo 163
Wells, Tom 25
Westerner 25, 215–216, 220, 228, 236
Westmoreland, William 12–15, 26, 29, 200, 204–205
Willbanks, James 121–122, 124, 127–128, 168, 171
Windy Hill 52, 60, 80, 100, 108–110, 141–143, 149, 167, 177

Xa Cam gate 164, 167–170, 182
Xuân Lộc 49, 218, 222, 236

www.ingramcontent.com/pod-product-compliance
Ingram Content Group UK Ltd.
Pitfield, Milton Keynes, MK11 3LW, UK
UKHW041934140426
5217IPUK00014B/467